Become Brighter

Ton manuel d'anglais, c'est une ouverture sur le monde anglophone et un outil d'apprentissage précieux ! Nous avons essayé de faire en sorte que tout soit réuni pour que tu progresses en ayant plaisir à apprendre.

Faciliter ton entrée en 2de

L'entrée en 2de est un moment important : nouvel établissement, nouveaux camarades de classe, nouveaux enseignants... Afin de rentrer en douceur dans l'année, le chapitre ***Celebrate English Worldwide*** te fera voyager à travers le monde anglophone et te permettra de réactiver tes connaissances de la langue anglaise grâce à des *challenges* stimulants.

Voyager loin et découvrir toujours plus

Afin de t'offrir un panorama complet, nous avons œuvré à proposer **24 chapitres** sur des **thématiques variées**. Du rêve hollywoodien aux liens intergénérationnels des familles indiennes, de la *sneaker culture* à l'histoire de l'indépendance des pays du Commonwealth, tu approfondiras tes connaissances à travers des chapitres aux **longueurs et approches pédagogiques variées.**

Varier les modalités d'apprentissage

Parce que tous les thèmes ne se ressemblent pas et que nous n'apprenons pas tous de la même façon et au même rythme, tu pourras, pour certains documents, télécharger une fiche d'accompagnement à la compréhension e-WB Différenciation grâce à deux options possibles (*ways*). Pour y accéder, **scanne le QR code** en haut de page, qui te permet aussi d'accéder à toutes les ressources (vidéos, audios, activités numériques).

Et comme ensemble, on est plus fort, de nombreux TEAM WORK te permettront de travailler en équipe.

Tu veux aller encore plus loin ? Tu trouveras dans les rubriques ***A little extra*** des documents supplémentaires.

Et pour la production ? Là aussi, les rubriques ***Your task*** te permettront de développer des compétences d'expression, avec parfois deux *ways* pour te laisser le choix.

Te fournir des outils pour maîtriser la langue

Pour mieux comprendre et t'exprimer, la maîtrise de la grammaire et de lexique sont nécessaires. Les ***Vocabulary spots*** et leurs MEMORISE your vocabulary ainsi que les infographies de grammaire et les GRAMMAR tuto te seront d'une aide précieuse.

Vérifier tes connaissances et compétences

Connaître ses forces et faiblesses, c'est important pour bien travailler. Grâce au Quiz TEST yourself tu pourras t'auto-évaluer régulièrement sur les éléments culturels et linguistiques abordés à travers les documents. Les pages ***Test your...*** sont aussi l'occasion de tester tes connaissances de façon ludique !

Et pour te préparer aux évaluations, la rubrique ***Yes you can*** dans les pages ***Your final*** task et les pages ***Practise & Shine*** seront de véritables atouts.

Nous avons eu à cœur de te proposer des chemins vers la réussite et te souhaitons un **voyage culturel et linguistique enthousiasmant** avec Shine Brighter 2de

Sommaire

Sommaire

Sommaire

AXE 4 DÉFIS ET TRANSITION • Challenges and transition

AXE 6 LES PAYS DU COMMONWEALTH : HÉRITAGE, UNITÉ, DIVERSITÉ

Commonwealth countries: heritage, unity, diversity

FILE 21 Paths to freedom p. 170 à 185

Objet d'étude 2
De l'empire aux indépendances : transitions postcoloniales

▶ How did British colonies gain their independence?

EXPLORE

1. A crumbling Empire
2. The way to freedom
3. New beginnings

Build your English!

- Les subordonnées temporelles
- La cause, le but et la conséquence
- La prononciation des diphtongues et triphtongues (2)
- Les pauses

YOUR FINAL TASK

Create an illustrated panel on decolonisation for a school exhibition.

TEST YOUR CULTURE → p. 178 PRACTISE AND SHINE → p. 184

SHORTFILE 22 Together in sport p. 186 à 193

Objet d'étude 4
Représenter le Commonwealth de sa conception à aujourd'hui

▶ How does sport reflect the evolutions of the Commonwealth?

EXPLORE

1. A common heritage
2. A unique sports tradition
3. Commonwealth Games… but what for?

Build your English!

- L'expression de la comparaison
- L'intonation des phrases exclamatives

YOUR FINAL TASK

Record a video to express your opinion about the importance of the Commonwealth Games.

SNAPFILE 23 The train from Rhodesia p. 194 à 197

Objet d'étude 1
La littérature anglophone, témoignage de l'histoire et d'histoires

▶ How does Nadine Gordimer's short story shed light on the consequences of colonialism in Africa?

GRAMMAR SPOT

- Le gérondif

PHONOLOGY SPOT

- Les lettres muettes

YOUR FINAL TASK

Rewrite the story from the old man's point of view.

FLASHFILE 24 From Westminster to Wellington p. 198 à 199

Objet d'étude 3
Permanence et rupture dans les héritages politiques britanniques

▶ How New Zealand and the UK have maintained political relationships since the creation of the Commonwealth?

GROUP WORK

In teams, **watch** and **read** the documents. **Share** information about the political relationships between New Zealand and the UK.

YOUR FINAL TASK

MÉDIATION

Write a letter to apply for the position of New Zealand's representative at the upcoming Commonwealth Day celebrations in London.

Sommaire

HOW to shine in AI

Les pictos de ton manuel

- Compréhension orale
- Compréhension écrite
- Expression orale
- Expression orale en interaction
- Expression écrite
- MÉDIATION : Médiation écrite ou orale
- e-WB Différenciation : E-workbook (fiche téléchargeable)
- Ai : Activités réalisables à l'aide d'un outil d'IA
- Video / Audio : Document vidéo ou audio
- Lexique ou activité de phonologie
- Quiz TEST yourself : Quiz sur les éléments culturels et linguistiques de la double page
- MEMORISE your vocabulary : Activités interactives de mémorisation
- GRAMMAR tuto : Ta leçon de grammaire en vidéo
- TEAMWORK : Travail en équipe
- BUILD YOUR ENGLISH → p. 61 : Renvoi aux pages de langue du chapitre
- HOW TO SHINE IN... Speaking → p. 208 : Renvoi aux pages de langue du chapitre

Proposition d'ordre de traitement des chapitres

Cette proposition respecte une progression linguistique tout en s'attachant à varier les formats, les aires géographiques et l'activité langagière de la tâche finale.

Aire Géographique	Chapitre	Grammaire	Activité langagière de la tâche finale
USA	**File 1 –** Hollywood : the dream factory	• Le présent simple et le présent en *be* + V-*ing* • Les questions	
United Kingdom	**Short File 18 –** Take it S.L.O.W.	• Les quantifieurs	
Canada	**Flash File 8 –** Growing green together		MÉDIATION
USA	**Short File 2 –** Cowboys ride back	• Présent *versus* prétérit	
United Kingdom	**Snapfile 11 –** Bowie's heirs	• Les démonstratifs	
United Kingdom	**Flash File 4 –** Star-crossed lovers		MÉDIATION
India and the USA	**File 5 –** Indian families	• Prétérit *versus past perfect* • Les articles	MÉDIATION
USA	**Snapfile 7 –** Family matters	• Le génitif et les pronoms possessifs	
United Kingdom	**Short File 6 –** Home sweet home?	• Les modaux	
USA	**File 17 –** Still I rise	• Prétérit *versus present perfect* • Le passif	
USA	**Flash File 16 –** Chicago skyline		MÉDIATION
Nigeria	**Snapfile 19 –** Building tomorrow's megacity	• L'expression du futur	
Commonwealth	**Short File 22 –** Together in sport	• L'expression de la comparaison	
USA	**File 9 –** #EveryBODY	• L'expression de l'addition et de l'opposition • Les phrases relatives	
United Kingdom	**Snapfile 15 –** Royals 3.0	• Les connecteurs	
USA	**Short file 10 –** Sneaker culture	• Le superlatif	
USA	**Flash File 20 –** Electric route 66		MÉDIATION
South Africa	**File 13 –** Healing the wounds	• L'expression du souhait ou du regret • Discours direct et indirect	
USA	**Snapfile 3 –** Wicked	• Les adjectifs en -*ed* et -*ing*	
Australia	**Short File 14 –** Walking in their tracks	• L'aspect *be* + V-*ing*	
Commonwealth	**File 21 –** Paths to freedom	• Les subordonnées temporelles • La cause, le but et la conséquence	
United Kingdom	**Flash File 12 –** A muse forever		MÉDIATION
Commonwealth	**Snapfile 23 –** The train from Rhodesia	• Le gérondif	
New Zealand	**Flash File 24 –** From Westminster to Wellington		MÉDIATION

L'AI, un allié pour apprendre ?

L'intelligence artificielle (*artificial intelligence* ou *AI* en anglais) est un outil puissant qui peut transformer votre façon de travailler, surtout en dehors de la classe. Que ce soit pour comprendre un cours, réviser avant une évaluation ou approfondir vos connaissances, l'IA peut être un véritable allié. Mais attention, il faut savoir l'utiliser efficacement et éviter les pièges.

A Utiliser l'IA pour apprendre efficacement

L'IA permet de travailler **à ton rythme** et **selon tes besoins**. Elle t'offre **une aide personnalisée**, comme un assistant toujours disponible pour répondre à tes questions, expliquer les notions complexes ou te guider dans tes révisions. Elle te donne aussi accès à **des ressources variées** et te permet de **mieux organiser ton temps**, tout en rendant tes études plus interactives et efficaces.

	Objectifs
PRODUIRE	Se faire accompagner dans ses productions (aide à la structuration, correction orthographique et grammaticale) et soigner sa présentation (créer des supports, générer des images ou simplifier des textes).
RÉVISER	Synthétiser ses cours (résumer, identifier les points clés), créer des exercices pour réviser et planifier son travail
S'ENTRAINER	Se préparer aux évaluations et améliorer ses compétences (qualité de l'expresion, de l'argumentation ou d'analyse de documents)
EXPLORER	Approfondir un sujet (trouver ou soumettre des idées, découvrir d'autres aspects) et apprendre à apprendre (méthodes et techniques)
COMPRENDRE	Obtenir des explications claires (définir des notions, illustrer avec des exemples concrets, apporter une aide personnalisée…)

L'IA À TON SERVICE

L'intelligence artificielle (IA) peut être une aide précieuse pour les élèves, notamment si tu as des besoins spécifiques.

Ce que l'IA peut faire pour toi :

- **Des contenus adaptés à ton niveau :** Si tu as du mal à lire un texte compliqué, des outils simplifient les phrases pour que tu comprennes mieux.
- **Apprendre à ton rythme :** l'IA peut repérer ce que tu as compris ou non, et te proposer des exercices pour t'aider à progresser sans te surcharger.
- **Un soutien en lecture et écriture :** Si tu as des troubles de la lecture ou de l'orthographe, des outils peuvent lire les textes à voix haute ou corriger tes erreurs.
- **Faciliter ton quotidien :** Les assistants vocaux peuvent t'aider à prendre des notes, à gérer ton emploi du temps ou à chercher des informations sans que tu aies besoin de tout écrire.

Les compléments numériques
e-WB
lycee.nathan.fr/2sb013

B Des familles d'IA

Il existe **plusieurs types d'IA** qui te permettent de faire des **tâches différentes**. Pour certaines, nous te proposons des **tutos vidéos** pour apprendre à les utiliser notamment en langues vivantes.

Famille d'IA	Tâches transversales	Caractéristiques
Moteurs de recherche augmentés par IA Tuto video	Recherche d'informations	Outils adaptés aux lycéens, fournissant des résultats synthétiques et respectant la vie privée.
IA de **traitement de texte**	Rédaction et correction	Correction orthographique et grammaticale, amélioration stylistique, multilingue.
IA de **traduction** Tuto video	Traduction et langues	Traductions précises et contextuelles, avec options multilingues pour les LV1/LV2.
IA pour l'**organisation des apprentissages**	Création de fiches de révision	Génération automatique de fiches et adaptation des révisions grâce à des algorithmes d'apprentissage.
IA pour générer des **illustrations**	Création de contenus visuels	Création d'illustrations ou de graphiques pour des présentations ou projets interdisciplinaires.
IA pour résumer et simplifier Tuto video	Synthèse et vulgarisation	Aide à la synthèse de textes complexes ou techniques.
IA pour l'**apprentissage** et les **quiz** Tuto video	Révision et entraînement	Aide personnalisée pour réviser les cours, quizz adaptatifs selon les résultats.

C Apprendre à utiliser l'IA

Utiliser l'IA demande de l'apprentissage et du discernement : éthique de la donnée, compréhension des biais algorithmiques, lutte contre la désinformation. Comme tout outil, elle peut être mal employée ou offrir des réponses inexactes. Il est donc essentiel de **comprendre ses limites** pour en tirer le meilleur tout en **évitant ses pièges**.

À faire	À ne pas faire
✔ Poser des questions précises et ciblées	✖ Copier-coller les réponses de l'IA sans les comprendre
✔ Utiliser l'IA pour résumer et expliquer	✖ Lui confier un devoir entièrement
✔ Vérifier les réponses avec d'autres sources	✖ Considérer les réponses comme toujours exactes
✔ Planifier tes études avec des outils numériques	✖ Réviser à la dernière minute

A LITTLE EXTRA Video

Watch the video from the beginning to 4'36 and **explain** why AI cannot replace learning a foreign language.

LET'S GO!

Celebrate English Worldwide!

MÉDIATION

Discover and **choose** an English-speaking country to celebrate on the European Day of Languages.

1 Game on!

MÉDIATION

- In groups, **roll** the dice and **move towards** the corresponding continent.
- **Answer** the list of questions about the continent.
  - If you fail, **skip** your turn and **start** from the beginning.
  - If you throw a six, **play** again!
- The **group** who **completes** the list of questions with no mistake **wins the continent**.
- The **group** who wins the most continents **win the game**!

EUROPE

1. Name at least three countries where English is an official language.
2. Name the capital city of one of them.
3. Name a must-see monument or a natural site.
4. Name two celebrities (singers, sportspersons, political or historical figures...).
5. Name a dish or a sport typical of one of these English-speaking countries.

2 English everywhere

Video

English through ages and continents, *OpenLearn_OU*, 2020.

a. **Watch** the video and **find** information about the origin of the English language.

b. **Note down** the countries mentioned in the video and the dates.

c. **Identify** the most important factor of the English language's expansion.

d. **Explain** why English is a global language today.

LET'S GO!

3 The SPEAKING challenge

AMERICA CANADA

▶ A school trip is organised in North America.

GRAND CANYON NATIONAL PARK

SAFETY TIPS Heat[1] is extremely dangerous and often underestimated, especially when hiking down into the Canyon.

YELLOWSTONE NATIONAL PARK

SAFETY TIPS The animals in Yellowstone are wild and unpredictable. The safest (and often best) view of wildlife is from inside a car.

BANFF NATIONAL PARK

SAFETY TIPS Temperatures can plummet[2] (and rise) quickly. To make sure you're prepared no matter what happens is to dress in layers[3].

GLACIER NATIONAL PARK

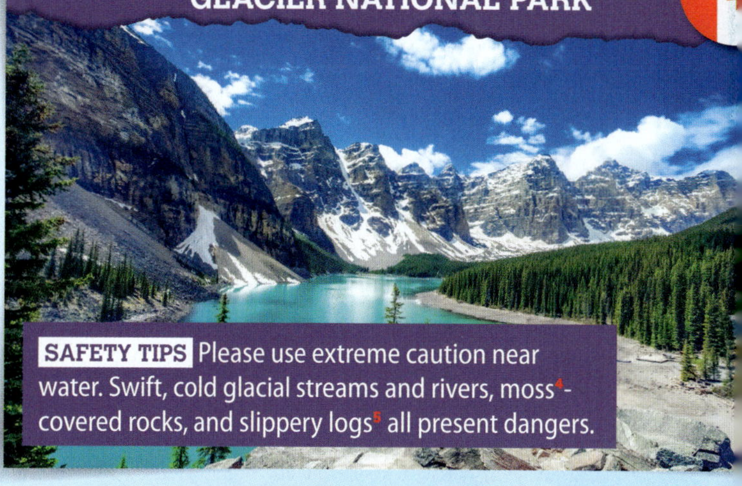

SAFETY TIPS Please use extreme caution near water. Swift, cold glacial streams and rivers, moss[4]-covered rocks, and slippery logs[5] all present dangers.

1. *chaleur* 2. fall rapidly 3. *épaisseurs* 4. *mousse* 6. *bûches glissantes*

VOCABULARY SPOT

- canyon
- lake
- meadow /ˈmed.əʊ/: *prairie*
- river /ˈrɪv.ər/
- trail: *sentier*

- breathtaking

- freezing
- mild /maɪld/ = not very cold

- climb /klaɪm/
- go hiking /ˈhaɪkɪŋ/: *faire une randonnée*
- kayak

MEMORISE your vocabulary

TEAM WORK

Team A works on the USA and Team B on Canada.

STEP 1 Make a one-minute oral presentation to convince your classmates to go and visit one park.

STEP 2 Then, **answer** their questions about potential dangers.

CHALLENGE

Now, **convince** your classmates to go and visit one park.

INDIA

4 The LISTENING challenge

▶ Now, **land** in India and learn more about Bollywood movies!

▲ Ekta Kapoor, *Badtameez Dil*, 2023.

Video
What is Bollywood, *What is*, 2022.

a. **Look at** the pictures and **describe** them. **Guess** what the films are about.

b. **Watch** the video and **pick out** information about Bollywood (dates, numbers).

c. **Identify** the characteristics of a Bollywood film.

d. **Explain** why Bollywood has become a massive industry.

CHALLENGE

Gather your notes to recap the document orally. How much have you understood?

▼ *Kanchana*, 2019.

LET'S GO!

5 The READING challenge

AFRICA

▶ **Land** in Africa and **discover** brilliant contemporary artists!

AFRICA

BRIAN OTIENO was raised in Kibera, where he documents the everyday realities of ordinary life. His passion and commitment[1] lie in capturing the stories of the vibrant community of Kibera and attempting to look beyond the chaotic appearance of his hometown.

storitellah.com, 2024

1. *engagement*

AFRICA

PHUMELELE TSHABALALA establishes his subjects within vibrant spaces that amplify the presence of each. The figures are dressed flamboyantly, with sumptuous folds of drapery, vivid patterns and pigments that express complex characters.

Arndt Art Agency, 2024.

▲ *Let him Reign*, 2021.

Europe Supported by Africa and America, 2015. ▶

AFRICA

SOKARI DOUGLAS CAMP's works reference the social and environmental impacts of the production, sale, and transportation of fossil fuels. As oil is one of the major exports of the Niger Delta, Camp decorates her figures with crowns made out of fuel cans to comment on the industry's impact on the region.

artsy.net, 2016

▲ *Untitled*, 2018.

CHALLENGE

Match the artist with the correct artwork and country.

6 The WRITING challenge

▶ **Travel to** in New Zealand and **write** an email to take part in an amazing activity!

▲ Haka Tours' activities in New Zealand, 2014.

a. Look at the document and **identify** its type. **List** the activities into two categories: discovering nature or extreme sports.

b. Explain what makes them unique.

CHALLENGE

Write an email to the tourist office to get information about one activity:
– **explain** why you are interested,
– **ask** details about the activity.

Build your skills! Écrire un email

➔ **Commencer** et **terminer** sa correspondance :
- *Dear Sir, Madam,*
- *Sincerely yours,*

➔ **Exprimer** les souhaits et les demandes :
- ***I would like to*** + BV, ***I feel like*** + V-ing
- ***I would appreciate*** *if you could tell me …*

MÉDIATION FINAL CHALLENGE

TEAM WORK

For the European Day of Languages, **choose** one country to celebrate. In groups, **go through** all the documents of this unit. **Debate** over which country should be celebrated. Then, **organise** a vote!

FILE 1

Hollywood: the dream factory

Les compléments numériques

lycee.nathan.fr/**2sb020-021**

To what extent has Hollywood always been a dream factory?

YOUR FINAL TASK

Write the scene of a screenplay about Hollywood.

> *Hollywood has bottled this idea of this intangible[1] magic that's inaccessible to most people.*
>
> Iconic America, *PBS*, 2023.

1. undefined

Brad Pitt and Leonardo di Caprio star in *Once Upon a Time in Hollywood* by Quentin Tarantino, 2019.

Video

Hollywood Sign history, *Tidbits of History*, 2022.

VOCABULARY SPOT

- celebrity
- fame /feɪm/ = stardom
- landmark = iconic place

- emblematic
- renowned /rɪˈnaʊnd/ = famous

- release (a movie)

MEMORISE your vocabulary

TEAM WORK

Team A
Observe the picture, **read** the caption and the quote. **Take notes** on the symbols of Hollywood.

Team B
Watch the beginning of the video. **Take notes** on the history of Hollywood.

Team C
Watch the video and **explain** the importance of the sign in the industry.

- Now **share** your findings with the other teams and **describe** the image of Hollywood today.

EXPLORE

The American Dream

1

▲ Hollywood Boulevard.

Audio

Hollywood Dreams Of Wealth, *NPR*, 2012.

a. **Look at** the pictures and **guess** why Hollywood is called "The American factory".

b. **Listen** to the audio and **pick out** the expressions used to identify Hollywood. **Explain** what they refer to.

c. **Identify** the issues hidden behind the glamorous appearance of Hollywood.

d. PHONOLOGY **Focus** on the pronunciation of the letter <o> in the following words: *comedy – factory – movie – California*. Do they all sound the same? **Listen** again and **repeat** the words.

◀ Chris Hemsworth gets a star on the Walk of Fame, 2024.

VOCABULARY SPOT

- expectations
- prospect = future
- self-made person
- self-reliance= autonomy

- idyllic /aɪˈdɪlɪk/ = idealised /aɪˈdɪəlaɪzd/

- make it = succeed
- shoot a movie
- strive /straɪv/: *faire tout son possible*

MEMORISE your vocabulary

2

Audio version

Mia is an aspiring actress, working at a café in L.A.

EXT.[1] STUDIO LOT - DAY

Mia runs, shirt stained with coffee. Jumps into her car. Eyes a COAT on her passenger seat.

INT.[2] AUDITION ROOM - DAY

Mia's in that coat, zipped up, looking odd indoors. On her cell–

MIA (CONT'D)[3]

(laughing, big smile on her face)
And I swear to God, she was wrecked. Pure lunacy. Oh God, I know...
(seems to be listening, then,) [...]
We PULL BACK...to see that Mia's auditioning for a CASTING DIRECTOR and ASSISTANT. And it's clear to us–there's something about her, a glow in her face. She's good.

ASSISTANT

Great. Could you try it again but–
(the CASTING DIRECTOR whispers in her ear; then, to Mia,)
Never mind. Thanks for coming in.
Beat. Mia manages a smile.

INT. LOBBY - DAY

Mia exits. [...] Enters the elevator with two other WOMEN–rail-thin, legs up to their ribs. Mia looks nothing like them.

INT. APARTMENT - DAY

Mia enters. Exhausted. [...] It's one of those tiny walled-off dens[4] not part of the original design, used to siphon off rent. An Ingrid Bergman poster hangs over the bed. Mia takes off her shoes. A blister[5] on her sole...

Damien CHAZELLE, *LA LA LAND*, 2013

1. = exterior 2. = interior 3. = continued 4. *appartement minable* 5. *ampoule*

a. Observe the poster and **imagine** what type of movie it is.

b. Read the text and **pick out** the specific elements in such a document.

c. GRAMMAR **Focus on** Mia. **Rephrase** what is happening to her.

d. Explain how she embodies the quest for the American Dream.

e. Explain what the scene reveals about the limits of the American dream.

▲ *La La Land* directed by Damien Chazelle, 2016.

YOUR TASK

DIFFÉRENCIATION

Rewrite the scene with a different ending.

WAY 1

1 Mia's performance is the same.
2 She reacts to the casting team's attitude.

WAY 2

1 Mia plays the scene one more time.
2 The casting team are impressed.

Build your skills! Caractériser, raconter et décrire

- Utilise le **présent simple** pour caractériser quelqu'un ou raconter une histoire :
  - *Mia **looks** nothing like them.*
  - *Mia **exits**.*
- Utilise le **présent en *be* + *-ing*** pour décrire une action en cours de déroulement :
  - *Mia's **auditioning** for a casting.*

Quiz
TEST yourself

BUILD YOUR ENGLISH → p. 30

EXPLORE Art is money

1

inews.co.uk, 2022.

Wickedly cynical: splitting the Wicked movie into two is a boring cash grab

The upcoming movie-musical, starring Cynthia Erivo and Ariana Grande, is the latest to succumb to Hollywood's habit of making two films where one would have sufficed

Audio

The Art of Filmmaking Versus Money, *Beyond Film School*, 2023.

Review: 'Minions' is a plotless cash grab starring annoying Twinkies

Despicable Me. The sidekicks set out on a journey for a new villain to serve, which

complex.comcomplex.com, 2017.

Do We Really Need More 'Avatar' Films?

Don't expect any originality in the upcoming 'Avatar' movies.

KYLE NEUBECK

APRIL 24, 2017

SHARE COMMENT

tampabay.com, 2015.

a. **Look at** the documents and **identify** their nature. **Guess** what these movies have in common.

b. **Read** the title of the audio and **make** hypotheses about its content.

c. **Listen to** the audio and **take notes** on the opposition exposed.

d. **Explain** the impact of money on filmmaking.

e. **Debate:** Is money necessary to make art?

VOCABULARY SPOT

- blank page
- blockbuster
- playwright = writer of plays

- creative
- greedy = interested in money
- lucrative = profitable
- torn between

- earn /'ɜːrn/ money
- rush = hurry

MEMORISE your vocabulary

2

e-WB **Différenciation**

Audio version

Young playwright Barton Fink discusses with his agent, Garland Stanford.

GARLAND

We have to talk a little business. I've just been on the phone to Los Angeles. Barton, Capitol Pictures wants to put you under contract. They've offered you a thousand dollars a week. I think I can get them to go as high as two.

BARTON

To do what?

GARLAND

What do you do for a living?

BARTON

I'm not sure anymore. I guess I try to make a difference.

GARLAND

Fair enough. No pressure here, Barton, because I respect you, but let me point out a couple of things. One, here you make a difference to five hundred fifty people a night-if the show sells out. Eighty-five million people go to the pictures every week.

BARTON

To see pap[1].

GARLAND

Yes, generally, to see pap. However, point number two: A brief tenure[2] in Hollywood could support you through the writing of any number of plays.

BARTON

I don't know, Garland; my place is here right now. I feel I'm on the brink of success—

GARLAND

I'd say you're already enjoying some.

Barton leans earnestly forward.

BARTON

No, Garland, don't you see? Not the kind of success where the critics fawn over[3] you or the producers like Derek make a lot of money. No, a real success-the success we've been dreaming about-the creation of a new, living theater of, about, and for the common man! If I ran off to Hollywood now I'd be making money, going to parties, meeting the big shots, sure, but I'd be cutting myself off from the wellspring of that success, from the common man.

He leans back and chuckles ruefully.

BARTON

I guess I'm spouting off[4] again. But I am certain of this, Garland: I'm capable of more good work. Maybe better work than I did in *Choirs*. It just doesn't seem to me that Los Angeles is the place to lead the life of mind.

Joel and Ethan Coen, *Barton Fink*, 1991

1. *bêtises* 2. job 3. flatter 4. speak without thinking

a. Read the introduction and **identify** the characters.

b. Read the script and **take notes** on Barton's situation (current job, job offer).

c. Identify the arguments used by Garland to convince Barton and **rephrase** them.

d. Explain how Barton feels and **sum up** his argument.

CULTURE SPOT

Barton Fink

The movie won the Cannes *Palme d'Or* in 1991, as well as awards for Best Director and Best Actor. Barton Fink is attracted to California. He discovers the harsh reality of Hollywood.

YOUR TASK

Act out the following scene between Barton Fink and Garland Stanford.

1. **Make** a decision for Barton's future and **brainstorm** arguments to justify his choice.
2. **Write**, then **act out** the dialogue between the two characters. **Include** questions and reactions.

Build your skills! Relancer une conversation

- Pose des **questions ouvertes** :
  - *To do what?*
  - ***What do you do** for a living?*
- Utilise des **questions rhétoriques** pour introduire les arguments :
  - *No, Garland, **don't you see**?*

BUILD YOUR ENGLISH → p. 31

Quiz **TEST yourself**

EXPLORE A dream in progress

1

Audio version

The Queen of Sugar Hill presents a fictional portrait of Hattie McDaniel, the first African-American woman to win an Academy Award in 1940.

Gone was the indescribable hunger I had back then, when I lived in a home haunted by my parents' memories of how they'd escaped slavery and their never-ending quest to give us a better life. [...]

I strained[1] to get a glimpse of my costars from *Gone with the Wind*. We were up for eleven awards, so they had prime seating near the stage. Their tables were round and held anywhere from ten to twenty-four people. I'd been led to the very back of the room, just outside the double door leading to the kitchen. There was seating only for three here. A grudging[2], mean little message meant for me: *Don't be too full of yourself. Never ever take up too much space.*

"Why is she here?" someone muttered from the table across from me. I recognized the woman as a character actress from a silent movie. I wanted to shout, *I deserve to be here!* but I nodded pleasantly at her. [...]

"I'm really especially happy that I'm chosen to present this particular plaque," Fay[3] began. I could hear the smile in her voice even if she was so far away I couldn't clearly see her expression.

"To me, it seems more than just a plaque of gold," Fay continued. "It opens the door of this room, moves back the walls and enables us to embrace the whole of America, an America that we love..."

I scooted[4] to the edge of my seat as her next words tumbled out. "...I present the Academy Award for Best performance of an Actress in a Supporting Role during 1939 to Hattie McDaniel."

ReShonda TATE, *The Queen of Sugar Hill*, 2024

1. make efforts 2. *à contre-coeur* 3. Fay Bainter, American actress 4. *bouger rapidement*

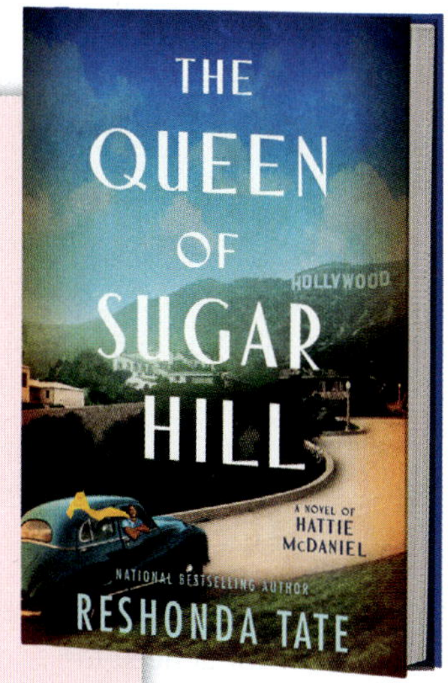

CULTURE SPOT

Hattie McDaniel
This African-American actress played Mammy in ***Gone with the Wind***. The 1939 movie tells the story of Scarlett O'Hara, the daughter of a Georgia plantation owner, during the Civil War and Reconstruction era.

2

Video

Ke Huy Quan wins best supporting actor, *Oscars*, 2023.

◄ Ke Huy Quan at the 2023 Oscars.

TEAM WORK

Team A works on doc 1 and Team B works on doc 2.

a. **Study** the document and **pick out** information about the actress/actor. **Explain** what is happening to her/him.

b. **Explain** the obstacles she/he has or had to overcome.

VOCABULARY SPOT

- assimilation
- land of plenty: *terre d'abondance*
- recognition
- affluent = wealthy
- penniless = poor
- achieve
- integrate
- overcome = surmount

MEMORISE your vocabulary

3

For Adrien Brody, his role in *The Brutalist* is more than an opportunity to win awards, though he has already done that. The film, which follows an architect who flees[1] postwar Europe for the United States, hits close to home.

"I definitely have an intimate understanding of the immigrant experience, as my mother is a Hungarian refugee," Brody told *Yahoo Entertainment*. "My grandparents and my mother fled Budapest in 1956 and came to America with hopes and dreams."

Like his character, László Toth, Brody's mom dedicated her life to "trying to leave behind something of great significance."

"Her experiences in the past informed her work, and her experiences have influenced me and my understanding of life and my own connection to art and yearnings[2] as an artist." [...]

The movie, he said, speaks to the "paradox" of the immigrant experience. Though it begins in the year 1947, it's still relevant today.

"One leaves behind all this hardship and oppression and comes to a nation such as the United States with all these hopes and dreams and assimilates and leaves behind a lot of that and becomes a member of the community and devotes themselves to it and yet is not still fully accepted or is looked down upon because they sound different, look different, have different beliefs or because of their name," he said. "It's just wrong, and it troubles me that it still exists."

Kelsey Weekman, *Yahoo!Entertainment*, 2024

▲ *The Brutalist* directed by Brady Corbet, 2024.

1. escape 2. *aspirations*

a. Observe the movie poster and **analyse** it (symbols, layout…).

b. Read the article and **pick out** information about the movie plot.

c. VOCABULARY **Pick out** the expressions related to immigration. What vision of immigration is given?

d. Explain how the actor's story has influenced his career.

A LITTLE EXTRA Video

Watch the trailer of *The Brutalist* and **see** how the immigrant experience is portrayed in the movie.

YOUR TASK

Write the script of the scene in *The Queen of Sugar Hill*.

1. **Write** the dialogues.
2. **Add** stage directions.
3. **Insert** the inner thoughts of the main character.

Ai Tu peux utiliser un outil d'IA pour transformer ton script en storyboard et le rendre plus attractif.

Build your skills! **Donner des indications scéniques**

Utilise des verbes précis pour **décrire les actions** des personnages :

- *She **strains** to get a glimpse of her costars.*
- *Someone **mutters** from the table.*
- *She **nods** pleasantly at her.*
- *She **scoots** to the edge of her seat.*

Quiz **TEST yourself**

TEST YOUR CULTURE AND VOCABULARY

"AND THE WINNER IS…"

HOW TO PLAY

Form two teams of three and **pick** a referee. You have 30 seconds to **write** as many words, expressions and names as you can as you go from theme 1 to 10. The team who has the most correct words or expressions wins an Oscar.

At the end, the team with the most Oscars reaches the Walk of Fame!

Build your English!

VOCABULARY

Les compléments numériques
e-WB
lycee.nathan.fr/2sb028-029

EXERCISES → p. 232

MEMORISE your vocabulary

HOLLYWOOD: THE DREAM FACTORY

The American Dream

- fame /feɪm/ = stardom
- success /sək'sɛs/
- wealth /welθ/
- magical
- unattainable
- chase /tʃeɪs/ = pursue /pər'sjuː/ one's dream
- make money = earn money
- reach one's goal

The industry

- casting director
- filmmaker = movie director
- film set
- part = role
- producer
- screenplay = scenario/script
- screenwriter
- stuntman: *cascadeur*
- audition
- shoot a movie

Business

- agent
- blockbuster
- lack = absence of
- wage /weɪdʒ/ = salary
- greedy = interested in money
- lucrative
- money-making = profitable
- release a movie

Stage directions

- frown /'fraʊn/
- grin = smile
- grumble = complain
- shake one's head ≠ nod
- shout = scream
- weep = sob
- whisper = mutter

Movie genres

- animated
- comedy
- drama
- fantasy
- horror
- musical
- romance/romcom (romantic comedy)
- thriller

NOUN · ADJECTIVE · VERB · ADVERB OR PREPOSITION

1 Name it! Then spot the odd one out.

a. A character played by an actor/actress.
b. The script for a movie, including descriptions of scenes and some camera directions.
c. Give a performance to try to get a part in a film.
d. The state of being recognised by many people.

2 Look at these faces. What type of film are they watching?

a. b. c. d.

3 Match the pictures with the job they refer to.

a. b. c. d.

screenwriter · stuntman · producer · movie director

4 Look at the still from *Once Upon a Time in Hollywood*. Describe it and imagine the corresponding stage directions.

Once Upon a Time in Hollywood, 2019.

Build your English!

GRAMMAR

EXCERCISES → p. 236-237

A Évoquer des faits présents à l'aide du présent simple et du présent en *be* + V-*ing*

GRAMMAR tuto

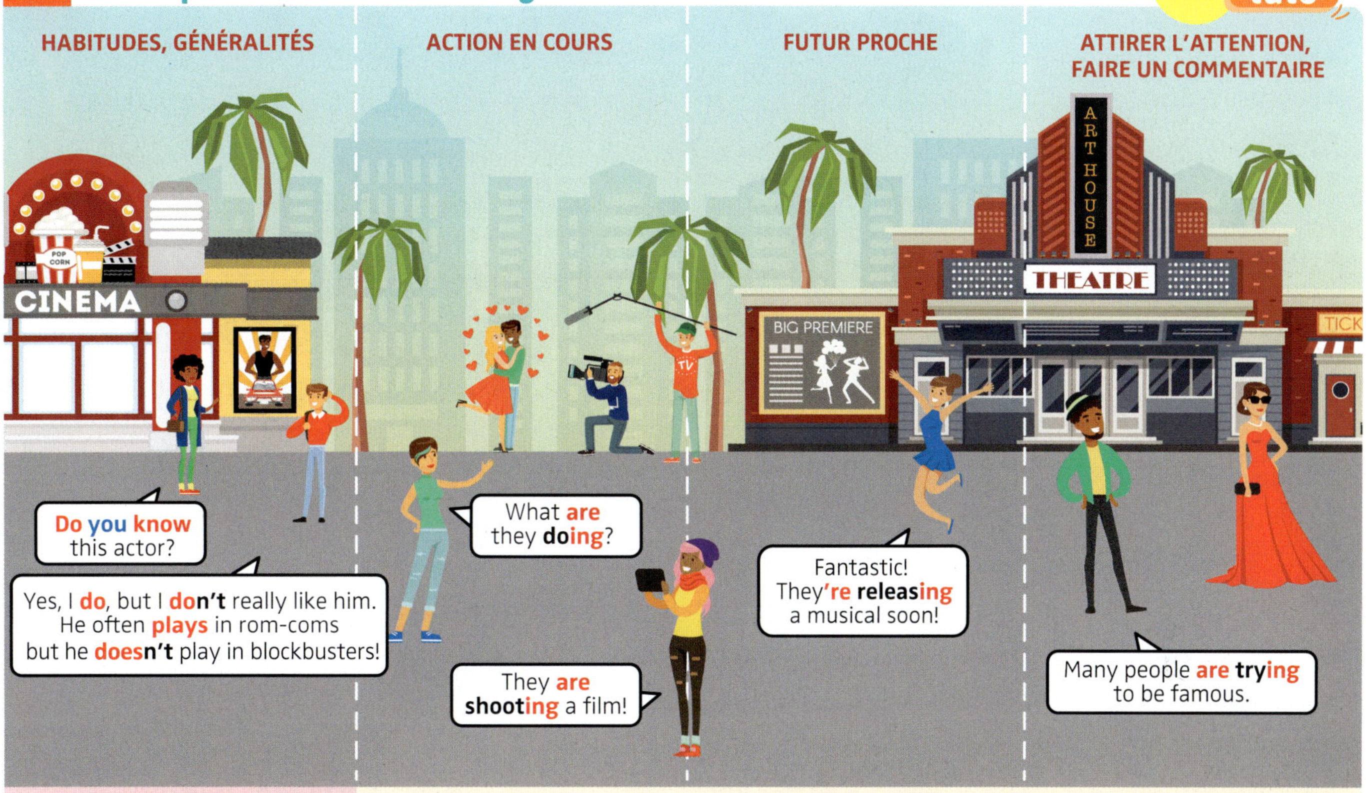

Présent simple	Présent *be* + V-*ing*
Auxiliaire : *do*/*does* ou *don't*/*doesn't* Attention au *s* à la 3e pers. du sing.	Auxiliaire : *be* au présent

1 Associe chaque phrase au complément de temps qui convient. Justifie ton choix.

a. I go to the cinema — in a few days.
b. They are auditioning for the role — once a week.
c. I'm writing a new screen play — at the moment.
d. They release an animated film — every month.

2 Conjugue les verbes au présent simple ou *be* + V-*ing* selon la situation et le sens de la phrase.

a. These days, film directors [become] less creative and greedier, films [lose] their magic.
b. A stuntman usually [play] the main actor's part but he [take] risks while the main actor [not / take] any!
c. Blockbusters always [attract] a lot of people! Fans often [rush] to the cinema.
d. Tonight, actors [receive] their Oscars during a ceremony. They usually [deliver] a speech to thank everyone.

3 Tu es guide dans les rues de L.A. Tu assistes à cette scène de tournage. Explique à ton groupe de quoi il s'agit en général et ce à quoi vous êtes en train d'assister.

▲ Margot Robbie on the set of *Once Upon a Time in Hollywood*, 2019.

B Se renseigner sur les faits et les personnes grâce aux questions

GRAMMAR tuto

Il existe **deux types de questions** en anglais.

LES QUESTIONS FERMÉES

= *Yes/No questions*

On peut y **répondre par oui ou non**.

Auxiliaire + Sujet + Verbe

Do you like romcoms? → Yes, I **do**.
Don't you like comedies? → No, I **don't**.
Does he play in comedies? → Yes, he **does**.

LES QUESTIONS OUVERTES

= *WH- questions*

Elles commencent par un **mot interrogatif** indiquant le **type d'information attendue**.

Mot interrogatif + Auxiliaire + Sujet + Verbe

What roles **do you like** playing?
→ I like playing heroes.
Where did they shoot the film?
→ They shot it in NYC.
Why do you play in musicals?
→ Because I love singing.

***BE* superstar ! À la fois verbe et auxiliaire.**

Are you a movie fan? → Yes, I **am**.
When is the film premiere? → It **is** next week.
Who is your favourite actress? → Zendaya **is** my favourite actress.

Quand le <u>mot interrogatif</u> est <u>sujet</u> de la question, il n'y a <u>pas d'auxiliaire</u>.

Who won the Oscar last year? → Emma Stone won the Oscar.
Which book **inspired** the film? → *The Queen of Sugar Hill* inspired it.

***How* peut être suivi d'un adjectif, d'un quantifieurs ou d'un adverbe.**

How <u>old</u> is Timothée Chalamet? *(âge)*
How <u>far</u> is Hollywood? *(distance)*
How <u>many</u> films have you seen? *(quantité)*

Whose + <u>chose possédée</u>
→ **Whose** <u>Oscar</u> is it?

1 Remets les mots dans l'ordre pour former des questions.

a. you / thrillers / like / Do / ?
b. auditioning / Is / your friend / ? / for the musical
c. are / When / releasing / the film / ? / they
d. is / Whose / it / ? / screenplay

2 Pose la question sur l'élément en bleu.

a. **Steven Spielberg** wrote the screenplay.
b. They shoot films **every day**!
c. This film lasts **three hours**!
d. I love horror films **because they are thrilling**!

3 Des taches d'encre sont tombées sur le bloc-notes du journaliste. Retrouve les questions posées à une réalisatrice. Aide-toi des réponses.

– ■?
– Yes, I do, I really love my job!
– ■?
– Yes, indeed! I'm shooting a comedy at the moment.
– ■?
– I wanted to be a film director because, when I was a kid, I was fascinated by Hollywood.
– ■?
– This comedy? On screens? Next summer, I think.
– ■?
– Of course I have a lot of projects, but it's a secret!

4 Tu es journaliste. Prépare quatre questions à poser à ces acteurs.

▲ Robert Downey Jr., Da'Vine Joy Randolph, Emma Stone and Cillian Murphy during the 96th Annual Academy Awards in Hollywood, 2024.

PHONOLOGY

Les compléments numériques
e-WB
lycee.nathan.fr/2sb032

A La prononciation de la graphie <o> Audio

En anglais, la voyelle **<o>** peut se prononcer :
- /ɒ/ *top* /'tɒp/,
- /əʊ/ *note* /'nəʊt/,
- /ɔː/ *short* /'ʃɔːt/,
- /uː/ *move* /'muːv/,
- /ə/ quand elle n'est pas accentuée : *parody* /'pærədi/.

1 Écoute ces mots, puis associe-les avec la prononciation correspondante.

role • actor • box office • who • political • producer • shoot • comedy • perform

/əʊ/

video

/uː/

movie

/ɒ/

Oscar

/ɔː/

popcorn

/ə/

director

2 Lis ces mots et trouve l'intrus. Vérifie, puis entraîne-toi à les prononcer.

a. blockbuster – comedy – studio – Hollywood
b. emotion – romance – producer – director
c. prohibit – hope – scenario – stardom
d. lose – sport – prove – shoes

3 Lis ce discours de Steven Spielberg. Écoute pour vérifier ta prononciation.

When I was young, I would observe old films and the way a single shot could convey so much emotion. I was born to shoot movie scenes, and to direct aspiring actors. I've reached my dream to become a popular director.

B L'intonation des questions Audio

L'intonation est différente selon le **type de questions** :
– **questions fermées** (*Yes/no questions*) : l'intonation **monte.** ↗
– **questions ouvertes** (*wh- questions*) : l'intonation **descend.** ↘
- *No Garland, don't you see?* ↗
- *Are these pastries gluten-free?* ↗
- *What is all this?* ↘
- *What do you do for a living?* ↘

4 Écoute ces questions et dis si l'intonation est montante ou descendante. Vérifie puis entraîne-toi à les prononcer.

a. What is your next film?
b. Do you like playing the villain?
c. How would you define your character?
d. Have you ever acted in a science-fiction movie?

5 Entraîne-toi pour ta future audition. Vérifie l'intonation des questions et répète.

Why did you leave me alone?

How could you do this to me?

Have you ever visited the Hollywood studios?

What have you been doing all these years?

6 Prépare cinq questions pour interviewer Emma Stone. Entraîne-toi à bien les prononcer.

▲ Emma Stone at the Award Gala Tribute to Diane Keaton, 2017.

YOUR FINAL TASK

I Write the scene of a screenplay about Hollywood.

You are an assistant screenwriter in Hollywood and you are going to contribute to the writing of a movie's script . The movie aims at celebrating Hollywood's 100th anniversary. It will gather ten different short films each illustrating a theme linked to the film industry. Write the first page of your script.

1. **Brainstorm ideas to start your script:**
   – choose a genre that will give the tone of the script,
   – select a period of the Hollywood industry you want to highlight,
   – choose a point of view (a movie director, an actor, a screenwriter…),
   – create a lead character (background, current career in Hollywood, dream…).

2. **Write a page of your script that you will send to your screenwriters' team:**
   – start with the dialogues between the different characters,
   – include technical indications to help the actors and the directing team.

YES YOU CAN!

Write a script

POSER LE DÉCOR

Pose le décor de cette première scène : on devra comprendre quand cela se passe et où. Les indications scéniques (intérieur/extérieur, lieu, date…) devront apparaître.

INT. APARTMENT – DAY

Mia enters. Exhausted. […]

It's one of those tiny walled-off dens not part of the original design, used to siphon off rent. An Ingrid Bergman poster hangs over the bed.

INSÉRER DU DIALOGUE

Rédige un dialogue entre les personnages. Prends en compte les spécificités de l'oral (phrases incomplètes, interruption, registre de langue, intégration de questions…).

BARTON

To do what?

GARLAND

What do you do for a living?

BARTON

I'm not sure anymore. I guess I try to make a difference.

INTRODUIRE LES PERSONNAGES

Introduis ton/tes personnages en présentant leur identité et/ou leur fonction ainsi que quelques éléments-clés les concernant.

Mia's auditioning for a CASTING DIRECTOR and ASSISTANT.

CONCLURE LA SCÈNE

Assure-toi de conclure la scène de manière logique et pense à une transition avec la scène suivante.

Mia exits. Enters the elevator with two other WOMEN – rail-thin, legs up to their ribs. Mia looks nothing like them.

DONNER DES INDICATIONS SCÉNIQUES

N'oublie pas de donner des indications aux acteurs (émotions, gestuelle).

Barton leans earnestly forward.

He leans back and chuckles ruefully.

Beat. Mia manages a smile.

HOW TO SHINE IN WRITING → p. 204

PRACTISE AND SHINE

Compréhension de l'oral

◀ Michelle Yeoh, Oscar for the best actress, 2023.

Audio

Michelle Yeoh about her leading role in *Everything Everywhere All at Once, NPR*, 2023.

A1›A2 **Step 1** Before listening to the audio, **observe** the picture and **read** the caption.

a. **Describe** the woman in the picture (clothes, attitude).

b. **Brainstorm** ideas about the topic of the audio.

A2 **Step 2** **Listen to** the audio once. **Take notes** about:

a. the different speakers b. the topic of the movie presented.

A2›B1 **Step 3** **Listen to** the audio again and **pick out** the key words about:

a. the actress b. the movie plot c. the message behind the movie.

B1›B1+ **Step 4** **Recap.**

WAY 1. **Link** the ideas and **recap**.

a. **Choose** the correct answers:

- The audio is an interview / a podcast / a radio ad about Michelle Yeoh's family story / new movie / Oscar.

b. **Complete** the recap using the prompt: Everything Everywhere All at Once *deals with…*

c. **Add** details using some of the elements below:

reach one's dream | believe in one's dream | patient | resilient | recognised

WAY 2. **Mets en lien** les informations recueillies et **récapitule** en français ou en anglais. Tu peux utiliser les aides contenues dans la *Way 1*.

B1+›B2 **Go further**

- **Identify** the tone of the interviewer and **explain** her attitude.

TIPS

- **Utilise** tes connaissances de la culture populaire et **relie-les** aux connaissances culturelles de l'unité pour anticiper le contenu de l'audio ou de la vidéo.

TIPS

- **Prête** une attention particulière aux différentes voix et intonations pour identifier les différents intervenants et leur rôle.

TIPS

- **Repère** les éléments en lien avec le rêve américain et **relie-les** aux éléments clés de l'audio.

TIPS

- **Repère** à qui/quoi fait référence la journaliste et **retrouve** les liens entre la fiction et la réalité.

e-WB **Grille d'autoévaluation**

Compréhension de l'écrit

Foreword

I was in Hollywood at the time, and my agent, Al Levy, talked me into performing a song at a party in Beverly Hills–which somehow led to an invitation to come to Warner Bros for a screen test. I didn't know at the time that my life was about to change forever, that I would be on the lot[1] for the next seven years, make seventeen pictures on its sets and backlots[2], record dozens of songs, and spend hundreds of hours working very hard in virtually every corner of the studio. I learned much during my days in Warner Bros.

When they first took me onto the *Romance on the High Sea* soundstage[3], I naively asked when we'd be leaving for the boat. Everyone laughed at me. But as I explored that film's intricate[4] ocean liner settings, I realized that this soundstage and its dozens of sisters on the lot had actually been the place where hundreds of the movies I had watched growing up in Cincinnati had really been made.

It astonished me that every location imaginable, from the high sea to tropical jungles could all be created, seemingly from scratch, in this remarkable place. Eventually it occurred to me that most of what I thought I knew about ships or jungles, or about a thousand other places I'd never actually visited, actually came from seeing these films.

To this day I can't decide if Hollywood takes its visual cues[5] from the real world, or if it is in fact, the other way around.

Doris Day[6]

Steven BINGEN, *Warner Bros. Hollywood's Ultimate Backlot*, 2018

1. studio 2. *plateaux* 3. *studio insonorisé* 4. complex 5. *signals* 6. American actress and singer born in 1922.

A1 › A2 **Step 1** Before reading the text, **focus on** the title.

a. Say what the subject of the book is.

b. Guess what a "foreword" is.

> **TIPS**
> • **Utilise** les informations que tu as retenues sur Hollywood.

A2 **Step 2 Read** the text once and **pick out** the information about:

a. the narrator **b.** the context (time, place, events).

> **TIPS**
> • **Repère** les dates et les noms propres pour dégager le contexte.

B1 **Step 3 Read** the text again and **find out**:

a. why the actress was invited to a screen test in 1948;

b. what she discovered about Hollywood and its studios.

B1 › B1+ **Step 4 Link** the ideas and **recap**.

a. Explain the difference between Doris Day's and Steven Bingen's roles.

b. Complete the recap using the prompt: ***After a while, Doris Day discovered…***

c. Enrich your recap using some of the words below:

unexperienced | amaze | mistaken | deceive | take for granted

d. Explain why a foreword adds a certain credibility to the book.

> **TIPS**
> • Pour mettre en avant la chronologie, **utilise** des mots de liaison comme *first, then, finally*…

B1+ › B2 **Go further**

• **Comment on** the last sentence: "I can't decide if Hollywood takes its visual cues from the real world, or if it is in fact, the other way around."

e-WB **Grille d'autoévaluation**

SHORTFILE 2

Cowboys ride back

▶ How has the archetypal figure of the cowboy evolved in American artistic creation?

YOUR FINAL TASK

Write a one-page comic that retells the myth of the cowboy.

19th century			20th century
(1803) After the **Louisiana Purchase**, which doubled the size of the USA many people "went West" : ranchers, pioneers and sheriffs/lawmen.	(1848-1855) **California Gold Rush.**	(1865) After the Civil War, more people went West. Railways arrived and there were **lots of jobs for cowboys** to herd cows to the railways.	(1910) **First Western movies in Hollywood.** Cowboys were white heroes, often fighting "Indians" (white actors with makeup).

1. An American hero

1

The cowboy stands as an iconic figure in American culture, embodying the rugged[1] individualism and frontier spirit that have come to define the nation's identity. Originating from the Mexican vaqueros, the American cowboy emerged as a symbol of freedom, self-reliance[2], and adventure on the open plains.

The cowboy's influence on American identity extends far beyond the historical realities of frontier life, shaping a national mythos that continues to resonate today. This romanticized image of the cowboy has permeated[3] literature, film, and popular culture, contributing to a collective imagination of what it means to be American.

simplytexan.com

1. *sauvage (ici)* 2. independence 3. *imprégnait*

2

▶ **Video**
Hollywood Cowboys, *American Experience* / *PBS*, 2022.

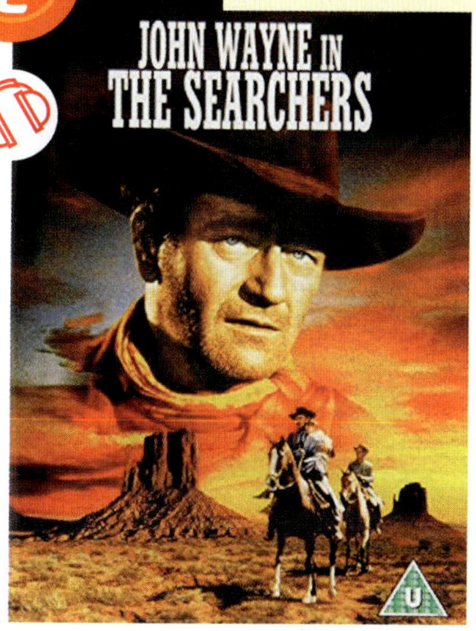

▲ Movie poster for *The Searchers*, John Ford, 1956.

TEAM WORK

Team A **read doc 1 and the timeline.**
Team B **observe the poster and watch doc 2.**

a. **Give** the characteristics of the cowboy.

b. **Find** information about his presence in Hollywood.

- Now **share** your information to define the cowboy archetype.

VOCABULARY SPOT

- gunfighter
- brave = courageous
- determined
- lonely /'ləʊnli/
- manly
- mysterious
- ruthless
- challenge
- duel /'djuːəl/
- embody
- ride a horse

MEMORISE your vocabulary

3

a. Look at the comic page and **list** all the visual elements that match the cowboy archetype.

b. Read the text and **sum up** the situation.

c. Analyse the attitude of the cowboy: to what extent is he an archetypal cowboy?

d. GRAMMAR *"What's a young lady like yourself doing carrying such a [...] sidearm in her purse?"* (frame 5) **Identify** the tense and **say** why it is used.

e. Comment on the way the woman is depicted in the page.

◀ Bunn Cullen, Hurtt Brian, *The Sixth Gun, book 2: Crossroads*, 2011.

1. nurse = drink very slowly
2. dull: *atténuer*
3. draw: *le moment auquel on dégaine*
4. pickled = drunk
5. sidearm = gun

YOUR TASK

As a fan of *The Sixth Gun*, you take part in a comic contest. Write the following frames.

1 **Describe** the meeting between the two characters after the last frame.

2 Don't forget to **give** the woman an important part.

Build your skills! **Écrire les dialogues d'une BD**

➔ Pose des **questions** pour rendre tes dialogues dynamiques :
- *How did you know?*

➔ Utilise des **contractions** dans un souci d'authenticité :
- *Yer in my seat, boy.*
- *Y'ever hear of Kid Bedlam...*

Quiz TEST yourself

HOW TO SHINE IN GRAMMAR ➔ p. 213

EXPLORE 2. Debunking the myth

1

Video
The Black Cowboys Hollywood Tried to Hide, *American Experience / PBS*, 2022.

a. **Watch** the video and **pick out** the reasons why people went West.
b. **Explain** why the American West was multiethnic.
c. **Explain** why this reality contrasts with the cowboy archetype.

2

VOCABULARY SPOT

- frontiersman(woman) = rural settler
- pioneer /paɪəˈnɪər/

- forgotten
- notorious = infamous
- underrated = underestimated

- acknowledge /ækˈnɒlɪdʒ/
- depict
- misrepresent
- recognise /ˈləʊnli/
- restore

MEMORISE your vocabulary

Video
Bass Reeves, an Untold Legend of the Old West, *CBS Sunday Morning*, 2023.

▲ *Lawmen: Bass Reeves*, Amazon Prime, 2023.

a. **Watch** the video and **pick out** information about Bass Reeves.
b. **Explain** why the host introduces the subject with these words: "[he] is finally getting his due."
c. PHONOLOGY **Listen to** these verbs: *lived, called, wrangled, wanted, roamed, worked, loaded, tried, packed, reached.* **Focus** on the <ed> endings: what do you notice?
d. **Comment on** the fact that the film is based on a true story.

3 e-WB Différenciation

Who is the 21st century cowboy?

As America has changed, so have our heroes. By the 1960s, as social revolutions forced conversations about gender, race, politics, and morality, the Western genre was wrestling with the meaning of heroism and villainy—and how and to whom both personae were ascribed[1]. The outlaws, bank robbers, and ruffians[2] who used to be the villains became the protagonists in films like *Butch Cassidy and the Sundance Kid* and *The Wild Bunch*. Suddenly, audiences were cheering for the man in the black hat as he kicked open the saloon doors—his motives had become as relatable[3] as the sheriff's.

While these "revisionist Westerns" flipped the tables on the Hollywood heroes and villains, the new antiheroes were still almost exclusively straight[4] white men. Americans of any other identity didn't see themselves reflected in the wide-open spaces of the Western plains. But both American society and the Western kept evolving and expanding our notions of who gets to be a worthy[5] hero. In the past couple decades, Westerns have told the stories of gay men *(Brokeback Mountain)*, black men *(The Hateful Eight)*, women *(Meek's Cutoff)*, and young girls *(True Grit)*, among others.

theatlantic.com, 2018

1. attributed 2. violent people 3. *reconnaissable* 4. *hétérosexuel* 5. *digne*

▲ *Calamity Jane* movie by Terry Miles, 2024.

a. Observe the picture and **react**.
b. Read the text and **explain** what has changed.
c. Analyse the evolution of this change.
d. GRAMMAR **Rephrase** "used to" (l.5).

A LITTLE EXTRA Video

Watch the trailer of *Calamity Jane* (2024) and **explain** the way it changes our vision of western movies.

YOUR TASK

DIFFÉRENCIATION

Take part in an interview on what is new about the retelling of the West.

WAY 1

Interview the directors of *Lawmen: Bass Reeves*.

1. **Ask** them about the reasons why they chose to portray this character.
2. As the movie directors, **explain** why it was about time black cowboys got their due.

WAY 2

Interview a historian specialised in the story of the West.

1. **Ask** him/her about the myths conveyed in movies that need to be debunked.
2. As the historian, **explain** the contrast between the archetypal cowboy in movies and real historical cowboys. **Use** recent examples.

Build your skills! **Contraster le passé et le présent**

- Utilise le **prétérit** pour raconter des faits passés :
  - *The outlaws **used** to be the villains...*
  - *Black folks **were** on the frontier.*
- Utilise le **présent simple** pour parler d'aujourd'hui :
  - *History **gives** us a cast of characters.*
- Utilise ***while*** pour exprimer le contraste :
  - ***While** these "revisionist westerns" flipped the tables...*

Quiz
TEST yourself

BUILD YOUR ENGLISH → p. 42
HOW TO SHINE IN GRAMMAR → p. 214, 216

EXPLORE

3. Expanding the myth

1

Audio version

"We don't like strangers."

The voice emerges from somewhere over my shoulder. It's cold and distant. A warning even more menacing than that of the growling[1] dog.

I pivot to face the speaker and barely stop myself from stumbling backward. I'm caught between the German Shepherd I just saw lumber[2] to its feet out of the corner of my eye and a woman with a rifle aimed at my kneecap. I can't see her face under the brim of her dusty baseball cap. She's wearing overalls and a flannel shirt, and her hair is one long dark braid dangling[3] over her shoulder.

"We?" I cautiously ask. Maybe she already found a farmhand[4].

"Me and Silas." She gestures toward the German Shepherd. [...] "Who are you and why are you here? [...]

"I saw the ad in the feedstore." I drop my hand because she's obviously not going to shake it.

She gives me a head-to-toe perusal[5]. "You don't look like you can handle this kind of work. Have you ever done manual labor a day in your life?"

Baseball is manual labor. People might think professional sports are glorified manual labor, but if I can hack hours of training, I can hack whatever this job is. "I've spent my whole adult life doing manual labor."

Her lips curl into a sneer[6]. "Your jeans and flannel might be faded, but they're designer label. And you're not even wearing steel-toed boots. You're dressed like someone who's trying to blend in[7], not someone who belongs."

"I'm not afraid of hard work."

"You wouldn't last a day. I eat boys like you for breakfast."

Andrea JENELLE, *No Excuses*, Willow Creek, Book 6, 2024

▲ *No Excuses* by Andrea Jenelle, 2024.

1. *qui grogne* 2. move heavily 3. hang loosely 4. *travailleur agricole* 5. scrutiny 6. *sourire moqueur* 7. have the correct appearance

a. **Look at** the book cover and **guess** what the genre of the novel is.

b. **Read** the excerpt and **find** information about the two characters (job, motives).

c. VOCABULARY **Pick out** each character's clothes and **explain** what they reveal about who they are.

d. **Compare** and **contrast** the man and the woman on the book cover and in the excerpt. What can you expect later in the novel?

e. **React**: to what extent does the figure of the cowboy embody modernity and tradition here?

VOCABULARY SPOT

- icon /'aɪkɒn/
- legacy
- romance
- trend

- authentic = genuine /'dʒɛnjuɪn/
- timeless

- adopt = embrace
- embody = represent

MEMORISE your vocabulary

Les compléments numériques
e-WB
lycee.nathan.fr/**2sb040-041**

2

How Cowboycore Became 2024's Defining Aesthetic

From Beyoncé's *Cowboy Carter* to Pharrell's Western runway[1] extravaganza, yeehaw style is everywhere you look right now.

You'd be hard-pressed to find a more potent symbol of America's ruthless self-determination and far-reaching wanderlust than the cowboy. From the wide-brimmed[2] hat and those body-hugging jeans to the snap-front shirt and the boots—he's an instantly recognizable cultural figure. Better yet, he's one which can be interpreted in a variety of ways.

So perhaps it's not so surprising that the cowboy has become the prevailing archetype of 2024—an election year, no less!—though he may not always look exactly as you remember him. Take, for example, our latest cover star Beyoncé's rendition[3] on her country-inspired album *Cowboy Carter*: flowing silver locks, red-white-and-blue chaps, sitting sidesaddle on a majestic white horse.

Or there's Pharrell Williams's fall-winter 2024 collection, his third as creative director of Louis Vuitton's menswear—faded denim with Western appliques, Nudie suits[4], fringed gaucho pants, Western shirts, bolo ties, and grommeted cowboy boots and hats made of luxe leather. Most notably there was the catwalk casting—a diverse group composed heavily of Black and Native American men—which added a very specific, slyly[5] political layer to Williams's grand vision. "When you see cowboys portrayed, you see only a few versions," Williams said backstage at the show. "You never really get to see what some of the original cowboys looked like. They looked like us, they looked like me. They looked Black. They looked Native American."

Max Berlinger, *gq.com*, 2024

1. *défilé de mode* 2. *à bords larges* 3. *interprétation* 4. suits decorated with fake diamonds 5. *malicieusement*

▲ Beyoncé, Best Country Album award for *Cowboy Carter*, 2025.

a. Look at the picture and **react**.

b. Read the article and **explain** why "*the cowboy has become the prevailing archetype of 2024*" (l. 8-9).

c. GRAMMAR **Focus** on "*a few versions*" (l.20). **Use** another quantifier to show what reality is.

d. Explain Pharrell Williams's vision of the cowboy and his message on the catwalk.

YOUR FINAL TASK

For the San Diego Comic-Con, create a one-page comic that retells the myth of the cowboy.

1. **Choose** a period and a hero to portray.
2. **Invent** a scenario that could be historically relevant.
3. **Add** some dialogues.
4. **Organise** your comic page using captions and (speech or thought) bubbles.

AI Utilise un outil d'IA pour créer ta page et ton illustration.

Build your skills! **Structure une planche de BD**

➔ Utilise des **connecteurs temporels et logiques** :

- **Début :** *Once upon a time – In the late 19th century – Back in the Old West…*
- **Événements :** *Then – Suddenly – Meanwhile – As soon as – After a while…*
- **Conclusion :** *In the end – Eventually – This is how he became a legend…*

Quiz TEST yourself

HOW TO SHINE IN GRAMMAR ➜ p. 216

Build your English!

GRAMMAR

EXERCISES ➜ p. 236-237

Contraster les faits passés et présents

GRAMMAR tuto

IN THE PAST
Pour évoquer des faits passés, révolus, datés
prétérit simple

⊕ The cowboy **was** fearless.
He **lived** on a ranch and had cattle.

⊖ He **didn't have** much sleep.

? **Did** he **live** in the West? Yes, he **did**!

NOWADAYS
Pour évoquer des faits présents, des habitudes, des généralités
présent simple

⊕ The cowboy **is** a popular figure.
He **represents** the West and **inspires** stories.

⊖ He **doesn't earn** much.

? **Do** they **live** on farms? Yes, they **do**!

PAST → PRESENT

I / He / She / It	was
You / We / They	were

They **weren't** cowards.

I	am
He / She / It	is
You / We / They	are

*Le **prétérit** peut s'utiliser avec des **marqueurs temporels** : yesterday, last week, a few years ago, in 1855…*

*Le **présent** peut s'utiliser avec des **marqueurs temporels** : nowadays, now, today…*

1 Choisis la forme verbale qui convient le mieux.

a. A few decades ago, Hollywood *gives* / *gave* us a stereotyped vision of the cowboy.

b. Not all cowboys *were* / *was* lawless, many didn't *robbed* / *rob* banks.

c. Many cowboys *went* / *go* West during the Gold Rush and *lived* / *live* in small towns.

d. Did you *see* / *saw* the latest Western movie? Yes, I did.

2 Recopie ces phrases en conjuguant les verbes au présent simple ou au prétérit simple.

a. Nowadays, the cowboy [*embody*] the West.

b. In the late 19th century, many people [*rush*] West and [*become*] cowboys who [*ride*] horses and [*wear*] boots with spurs.

c. In the 1860s, cowboys [*be / not*] all white, some [*be*] former slaves who [*look*] for freedom in the West.

d. Nowadays, cowboys still [*break*] horses but they [*do /not*] outlaws anymore. [*you / know*] a famous cowboy?

PHONOLOGY

La prononciation de la terminaison *-ed*

La terminaison *-ed* du **prétérit**, et du **participe passé** des verbes **réguliers**, peut se prononcer de trois façons différentes.

Son précédant *-ed*	/p/, /k/, /f/, /s/, /ʧ/, ou /ʃ/	/t/ ou /d/	Tous les autres sons !
Prononciation de *-ed*	/t/	/ɪd/	/d/
Exemples	stopped • looked • laughed • missed • watched • washed	wanted • decided	lived • changed

3 Écoute chaque série de mots et trouve l'intrus.

a. dressed – liked – noticed – buckled

b. wanted – decided – started – robbed

c. planned – missed – worked – stopped

d. buried – dropped – roamed – sued

4 Écoute ces mots et place-les dans la bonne colonne.

shaped faded evolved reinvented concealed nursed originated emerged liked

/t/	/ɪd/	/d/

Les compléments numériques
lycee.nathan.fr/2sb042-043

VOCABULARY

EXERCISES → p. 234

MEMORISE your vocabulary

COWBOYS RIDE BACK

Cowboy

- cattleman = cowboy
- outlaw
- lasso /læ'suː/
- rancher: *éleveur de bétail*
- sheriff = lawman
- brave = fearless
- independent
- lawless
- lonely
- resilient
- tough /'tʌf/

Outfit

- belt
- chaps: *jambières*
- leather vest
- pistol = gun
- spurs: *éperons*
- Stetson = cowboy hat
- denim
- buckle /'bʌkəl/: *boucler*

Archetype

- hero ≠ villain
- myth
- symbol
- authentic = genuine /'dʒɛnjuɪn/
- everlasting
- iconic
- traditional
- endure = last
- evolve
- reinvent
- historically

Life

- bull /bʊl/
- campfire
- cattle: *bétail*
- meadow = prairie
- saloon
- wagon /'wægən/
- wild /'waɪld/
- ride
- roam: *errer*

NOUN ADJECTIVE VERB ADVERB OR PREPOSITION

1 Name it!

a. A vehicle the settlers used to go west.
b. Not respecting the law.
c. A synonym for "last".
d. A synonym for "resistant".

2 Rebuild the words. Watch out, some syllables are useless!

a. MAN TIONAL CAMP LOON CATTLE LONE SA INDE LY FEAR TRADI LESS

b. TOL BOY DOW DE NI PIS PEN MEA IN DENT

3 Separate the words then use them to say what cowboy representation is given here.

SNAPFILE 3

Wicked!

▶ How has the Wicked Witch of the West evolved to mirror society's concerns?

YOUR FINAL TASK

You are the director of an upcoming adaptation of *Wicked*.

Introduce Elphaba to the cast and crew.

FOLLOW THE STEPS

1

Audio

Author Gregory Maguire on creating *Wicked*, *NPR*, 2024.

▲ *Wicked* movie poster, 2024.

a. **Look** at the poster and **describe** the characters. **Imagine** what the story might be about.

b. **Listen** to the audio and **identify** the origin of *Wicked*.

c. **Explain** who Elphaba is and how she was seen in the original story.

d. **Comment on** the author's choice regarding Elphaba.

A LITTLE EXTRA Video

Watch the trailer of *Wicked* and **comment on** the various characters.

PHONOLOGY SPOT

adaptation • conversation • fear • frightened • nameless • terrified

Écoute ces mots. Que remarques-tu concernant la prononciation des lettres en rouge ? Comment appelle-t-on ces sons ?

VOCABULARY SPOT

- main character
- retelling: *réécriture*
- villain

- determined = self-assured
- magical
- wicked = mean

- cast a spell on
- torment

MEMORISE your vocabulary

2

Audio version

The wicked woman was greatly pleased with the success of her trick[1], for as long as she had one of the shoes she owned half the power of their charm, and Dorothy could not use it against her, even had she known how to do so.

The little girl, seeing she had lost one of her pretty shoes, grew angry, and said to the Witch, "Give me back my shoe!"

"I will not," retorted the Witch, "for it is now my shoe, and not yours."

"You are a wicked creature!" cried Dorothy. "You have no right to take my shoe from me."

"I shall keep it, just the same," said the Witch, laughing at her, "and someday I shall get the other one from you, too."

This made Dorothy so very angry that she picked up the bucket[2] of water that stood near and dashed it over the Witch, wetting her from head to foot.

Instantly the wicked woman gave a loud cry of fear, and then, as Dorothy looked at her in wonder, the Witch began to shrink[3] and fall away.

"See what you have done!" she screamed. "In a minute I shall melt away."

"I'm very sorry, indeed," said Dorothy, who was truly frightened to see the Witch actually melting away like brown sugar before her very eyes.

"Didn't you know water would be the end of me?" asked the Witch, in a wailing[4], despairing voice.

"Of course not," answered Dorothy. "How should I?"

"Well, in a few minutes I shall be all melted, and you will have the castle to yourself. I have been wicked in my day, but I never thought a little girl like you would ever be able to melt me and end my wicked deeds. Look out—here I go!"

L. Frank BAUM, *The Wonderful Wizard of Oz*, 1900

1. *ruse* 2. container 3. become smaller 4. *plaintive*

CULTURE SPOT

The Wizard Of Oz is a famous American classic tale by L. Frank Baum. Dorothy, a girl carried by a tornado to the magical land of Oz, seeks the help of the Wizard. Helped by her friends, she will have to face the Wicked Witch of the West to go home to Kansas.

▲ The Wicked Witch of the West and Dorothy in *The Wizard of Oz*, 1939.

a. Observe the picture and **imagine** what the situation might be.

b. Read the text and **identify** the source of the conflict.

c. VOCABULARY **Pick out** adjectives describing the characters' emotions and **comment on** their personality.

d. GRAMMAR **Spot** the modal auxiliaries used on lines 7 and 10 and **say** what they reveal about the witch.

e. Explain Dorothy's reaction at the end of the passage and **comment on** the consequence for the witch.

GRAMMAR SPOT

- *…who was truly **frightened**…*
- *I was **terrified** of her.*
- *a **wailing**, **despairing** voice*

Observe les mots en gras. Quelle est la différence entre les adjectifs en *-ing* et les adjectifs en *-ed* ?

STEP 1

Start your presentation to the cast and crew.

1. **Present** the origins of Elphaba's story and Gregory Maguire's artistic choices.
2. **Describe** her personality.

Build your skills! Présenter un personnage

➔ Caractérise le personnage grâce à des **adjectifs** et des **adverbes** :
- *… the **wicked** witch was **greatly pleased**.*

➔ Utilise la structure ***so*** **+ adjectif +** ***that*** pour expliquer un comportement :
- *- … she was **so angry that** she picked up the bucket of water…*

HOW TO SHINE IN GRAMMAR ➔ p. 211

3

Audio version

They didn't talk much. Galinda was too busy forging alliances with the better girls who had been her rightful roomie[1] prospects. No doubt she could switch rooms at half-term[2], or at any rate next fall. So Galinda left Elphaba alone, and she flew down the hall to gossip with her new friends. Milla, Pfannee, Shenshen. Just as in children's books about boarding school, each new friend was wealthier than the one before. At first Galinda didn't mention who her roomie was. And Elphaba showed no sign of expecting[3] Galinda's company, which was a relief[4]. But the gossip had to start sooner or later. The first wave of discussion about Elphaba concerned her wardrobe[4] and her evident poverty, as if her classmates were above noticing her sickly and sickening color.

Gregory MAGUIRE, *Wicked*, 1995

1. roommate 2. the middle of the trimester 3. *s'attendre à quelque chose* 4. *soulagement* 5. clothes

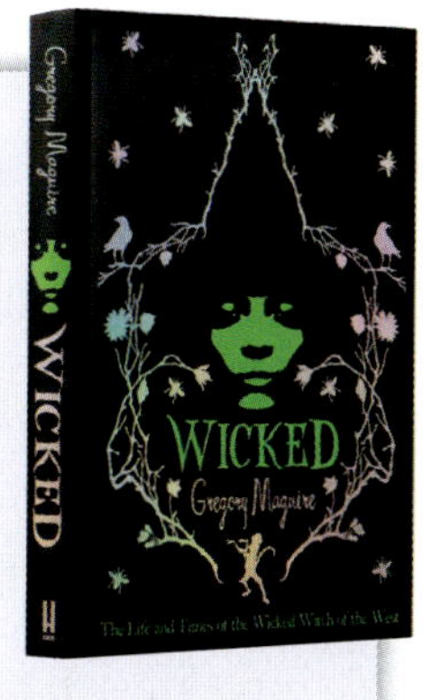

Gregory Maguire's first book of his *Wicked* series.

a. Read the text and **identify** the two main characters.

b. Describe Galinda's attitude towards Elphaba and **compare** the two characters' personalities.

c. PHONOLOGY **Focus on** the adjectives "*sickly and sickening*" (l.14). **Comment on** the effect of their sound.

d. Guess the message the author wants to convey.

4

Something has changed within me
Something is not the same
I'm through with playing
by the rules of someone else's game
Too late for second-guessing
Too late to go back to sleep
It's time to trust[1] my instincts
Close my eyes and leap[2]
It's time to try defying gravity
I think I'll try defying gravity
And you can't pull me down[3] [...]
So if you care to find me
Look to the western sky
As someone told me lately
"Everyone deserves the chance to fly"
And if I'm flying solo
At least I'm flying free
To those who ground[4] me
Take a message back from me
Tell them how I am defying gravity
I'm flying high, defying gravity
And soon, I'll match them in renown

And nobody in all of Oz
No wizard that there is or was
Is ever gonna bring me down
I hope you're happy
(Look at her! She's wicked, get her)
Bring me down!
(No one mourns[5] the wicked!
So we've got to bring her)
Oh! (Down)

Stephen SCHWARTZ, "Defying Gravity", 2003

1. *faire confiance* 2. *faire le grand saut* 3. destroy 4. imprison 5. be sad about

Cynthia Erivo as Elphaba, *Wicked* film, 2024.

a. Read the lyrics of the song and **rephrase** Elphaba's project in the first stanza.

b. Turn to the end (l.23-31) and **explain** Elphaba's feelings.

c. Comment on the quote "*Everyone deserves the chance to fly*" (l.15).

d. In your own words, **rephrase** the message of the song.

Les compléments numériques
e-WB
lycee.nathan.fr/2sb046-047

5

▲ Four artists recalling being in *Wicked* for the show's 20th anniversary, 2023.

Video
A wicked roundtable, *Wicked The Musical*, 2023.

a. Look at the picture and the caption. **Comment on** the event and **guess** the common point between the women.

b. Watch the video and **describe** Elphaba's attitude at the beginning of the show.

c. Guess why she changes attitude over the course of the story.

d. Sum up the lessons learned by the various actresses.

e. Explain why Elphaba is an inspirational character.

VOCABULARY SPOT

- bullying
- outsider = outcast

- isolated /ˈaɪsəleɪtɪd/
- lonesome = lonely, alone, solitary
- self-confident

- assert oneself: *s'affirmer*
- face obstacles
- gossip about someone = backbite

MEMORISE your vocabulary

A LITTLE EXTRA Video

Watch Cynthia Erivo speaking about her role as Elphaba in Jon Chu's movie adaptation.

STEP 2

Carry on with your presentation to the cast and crew.

1 **Mention** the obstacles Elphaba had to overcome and the consequences on her personality.

2 **Explain** why she remains such an inspirational character.

Build your skills! Mettre en avant la force d'un personnage.

➔ Utilise le modal ***can*** pour exprimer la capacité :
- *… we **can** make our ways on our own, we **can** be strong within ourselves …*

➔ Pense au **présent simple** pour évoquer une généralité :
- *Everyone always **identifies** with Elphaba.*

HOW TO SHINE IN GRAMMAR ➔ p. 214, 216

Quiz
TEST yourself

FLASH FILE 4

Star-crossed lovers

▶ How can *Romeo and Juliet* transcend time?

YOUR FINAL TASK — MÉDIATION

In teams, **listen**, **read** and **watch** the documents. **Compare** and **contrast** the different versions of *Romeo and Juliet*. Then **write** a free adaptation of the balcony scene.

e-WB

1

Audio

William Shakespeare, *The Tragedy of Romeo and Juliet*, Act 2 scene 2, 1597.

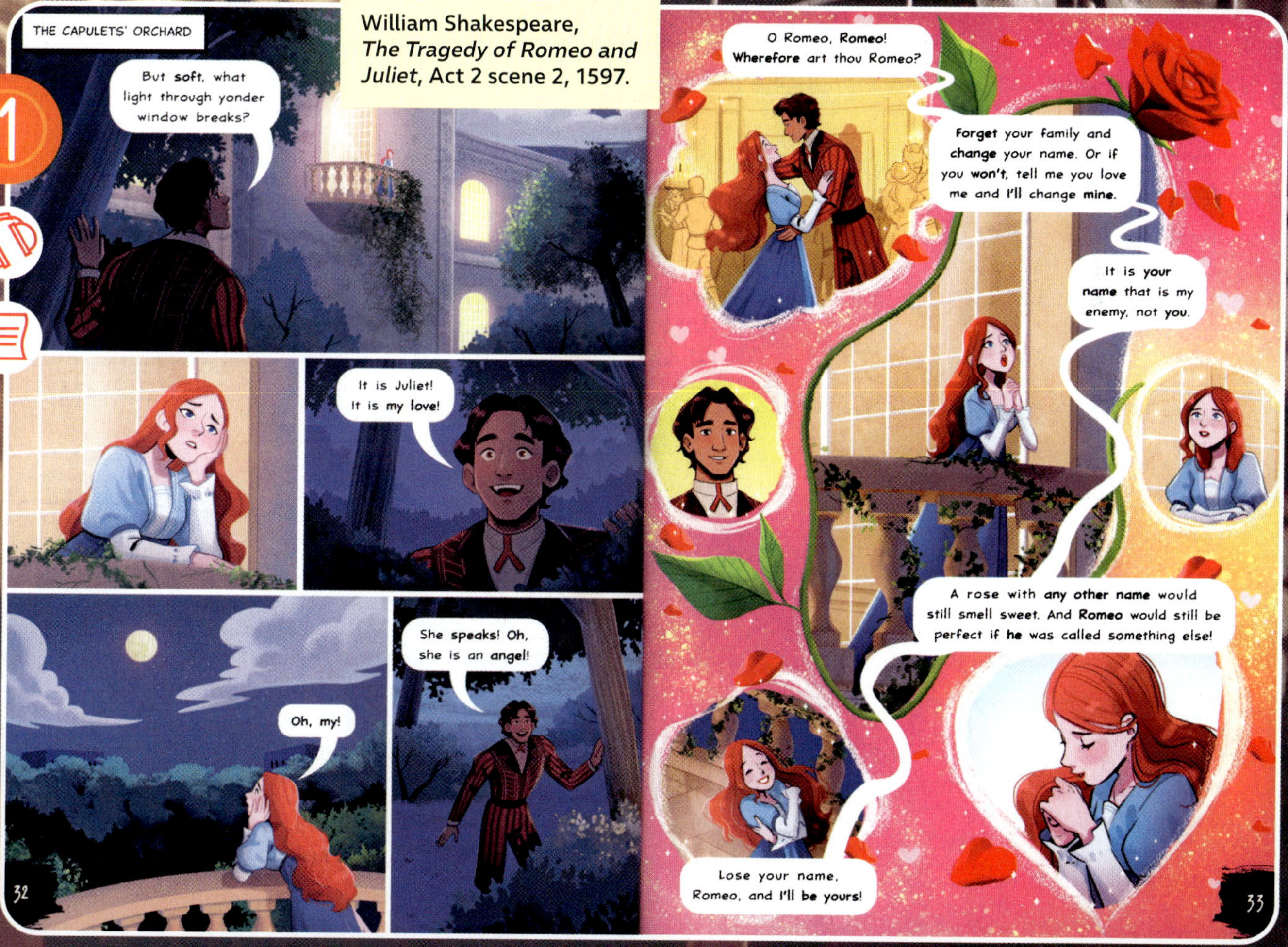

▲ Steve Barlow, Steve Skidmore et Wendy Tan, *Shakespeare's Romeo and Juliet: A Graphic Novel*, 2022

Tony and Maria in NYC in the 50s in 1961 *West Side Story*

Les compléments numériques

lycee.nathan.fr/2sb048-049

2

Audio

West Side Story (Musical) Plot Summary, Stage Agent, 2021

3

A poster of the BBC series adapted from the book, 2020

Video

Dua Lipa In Conversation With Malorie Blackman, Author Of *Noughts & Crosses*, Service 95, 2024.

4

Audio version

Roma and Juliette

In Shanghai in the 1920s, there are two rival gangs: the Scarlet Gang, who are Chinese, and the White Flowers, who are Russian.

“Really?” Juliette demanded through the glass door. “You climbed my house? You couldn’t have simply thrown a few pebbles[1]?”

Roma looked down into the gardens below. “You don’t have any pebbles.”

Juliette rubbed her eyes again, forcefully this time. Maybe if she rubbed hard enough, she would realize this was all a fever dream and she’d wake up peacefully alone in her room.

She removed her hand from her eyes. Roma was still there.

They really needed to upgrade their security.

“Roma Montagov, this is unacceptable,” Juliette declared tightly. This was all too reminiscent, too wistful[2], too much. “Leave before you get shot.”

Even with his face shrouded in the shadows, Roma managed to convey a frown[3] that reached Juliette with maximum effect. He looked around, seeing no one in the gardens below him.

“Who will shoot me?”

“I’m going to shoot you,” Juliette snapped.

“No, you’re not. Open the door, dorogaya[4].”

Chloe GONG, *These Violent Delights*, 2020.

1. stone 2. nostalgic 3. make a face 4. dorogaya = darling in Russian

FILE 5

Indian families

MEA (Ministry of External Affairs), December 25, 2021.

Les compléments numériques
e-WB
lycee.nathan.fr/2sb050-051

How are intergenerational bonds part of Indian culture?

YOUR FINAL TASK

MÉDIATION

Record a report to share stories about the Indian diaspora.

VOCABULARY SPOT

- bond = link = tie /'taɪ/
- diaspora /daɪ'æspərə/
- roots

- close-knit = united
- multigenerational

- move to (a new country) = migrate /maɪ'greɪt/
- preserve

- abroad = overseas

MEMORISE your vocabulary

Video
How Indian is the world?, *Let's Go*, 2024.

TEAM WORK

Team A
Observe the map and the picture. **Imagine** what brings these people together and where it may take place.

Team B
Watch the video and **find** information about the Indian diaspora.

- Now **share** your findings with your friends focusing on the importance of family bonds in Indian culture.

EXPLORE Living together

1

▶ Video
Living in a joint family, *Kannika's Korner*, 2023.

a. **Watch** the video and **pick out** information about the speaker's childhood.

b. GRAMMAR **Rephrase** this sentence with a preterite form:
We would go to meet our relatives.
Does it change the meaning?

c. VOCABULARY **Explain** the difference between her *nuclear family* and her *joint family*.

d. **Identify** the advantages and drawbacks of such a family organisation.

e. **React:** Would you be ready to live in a joint family? Why or why not?

VOCABULARY SPOT

- ancestor
- encounter = meeting
- extended family
- household: *foyer*
- privacy /ˈpraɪvəsi/
- relatives
- interconnected
- welcoming

- dither over something = face a dilemma
- hesitate about
- share
- support = help
- weigh the pros and cons

MEMORISE your vocabulary

CULTURE SPOT

The Indian family
In India, 16% of the population lives in **joint families** or **extended families**. They live with several generations and maintain daily ties. Some even have dozens of **relatives** living under the same roof.

A LITTLE EXTRA ▶ Video
Watch this video to learn more about the consequences of living in a joint family. How much of a caricature do you think this is?

2 e-WB Différenciation

Ghosh, an Indian businessman, and Ashoke, a young Indian student, meet on a train in India.

Ghosh extended his arm out the windows, flicking the glowing tip of his cigarette into the night. "Not this world," he said, glancing[1] disappointedly about the interior of the train. He tilted his head towards the window. "England. America," he said, as if the nameless villages they passed had been replaced by those countries. "Have you considered going there?"

"My professors mention it from time to time. But I have a family," Ashoke said.

Ghosh frowned[2]. "Already married?"

"No. A mother and a father and six siblings. I am the eldest."

"And in a few years you will be married and living in your parents' house," Ghosh speculated.

"I suppose."

Ghosh shook his head. "You are still young. Free," he said, spreading his hands apart for emphasis. "Do yourself a favor. Before it's too late, without thinking too much about it first, pack a pillow and a blanket and see as much of the world as you can. You will not regret it. One day it will be too late."

"My grandfather always says that's what books are for," Ashoke said, using the opportunity to open the volume in his hands. "To travel without moving an inch."

Jhumpa LAHIRI, *The Namesake*, 2003

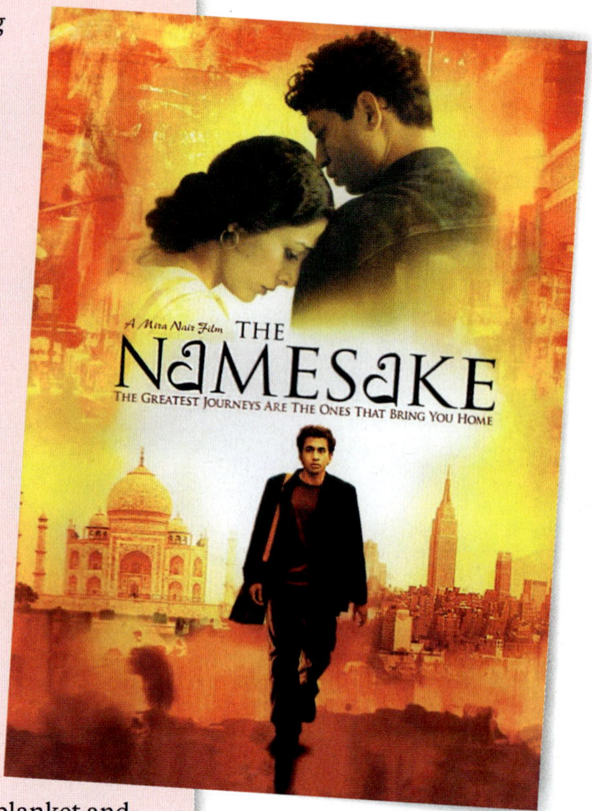

1. look 2. *froncer les sourcils*

a. **Observe** the movie poster and **read** the first paragraph. What opposition is highlighted?

b. **Continue** reading Ashoke's dilemma. **Rephrase** Ghosh's advice to Ashoke.

c. VOCABULARY **Focus** on this sentence *"A mother [...] the eldest"* (l.11-12) and **draw** Ashoke's family tree.

d. **Explain** how this could impact Ashoke's decision.

e. **Explain** how the encounter may impact Ashoke's decision for his future.

YOUR TASK

Record the testimony of an Indian person who used to live in a joint family as a child.

1. **Take notes** on the place of this person in the family and his/her relationship with other family members (difficulties, advantages).
2. **Include** memories of the daily life in this joint family.

Build your skills! **Décrire son environnement.**

→ Utilise les **articles** appropriés pour décrire les choses qui t'entourent.

- *Pack **a** pillow and **a** blanket and see as much of **the** world as you can.*
- *We would go to meet relatives or meet friends.*

BUILD YOUR ENGLISH → p. 61

Quiz TEST yourself

EXPLORE The heart of the diaspora

1

Audio

Kunal Nayyar Q&A Oxford Union, *OxfordUnion*, 2020.

▲ Kunal Nayyar answers questions about his childhood.

a. **Read** the Culture Spot and **brainstorm** ideas about the content of the audio.

b. **Listen to** the audio and **take notes** on Kunal Nayyar's childhood.

c. **Compare** his childhood with his life in the USA.

d. GRAMMAR **Focus on** the sentence *"So if the acting didn't work out I'd still need a way to take care of them, so it was important for me to have something to fall back on."*. **Say** what modal auxiliary "'d" is.

e. **Imagine** what Kunal could have done if the acting had not worked.

VOCABULARY SPOT

- activist
- diaspora
- duty /'dju:ti/ = responsibility
- family values

- committed to
- lonely

- responsible for

- give back
- instill [sth] in [sb] = *inculquer [qch] à [qqn]*
- provide for = *subvenir aux besoins de*

MEMORISE your vocabulary

CULTURE SPOT

Kunal Nayyar
This **British actor** spent his childhood in India. He became famous for his role as Raj in the American TV show *The Big Bang Theory*.

Les compléments numériques
e-WB
lycee.nathan.fr/2sb054-055

2

Explore Search
Monday, Sep 09, 2024 **Hindustan Times** Games E-Paper Sign in
Start 14 Days Free Trial Subscribe

Kamala Harris praises her Indian roots.

By Sanya Jain

U.S. former Vice President Kamala Harris remembered her Indian grandparents and her childhood visits to India on the occasion of National Grandparents Day.

The Democratic Party presidential candidate shared a throwback[1] photograph that shows her with her grandparents, PV Gopalan and Rajam Gopalan, as she remembered the conversations she had with her grandfather.

"As a young girl visiting my grandparents in India, my grandfather took me on his morning walks, where he would discuss the importance of fighting for equality and fighting corruption. He was a retired civil servant who had been part of the movement to win India's independence," claimed Kamala Harris. PV Gopalan had joined the Imperial Secretariat Service during British rule in India. [...]

"My grandmother traveled across India—bullhorn[2] in hand—to speak with women about accessing birth control," Harris, 59, added, crediting her grandparents for instilling in her a love for public service.

1. old 2. *porte-voix*

▲ Kamala Harris's Indian ancestral village honors her as a "daughter of this land", 2024.

A LITTLE EXTRA Video

Watch Kamala Harris sharing memories of her childhood visits to India.
Observe the context and **imagine** why it is important for her to talk about her Indian roots.

a. **Observe** the picture and **read** the caption. What can you **say** about Kamala Harris's origins?

b. **Read** the text and **check** your hypotheses.

c. **Say** how her relationship with her grandparents has influenced her political career.

d. **Draw conclusions** about the tight relationships between Indian people across the diaspora.

e. **Comment on** this visit during the presidential campaign.

YOUR TASK

DIFFÉRENCIATION

Write a passage from the autobiography of an Indian personality.

WAY 1

Choose Kamala Harris's autobiography. **Express** her feelings towards her Indian roots.

WAY 2

Choose an Indian personality who now lives abroad. **Express** both positive and negative feelings when describing his/her childhood.

Build your skills! **Exprimer son opinion sur des habitudes passées.**

➔ Utilise des **verbes d'opinion** pour partager ton ressenti :
- *I really **missed** that living in LA.*
- *I really **loved** that you know, I **don't like** being alone so much.*

➔ **Utilise *would*** pour parler d'habitudes passées :
- *My grandfather **would** discuss the importance of fighting for equality.*

HOW TO SHINE IN GRAMMAR ➔ p. 215

Quiz
TEST yourself

EXPLORE Preserving family traditions?

1

Bollywood–It Brings the Indian-American Family Together

Once my mom walked into my freshman[1] dorm room during Parents Weekend, a sense of comfort accompanied me for the first time in weeks. I hadn't seen my parents in a month, and that was the longest I had ever been without them. So, naturally, I suggested we do the one thing we always did together as a family.

"Let's go watch a Bollywood movie." We left campus, and drove 45 minutes away to a theatre that was showing a two-hour Hindi movie. And in those two hours, I felt at home for the first time in ages. But that is what a Bollywood movie does! It connects me with my parents and my Indian culture in such a unique manner. [...]

It creates a tradition where everyone, whether they're 6 or 60, sits down and just has some great entertainment. Furthermore, these movies (which are usually set in India) provide a great reference to see the type of culture my parents (and other Indian-American parents) grew up in. It provides great context about personality and lifestyle which helps bridge the gap between Indian-American kids and their parents.

Gaurav S., *Majmudarhuffpost.com*, 2016

1. 1st-year student at university

Kalbeliya folk dancer, Jodhpur Rajasthan, India.

TEAMWORK

Team A works on doc 1 and Team B on doc 2.

a. **Read** the text and **pick out** information about the narrator.

b. **Find out** which elements represent Indian culture and **say** how the young generation reacts to it.

c. GRAMMAR **Focus** on tenses and **create** a timeline with verbs in different tenses (present, preterite and past perfect) to emphasise the chronology.

d. **Share** your findings with the other team and **react** to the importance of family traditions in the Indian diaspora.

2

The life of a dancer—as I learned from my grandmother—isn't always adoring audiences, standing ovations or beautiful garlands of flowers. In my own dance incarnation there were the inevitable highs and lows. It was when I was recruited as a guinea pig for the Artists in Schools Programme in Maine that I encountered some of my lows. [...]

One of my gigs[1] was an invitation to perform at my sons' elementary school in Harpswell Island, Maine. When I stepped on stage the student's jaws dropped... (did they think I had descended from the moon?). They received my performance with much enthusiasm and bombarded me at the end with questions: "Why do you have a red dot on your forehead? Why are your feet and the palms of your hands painted orange? Are those real flowers in your hair? Do all the women in India wear bells around their ankles?"

Once back home, as we were sitting down to dinner, my older son turned to me and said, "Ma, don't ever come to our school dressed like that again." I complied... thinking back to the times the grown-ups in my family had mortified me with their behaviour.

Sukanya RAHMAN, *Dancing in the Family: An Unconventional Memoir of Three Women*, 2005

1. performances

Les compléments numériques
e-WB
lycee.nathan.fr/2sb056-057

3

▲ A traditional Pookalam made to celebrate Onam.

Video

This Indian American family keeps tradition alive, *PBS News Student Reporting Labs*, 2023.

a. Watch the video from the beginning to 0'18 and **find** information about Anjali's life (date, reason for moving...).

b. Continue watching and **identify** what Anjali does to stick to her Indian roots.

c. Explain how this tradition also benefits her family.

d. Imagine why the journalist says "*It is different than in India*".

VOCABULARY SPOT

- festivities = celebrations
- heritage = legacy

- ashamed of = embarrassed by
- attached to
- proud /'praʊd/ of

- bond
- gather
- inherit
- live on: *perdurer*
- take part in = participate in

MEMORISE your vocabulary

CULTURE SPOT

Indian festivals

Indians around the world preserve their **traditions** through the celebration of various **festivals**: Diwali (festival of lights), Holi (festival of colours), Onam (festival of Kerala), etc.

A LITTLE EXTRA

Read more testimonies from Indian Americans and **identify** the challenges of trying to keep home traditions alive.

YOUR TASK

Write a post on the Indian Diaspora Network website recalling a personal anecdote.

1. **Brainstorm** ideas about a past event showing how you kept family traditions alive in your new country.
2. **Compare** it to your traditions when you still lived in India.

Build your skills! Rapporter un récit familial, de manière chronologique.

→ Utilise le **prétérit** et le ***past perfect*** pour organiser les événements dans le passé.

- *I **hadn't seen** my parents in a month, and that **was** the longest I **had** ever **been** without them. So, naturally, I **suggested** we do the one thing we always **did** together as a family.*
- *I **complied**… thinking back to the times the grown-ups in my family **had mortified** me with their behaviour.*

BUILD YOUR ENGLISH → p. 60

Quiz
TEST yourself

TEST YOUR CULTURE, VOCABULARY AND GRAMMAR

HAPPY INDIAN FAMILIES

HOW TO PLAY

This game has three Indian families. Each family has four cards. Collect as many families as possible.

1. In pairs, **deal** about all cards equally.
2. One player **asks** for a card needed to complete a family.
   Ex.: *"In the Gupta family, I would like the mother."*
3. Your teammate **reads** the question written on the corresponding card.
   ➡ **Correct answer: get** the card and **keep** asking.
   ➡ **Wrong answer: pass** your turn.
4. The player who completes the most families at the end of the game is the winner!

The Guptas

Which film industry comes from India?

The Guptas

Who is the first-born child of a family?

The Guptas

What's the preterite form of "grow"?

The Guptas

Define "diaspora".

The Pastels

Give a synonym for "link".

The Pastels

Put the verb in the correct form.
I (*leave*) New Delhi at the age of 5.

The Pastels

Regular or irregular verb?
Meet

The Pastels

Why does the eldest have a special responsibility?

The Borahs

Who are all the brothers and sisters of a family?

The Borahs

Regular or irregular verb?
migrate

The Borahs

Complete with the right tense.
I (*never visit*) India when I (*get*) there for the holidays.

The Borahs

Give two advantages of life in a joint family.

VOCABULARY

Les compléments numériques
lycee.nathan.fr/2sb058-059

EXERCISES → p. xxx

MEMORISE your vocabulary

INDIAN FAMILIES

Family

- household
- in-laws /'ɪnlɔːz/: *belle famille*
- joint family ± extended family
- nuclear /'njuːkliər/ family
- relatives
- siblings
- the eldest (child) ≠ the youngest (child)

Relationships

- bond = link = tie /'taɪ/
- childhood, adulthood, parenthood
- generation gap
- close-knit = united /juː'naɪtɪd/
- break free from
- bring up = raise
- provide for
- take care of = look after

Traditions

- customs = habits
- heritage = legacy
- roots
- long-standing = ancient /'eɪnʃənt/
- nostalgic
- celebrate = commemorate
- honour /'ɒnə/
- live on: *perdurer*
- stick to = preserve

Feelings

- pride
- privacy
- shame
- ashamed of = embarrassed by
- nostalgic
- lack
- miss

The diaspora

- expectation
- homeland = birth country
- opportunities
- foreign-born
- hope for = long for
- improve = get better
- move to = migrate /maɪ'greɪt/
- settle
- abroad = overseas

NOUN · ADJECTIVE · VERB · ADVERB OR PREPOSITION

1 Observe the family tree. Complete the following statements.

a. Sanya and Arjun are Anjali's ... .
b. Rahul and Pria are Kari's ... .
c. Manish is the ... child of the family.
d. Arjun and Sanya are Manish's ... .

2 Paint has fallen on this text. Figure out the missing words to understand what it is about.

Anjali and Amit met in India and then decided to set... in the UK. They are ...ign-b... British citizens. Their son, Manish, was born in London and has never visited his ho... yet. But they are attached to sharing their cultural ro... with him so that their traditions can li... .

3 Choose a person and make your partner guess who he/she is, by describing his/her family links.

Build your English!

GRAMMAR

+ EXERCISES ➜ p. xxx

A Situer les événements passés grâce au prétérit et au *past perfect*

GRAMMAR tuto

Le *past perfect* permet d'évoquer un événement antérieur à un autre au prétérit.

She **had dressed** for performance { ***when* / *before* / *by the time*** } she **arrived** at her son's school.

- had: *auxiliaire* **have** *au prétérit*
- dressed: *verbe* **dress** *au participe passé*
- when / before / by the time: *marqueur de temps*
- arrived: *verbe* **arrive** *au prétérit*

⚠ *L'ordre des propositions dans la phrase ne correspond pas toujours à l'ordre chronologique !*

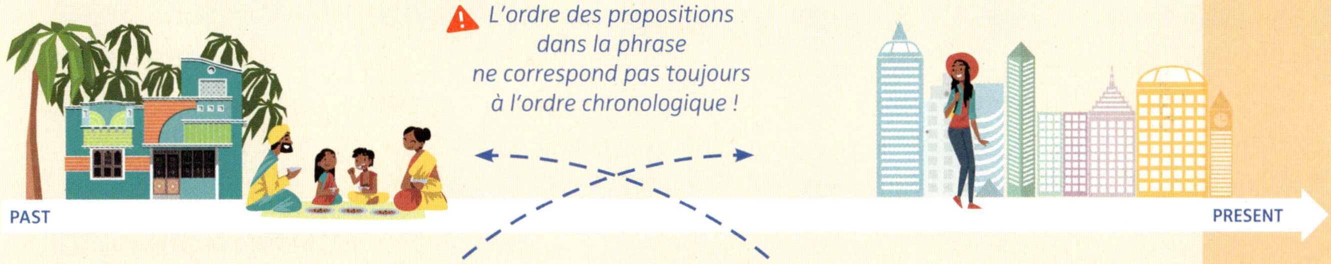

Before she **lived** in the US, she **had spent** her childhood in India.

1 Conjugue les verbes entre parenthèses au prétérit ou au *past perfect* selon le sens de la phrase.

a. Sanya [study] abroad for a few years before she [meet] her husband and [come] back to India.

b. Before Amit [become] a dancer, he [study] Indian music.

c. Manish [decide] to be an actor after he [watch] a Bollywood film.

d. Priya [not / meet] her Indian family before they [visit] her last year.

2 Finis ces phrases de façon logique en utilisant le prétérit ou le *past perfect* selon le sens.

a. Anjali had never celebrated her Indian roots before … .

b. Ghosh went overseas after … .

c. Vikash had lived with all his family when … .

d. Meerah learned how to cook traditional meals after … .

3 Raconte le parcours de vie de cet indien en utilisant le prétérit et le *past perfect*. Lie les événements entre eux.

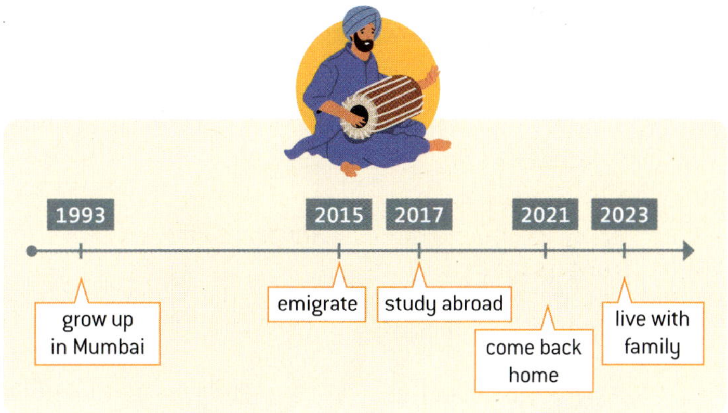

4 Raconte à tes camarades américains les habitudes de ton enfance en Inde. Rédige cinq phrases, dont une négative. Aide-toi des expressions suivantes.

gather · tell stories · have dinners · spend time together · celebrate special events · watch Bollywood films

B Désigner des éléments grâce aux articles

GRAMMAR tuto

En anglais, il existe **trois types d'articles**. On les utilise dans des situations différentes.

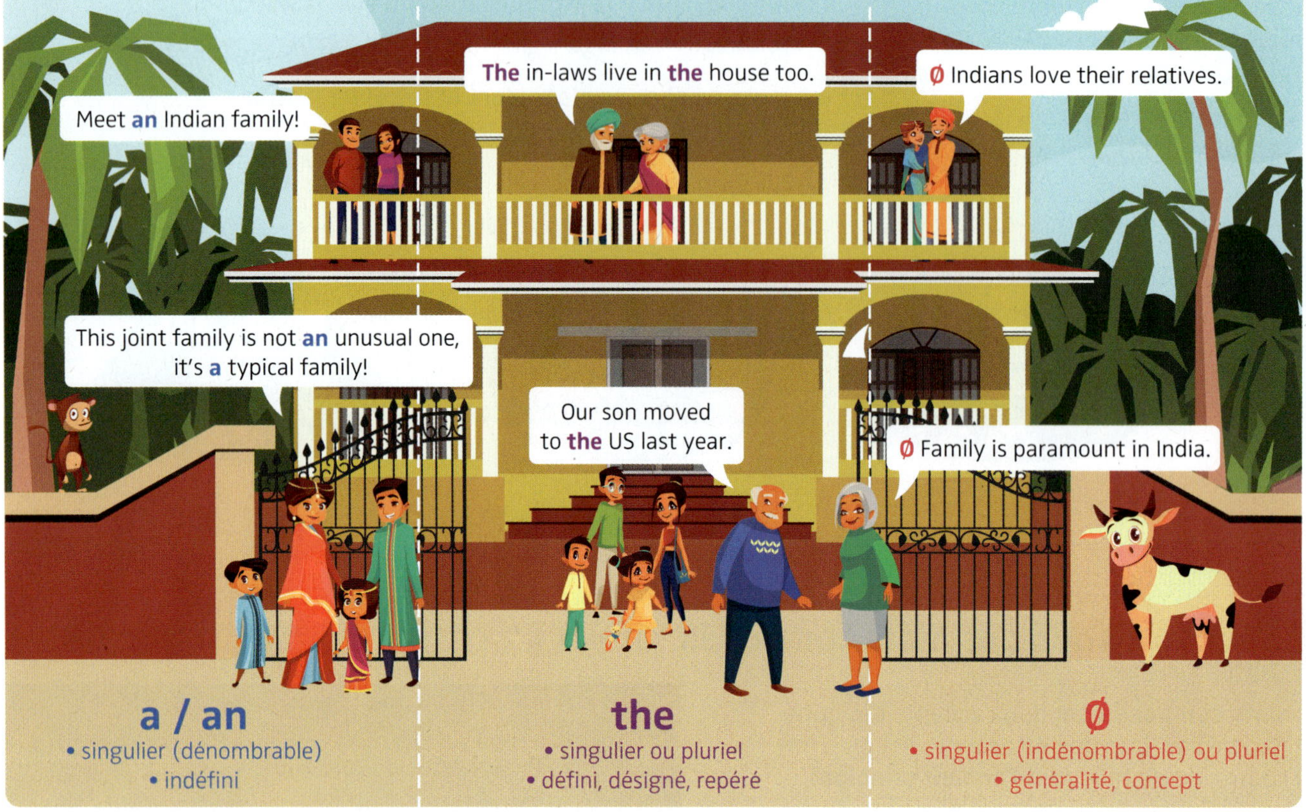

1 Choisis l'article adéquat et justifie ton choix.

a. As *ø* / *an* Indian American, I'm proud to have *the* / *ø* Indian roots.

b. *The* / *ø* Indian festivals are always full of *the* / *ø* colours.

c. *ø* / *The* traditional dances are *the* / *an* amazing show.

d. Usually, *ø* / *the* whole family is involved in *a* / *the* preparation of *a* / *ø* meals.

2 Complète avec l'article qui convient : *ø, a/an* ou *the*.

a. ... traditions are essential to bond with ... ancestors.

b. Living together is typical of ... Indian culture.

c. In ... evening, I would watch ... Bollywood film with my siblings, it was like ... tradition at home!

d. We watched ... traditional Indian dance performance yesterday. ... dancer was amazing and ... costumes were great.

3 Les articles de ce témoignage ont été effacés. Retrouve-les : *ø, a/an, the*.

When I was ___ kid, I dreamt of becoming ___ Bollywood actor! We would go to ___ movies every weekend with my grandpa and I would admire ___ actors on screen. It was such ___ pleasure to go to ___ cinema. Being ___ Bollywood actor in ___ India is ___ dream come true! ___ Bollywood films provide ___ tips about ___ Indian culture and what it's like to live in ___ traditional Indian family.

4 Rédige des phrases pour décrire cette image. Imagine où se trouvent ces personnes, d'où elles viennent, pour quelle occasion… Choisis bien les articles !

PHONOLOGY

A La prononciation de la graphie <i> Audio

En anglais, la lettre <i> peut se prononcer de **trois manières** différentes :

1. /ɪ/ → *live* • *link*
2. /aɪ/ → *migrate* • *tie*
3. /ɜː/ → *third* • *bird*

1 Écoute et répète ces mots. Puis classe-les selon la prononciation du <i>.

diaspora • relatives • siblings • girl • childhood • bring up • provide for

2 Lis les mots de chaque plat coloré et retrouve l'intrus. Écoute pour vérifier.

a.

b.

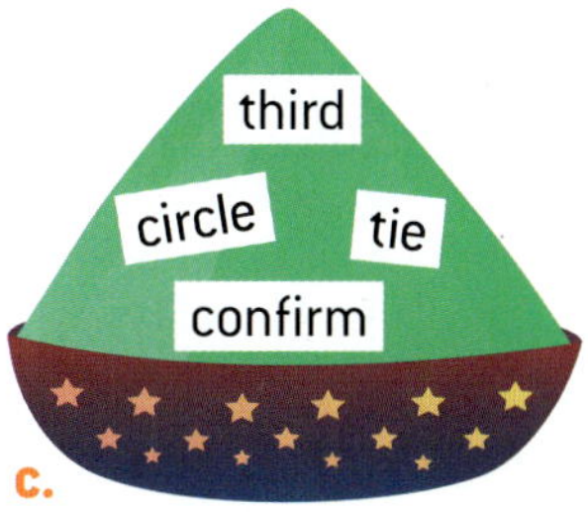

c.

B L'accentuation des mots composés Audio

Les **mots composés** ont deux accents toniques (un par partie). L'un de ces accents est plus fort que l'autre, on dit que c'est l'**accent principal** (noms). Celui-ci tombe soit sur la première partie, soit sur la seconde partie du mot (adjectifs).

gr**o**wn-**u**ps • m**u**lticu**l**tural
2 1 1 2

3 Écoute et repère l'accent tonique principal des mots suivants. Entraîne-toi à les répéter.

grandparent • Indian-American • hard-working • in-laws • multigenerational

4 Prononce les mots suivants et dis où se trouve l'accent principal. Écoute pour vérifier.

intergenerational • overseas • close-knit • brother-in-law • household

5 Lis à voix haute la lettre d'Anil à sa famille qui vit en Inde. Fais attention à la prononciation des mots composés.

Dear Family,
I miss our household so much. I often think about our grandmother's cooking and our Bollywood film sessions. Having such a close-knit family relationship is so precious!
I hope to see you all soon.
Anil

YOUR FINAL TASK

MÉDIATION

Record a report to share stories about the Indian diaspora.

For the celebration of Diwali, record a report including testimonies from various Indians living around the world.

1. **Form your groups and decide on the role you will each play:**
– the **journalist** who will present the topic and introduce each speaker;
– one **member** of the **diaspora** who will share his/her story.

2. Together, **choose** the stories you want to share in order to give a diverse image of the diaspora: your generation, memories of your life in India, your new country, reasons why you moved, time spent outside of India, your family organisation now.

3. **Take notes** about the way you connect with your Indian roots: the importance of family, the challenges of preserving traditions, your feelings about this new life…

4. **Record** the report together.

YES YOU CAN!

MÉDIATION

Record a report

Journaliste
DONNER LE CONTEXTE

Explique à quelle occasion le reportage a lieu.

"Tomorrow is Diwali, the festival of lights. It is celebrated throughout the world by the Indian diaspora."

Invité(e)
RACONTER SON HISTOIRE

Donne des repères chronologiques et géographiques pour mettre en avant ton parcours.

–I was only ten when we left India…

–During my childhood…

–At the beginning we lived in New York, and then we moved to Chicago.

Invité(e)
PARTAGER SES ÉMOTIONS

Exprime ce que tu as ressenti à chaque étape de ton parcours.

–It always felt like we were more than the four of us.

–We were 6, 8, and absolutely had great fun.

–I found it very difficult to assimilate.

–It's important for me to stick to my traditions.

Journaliste
PRÉSENTATION DES INVITÉS

Fais une rapide présentation de chaque invité.

–Anjali and her family currently reside in the United States.

–She spent a majority of her childhood in India.

–Let's meet Anjali… Now, let's move to Priya.

Journaliste
CONCLURE SON REPORTAGE

Remercie tes invités et fais une synthèse des témoignages.

–Thank you all for your stories.

–We saw how diverse the Indian diaspora is.

HOW TO SHINE IN… Speaking ➜ p. 208

PRACTISE AND SHINE

Compréhension de l'oral

Video
Growing Up Indian American (the struggle!), *Harshibar*, 2021.

A1 › A2 **Step 1** Before watching the video, **focus on** the picture.

a. **Read** the title and **observe** the picture. **Pick out** information about the girl.

b. **Focus** on the picture: what is the girl doing?

c. **Make hypotheses** about the video: type of document, topic…

TIPS
- **Appuie-toi sur l'image et le titre** pour anticiper le contenu de la vidéo. Imagine plusieurs scénarios et fais le lien avec les éléments culturels de l'unité.

A2 **Step 2** **Watch** the video once and **take notes** about:

a. the speaker, her identity (origins, current situation…);

b. the three parts of the video.

TIPS
- **Appuie-toi sur l'organisation de la vidéo** pour repérer les points importants du discours de l'interlocutrice.

A2 › B1 **Step 3** **Watch** the video again and **take notes** about:

a. the struggles the girl faces;

b. the different possible solutions.

TIPS
- **Repère** les mots répétés et ceux issus du champ lexical de chaque partie.

B1 › B1+ **Step 4** **Recap.**

WAY 1. Link the ideas and **recap**.

a. **Choose** the correct answers:

- The video is a **news report** / **testimony** / **critic** by a girl of **Indian** / **American** / **British** origins who lives in **India** / **the US** / **Great Britain**.
- She talks about her struggles to **discover a new culture** / **stay in touch with her roots** / **live with two cultures**.

b. **Complete** the recap using the prompt: ***She found three solutions to do so…***

For each solution, **include** details using the following words:

1. parents' help — YouTube videos
2. connect with — variety
3. improve — advice

WAY 2. Mets en lien les informations recueillies et récapitule-les en français ou en anglais. Tu peux utiliser les aides contenues dans le *Way 1*.

B1+ › B2 **Go further**

- **Explain** the intention of the girl while filming and posting such a video.

e-WB **Grille d'autoévaluation**

Compréhension de l'écrit

I'VE RARELY FELT COMFORTABLE WITH MY CULTURE. THIS SUMMER, THAT CHANGED

I've never had the privilege of knowing where I belong. I've always had each foot in a different country—I'm too Indian for America and too American for India. But unlike most of my other first-generation friends, I have one more nuance to my relationship with my culture: language.

For the first time in twelve years, both of my grandmothers from India came to visit my family in Maryland at the same time this summer. They primarily speak Tamil, a South Indian language, and though they could get by speaking in English, they have a hard time understanding American accents. [...] But what I've come to realize, especially after seeing my maternal grandmother again for the first time in five years, is that there is one language we can all communicate freely in: food. [...]

She likes to say that cooking is her meditation. But deeper than that—and perhaps she doesn't even realize it—cooking is her communication.

As my grandmothers' visit went on, my discomfort in my own culture began to lessen. Each morning, our first conversation was about breakfast: idlis or upma? [...] By the afternoon, the smell of spicy sambar or crisp dosa would be wafting[1] into my room, and we'd spend dinner talking about how the dish was made and family stories it reminded us of.

Laya Neelakandan, *today.com*, 2022

1. *flotter*

A1 › A2 **Step 1** Before reading the text, **focus on** the headline and the picture.

a. Brainstorm ideas about who the pronoun "I" in the title refers to.

b. Observe the presentation and **identify** the type of document.

c. Make hypotheses about the content of the text.

TIPS
- **Appuie-toi** sur l'ensemble du paratexte (titre, nom de l'auteur, source, photographie) pour anticiper le contenu du texte.

A2 **Step 2** **Read** the text once and **take notes** about:

a. the author (living place, origins, language);

b. her grandmothers (living place, language).

TIPS
- **Repère** les différentes personnes mentionnées dans le texte et leurs caractéristiques.

B1 **Step 3** **Read** the text again and use it to:

a. say what challenge the girl faces with her grandmothers;

b. explain the headline.

TIPS
- **Repère** les éléments répétés dans le titre et l'article pour comprendre les informations essentielles.

B1 › B1+ **Step 4** **Link** the ideas and **recap** in English.

a. Choose the correct answers:

- The text is an excerpt from **an article** / **a novel** / **a diary**. The author is a girl of **American** / **Indian** / **Australian** origins living in **the US** / **India** / **Australia**.

b. Complete the recap using the prompt: ***It is difficult for the author to ...***

c. Explain the sentence "cooking is her communication" (l.16-17) using the following elements:

universal language | share | no barrier

B1+ › B2 **Go further**

- **What does this last sentence show?:** *"we'd spend dinner talking about how the dish was made and family stories it reminded us of."*

e-WB **Grille d'autoévaluation**

SHORTFILE 6

Home Sweet Home?

▶ How does housing represent a challenge for younger generations in London?

YOUR FINAL TASK

Take part in a talk show about the difficulties of renting and buying a flat in London.

1. Expensive London

1

Audio

Something is Missing from London: Children, *NPR*, 2024.

▲ Londoners protesting for housing solutions, Oxford Street (London), 14th December 2024

a. Observe and **describe** the picture. **Guess** the issue.

b. Listen to the document and **pick out** information about Hackney.

c. GRAMMAR *"Even those that are staying **might** be actually just deciding to have less or potentially no children."* What does "might" mean here?

d. PHONOLOGY **Listen to** the sentence again. Which words are particularly stressed and why?

e. Explain why the school was closed and how people feel about it.

f. Comment on the link between housing and the decline in the number of families.

VOCABULARY SPOT

- demonstration
- placard

- affordable
- costly ≠ cheap
- expensive
- neighbourhood /ˈneɪbəhʊd/
- overpriced
- shortage of = lack of

- earn one's living
- make ends meet

- They can't afford it!

MEMORISE your vocabulary

Les compléments numériques
e-WB
lycee.nathan.fr/2sb066-067

2

e-WB Différenciation

I will never be able to afford to live where I grew up

I will never be able to afford to live where I grew up. It's true that I don't know what the future will bring, but given the state of the British economy, I doubt that I'm going to become a millionaire anytime soon. And thanks to the rocketing[1] cost of housing in the corner of London that I call home, I would need to be a millionaire to carry on living here. […]

Southwark, the south London borough where I have spent my entire life, is in the grip of a particularly cruel crisis of affordable housing. We have a council housing[2] waiting list of 16,500 and council housing stock decreased by 18,000 between 1994 and 2020. Despite this, Southwark council has been engaged for many years in two controversial "regeneration" projects: knocking down one of western Europe's largest housing estates, the Aylesbury, as well as the Heygate estate in Elephant and Castle, to make room for mainly privately owned flats. This is not regeneration. It is gentrification. […]

I am an elected representative in the Southwark Youth Parliament; I care deeply about my community and I love many things about Southwark, not least its incredible diversity. But Southwark council's decision to demolish the homes of largely working-class, often minority-ethnic, residents and replace them with sanitised apartment blocks where a flat can cost more than £1m, all while having the audacity to claim that it is creating the new "life and soul of London"—as one billboard[3] puts it—is not only harming said community, but erasing it.

Elsie McDowell (17-year-old student, Winner of the 2023 Hugo Young Award), *theguardianfoundation.org*, 2023

▲ The Shard building in the Southwark borough, London

CULTURE SPOT

London is made up of **thirty-two boroughs**, each with its own local government. They vary in size, culture, and character. Some, like Westminster, are known for landmarks, while others, like Hackney, are famous for creativity and diversity.

1. rising 2. *logement social* 3. *panneau publicitaire*

a. Read the article and **find** information about the author (age, occupation, place).

b. VOCABULARY **Pick out** the noun describing the evolution of the area and **define** it.

c. Comment on the way the issue of housing affects the community.

d. Explain Elsie McDowell's commitment.

A LITTLE EXTRA Video

Watch the video about living conditions in council houses and **react**.

YOUR TASK

You interview a Londoner about the impact of the recent demolition of housing estates in his/her neighbourhood.

1 **Introduce** the person and **ask** him/her questions about the issue.

2 He or she **answers** expressing what might happen in the future.

Build your skills! Exprimer des probabilités

➜ Utilise les **modaux** pour exprimer une probabilité plus ou moins grande :
- *… it **could** be a bad sign for the future.*
- *… those that are staying **might** be actually just deciding …*
- *London **may** have the worst of it.*

➜ Ajoute des **adverbes** de probabilité :
- *probably, certainly, maybe, perhaps…*

BUILD YOUR ENGLISH ➜ p. 72

Quiz
TEST yourself

EXPLORE

2. Becoming an owner: a shared dream?

1

Video

Teen Millionaire's London Penthouse Search Real Estate TV, *Banijay Home and Garden*, 2022.

VOCABULARY SPOT

- budget
- ladder: *échelle*
- loan /ləʊn/ = mortgage /mɔː.gɪdʒ/ = credit
- rent: *loyer*
- tight/small budget ≠ healthy budget

- impressive
- prime = excellent

- own /əʊn/: *posséder*
- purchase = buy
- rent: *louer*
- struggle

MEMORISE your vocabulary

a. Imagine what main challenges buyers might face in London.

b. Watch the video and **pick out** information about the buyers.

c. GRAMMAR **Pick out** superlative forms and **explain** what they show about London.

d. Comment on the impact of buying in London.

2

'I was given a London flat, mortgage-free[1]—here's how I feel'

Can you tell me a bit about you and your life?

I'm nearly 30 years old and run a business in the cultural sector. My parents worked very hard when I was growing up, so we had plenty of money—I went to private school and we frequently went on nice holidays.

How did you come to own the flat?

When I was 20 and in my second year of university, my parents bought me a flat in central London mortgage-free. I always knew we were well off[2] but this definitely shifted my perspective on the family wealth and my life significantly.

How did it change your perspective?

I suddenly struggled to relate to many of the things that other people my age were facing, predominantly the London rental market and thinking about saving for a property deposit[3]. Because I didn't need to pay rent I decided to pursue what I wanted to do – set up my business.

gfy.co.uk, 2023

▲ Kensington neighbourhood, London.

1. *sans hypothèque = acheté comptant* 2. rich 3. *acompte*

a. Look at the structure of the article and **identify** its nature.

b. Read it and **find** information about the woman's background.

c. Say how the woman got her flat.

d. Explain her reaction.

A LITTLE EXTRA Video

Watch the video and **comment on** young adults' reasons for living with their parents.

Les compléments numériques
e-WB
lycee.nathan.fr/**2sb068-069**

3

Buying a home with friends: how these pals[1] joined forces to escape London's rental trap

Soyemi and Farleigh, who are both 27, headed to London after graduating from Lincoln University and in 2019 they started toying with the idea of buying a place. "We were freelancing and making good money, but neither of us could buy a place on our own," says Farleigh.

"Then a friend said he knew this really good mortgage broker[2] who could get us a loan. Within a week we had a mortgage in principle."

In early 2020, just before the pandemic first hit, they found themselves the proud co-owners of a £450,000 three-bedroom terrace[3] in Waltham Forest.

Ruth Bloomfield, *standard.co.uk*, 2022

▲ Best friends Olamide Soyemi and Cullen Farleigh.

1. friend 2. *courtier* 3. *maison mitoyenne*

TEAM WORK

Team A works on doc 3 and
Team B on doc 4.

a. **Look at** the picture and **guess** the solution found by these young Londoners to buy a property.
b. **Study** your document and **check** your hypotheses.
c. **Explain** why this strategy has been chosen.
d. **Share** your findings and **comment on** the young Londoners' choices.

A LITTLE EXTRA Video

Watch the video and **explain** these friends' decision.

4

Video

I pay £50 a month to live in a skip in London, *PoliticsJOE*, 2023.

YOUR TASK

MÉDIATION

With your team, choose an option to live in London and be ready to explain your choice.

1. **Gather** arguments about your choice and **discuss** them with your team.
2. Once your team agrees, **describe** your option to the class and **justify** your point.

Build your skills! **Savoir échanger et convaincre**

➔ Utilise des **adverbes** pour donner de l'intensité à une idée :
- *This **definitely** shifted my perspective on the family wealth and my life **significantly**.*

➔ Utilise des **questions ouvertes** pour obtenir une réponse étoffée :
- ***Can you tell** me a bit about you and your life?*
- ***How did you** come to own the flat?*

Quiz
TEST yourself

BUILD YOUR ENGLISH ➜ p. 211

EXPLORE

3. Housing in fiction

1

Audio version

Chelsea's empty houses

These beautiful big houses in Chelsea are not homes in any sense that I understand. For most of the year they stand empty. Or at least, you think they are empty, but inside, there is a kind of life taking place. A phantom life. Members of staff – cleaners and cooks and chauffeurs – dust[1] haunted rooms and polish cars in underground garages during the morning, and then gather together in the kitchen at midday to eat silent lunches. Dogs sit by windows and look out into gardens and wonder why their owners bothered to buy them in the first place. Meanwhile, the family is...where? The father is in Singapore, the mother is in Geneva, the children...who knows?

Other houses here are even emptier. They contain no furniture, no curtains at the windows, no pictures on the walls. They are always dark. In the winter, when I come back from the park or the cemetery to return the last of my dogs to its owner's house, the silence and darkness of these streets begins to frighten me. It is as if some terrible plague[2] has come to London and everybody has had to leave but nobody has told me. Once I walked back from the park with Jane, through the streets of Chelsea, and she explained to me that people buy these houses now – rich people –and then just let them stand there, watching money attach to them like barnacles[3] to a sunken ship.

Jonathan Coe, *Number 11*, 2015

1. *poussière* 2. *peste* 3. *type de crustacés*

a. **Observe** the book cover and **identify** the nature of the text.
b. **Find** the characteristics of the houses in Chelsea.
c. **Identify** the people who are there.
d. VOCABULARY **Find** words describing the atmosphere and **say** what lexical field is used.
e. **Explain** why other houses are even emptier (l.14).
f. **Comment on** the tone of the extract.

A LITTLE EXTRA Video

Watch the video to 1'50 and **comment on** the hidden particularity of luxury homes in London.

VOCABULARY SPOT

- speculation
- trap

- available
- death-like
- gorgeous = beautiful
- worried = uneasy

- be a shift worker
- be in dire straits
- keep the prices high
- look for a flatmate
- share
- sublet

MEMORISE your vocabulary

2

Audio version

Sharing a bed

"So, anyway, " I say brightly, withdrawing my hands to wipe my eyes, "I need to move out. Now. Even if I wanted to stay and risk him bringing Patricia back again, I can't afford the rent, and I owe[1] Justin a ton of money, and I really don't want to borrow[2] from anyone, I'm kind of sick of not paying for things myself, to be honest, so... Yes. It's this or the flatshare."

Mo and Gerty exchange a look. Gerty closes her eyes in pained resignation.

"Well, you clearly cannot live here." She opens her eyes and holds out a hand. "Show me that advert again."

I hand her my phone, flicking from Justin's message to the Gumtree ad for the flatshare.

Double bedroom in sunny one-bed Stockwell flat, rent £350 per month including bills. Available immediately, for six months minimum.

Flat (and room/bed) is to share with twenty-seven-year-old palliative care nurse[3] who works nights and is away weekends. Only ever in the flat 9 a.m. to 6 p.m. Monday to Friday. All yours the rest of the time! Perfect for anyone with 9 to 5 job.

To view, contact L. Twomey—details below.

"It's not just sharing a flat, Tiff, it's sharing a bed. Sharing a bed is *odd*[4]", "Mo says worriedly.

Beth O'Leary, *The Flatshare*, 2019

1. be in debt to. 2. *emprunter*. 3. *infirmier* 4. strange, bizarre

a. **Look at** the book cover and **imagine** what this novel may be about.

b. **Read** the excerpt and **sum up** the advert.

c. **Explain** why this ad is odd (l. 22).

d. **Find out** why Tiff is ready to answer the ad.

e. **Comment on** her friends' reaction.

A LITTLE EXTRA — Video

Watch the trailer of the movie adaptation *The Flatshare* and **react**.

YOUR FINAL TASK

Take part in a talk show about the difficulties of renting and buying a flat in London.

1. **Define** your roles: pupil A is a journalist for Channel 4 and asks questions to young Londoners (other pupils) about the housing crisis.
2. **Collect** your ideas, focusing on:

   Pupil A:
   - the identity of your guests;
   - the questions you may ask about their current housing situation (difficulties/possibilities and their projects).

   Other pupils:
   - your personal details and the positive aspects of living in London;
   - your current living conditions, the reasons why you can't afford buying in London and your future plans.
3. **Act out** the talk show.

Build your skills! **Parler de manière convaincante**

Rebondir sur ce qui vient d'être dit.
- ***Yes, I suppose so, however*** *when you can't afford...*
- ***It depends on the situation:*** *if you earn a decent living...*

Utilise l'**intonation** pour donner du rythme et du sens :
- *Are you buying a house?* (intonation montante)
- *When did you move to London?* (intonation descendante)

HOW TO SHINE IN PHONOLOGY → p. 238

Quiz — TEST yourself

Build your English!

GRAMMAR

+ EXERCISES → p. 236-237

Exprimer la probabilité d'une action avec les modaux *must, may, could, might, can't*

GRAMMAR tuto

Les modaux de **probabilité** indiquent les **chances de réalisation** d'un fait.

PASSÉ modal + ***have*** + V-***en*** **ou** modal + ***have been*** + V-***ing***		**PRÉSENT / FUTUR** modal + BV **ou** modal + ***be*** + V-***ing***
He must **have looked** for a flat before he decided to live in a skip.	**La certitude = MUST** C'est sûr, je le déduis. (Tu as dû... Tu dois... / Il est certain que...)	Jane must **be considering** other options.
We could **have shared** a flat.	**Le possible = COULD** C'est possible si les conditions sont réunies. (Ils auraient pu... Ce pourrait...)	The housing issue could **become** a bigger problem in the future.
They may **have made** a lot of money to afford a house in Chelsea.	**La probabilité moindre = MAY** C'est possible, mais pas sûr. (Il se peut que... / Il est possible que...)	Some Londoners may **feel** anxious about the housing issue.
She might **have found** a flat to share on the internet.	**Le possible très restreint = MIGHT** Il y a une chance, un risque pour que... (Il se pourrait que...)	One day, I might **buy** a tiny flat in London.
She can't **have considered** living there, it's impossible!	**L'impossible = CAN'T / CANNOT** C'est impossible. (Tu ne peux pas...)	You can't **ignore** the housing problem in London.

1 Reformule les phrases suivantes à l'aide d'un modal suivi d'une base verbale ou de *have* + *V-en* selon le sens de la phrase.

a. I'm not sure but I think Jack found a flat to share.

b. I guess staying at my parents' house is an option.

c. Leaving London is a possibility.

d. I'm sure they bought a two-bedroom flat.

2 Recopie et complète ces phrases en exprimant la probabilité au présent ou au passé. Tu peux utiliser les verbes proposés.

buy afford increase find

a. When Londoners look for a place to live, they ...

b. The housing issue is becoming worrying, it ...

c. Few people can afford a London house, these people ...

d. I'm considering moving to London, but I ...

PHONOLOGY

L'accent de phrase

L'accent de phrase consiste en la mise en valeur des **mots clés** d'une phrase pour souligner **l'information principale**. Cela permet de guider l'interlocuteur sur **l'intention du locuteur**.

- *Rent is too **high** for most people to afford in central London.*
→ L'accent de phrase est sur *high* pour souligner l'idée principale du problème : les loyers sont trop élevés.

3 Écoute ces phrases et repère les mots particulièrement accentués. Puis répète les phrases.

a. The cost of rent in London is extremely high.

b. Many families are struggling to find affordable housing.

c. There are not enough homes for the growing population.

d. People are forced to live in small and overcrowded flats.

4 Prononce ces phrases, puis écoute et vérifie l'accentuation de phrase.

a. Is it difficult to find affordable housing in London?

b. Young people are finding it impossible to buy their first home.

c. The waiting lists for council housing are extremely long.

d. Many people are forced to share their homes.

VOCABULARY

+ EXERCISES → p. 231

MEMORISE your vocabulary

HOME SWEET HOME?

Accommodation

- bills: *factures*
- council housing
- flat = apartment
- terraced house: *maison mitoyenne*
- furnished
- purchase = buy
- rent
- share
- sublet: *sous-louer*

Real estate

- buyer = owner
- cost
- deposit /dɪˈpɒz.ɪt/
- housing estate: *cité (ou quartier de logements sociaux)*
- loan = mortgage /ˈmɔː.ɡɪdʒ/
- property = flat or house
- expensive = costly
- extraordinary ≠ normal
- own /əʊn/: *posséder*

Housing crisis

- gentrification
- shortage of = lack of
- speculation
- affordable ≠ unaffordable
- (un)available
- disappearing
- afford
- fail to ≠ manage to
- protest
- rise ≠ fall

Urban life

- borough /ˈbʌr.ə/
- city centre
- diversity
- infrastructure
- neighbourhood
- public transport system
- residential area
- working-class
- central
- commute = travel to work

NOUN ADJECTIVE VERB

1 Separate the words and use them to write five sentences referring to this picture.

protestexpensiveunavailableafford shortagerentflatrise

2 Name it!

a. A sum of money paid in advance as part of a total cost.

b. A district or an area in a town or city.

c. An agreement made with the bank to buy a house.

d. Something that is reasonably priced and easy to pay for.

3 Name the opposite.

a. rise b. cheap c. normal d. succeed

4 Complete the advert with the following words!

available deposit flat flatshare location rent

LOOKING FOR RENT?

A lovely 2-bedroom ... for ... in Hackney, London. The ... is spacious and the ... is amazing, perfect for those looking for a comfortable home. The ... is £1,000 per month with a £500 ... The property is ... in two weeks, and there is the option for a ... Contact now to arrange a viewing!

SNAPFILE 7 Family matters

▶ In what ways do family sitcoms reflect the changing American family?

YOUR FINAL TASK

You are a Youtuber and a fan of American family sitcoms. **Study** the following documents and **gather** information about the representation of the American family over time.

Record a 2-minute video on the evolution of the American family in TV shows.

FOLLOW THE STEPS

1

FACTS ABOUT THE AMERICAN FAMILY TODAY

Family life is changing. Two-parent households are on the decline in the United States as divorce, remarriage and cohabitation are on the rise. And families are smaller now, both due to the growth of single-parent households and the drop in fertility.

For children, growing diversity in family living arrangements
% of children living with...

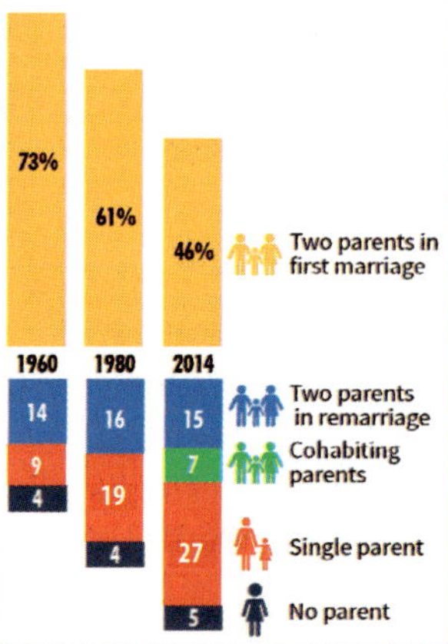

Not only are Americans having fewer children, but the circumstances surrounding parenthood have changed. While in the early 1960s babies typically arrived within a marriage, today fully four-in-ten births occur to women who are single or living with a non-marital partner.

THE TWO-PARENT HOUSEHOLDS IN DECLINE

% of children living with...

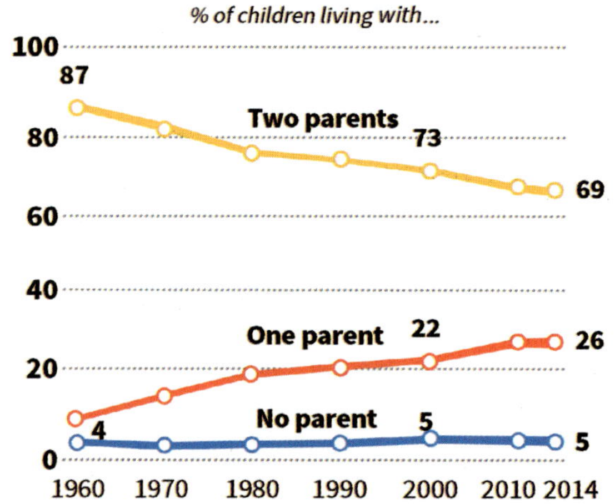

The share of children living in a two-parent household is at the lowest point in more than half a century: 69% are in this type of family arrangement today, compared with 73% in 2000 and 87% in 1960.

◀ "Facts about the American family today", *houstonnationalinsurance.com*, 2018.

▶ Video

"The changing American family", *CBS Sunday Morning*, 2014.

TEAM WORK

Team A works on the infographic **Team B** on the video.

a. Look at the infographic or **watch** the video. **Identify** what it is about.

b. Pick out figures about the American family between 1960 and 2014. **Comment on** how it has evolved over time.

c. Share your findings with the other team. **Explain** in what ways American family life has changed since 1960.

VOCABULARY SPOT

- blended family: *famille recomposée*
- breadwinner: *soutien (de famille)*
- housewife (-husband)
- lone-parent family = single parent
- nuclear /ˈnjuːkliər/ family

- idealised /aɪˈdɪə.laɪzd/
- unrealistic

- decrease = fall
- depict = represent
- increase = rise
- resonate with

- accurately /ˈæk.jə.rət.li/ = correctly

MEMORISE your vocabulary

2

"The Evolution of Family Sitcoms"

There's something eternal about the way family, comedy, and television go together. It just seems obvious and inevitable: if audiences are going to watch fictional stories on a small screen in their own home, many of those stories are going to be about families, and they're going to be funny and insular[1] and expected, with just a dash of[2] surprise to delight viewers.

Because of this, the history of the sitcom is the history of America. The variations that come along tell the story of what's changing in the zeitgeist[3], in our conception of family. The modern memory of early sitcoms begins with *I Love Lucy*, which began in 1951 and was focused on a married, child-free couple and their friends before stars Lucille Ball and Desi Arnaz became parents in real life, forcing the birth of their onscreen son, Little Ricky. […]

The family began to look a bit more modern in the '60s with *The Dick Van Dyke Show*'s sexy young couple, Rob and Laura Petrie, at its center. […] But the biggest shift[4] came in the '70s with *All in the Family*, which brought us a working-class white family whose love language was loud, uncomfortable political squabbles[5].

peabodyawards.com

1. *bornés* 2. a small amount of 3. *esprit de l'époque* 4. change 5. arguments

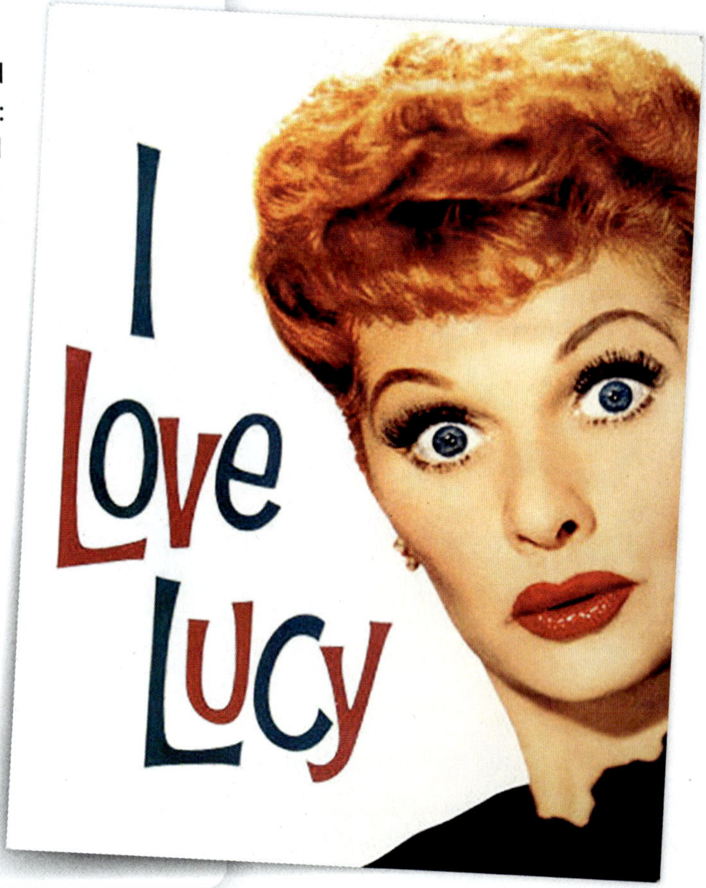

▲ *I Love Lucy*, 1951-1957.

a. Look at the poster and **imagine** what the sitcom might be about.

b. Read the text and **identify** why *I Love Lucy* is a landmark.

c. Pick out the dates and **find** what they correspond to regarding sitcoms.

d. Explain how the family sitcoms evolved from the 50s to the 80s.

A LITTLE EXTRA Video

Watch the trailer of the TV show *I Love Lucy* from 2'08 to 3'12. **Explain** what it shows about American family life in the 1950s.

STEP 1

Introduce the subject.

1 **Describe** the evolution of the American family from the 1950s.

2 **Explain** how the American family was represented in the 1950s-1960s sitcoms.

Build your skills! **Décrire l'évolution d'une situation**

- Pense au **présent en *be* + V-*ing*** pour commenter une situation présente :
  - *Family life **is changing**.*
- Utilise le **prétérit simple** pour faire référence à des faits passés sans lien avec le présent :
  - *While in the early 1960s babies typically **arrived** within a marriage, today…*
- Utilise le ***present perfect*** pour décrire une évolution qui a une incidence dans le présent :
  - *We**'ve** just **lived** through a huge period of social change.*

HOW TO SHINE IN GRAMMAR → p. 214

3

▲ *Father Knows Best*, 1954-1960.

What's the Story?

The classic series *Father Knows Best* (1954 -1960) is a situation comedy about the day-to-day antics[1] of the Andersons, a middle-class nuclear family living in the fictitious suburban town of Springfield. Insurance salesman Jim Anderson (Robert Young) heads up the tight-knit[2] gang, which includes his wife Margaret (Jane Wyatt), teenage daughter Betty (Elinor Donahue), his teen son Bud (Billy Gray), and "Kitten," his precocious youngest daughter Kathy (played by Lauren Chapin). From making sure that Bud knows how to dance in time for the spring formal[3], to testing his marriage by teaching Margaret how to drive, Jim helps his family through their ups and downs, and makes the most of every event to teach the family about the best way to handle every situation that comes their way.

Melissa Camacho, *commonsensemedia.org*, 2023

1. silly behaviours 2. united 3. *bal de printemps*

TEAMWORK

Team A works on doc 3 Team B on doc 4.

a. **Look at** the family picture and **describe** it. **Imagine** what the TV show is about.

b. **Read** the text or **listen to** the audio. **Pick out** information about the main characters.

c. **Explain** what role the man plays in the family.

d. **Share** your findings with the other team. **Compare** and **contrast** the way the American family is depicted in each sitcom.

VOCABULARY SPOT

- bias /'baɪəs/: *parti pris*
- expectation

- diverse
- in keeping with = typical of
- subversive

- challenge
- expand = develop
- feature
- shape

MEMORISE your vocabulary

4

◀ *Who's the Boss?*, 1984-1992.

Video

'Who's the Boss' Reunion ft. Tony Danza, Alyssa Milano, and Judith Light, *People*, 2022.

Les compléments numériques
e-WB
lycee.nathan.fr/2sb076-077

5

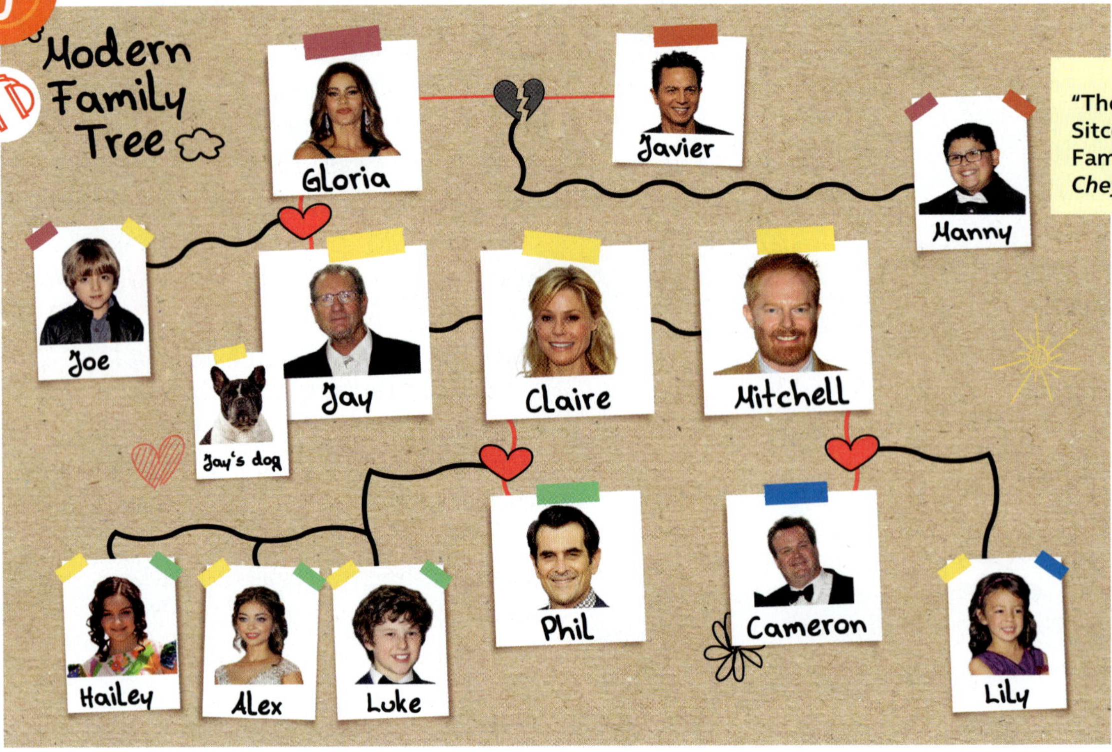

◀ *Modern Family*, 2009-2020.

Audio

"The Last Great Sitcom?" A Modern Family Retrospective, *Cheyenne Lin*, 2023.

a. **Observe** the family tree and **say** what is not traditional about this family.

b. **Listen to** the audio and **identify** its nature.

c. **Pick out** information about the characters and **describe** how they are related.

d. **Explain** what is "modern" about this family.

e. **Sum up** the speaker's opinion about *Modern Family*.

PHONOLOGY SPOT

show • 2020 • modern • nuclear • father • popular

Écoute ces mêmes mots prononcés avec l'accent britannique puis américain. Quelle différence constates-tu ?

GRAMMAR SPOT

- *… there's Jay**'s** family*
- *… **his** precocious youngest daughter Kathy …*
- *… wife and homemaker Claire and **her** realtor husband*

Observe les phrases ci-dessous. Qu'expriment les éléments en gras ?

STEP 2

Explain how the representation of the American family in sitcoms has evolved since the 1950s.

1. **Provide** examples from family sitcoms and **give** details about the characters. **Use** pictures to illustrate your presentation.
2. **Give** your opinion.

Build your skills! Enrichir ses descriptions

➔ Décris les relations entre les personnages à l'aide du génitif :

- *Next, there's Claire**'s** brother Mitchell.*
- *Jay is Claire and Mitch**'s** father.*

➔ Pense à utiliser des adjectifs composés pour donner plus de détails.

- *…the **ever-clueless** Luke*
- *… an incredibly **cutting-edge** show*

HOW TO SHINE IN GRAMMAR ➔ p. 210-211

Quiz
TEST yourself

AXE 2. VIVRE ENTRE GÉNÉRATIONS
→ Objet d'étude 4

FLASH FILE 8

Growing green together

▶ Is there a generational divide on ecological issues in Canada?

YOUR FINAL TASK

In teams, **watch** and **read** the documents. **Share** information about the way the different generations are involved in the protection of the environment. e-WB

Then **record** a 120-second podcast about how different generations fight together against climate change.

1

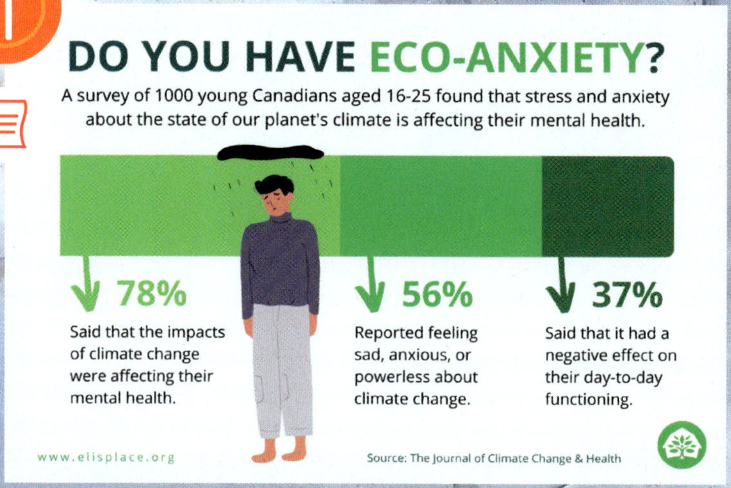

elisplace.org

2

Generational conflict over climate conflict is a myth

The idea that young people are ecowarriors, battling against selfish older generations is a common trope[1] in representations of the environment movement. It has been stoked[2] by instances including *Time* magazine naming Greta Thunberg their person of the year in 2019, for being a "standard bearer[3] in a generational battle".

The stereotypes were further strengthened when generation Z, US singer Billie Eilish said: "Hopefully the adults and the old people start listening to us [about the climate crisis]. Old people are gonna die and don't really care if we die, but we don't wanna die yet."

But a new [...] study, Who Cares About Climate Change: Attitudes Across The Generations, has found that the generational divide over climate action is a myth. [...]

Prof Bobby Duffy [...] said the fake conflict between generations over the climate crisis is "dangerous and destructive". It had, he said, "crept[4] into so many discussions about climate concern that it's become an accepted truth that the young are at war with older generations who are not only utterly unfussed[5] about the future of the planet, but are culpable for the current crisis.

"Parents and grandparents care deeply about the legacy they're leaving for their children and grandchildren – not just their house or jewelry, but the state of the planet. If we want a greener future, we need to act together, uniting the generations, rather than trying to drive an imagined wedge between them," he added.

Amelia HILL, *The Guardian*, 15 September 2021

1. stereotype 2. revive 3. *porte-parole* 4. invade 5. unworried

3

"Every generation has its own struggle and will either conquer it or fail. Now we have this young generation that is just trying to save the world to just live a life, because they can see what we couldn't see when we were living our lives in, trying to have what we thought was an infinitely good life. And now we know that nothing is infinite. And so this generation was born with the idea of finiteness".

Sheila OCHUGBOJU, Global climate expert, 2024.

Video
Generation gap: Young Canadians blame boomers for growing disparity, study finds, *Global News*, 2021.

4

Video
The Water Walker Trailer, *Seeing Red Media*, 2023.

VOCABULARY SPOT

- activist
- carbon footprint
- climate change
- gap = divide
- legacy
- lifestyle

- committed (to) = involved (in)
- environmentally-conscious
- sustainable

- address an issue
- advocate for
- be likely to
- feel concerned by
- inherit /ɪnˈhɛrɪt/
- raise awareness about

MEMORISE your vocabulary

A climate change-themed mural in Toronto, 2021.

FILE 9 #EveryBODY

We live in a day and age where people make it impossible for women, men, anyone to embrace themselves exactly how they are. Diversity is sexy!"

Ariana GRANDE, *Teen Vogue*, 2015.

Ad campaign for Good American, an inclusive fashion brand co-founded by Khloé Kardashian, 2022.

Les compléments numériques

e-WB

lycee.nathan.fr/**2sb080-081**

How are beauty standards in the USA questioned?

YOUR FINAL TASK

Write an article about the evolution of beauty standards in the USA.

Video

What does beauty mean?, *Thoraya YouTube channel*, 2017.

VOCABULARY SPOT

- confidence
- corpulence
- figure = body shape
- height /'haɪt/

- curvaceous /kɜr'veɪʃəs/ = voluptuous
- inclusive
- self-conscious
- slender = slim

- assert oneself
- identify with = relate to

MEMORISE your vocabulary

TEAM WORK

Team A

Describe the main picture and **read** the caption. **React** to the strategy of this brand.

Team B

Read the quote. **Rephrase** what the singer means and **react**.

Team C

Watch the video and **sum up** the interviewees' definitions. **React** to their answers.

- Now **share** your findings with the other teams and **explain** the complexities of beauty standards.

EXPLORE Iconic beauties?

1

◀ Michelle Williams, *My Week with Marilyn*, 2011.

Lana Del Rey, ▶ *A.K.A. Lizzy Grant*, 2010.

Marilyn Monroe: The Ultimate Fashion Icon

Marilyn Monroe[1], the iconic blonde bombshell of Hollywood's golden era, captivated audiences with her beauty, charm, and undeniable talent. Her unique style and timeless beauty have made her an enduring cultural icon, inspiring generations of women around the world. She continues to influence the fashion and beauty industry even today.

Marilyn Monroe, the epitome[2] of glamour and timeless beauty, left an undeniable mark on the world of fashion with her impeccable style choices. Her outfits not only reflected her status as a Hollywood icon but also set trends that continue to inspire designers and fashion enthusiasts to this day.

elminimarian, *thefashionguideofmarian.com*, 2024

1. 1926-1962 2. perfect example

▲ Violet Chachki, winner of the seventh season of *RuPaul's Drag Race*, 2015.

a. **Look at** the three pictures. **Describe** them and **say** their common points.

b. **Read** the text. **Identify** the characteristics attributed to Marilyn Monroe.

c. GRAMMAR **Focus** on the last sentence and **explain** what the author insists on with the expression *"not only … but also"*.

d. **Explain** why Marilyn Monroe is still relevant today.

e. **Comment on** the way the pictures illustrate her iconic status.

VOCABULARY SPOT

- body shaming ≠ body positivity
- frame = stature
- self-acceptance
- weight /weɪt/

- bold = daring
- discriminated against
- plus-size

- accept one's image
- fit the norm
- promote

- despite + V-*ing*/ N = in spite of + N
- regardless

MEMORISE your vocabulary

Les compléments numériques
e-WB
lycee.nathan.fr/2sb082-083

2

◀ Timothée Chalamet at the Los Angeles Premiere of *Wonka*, 2023.

Audio

Timothée Chalamet on *Losing out roles over his body type*, *The Hollywood Reporter*, 2024.

TEAMWORK

Team A works on doc 2 and Team B on doc 3.

a. **Look at** the picture and **read** the title. **Make** hypotheses about the document.

b. **Watch** or **listen to** your document and **identify** the message delivered by each celebrity.

Team A

c. **Analyse** the role played by the cinema industry.

d. GRAMMAR **Explain** the use of the word *However* in the sentence *"However, he was consistently shut down."*

e. PHONOLOGY **Focus** on the pronunciation of "*Oscar-nominated*": **identify** the most stressed word.

Team B

c. Analyse the role played by the social media.

d. GRAMMAR **Rephrase** this sentence: "*I just love posting photos that I wish I could have seen when I was a little girl.*" **Say** what it shows about Ashley Graham's motivation.

Video

Ashley Graham speaks on body positivity, *Arise News*, 2023.

3

▲ Ashley Graham at a fashion show, 2023.

YOUR TASK

DIFFÉRENCIATION

Interview a celebrity about the way his/her looks have influenced his/her career.

WAY 1

Interview Timothée Chalamet about the way his appearance impacted his debut in the cinema industry.

WAY 2

Interview Michelle Williams about the way her appearance opened her doors. **Include** elements showing the limits of this idea.

Build your skills! Présenter des situations contrastées

- Utilise des **connecteurs logiques** :
  - *However, he was consistently shut down.*
  - *So, I went to what I thought was a more humble door, but actually ended up being explosive for me.*
- Utilise des structures exprimant **le regret** :
  - *I wish I could have seen photos of natural bodies…*

BUILD YOUR ENGLISH ➜ p. 90

Quiz
TEST yourself

EXPLORE Accepting one's body?

1

e-WB **Différenciation**

a. **Look at** the pictures and **react** to the way they differ.

b. **Watch** the video and **pick out** some features of social media.

c. **Explain** the consequences on social-media users.

d. **Give** a definition of "social media dysmorphia".

e. **Discuss**: What do you think about the influence social media may have?

Video

Social-media dysmorphia, *The Take*, 2023.

2

Billie Eilish credits controversy-ridden Brandy Melville as the start of her 'body problems'

Billie Eilish has claimed that the controversial fashion line Brandy Melville contributed to the start of her "body problems."

The 22-year-old singer spoke candidly about growing up with the brand, which famously sells all of its clothing in one size, during a cover story interview with *Complex* published on Thursday (December 5). She explained that she loved Brandy Melville so much as a child that it caused her to develop a negative view of her appearance.

"I never wore pants or shorts when I was a little kid," she explained, noting that she loved wearing skirts and large dresses growing up. "But when I got to be about 11, I got obsessed with this brand called Brandy Melville. And they only sold clothes in one size. I was chubbier[1] and I was obsessed with these clothes, but I'd buy a shirt and it wouldn't fit me. That's when my body problems started."

Amber Raiken, *independent.co.uk*, 2024

1. plumper

Singer Billie Eilish at the 2024 *Vanity Fair* Oscar Party.

a. **Read** the text and **identify** the brand discussed in the text: what makes it particular?

b. **Explain** how this brand influenced Billie Eilish.

c. GRAMMAR **Comment on** the effect of the use of direct speech (l.9 and l.11-14).

d. **Analyse** the role played by brands in the issue of body acceptance.

e. **Comment on** the impact of Billie Eilish's revelation may have on teenagers.

VOCABULARY SPOT

- (medical) disorder
- self-esteem

- bodily = physical
- distorted = twisted
- filtered ≠ unretouched (photographs)

- embrace
- empower
- undergo (cosmetic) surgery: *subir une opération (de chirurgie esthétique)*

MEMORISE your vocabulary

3

What is Aerie doing differently to continue to prosper? It starts with several strategic decisions it made many years ago. One of those is a focus on diversity and inclusivity. While this is a buzz word in 2024 Aerie stepped out and made a decision to use more diverse models ten years ago. […]

There are companies that talk about diversity and inclusion and others that walk the talk. A decade ago in 2014 Aerie launched its first #AerieReal campaign featuring models that were not re-touched. Speaking about the campaign a spokesperson for Aerie said: "we left beauty marks, we left tattoos, what you see is really what you get with our campaign." Some of the other "flaws" that are not retouched are: lines, dimples[1], fat, puckering[2] and slight stretch marks[3].

In 2019 Aerie took its focus on realness a step further when it began featuring people with disabilities and illnesses on its website. In a step away from the models brands typically use, Aerie showcased a model wearing intimate apparel in a wheelchair as well as a model with crutches[4]. "As a brand, Aerie has been a leader in empowering women and celebrating inclusivity and body positivity since our launch of #AerieREAL in 2014. Our newest bra models are part of our brand's ongoing commitment to show real, authentic and unretouched women, who are at the core of everything that we do," said Jennifer Foyle, president and executive creative director of American Eagle & Aerie.

Tricia McKinnon, *indigo9digital.com*, 2024

1. *fossettes* 2. *plis* 3. *vergetures* 4. *béquilles*

▲ Aerie's #AerieReal campaign, spring 2019.

a. Observe the picture and **identify** its nature. How effective do you find it?

b. Read the article and **find** information about Aerie.

c. VOCABULARY **List** the words linked to body features. **Explain** what makes Aerie so diverse and inclusive.

d. GRAMMAR **Replace** *that* by another relative pronoun: "*There are companies that talk…; Aerie launched its first #AerieReal campaign featuring models that were not re-touched.*" (l.9-14)

e. Comment on the impact this type of campaign may have on people.

A LITTLE EXTRA

Watch this ad and **reflect** on the impact of Artificial Intelligence (AI) on beauty standards.

YOUR TASK

Write a post on a social network about the dangers of beauty representation on social media.

1. **Present** the way social media distorts people's images online.
2. **Describe** the impact it has on its users.
3. **Show** the role played by some brands to solve this problem.

Build your skills! Décrire un phénomène de société

➜ Appuie-toi sur différents témoignages, à l'aide du **discours direct et indirect** :
- *Billie Eilish explained that she loved Brandy Melville…*
- *"As a brand, Aerie has been a leader in empowering women"…*

➜ Caractérise le phénomène grâce à des **propositions relatives** :
- *…unretouched women, who are at the core of everything that we do.*

BUILD YOUR ENGLISH ➜ p. 91

Quiz
TEST yourself

EXPLORE Hair empowerment

1

The Impact of The 'Fro In The Civil Rights Movement

The afro is more than just a hairstyle, it was an incredibly powerful symbol of the civil rights movement.

During and after the period of slavery in the United States, most Blacks styled their hair in an attempt to mimic their oppressors. European settlers considered kinky[1] or "nappy"[2] hair unattractive and undesirable.

The hair of Africans was often referred to as cottony and woolly. Europeans deemed their straight and fine hair texture as the ideal. Black hair was the antithesis of the Euro-American standard of beauty thus possessing nappy hair was negative and shameful.

The Civil Rights Movement sparked a change in the way Blacks viewed their hair and themselves. The movement was a catalyst for Blacks to embrace who they were naturally including their hair texture. In the African American community, there was a renewed appreciation for the Black aesthetic resulting in the popular phrase "Black is Beautiful".

The afro became a powerful political symbol that reflected the pride one had in their African ancestry. No longer were Blacks attempting to assimilate. Prominent Civil Rights activist, Angela Davis, one of my inspirations, rocked a picked out 'fro which led many women to follow in her footsteps. [...]

It is important for us to remember our history and the power symbols possess. For me, rocking my hair in its afro texture meant I was choosing to love and accept my Black self and I would no longer use abrasive methods in an attempt to alter who I was naturally.

Chime Edwards, *essence.com*, 2020

1. curly 2. curly (historically pejorative)

▲ Angela Davis photographed by Abby Weintraub, 1969.

CULTURE SPOT

Angela Davis (born in 1944) is a prominent political **activist**, **scholar**, and **author**. She emerged as the leader of the Communist Party USA in the 1960s and had close ties to the **Black Panther Party** during the **Civil Rights movement**. She embraced the "Black is beautiful" movement, wearing her hair in an afro.

a. **Look at** the picture and **read** the Culture spot. **Sum up** what you have learnt about Angela Davis.

b. **Read** the first two paragraphs and **take notes** on the way European settlers influenced the way Black people considered their hair.

c. PHONOLOGY **Check** the pronunciation of the -*s* in the following words and **practise** pronouncing them: *resulting – possess – symbols – oppressors*

d. **Continue reading** and **explain** how the situation evolved with the Civil Rights movement.

VOCABULARY SPOT

- hairstyle
- prejudice against sb
- implemented = executed (law)
- straight ≠ curly (hair)
- assimilate
- do one's hair
- resemble /rɪˈzɛmbəl/ = look like
- straighten /ˈstreɪtən/ one's hair

MEMORISE your vocabulary

2

▲ Student Darryl George surrounded by (left) Candice Matthews, member of the New Black Panther Nation, and (right) his mother, Texas, 2023.

Video

Black student legally suspended for his hair style, *Scripps News*, 2024.

CULTURE SPOT

The **CROWN (Create a Respectful and Open Workplace for Natural Hair) Act** is a 2019 California law which prohibits **discrimination** based on hair style and hair texture. Other states have adopted this law since then (Texas, New York, Michigan, etc.).

TEAM WORK

Team A **works on** doc 2 **and**
Team B **on** doc 3.

a. **Watch** the video. **Take notes** on the person at the heart of the document.

b. **Identify** the issue presented.

c. **Explain** how this topic surpasses the subject of hair.

d. **Share** your findings with the other team and **comment on** the place of this topic in American society.

3

Chimamanda Ngozi Adichie ▶

Video

"Hair is political", *Channel 4 News*, 2013.

A LITTLE EXTRA

Video

Watch this trailer and **identify** the different topics linked to Black women's hair.

YOUR TASK

Write the back cover of the book entitled Textures: The History and Art of Black Hair.

1. Briefly **account for** the history of black hair in the USA.
2. **Denounce** the discrimination faced by African Americans because of their hair.

Build your skills! Évoquer des problèmes

- Utilise des **subordonnées relatives** pour affiner tes arguments :
  - *Angela Davis rocked a picked out 'fro which led many women to follow in her footsteps.*
  - *You have young girls who are growing up with that in their heads.*
- Utilise l'**emphase** pour mettre en lumière la situation :
  - *What we know is that Darryl George had been told that he was breaking the rules.*

BUILD YOUR ENGLISH ➔ p. 91

Quiz
TEST yourself

TEST YOUR CULTURE

HOW MUCH OF A BEAUTY VOCABULARY EXPERT ARE YOU?

HOW TO PLAY

- **Read** the first question and **choose** the correct answer.
- **Follow** the arrows to answer the following questions.
- **Discover** your vocabulary profile at the bottom.

START

1 The fact of including all types of people and treating them all in the same way.
- A diversity
- B inclusivity

2 A condition in which people falsely believe there is something wrong with the size or shape of their body.
- A body shaming
- B body dysmorphia

3 Criticism of someone based on the shape, size, or appearance of their body.
- A self-acceptance
- B body shaming

4 A very famous person considered as representing a set of beliefs or a way of life.
- A leader
- B icon

5 The fact of feeling good about your body and the way it looks.
- A attractiveness
- B body positivity

6 A fault, mistake, or weakness.
- A stature
- B flaw

7 Pulled into or appearing as a strange or unnatural shape.
- A distracted
- B distorted

8 A physical or mental condition that makes someone unable to act in a way that is considered usual for most people.
- A inequality
- B body-conscious

9 Preoccupied with one's body or physical appearance.
- A self-confident
- B body-conscious

10 A style for curly hair, particularly Black people's hair, in which it is allowed to grow naturally into a thick, rounded shape.
- A locks
- B afro

Nice try!
You are a vocabulary novice. Keep on practising!

Well done!
Nice vocabulary, you are very competent! Keep on practising to become an expert!

Amazing!
You are a vocabulary expert!

VOCABULARY

Les com
numérique
lycee.nathan.fr/2s

+ EXERCISES → p. 228

MEMORISE your vocabulary

Body types

- figure = body shape: *silhouette*
- height /'haɪt/
- weight /'weɪt/
- curvaceous /kɜr'veɪʃəs/
- plump = overweight
- petite /pə'tiːt/: *menu(e)*
- slim = slender
- put on ≠ lose weight

Acceptance

- body positivity ≠ body shaming
- (self-)confidence
- self-esteem
- body-conscious
- insecure ≠ confident
- accept one's image
- embrace
- empower
- overcome criticism

Appearance

- charisma /kə'rɪzmə/
- stature
- blonde/red/black-haired
- bodily = physical
- good-looking = attractive
- homely = unattractive
- consider + *adj.* / sb as + *n.*
- look + *adj.* = seem + *adj.*
- straighten /'streɪtən/ one's hair

Social media

- anxiety /æŋ'zaɪəti/
- body dysmorphia
- fake ≠ real
- (un)filtered
- (un)healthy
- (un)retouched
- affect sb's (physical, mental) health
- distort (reality)

Representation

- diversity
- inclusivity
- disabled /dɪ'seɪbəld/
- discriminated against
- plus-size
- assimilate
- fit the norm
- identify with
- resemble /rɪ'zɛmbəl/

NOUN · ADJECTIVE · VERB · ADVERB OR PREPOSITION

1 List the following expressions depending on what they refer to.

promote inclusivity
suffer from body dysmorphia
lead to unhealthy habits
boost one's self-esteem
feel insecure
gain confidence
affect one's mental health

Body positivity	Body shaming

2 Find the corresponding words based on the definition.

a. Of a photograph posted without being altered.
b. Short and slim.
c. Correspond to society's standards.
d. Surmount criticism.

3 Complete this Instagram post with the corresponding words.

thecrownact • Happy NATIONAL Crown Day! • Following

National CROWN Day is a day to encourage everyone to ... their natural black hair. Black people should no longer be asked to ... by ... their hair. They should no longer be ... against because of their hair. Raise awareness about #TheCROWNAct and help ... our community.
#CROWNLove# CROWNProud#TheCROWNAct
#CROWNMovement#PassTheCROWN#CROWNDay

♥ 3 290 likes

GRAMMAR

A Ajouter ou opposer des idées

GRAMMAR tuto

Pour **ajouter** ou **opposer** des **idées**, tu as besoin de **mots de liaison**.

ADDITION	OPPOSITION
+ nom / GN	
In addition to **In addition to** unfiltered bodies, they show plus-size ones. **Not only... but also** They celebrate **not only** curvy women **but also** every woman.	**contrary to** / **unlike** **Unlike/Contrary to** retouched ads, this one honours real bodies.
+ proposition	
Not only... but also They **not only** empower black people **but** they **also** boost their confidence. **furthermore** / **what's more** / **moreover** She is natural, **moreover**, she's beautiful.	**while** / **whereas** / **but** This brand promotes body positivity **while** others use body shaming in their ads. **and yet** / **however** He's a good actor, **and yet**, he didn't get the role. He didn't fit the norm. **However**, he's self-confident.

1 **Reformule ces phrases à l'aide des expressions entre parenthèses.**

a. She's real and good-looking. *(not only ... but also)*

b. This brand empowers women and embraces body positivity. *(what's more)*

c. His actions inspire and help men feel confident. *(furthermore)*

d. They overcome difficulties and show the way. *(not only ... but also)*

2 **Associe deux éléments afin de créer des oppositions en utilisant *However* et *yet*.**

- they are models for a campaign
- She fits the norm
- Some brands promote diversity
- they are discriminated against.
- These teenagers don't fit the norm
- They have great Afro hair,
- she suffers from body shaming
- our society still criticises differences

3 **Utilise les éléments ci-dessous pour rédiger des phrases en utilisant soit *not only ... but also* soit *however*, selon le sens des mots.**

a. She suffers from body shaming / she's confident.

b. This campaign promotes diversity / it shows only petite women.

c. This campaign promotes diversity / it boosts people's self-confidence.

d. Angela Davis was an icon / she empowered black people.

4 **Tu es chargé(e) de préparer un paragraphe sur le thème du *body positivity* pour le journal du lycée. Rédige six phrases en utilisant *however*, *yet* et *not only ... but also*.**

B Donner des précisions à l'aide des phrases relatives

GRAMMAR tuto

La **subordonnée relative** est liée à la phrase principale par un **pronom relatif** qui reprend le nom placé juste avant : l'antécédent. Il faut faire attention à l'**antécédent** pour choisir le bon pronom relatif !

THAT

- WHO — This campaign celebrates **women** **who** don't fit the norm. ***(personne)***
- WHICH — The brand **which** empowers women is Aerie. ***(chose)***
- WHEN — It's the moment **when** she decided to accept her Afro hair. ***(moment)***
- WHERE — California is the state **where** discrimination based on hair is forbidden. ***(lieu)***
- WHOSE — Angela Davis is the woman **whose** self-confidence inspires me! ***(lien d'appartenance, de parenté)***

TIPS! Comment savoir si le pronom est sujet ou complément de la relative ?

Sujet : The brand **that** empowers women.
sujet

Complément : The brand **that** I prefer.
COD → I prefer the brand.

⚠ Si le **pronom relatif** est **complément**, alors on peut le **supprimer**.

1 Recopie et complète avec le pronom relatif qui convient.

a. I love the campaigns ... promote body positivity!
b. I admire my best friend ... fights body shaming.
c. The 1960s were the decade ... the Civil Rights movement intensified.
d. Actors ... goal is to denounce discrimination are my favourite!

2 Relie les deux propositions grâce à un pronom relatif. Attention aux modifications engendrées.

Ex.: This ad shows various bodies. These bodies are real.
*→ This ad shows various bodies **that** are real.*

a. This brand sells clothes in one size only. This brand doesn't celebrate differences.
b. My friend suffers from discrimination. My friend is determined to make things change.
c. More and more campaigns show diverse bodies. These bodies are awesome.
d. Angela Davis was an activist. Angela Davis's determination inspired other African Americans.

3 Donne des précisions sur l'élément souligné à l'aide d'une proposition relative.

a. This actress supports body-positivity campaigns.
b. This brand sells clothes all over the world.
c. This campaign is inspiring.
d. The next generation will be more self-confident.

4 Tu travailles pour une marque qui promeut l'inclusion et les différences. Appuie-toi sur l'image ci-dessous pour expliquer à un nouveau collègue les valeurs de la marque et quels acteurs vous recherchez pour la prochaine campagne. Utilise des relatives !

PHONOLOGY

Les compléments numériques
lycee.nathan.fr/2sb092

A La prononciation des adjectifs composés Audio

Généralement, les **adjectifs composés** sont **accentués** sur le **second mot** : *beauty-enhancing*. Attention ! Certains adjectifs composés sont accentués sur le premier mot : *body-conscious*.

1 Écoute ces adjectifs composés : retrouve l'accent principal et entraîne-toi à les prononcer.

a. self-confident
b. plus-size
c. hard-working
d. well-known

2 Écoute la prononciation des adjectifs composés suivants et repère l'accent principal. Utilise-les pour décrire Taylor Swift.

good-looking
blonde-haired
blue-eyed
light-skinned

▲ Singer Taylor Swift at the 2024 Grammy Awards in Los Angeles.

B La prononciation du <s> en fin de mot Audio

Située en **fin de mots**, la **graphie <s>** peut se prononcer de **trois manières** différentes : /s/, /z/ ou /ɪz/. Sa **prononciation** dépend du **son précédent** le <s> final.

Prononciation du <s>	/s/	/ɪz/	/z/
Après les consonnes :	• sourdes comme : /p/, /t/, /k/, /f/, /θ/	• sifflantes comme : /s/, /z/, /ʃ/, /tʃ/, /ʒ/, /dʒ/	• sonores comme : /r/, /v/ ou /l/
Exemples	caps, looks, cats…	buses, brushes, ages…	hairs, lives, girls…

3 Écoute et répète ces mots, puis classe-les selon la prononciation du <s> final.

trends — standards — actresses — filters — audiences — conscious — curvaceous

/s/	/ɪz/	/z/

4 Trouve l'intrus parmi les mots suivants. Écoute et vérifie.

a. followers – trolls – photos – apps
b. marks – curls – locks – lips
c. jeans – rights – designers – inspires
d. blushes – choices – experiences – clothes

5 Entraîne-toi à bien lire ces courtes biographies à voix haute. Puis, choisis une personnalité, décris-la en 30 secondes pour la faire deviner à ton/ta camarade.

ZACH MIKO

He is one of the most famous plus-size male models today. He hosts a podcast in which he talks to positive, diverse and inclusive guests.

SELENA GOMEZ

Actress Selena Gomez' body has been scrutinised these past years. Because of that, she now raises teenagers' awareness about the dangers of beauty filters on social media apps.

ALICIA KEYS

A few years ago, the singer Alicia Keys decided to stop wearing make-up. She said she didn't want to cover up her soul, her thoughts, her dreams, her struggles.

YOUR FINAL TASK

Write an article about the evolution of beauty standards in the USA.

You are a journalist for *Teen Vogue* magazine. Write an article to report on the evolution of beauty standards. Focus on icons and trends from the mid-20th century to the present.

1. **Brainstorm** ideas about what traditional American beauty standards are.
2. **Identify** some moments that made them evolve.
3. **Explain** the impact beauty has on society: negative (discrimination, anxiety, etc.) and positive (self-acceptance, inclusivity, etc.).
4. **Include** testimonies from different speakers: representatives of the beauty and fashion industry, celebrities (actors and actresses, models, singers, etc.), activists, teenagers, etc.

YES YOU CAN!

Write an article

LE TITRE

Choisis un titre percutant et accrocheur (phrase non verbale) ou un titre plus explicite et détaillé (phrase verbale).

The Impact of The 'Fro In The Civil Rights Movement

Billie Eilish credits controversy-ridden Brandy Melville as the start of her "body problems."

LA PHOTO

Illustre ton article à l'aide d'une photographie dynamique et directement compréhensible des lecteurs(-trices) pour donner envie de lire l'article. Complète-la d'une légende (personne(s), lieu, date, etc.).

Angela Davis photographed by Abby Weintraub, 1969.

Aerie's #AerieReal campaign, spring 2019.

Singer Billie Eilish at the 2024 Vanity Fair Oscar Party.

LE SOUS-TITRE

Annonce le contenu de l'article en une phrase courte qui donne le sujet et éveille la curiosité, en particulier si tu as choisi un titre court.

The afro is more than just a hairstyle, it was an incredibly powerful symbol of the civil rights movement.

LES TÉMOIGNAGES

Inclus des témoignages afin de montrer le travail documentaire fait en amont de la rédaction de l'article.

Speaking about the campaign a spokesperson for Aerie said: "we left beauty marks, we left tattoos, what you see is really what you get with our campaign."

She explained that she loved Brandy Melville so much as a child that it caused her to develop a negative view of her appearance.

LE CONTEXTE

Replace le sujet dans son contexte afin de justifier son importance, à l'aide d'informations historiques et contemporaines factuelles.

During and after the period of slavery in the United States, most Blacks styled their hair in an attempt to mimic their oppressors.

A decade ago in 2014 Aerie launched its first #AerieReal campaign featuring models that were not re-touched.

The 22-year-old singer spoke candidly about growing up with the brand […] during a cover story interview with Complex.

HOW TO SHINE IN WRITING → p. 204

Compréhension de l'oral

Video
Positive Body Image, *CVS Health*, 2023.

A1 > A2 **Step 1** Before watching the video, **focus on** the title and the picture.
a. **Describe** the picture.
b. **Brainstorm** elements linked to "positive body image".

TIPS
• **Note** des mots et expressions vus dans le chapitre qui peuvent être mis en lien avec les éléments du titre et de l'image.

A2 **Step 2** **Watch** the video once and **take notes** about:
a. the different speakers and their role;
b. the programme presented (pay attention to the images as well).

TIPS
• **Repère** les passages où les intervenants sont présentés. Dans les vidéos, les présentations écrites peuvent t'aider à compléter les informations sur leur rôle.

A2 > B1 **Step 3** **Watch** the video again and **identify**:
a. the issues raised (social media transformations, consequences);
b. the objective of the programme and the way it will reach it.

TIPS
• **Repère** les mots répétés et les synonymes utilisés pour comprendre quel est le cœur du document.

B1 > B1+ **Step 4** **Recap.**
WAY 1. **Link** the ideas and **recap**.
a. **Present** the document, using the following checklist:
- ☑ *type of document*
- ☑ *creator of the document*
- ☑ *main subject*
- ☑ *people present in the document*

b. **Complete** the recap using your notes from Step 3. **Use** some of these elements:
- *The program aims at…*
- *They intend to…*
- *Its goal is to…*
- *They wish they could…*

c. **Link** the messages to the corresponding woman and **include** these elements in your recap:

personal goal | instill confidence | imperfect | distorted reality | unattainable beauty standards | isolation

WAY 2. **Mets en lien** les informations recueillies et **récapitule** en français ou en anglais.
Tu peux utiliser les aides contenues dans la ***Way 1***.

B1+ > B2 **Go further**
• **Identify** the precise nature of the document and its goal.

e-WB **Grille d'autoévaluation**

Compréhension de l'écrit

My Beautiful Black Hair

These days, it's not uncommon to see Black women wearing their natural hair. Something unheard over twenty years ago. Back then, sporting one's kinks, coils, and curls was not socially acceptable. Forcing women to chemically alter their hair texture. Giving them that desired bone, straight, European look, that attracted the eyes of many.

This all changed with the onset[1] of the "natural hair movement". […] While there is more acceptance surrounding Black women's hair, there are some who are still singled out because of it. From boardrooms to classrooms, many women sometimes experience ridicule and harsh criticisms. Often resulting in them feeling shame or questioning their beauty. One woman, however, is on a mission to encourage Black women to celebrate their hair with her new book, *My Beautiful Black Hair*. In it, author and photographer, St. Clair Detrick-Jules collected 101 empowering stories. Resulting in a natural hair love letter to Black women across the country. […]

Aside from a celebration of hair, would you say that the universal theme of *My Beautiful Black Hair* is self-love?

St. Clair Detrick-Jules: Definitely. I think everyone of all demographics should love themselves. It is an ongoing journey for a lot of us. And I think it's hard to be at a place where we love ourselves all the time. For me, there are days when I don't love myself as much as I should. Even though I'm an advocate for self-love, I constantly have to affirm myself.

Racquel Coral,
Chicago Defender, 2021

1. start

A1 › A2 **Step 1** Before reading the text, **focus on** its title and the picture.

a. Make hypotheses about the content of the text.

b. Then, **browse** the text and its structure: **deduce** the nature of the document.

TIPS
- **Appuie-toi** sur l'organisation visuelle du texte pour en déduire sa nature.

A2 **Step 2** **Read** the text once and **take notes** about:

a. the topic of black hair in the USA;

b. the book and its author.

TIPS
- **Repère** les marqueurs de temps pour retracer l'évolution historique.

B1 **Step 3** **Read** the text again and:

a. explain how black hair has been perceived throughout history;

b. say what the situation is today;

c. identify the author's objective.

TIPS
- **Repère** les adverbes et mots de liaison pour comprendre les liens entre les informations (opposition, nuance, concession, etc.).

B1 › B1+ **Step 4** **Link** the ideas and **recap**.

a. Present the document, completing the following sentences:

The text is an excerpt from an … *with St. Clair Detrick-Jules, who is a* … *Her book,* My Beautiful Black Hair, *tells* …

b. Put the release of the book **in context**, using some of the following elements:

discriminated against | criticised | ashamed | natural hair | inappropriate

c. Include the author's experience, using some of the following elements:

struggle | long process | it takes time to

B1+ › B2 **Go further**

- **Analyse** the use of the expression "on a mission" (l.13).

e-WB **Grille d'autoévaluation**

SHORTFILE 10 Sneaker culture

▶ How have sneakers risen from a tool of rebellion to mainstream uniforms?

YOUR FINAL TASK

As a famous online sneakerhead, **convince** an American celebrity to make a commercial for a new pair of sneakers.

1. Off the beaten track

1

▲ Matthew Laurence Knott, 2019.

▶ Video
The Origins of Sneakers, *@pbsvoices*, 2024.

▲ *Cinderella*, Mimi Yoon, 2023.

CULTURE SPOT

Sneaker culture is a subculture that revolves around the love of sneakers. It's an ever-growing **community of people** who **collect**, **trade** and **wear** sneakers as a form of **self-expression**, **personal style** and **investment**.

a. Look at the title of the video and **make** hypotheses about its content.
b. Watch the video and **identify** the topic.
c. Pick out the dates and what they correspond to.
d. Explain why sneakers are more than shoes.
e. Choose one picture, **describe** it and **say** why it illustrates question **d**.
f. Imagine it is an advert. **Write** a slogan.

VOCABULARY SPOT

- footwear = shoes
- laces
- leather
- tape

- distorted: *déformé(e)*
- iconic

- mainstream
- messy = untidy
- tangled: *emmêlé(e)*

- stand out
- wink = blink one eye

MEMORISE your vocabulary

Les compléments numériques
e-WB
lycee.nathan.fr/2sb096-097

2

From Jock to Punk: How Converse's Iconic Shoes Went From the Basketball Court to the Mosh Pit[1]

The Chuck Taylor's, officially the Converse All-Star, has a unique place in pop culture, mostly because of how ubiquitous[2] it is across various subcultures, from sneakerheads and sports fans, to graffiti artists, and of course, the punk scene. It's as American as Apple Pie and Baseball, despite being a product of a Canadian sport. In a recent study, a staggering[3] 60% of the entire population of the country has stated owning at least one pair of All-Stars in their lifetime. Even today, it is still the highest selling sneaker in history, bar none[4].

Its place in punk rock history, of course, is probably the best documented, from The Ramones and Nirvana, to Taking Back Sunday and Dashboard Confessional; it's the footwear of choice for anti-establishment, angst[5], and youthful indiscretions, a true testament to punk's use of corporate irony and turning their products into a weapon against the system itself. […]

In fashion, punk brought to the fore the idea of DIY-ing your wardrobe as a show of rejecting society's customs. It is in this vein that The Ramones first started wearing Chuck Taylors regularly. In his mind, Johnny Ramone saw it as a way to show disdain[6] over "proper" clothing, as sneakers were only supposed to be worn in the gymnasium or in training. […]

With a storied past and a bright future, Converse All-Stars, or 'Chucks' as fans call them, are more than just a pair of shoes: they're a lifestyle.

Ethan Reynolds, *cottonable.com*, 2019

1. *fosse de concert* 2. everywhere
3. impressive 4. *sans exception*
5. anxiety 6. disrespect

◀ Kurt Cobain and the other members of Nirvana wearing Converse, 1990.

a. **Read** the headlines and **identify** what footwear the article deals with.

b. **Read** the article and **explain** why this footwear has a unique place in pop culture.

c. VOCABULARY **Find** a synonym for "transform something into something".

d. **Identify** the subculture highlighted and **explain** why this movement chose this footwear as a symbol.

A LITTLE EXTRA Video

Watch the video and **explain** the specificities and evolution of the skaters' sneakers.

YOUR TASK

You are working for the Sneakertopia Museum Website in Los Angeles. Write the introductory post for its website.

1. **Explain** how popular this footwear is, giving facts and figures.
2. **Say** what famous people claimed through them.
3. Be convincing using *so* and *such*. **Illustrate** your post.

Build your skills! **Renforcer l'intensité de tes propos**

Utilise *so* et *such* pour marquer l'emphase :
- *How did a piece of rubber, leather and canvas become* ***such*** *big business?*
- *They are* ***so*** *popular everybody wears them.*
- *The shoe was* ***so*** *different that you had to love it.*

HOW TO SHINE IN GRAMMAR → p. 211

Quiz
TEST yourself

EXPLORE 2. Sport and Hip Hop

1 e-WB Différenciation

Run DMC x Adidas: The Original Collab That Changed Sneakers Forever

▲ Run DMC, 1986.

The legendary rap group from Queens, New York, made history by not only popularizing the iconic Adidas Superstar silhouette but also reshaping the entire sneaker industry. […]

Run DMC emerged on the hip-hop scene in the early '80s with a sound characterized by hard-hitting beats, clever rhymes, and a rebellious attitude that resonated with the youth. They were more than just rappers; they were cultural icons who blended music and fashion in ways that no one had ever done before.

The game-changing moment occurred in 1986 when Run DMC dropped their hit single "My Adidas." The song, an ode to the iconic Three Stripes, celebrated the group's love for Adidas—particularly a certain pair of shell toes. What made it truly groundbreaking[1] was that it wasn't just a song; it was a movement. Fans in the crowd, inspired by the track, started holding up their adidas sneakers in the air at concerts, and soon the brand took notice.

In response to this grassroots fandom[2] galvanized by Run DMC, Adidas made a huge gamble. They approached the group with an eye-watering[3] endorsement deal[4], becoming the first major sports brand to partner with hip-hop artists. The partnership was a turning point in the sneaker industry, bridging the gap between sports and music, and forever changing the way sneakers were marketed.

The Adidas Superstar became the star, if you will, of Run DMC's partnership. The group famously rocked[5] them laceless with the tongues pushed out, a look that would become forever linked to their singular style. This unorthodox fashion set a new trend in the hip-hop community, turning the Superstar into a symbol of authenticity and street cred.

Daniel So, *highsnobiety.com*, 2023

1. *avant-gardiste* 2. ordinary people 3. surprising 4. *contrat publicitaire* 5. wear

Video

The full history of Air Jordan Sneakers, *NachoAverageFinds*, 2023.

2

Michael Jordan ▶ #23 of the Chicago Bulls during an NBA game, 1985.

TEAM WORK

Team A works on doc 1 and Team B on doc 2.

a. **Look at** the picture and **guess** the people's professional activities.

b. **Watch** the video or **read** the text and **find** information about the footwear. **Say** what happened.

c. GRAMMAR **Pick out** the comparisons.

d. **Explain** how the brands took advantage of the situation.

VOCABULARY SPOT

- advertising (ads)
- endorsement (of products): *promotion/publicité*

- controversial
- inappropriate

- exploit /ɪk'splɔɪt/
- merge: *fusionner*
- monetise
- take advantage of

MEMORISE your vocabulary

Les compléments numériques
e-WB
lycee.nathan.fr/2sb098-099

3

▲ New York, Brooklyn Breakdancers, 1984.

Video

How Hip Hop and Basketball created sneaker culture, *wearepushblack*, 2022.

a. Observe the picture and **imagine** who these people may be.

b. Watch the video and **define** sneaker culture.

c. Identify the positive and negative effects.

d. Comment on the partnership between the African-American communities and the sneaker brands.

PHONOLOGY SPOT

Écoute et **entraîne-toi** à dire ces phrases comme le rappeur de Run DMC. Aide-toi des lettres en gras pour bien respecter le flow !

My Adidas
W**a**lk through concert d**oo**rs
And r**oa**m all over coliseum fl**oo**rs
I st**e**pped on st**a**ge, at Live **Ai**d

YOUR TASK

DIFFÉRENCIATION

For the 50th anniversary of hip-hop culture, you must do a series of radio reports about the history of sneaker culture.

WAY 1

Interview the band Run DMC on the importance of their partnership with Adidas.

1 **Present** the historical context.

2 **Ask** them about their collaboration and its consequences.

WAY 2

Interview breakdancers on the importance of sneaker culture.

1 **Present** the historical context.

2 **Ask** them what sneakers represent for them.

Build your skills! Établis la supériorité d'un élément

→ Utilise le **superlatif** pour souligner l'importance d'un élément :

- *Jordans became* ***the hottest*** *shoes ever.*
- *What happened next was one of* ***the most brilliant*** *marketing moves in history.*

BUILD YOUR ENGLISH → p. 102

Quiz
TEST yourself

3. Sneakerheads everywhere

1

▲ Rihanna's brand Fenty collab with Puma, 2024.

Video

Women sneakerheads, *Complex*, 2017.

VOCABULARY SPOT

- activist
- carbon footprint
- empowerment
- hype = trend

- state of the art

- emphasise
- highlight = shed light on
- matter = be important
- save (money)

MEMORISE your vocabulary

a. **Watch** the video and **identify** the place and the speaker.

b. GRAMMAR **Pick out** expressions with *so* and *such* and **say** what they reveal about the speaker.

c. **Find** information about Rihanna and the brand and **explain** the evolution mentioned.

d. Now **look at** the picture and **comment on** the communication strategy.

A LITTLE EXTRA Video

Watch the video about the exhibition: *50 years of Sneaks and Beats* and **pick out** more details about sneaker culture and hip hop for your final task.

Les compléments numériques
e-WB
lycee.nathan.fr/2sb100-101

2

Sneakerhead Culture: Why Gen Z is Obsessed with Shoe Collecting

In recent years, sneakerhead culture has skyrocketed[1], particularly among Generation Z, who have embraced and propelled[2] this trend to unprecedented levels of popularity. For Gen Z, sneakers are not just shoes; they are a canvas[3] for self-expression, a sound financial investment, and a vital part of their digital and real-life communities. […]

As Generation Z continues to define its place in the world, its members are actively influencing the sneaker industry with a strong push towards sustainability[4] and environmental responsibility. This generation, known for its environmental activism, is demanding more than just style and brand name from their sneakers; they seek innovation in sustainability that aligns with their values of ecological stewardship[5]. […]

They advocate for the use of sustainable materials such as organic cotton, recycled plastics, and natural rubber, which not only minimize environmental impact but also promote a more ethical approach to fashion. […] Recycling programs are another area where Gen Z's influence is noticeable. They are enthusiastic about initiatives that repurpose old sneakers into new products or that responsibly dispose of shoes at the end of their life cycle. […]

Sneakerhead culture among Gen Z is a vibrant intersection of fashion, finance, technology, and social interaction. It reflects the values of a generation that prizes individuality, connectivity, and responsibility.

ankitamishra, *furyblades.com*, 2024

◀ GenZ and sustainable sneaker culture, 2024 (AI generated picture).

1. increase rapidly 2. move forward 3. *toile*. 4. *durabilité* 5. *responsable des ressources*

a. React to the picture.

b. Read the article and **identify** what sneakers mean to Gen Z.

c. VOCABULARY **Pick out** the words linked to sustainability.

d. Explain how Gen Z influences footwear brands' strategy.

e. Comment on "*a generation that prizes individuality, connectivity, and responsibility.*" (l.20-21)

YOUR FINAL TASK

As a famous online sneakerhead, you want to launch your own brand. Convince an American celebrity to make a commercial for a new pair of sneakers.

1. **Create** your pair of sneakers and **choose** the American celebrity that could embody your creation.
2. **Prepare** your arguments: historical, cultural, financial…
3. **Act out** the conversation. Be convincing!

AI Tu peux utiliser un outil d'IA pour créer ta nouvelle basket.

Build your skills! **Convaincre quelqu'un**

➜ Pose des **questions** pour interpeller et faire réfléchir :

Questions ouvertes

- *Tinashe, what do you think it is about Jordans that everyone loves so much?*

Questions fermées

- *Do you know which […] ones you would get two pairs of?*
- *Do you know the origins of sneakers?*

HOW TO SHINE IN GRAMMAR ➜ p. 213

Quiz
TEST yourself

Build your English!

GRAMMAR

Évoquer une qualité extrême grâce au superlatif

GRAMMAR tuto

Superlatif de supériorité

These beautiful shoes are **the most popular** sneakers ever!
(popular : adjectif long)

They were **the boldest** on the market!
(bold : adjectif court)

Sneakers are **the trendiest** shoes for Gen Z!
(trend : adjectif court)

This sneakerhead has **the biggest** collection in the world!
(big : adjectif court)

Superlatif d'infériorité

These sneakers are **the least comfortable**
(comfortable : adjectif long)

and **the least cool** too!
(cool : adjectif court)

Superlatifs de supériorité irréguliers

Good → the best **Far → the farthest/furthest**
These are **the best** sneakers for sport!

Bad → the worst
These are **the worst** sneakers I have!

1 **Recopie et complète ces phrases avec les adjectifs ci-dessous au superlatif de supériorité ou d'infériorité.**

fashionable | unexpected | interested in | ugly | great

a. Gen Z is ... in sneakers.

b. These awful sneakers are ... and ... I've ever seen!

c. For Michael Jordan his endorsement with Nike was ... in his career.

d. Collaborations with singers were ... ever for sneakers.

2 **Tu travailles pour une célèbre marque. Rédige le texte explicatif de cette paire de sneakers. Utilise les adjectifs suivants et le superlatif.**

colourful | expensive | original | bold | good (quality)

PHONOLOGY

La prosodie

- Elle désigne l'**intonation** et le **débit** propres à une langue.
- Dans la **poésie** ou le **rap**,… ce « flow » est rendu par le choix des **allitérations** (répétition d'un même son produit par des consonnes) et **assonances** (répétition d'un même son produit par des voyelles) qui sont **accentuées** et donnent un **rythme** entre les pauses.
  - *I stepped on stage*
  - *Walk through concert doors*
  - *My Adidas touch the sand of a foreign land*

3 **Écoute la chanson de Run DMC. Indique les allitérations et les assonances qui rythment ces phrases. Répète-les.**

All the people gave and the poor got paid
And out of speakers I did speak
I wore my sneakers but I'm not a sneak
With mic in hand I cold took command.

4 **Rédige la strophe d'un rap sur la culture des baskets. Utilise des assonances et des allitérations, puis lis ton texte à voix haute.**

VOCABULARY

+ EXERCISES → p. 230

MEMORISE your vocabulary

SNEAKER CULTURE

Identity

- rebel
- self-assertion
- self-esteem
- mainstream
- self-confident
- unconventional
- be in tune with: *être en accord avec*
- embody
- express

Sneakers

- canvas = fabric
- heel
- kicks = sneaks (fam)
- nose: *bout de la chaussure*
- shoelace (GB) = shoestring (US)
- sole: *semelle*
- tongue: *languette*
- trainers (GB) = sneakers (US)
- rubber-soled
- customise

Sneakerheads

- collector
- fashion-addict
- iconic
- ID = Individually Designed
- knowledgeable
- staunch /ˈstɔːntʃ/ = devoted
- talk the talk = speak impressively about sth
- walk the walk: *être en accord avec ses convictions*

Environmental issues

- organic cotton
- brand new in box
- eco-friendly
- ethical
- sustainable
- pollute
- wear out: *s'user*

● NOUN ● ADJECTIVE ● VERB

1 Find the word behind each definition.

a. Somebody who likes to buy a lot of clothes.
b. Confidence in one's own worth and abilities.
c. Regarded as a representative symbol.
d. Not harmful for the environment.

2 Unscramble the letters and discover the mystery word!

a. LAHOSECE : ...
3 8 1

b. SENCONTLFFIDE : ...
6

c. IENCOEFRDLY: ...
2 9 4

d. TABLSUSINAE : ...
7 5

Mystery word! 1 2 3 4 5 6 7 8 9 = ...

3 Write down as many elements as you can to describe these rappers and their shoes.

4 a. Do you speak sneakerhead? Check the meaning of these idioms.

Have you seen my kicks?
These shoes are BNIB!
I wear these beaters every day, they are so comfy!
Mine are very expensive IDs!

b. Imagine you are talking with your friend about sneakers. How many idioms will you be able to include?

SNAPFILE 11

Bowie's heirs

▶ How has David Bowie's creation influenced new generations of artists?

YOUR FINAL TASK

MÉDIATION

As an artist invited to an exhibition on David Bowie's legacy, create an artwork made of pictures, quotes and short texts in prose or poetry. Your artwork reflects the link between Bowie and the young generation of artists.

Then present it to the exhibition's curator.

FOLLOW THE STEPS

1

▲ Lady Gaga singing a Bowie medley at the Grammys, 2016.

Audio

Lady Gaga on Bowie, *NPR*, 2016.

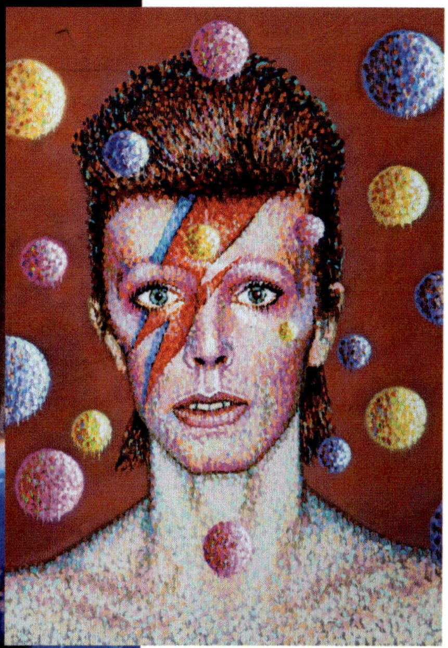

▲ David Bowie in Ziggy Stardust, mural in Brixton, London, 1016.

a. **Compare** the two pictures and **guess** the link between Lady Gaga and David Bowie.

b. **Listen to** the journalist and **say** why Lady Gaga has been compared to Bowie.

c. **Focus on** the journalist's questions and **rephrase** them in a simple way.

d. GRAMMAR **Listen to** Lady Gaga. **Pick out** the verbs she uses. What tense is used to show the succession of actions in the past?

e. **Sum up** Lady Gaga's answer.

PHONOLOGY SPOT

the • that • there

birth • something • through

Écoute puis **répète** les deux listes de mots. Dans quelle liste le son <th> est sonore /ð/? sourd /θ/?

Les compléments numériques
e-WB
lycee.nathan.fr/2sb104-105

▲ The Changing Faces of David Bowie by illustrator Vitoria Bas, 2017.

2

David Bowie was unfathomable[1]. Everything from his life to his career made him a true artist, the kind that only comes up every few generations. There was something about him, an undefinable quality. Something that captured audiences and continues to enthral[2] listeners to this day. And it is exactly that something that shaped the modern Western music industry.

Bowie changed music forever. He did that by constantly reinventing himself, a quality very much present in today's music industry. In a 1976 *Rolling Stone* interview, the British artist said "I always thought that I should change all the time. […] I stripped myself down, chucked things out[3] and replaced them with a completely new personality. When I heard someone say something intelligent. I used it later as if it were my own. When I saw a quality in someone that I liked. I took it. I still do that. All the time."

It was this chameleon-like approach that made him one of the most influential artists of all time and inspired modern-day musicians. Bowie wasn't afraid of experimenting, and he kept reinventing himself through his music. His style constantly shifted, but it was always recognizable as Bowie. […]

Bowie gave artists the freedom to explore their musical styles, who they were, and reflect on what they have to offer to the world.

Ariane Triebswetter, *meer.com*, 2023

1. difficult to understand 2. fascinate 3. throw away

a. React to the drawing.

b. Read the text and **explain** why David Bowie was difficult to understand.

c. GRAMMAR **Focus** on "**the** modern Western music industry" (l.5) and "**Ø** music" (l.6). **Explain** why the determiners are different.

d. Sum up how David Bowie has changed music forever.

STEP 1

Use what you have learned to introduce David Bowie as a multi-faceted artist who influenced the modern music industry.

1 **Gather** the pictures, texts and quotes about David Bowie to start your collage.

2 **Prepare** the first part of your oral presentation about David Bowie.

Build your skills! **Décrire un artiste**

- Utilise les **déterminants** pour donner des précisions :
  - *His career made him **a** true artist / **the** British artist / **this** chameleon-like approach*
- Développe une caractéristique à l'aide d'une **proposition relative** :
  - *an approach **that made him one of the most influential artists of all time***
  - *an artist **who reinvented himself***

HOW TO SHINE IN GRAMMAR → p. 210, 218

3

▲ Halsey in *The Advocate*, 2020.

Audio

Halsey On The Death Of David Bowie, *Pedestrian* TV, 2016.

VOCABULARY SPOT

- heir /'ɛər/ = successor
- androgynous /æn'drɒdʒɪnəs/
- inspiring
- influence
- mimic = imitate
- renew = reinvent
- shape
- shift = change
- trailblazer /'treɪlbleɪzər/: *innovateur(trice)*

MEMORISE your vocabulary

GRAMMAR SPOT

- ***This** androgynous beauty / **these** stereotypes*
- *At **that** time / in **those** years*

Observe les **démonstratifs**. Lesquels sont singuliers ? Pluriels ?

Lesquels expriment la proximité ? L'éloignement ?

TEAM WORK

Team A works on doc 3 and Team B on doc 4.

a. **Look at** the picture and **guess** why David Bowie may be a source of inspiration.

b. **Listen to** the audio and **pick out** the Bowie elements that influenced her/his music.

c. **Share** your findings.

A LITTLE EXTRA — **Video**

Watch David Bowie speaking about his art.
Pick out some of his advice to young artists.

4

Audio

Declan McKenna reveals why David Bowie is such an essential artist, *Radio X*, 2020.

◀ Declan McKenna, *Zeros*, 2020.

Les compléments numériques
e-WB
lycee.nathan.fr/**2sb106-107**

5

Harry Styles: The new Bowie or a marketing dream?

There's been a lot of comparisons made in recent months about the former One Direction heart throb being right up there with the legendary Thin White Duke.

In musical terms, Styles clearly has some way to go if he wishes to sit on the same podium as Bowie when it comes to legendary status (although he's made a decent start in terms of record sales–having the record for the most streamed track in 24 hours).

Individualism is what made Bowie stand out from the chasing pack. Devising[1] different on-stage personas time and time again to leave his audience guessing, and shocking parents watching him perform on *Top of the Pops*.

"Is he a man? Is he a woman? Is he an alien?" gasped a tutting[2] older generation who were more accustomed to four white guys dressed slickly as if going to a job interview on a Monday morning.

Styles is credited for a similar approach to androgyny. A strong sense of fashion, wearing a dress on the front page of *Vogue*, painting nails. This is for sure breaking down barriers and rightly so, but is it just the former One Directioner working alone, or does he have a team providing the tools?

cwa.co.uk, 2023

1. conceive 2. disapproving

a. Look at the title and **rephrase** the issue.

b. Read the article and **give** the similarities between David Bowie and Harry Styles.

c. Explain why this legacy could be a marketing approach.

d. VOCABULARY **Find** two phrasal verbs which mean "emerge from" and "remove".

Harry Styles in 2021 and David Bowie in 1971.

STEP 2

Present your artwork and explain the links between David Bowie and his heirs.

1 **Gather** the pictures, texts and quotes about David Bowie's heirs and **finish** your collage.

2 **Make** the second part of your oral presentation insisting on David Bowie's legacy.

Tu peux utiliser un outil d'IA pour assembler les éléments de ton projet artistique.

Build your skills! **Exprimer une filiation**

Emploie la **comparaison** :
- ***similar to …***, *sing* ***alike***, ***both*** *reinvent themselves*, ***the same*** *approach* ***as …***
- ***as*** *innovative / creative* ***as …***

HOW TO SHINE IN GRAMMAR ➜ p. 211

Quiz
TEST yourself

FLASH FILE 12 A muse forever

▶ How has Elizabeth Siddal become a beauty standard?

YOUR FINAL TASK

In teams, **watch** and **read** the documents and share your information. e-WB

Then **use** an AI tool to create a Pre-Raphaelite muse for a fashion show project. **Present** it to the class.

1

▲ Dante Gabriel Rossetti, *Portrait of Elisabeth Siddal* (1854).

Video

The artist who modelled for *Ophelia, Jessye Seth Bloomfield*, 2018.

VOCABULARY SPOT

- (fair) complexion = (pale) face
- (stately) demeanour /dɪˈmiːnə/: *port de tête (altier)*
- (loose / ethereal /iˈθɪəriəl/) dress
- (curly / long / wavy) hair
- bucolic = pastoral
- flowery
- melancholic = sad
- red-headed
- slender = slim
- embody = stand for
- look like = resemble

MEMORISE your vocabulary

2

The first supermodel

The Pre-Raphaelite Brotherhood, a movement Rossetti co-founded in the 19th century, loved symbolism, but I'm more interested in Siddal the person, who was herself an artist. What does it mean that we remember her life stories far better than we do the craft to which she dedicated her life?

Her life stories are, to be fair, exciting: art historical myths in their own right. One of the most famous is that she was discovered behind the counter at a milliner's shop[1] by Sir Walter Deverell, who cast her as Viola in a painting of scenes from *Twelfth Night*. One of my favorites is that her first exposure to poetry was a poem by Tennyson that had been used to wrap[2] butter.

▲ Elizabeth SIDDAL, *St Agnes' Eve*, 1853-60.

But beyond the stories are the facts: Elizabeth Siddal was born Elizabeth Siddall to a lower-middle class family and changed her name when Rossetti suggested that dropping an L would improve her aesthetic; she was a painter and poet who had to work for her money; and her red hair and long, lanky[3] frame were not considered attractive until she became the foremost muse to the Pre-Raphaelites. She was, in many ways, the first supermodel, shaping the cultural landscape with her image.

Amina KHAN, *artic.edu*, 2023

1. *boutique de chapeaux* 2. *envelopper*
3. thin and tall

3

Video

Karen Elson on Millais's *Ophelia*, *TateShots*, 2012.

▲ Dante Gabriel ROSSETTI, *Regina Cordium* (1860).

John Everett MILLAIS, *Ophelia*, 1851-1852, Tate Britain, London.

FILE 13 Healing the wounds

Reconciliation means working together to correct the legacy of past injustice."

Nelson MANDELA, 1995.

VOCABULARY SPOT

- apartheid /əˈpɑːrthaɪt/
- legacy: *héritage*

- racially-divided /ˈreɪʃəli-dɪˈvaɪdɪd/
- reconciled /ˈrɛkənsaɪld/
- unforgettable

- acknowledge the past
- gather
- wave a flag

MEMORISE your vocabulary

Les compléments numériques

e-WB

lycee.nathan.fr/**2sb110-111**

How is South Africa dealing with the legacy of apartheid?

YOUR **FINAL** TASK

Record and **publish** a collection of testimonies on Day of Reconciliation.

Children celebrate 30 years of democracy in Pretoria, South Africa, 2024.

Video

Singing in Harmony, *PBSNewsHour*, 2024.

TEAM WORK

Team A

Look at the main picture, **read** the caption and **react**.

Team B

Read the quote and **rephrase** Nelson Mandela's idea.

Team C

Watch the video and **comment on** the aim of the musical band.

- Now **share** your findings with the other teams and **explain** why it is important for South Africans to deal with their past.

EXPLORE A traumatic past

1652 The **Cape Colony** was founded by the Dutch

1795-1806 The British took the Cape Colony

The **Boer War** (The Dutch Afrikaaners vs the British)

1948 Beginning of **apartheid**

1960 Black civilians were killed while peacefully demonstrating during the **Sharpeville Massacre**

1964 **Nelson Mandela** was imprisoned for life

1976 **Soweto riots**: school children demonstrated against being taught in Afrikaans

1990 **Nelson Mandela** was released after **27 years in prison**

1990-1994 Several negotiations led to the **end of apartheid**

1994 **Nelson Mandela** was elected **president**

19th century — 20th century — 21st century

1

▲ A woman sitting in the white section of a train in South Africa, 1952.

Video
Apartheid, *Encyclopaedia Britannica*, 2024.

a. **Observe** the picture and **check** the timeline. **Guess** why the woman chose to sit there.

b. **Watch** the video and **pick out** elements on the apartheid system.

c. **Describe** black people's living conditions back then.

d. **Identify** and **sum up** the two events which showed the population's resistance to apartheid.

e. **Recap** the different international actions taken to oppose the system.

f. **Explain** how apartheid was ended and the first consequences for the population.

VOCABULARY SPOT

- discrimination

- discriminated against
- hopeful ≠ hopeless
- separate

- be allowed to
- be kept apart
- speak out against

- unfairly

MEMORISE your vocabulary

A LITTLE EXTRA — **Video**

Watch the video and **pick out** elements on the story of District 6 during apartheid and now.

Les compléments numériques

e-WB

lycee.nathan.fr/**2sb112-113**

2

▲ The Nelson Mandela Foundation with Umlando Wezithombe, *Nelson Mandela: the Authorized Comic Book*, 2009.

a. **Read** the comic book page and **identify** the event.

b. GRAMMAR **Name** the tenses used in the first vignette. **Explain** the succession of actions.

c. **Describe** the different people's reactions to the main event.

d. **Focus** on Nelson Mandela's speech. **Spot** the repetitions and **sum up** his vision for his country.

e. **Observe** the colours and illustrations used and **explain** what the illustrator wanted to convey.

CULTURE SPOT

The Rainbow Nation is an expression created by **Archbishop Desmond Tutu**. **Nelson Mandela (Madiba)** used it a lot to define **South Africa's cultural diversity** and promote **unity** and **peace** in **a post-apartheid country**.

1. concession speech: *discours de défaite* 2. exhausted = extremely tired 3. trademark: *marque de fabrique* 4. fledgling = newborn

YOUR TASK

Write a post on the Nelson Mandela Foundation's website entitled "The end of apartheid".

1. **Explain** the rules during apartheid.
2. **Mention** the changes with Nelson Mandela's election and his vision for South Africa.

Build your skills! Évoquer des faits marquants et exprimer un besoin de changement

➜ Mentionne des faits passés avec le **prétérit** :
- *Black children **didn't get to go** to the same schools as white children…*

➜ Mentionne des faits antérieurs avec le ***past perfect*** :
- *The people of South Africa **had spoken**.*

➜ Utilise la **mise en relief** pour évoquer une transition :
- ***This is the time** to heal old wounds and build a new South Africa!*

Quiz

TEST yourself

HOW TO SHINE IN GRAMMAR ➜ p. 215

EXPLORE Towards reconciliation

1

▲ Archbishop Desmond Tutu on the first day of the Truth and Reconciliation Commission, April 1996.

a. **Observe** the picture and the saying. **React**.

b. **Read** the culture spot and **explain** the context of the picture.

c. Now **read** the poem and **identify** the situation and the people present.

d. VOCABULARY **Pick out** the repeated verb and words belonging to the same lexical field. **Identify** the emotion.

e. PHONOLOGY **Spot** the repeated sound on lines 21 and 22 and **guess** why the author is using it.

f. **Comment on** the poet's message.

A LITTLE EXTRA Video

Watch the video and **find out** more about Archbishop Desmond Tutu's role in the commission.

CULTURE SPOT

The Truth and Reconciliation Commission (TRC) (1996-2000), was created by the South Arfrican government. Led by **Archbishop Desmond Tutu**, the commission listened to **testimonies** from **victims** and **oppressors** to overcome the trauma of apartheid and promote national reconciliation. The Commission acknowledged that **apartheid** was a clear **violation of human rights**.

2

Audio version

The Archbishop chairs[1] the first session

On the first day
after a few hours of testimony
the archbishop wept[2].
He put his grey head
on the long table
of papers and protocols
and he wept.

The national
and international cameramen
filmed his weeping,
his misted[3] glasses,
his sobbing[4] shoulders,
the call for a recess[5].

It doesn't matter what you thought
of the archbishop before or after,
of the settlement, the commission,
or what the anthropologists flying in
from less studied crimes
and sorrows
said about the discourse,
or how many doctorates,
books, and installations followed,
or even if you think this poem
simplifies, lionizes[6]
romanticizes, mystifies.

There was a long table, starched[7]
purple vestment[8]
and after a few hours
of testimony,
the archbishop,
chair of the commission,
laid down his head and wept.
That's how it began.

Ingrid DE KOK, *Terrestrial things*, Kwela/Snailpress, 2002

1. preside over 2. cry (weep) 3. *embuées* 4. cry 5. break 6. *idôlatrer* 7. *amidonné* 8. clothes

3

Video

Reconciliation Day, *SABC News*, 2020.

Knzmuseum • Following

National Reconciliation Day is commemorated annually in South Africa with the aim of promoting social cohesion, healing and nation building following years of turmoil and division in the country.

This year's edition of National Reconciliation Day is celebrated under the theme, "Strengthening Unity and Social Cohesion in a Healing Nation" and calls on each and every South African to play an active role in promoting peace and stability in a democratic South Africa.

#Knzmusemum#ReconciliationDay

119 likes

▲ The Kwazulu-Natal Museum Instagram post on Reconciliation Day (16 December), 2023.

a. **Describe** the post and **rephrase** what Day of Reconciliation is about.

b. **Comment on** the use of Instagram to promote that day.

c. **Watch** the video and **pick out** information on the event.

d. **Describe** the remaining problems in South Africa.

e. **Sum up** the question raised by the journalist.

f. **Recap** the positive aspects mentioned by the speaker.

VOCABULARY SPOT

- forgiveness: *pardon*
- healing: *guérison*
- human rights abuse
- testimony

- divided ≠ united

- chair: *présider*
- heal the wounds: *soigner les blessures*
- provide reparations
- seek reconciliation
- testify

MEMORISE your vocabulary

YOUR TASK

DIFFÉRENCIATION

Record a short podcast on reconciliation is South Africa.

WAY 1 You are a historian.

1 **Present** the TRC.

2 **Explain** what happened during the first session of the TRC.

WAY 2 You are a journalist.

1 **Present** the TRC.

2 **Explain** its goals.

3 **Mention** today's issues.

Build your skills! Faire un état des lieux

➔ Utilise le ***present perfect*** pour faire un bilan :

- *It's **been** 26 years since we attained political freedom.*
- *South Africa as a democracy **has managed** to achieve political freedom.*

➔ Évoque ce qui doit être envisagé avec ***need*** :

- *We need to take the positives…*

HOW TO SHINE IN GRAMMAR ➔ p. 215

Quiz
TEST yourself

Living together

1

Audio version

Rise: The Siya Kolisi Story, documentary poster, 2023.

When I was on the field and I looked into the crowd, I saw people of all races and social classes. We as players represented the whole country. I told my teammates: "You should never play just to represent one group. You can't play to be the best black player or to be the best white player to appeal[1] to a community. You have to play to be the best for every South African. We represent something much bigger that we can imagine."

It wasn't just the destination that was important, but the journey too. Being the first black captain was made immeasurably more meaningful by the journey I'd taken to get there, because that journey was one which had been denied[2] to thousands of talented players before me purely because of the colour of their skin. I was, as far as I know, the first Springbok captain to speak in isiXhosa[3] at a press conference, certainly for more than a few words. IsiXhosa was the language of those players of colour who had missed out until now. No longer.

There were even comparisons to Mr Mandela. It was an honour and very flattering, but it was also wrong. I played rugby, I existed in a smaller world. He spent all those years in prison and then achieved so much when he was freed. I had to do what I could as a rugby player to help people, especially those in the townships, but it was nothing compared to what Mr Mandela did.

Siya Kolisi, *Rise*, 2021

1. please
2. refuse
3. one of the most spoken African languages in South Africa

a. **Describe** the poster and **imagine** what the documentary is about.
b. **Read** the text and **pick out** information on the narrator.
c. GRAMMAR **Focus on** the direct speech (l. 2-5). **Rephrase** the narrator's message and **comment on** the use of direct speech here.
d. **Identify** who the narrator is compared to and **imagine** why.
e. **Explain** the narrator's mixed reaction to the comparison.

A LITTLE EXTRA

Video

Watch the video and **pick out** actions taken by the Siya Kolisi foundation.

VOCABULARY SPOT

- role model
- spokesperson

- diverse
- multicultural

- gather
- raise awareness

- reckon with the past = deal with the past
- unite the country

MEMORISE your vocabulary

Les compléments numériques
lycee.nathan.fr/2sb116-117

2

▲ Schoolgirls in a history class in Cape Town, 2019.

Video

South African pupils open up to wounds of apartheid past, *AFP News Agency*, 2019.

3

Video

Honouring Mandela's legacy, *eNCA*, 2023.

▲ Mandela Day in Johannesburg (18 July), 2023.

TEAM WORK

Team A **works on doc 2 and**
Team B **on doc 3.**

a. **Watch** the video. **Identify** the type of document and the speakers.
b. **Explain** the context of the video and **sum up** the main ideas.
c. **Describe** the images used in the video and **say** how they help to convey a message.
d. **Share** your findings with the other team, then **compare** and **contrast** both videos.
e. **Comment on** the different ways South Africa is dealing with its past today.

YOUR TASK

Interview young South Africans on the impact of the past in today's South Africa.

1. **Ask** questions about dealing with the past.
2. **Mention** how the country is coming together as a nation.

AI Vous pouvez utiliser un outil d'IA pour **mettre en forme** votre projet (insertion de musique, transitions, etc.).

Build your skills! **Mentionner l'héritage du passé et évoquer un souhait pour l'avenir**

➜ Utilise **l'adverbe *still*** pour parler d'éléments qui subsistent :
- *… but it **still** casts a shadow over their lives …*
- *… the country **still** remains a racially-divided one …*

➜ Pense aux modaux et équivalents pour évoquer des **souhaits** :
- *You **should** never play just to represent one group.*
- *You **have to** play to be the best for every South African.*
- *… this is what we **can** do together.*

BUILD YOUR ENGLISH ➜ p. 120

Quiz
TEST yourself

TEST YOUR CULTURE AND VOCABULARY

MANDELA DAY CHALLENGE!

HOW TO PLAY

In pairs, **answer** as many questions as possible in 6 minutes and 7 seconds* to honour Mandela's legacy.

The first team to **answer** all the questions **wins** and is ready to celebrate Mandela Day!

*"67" being the number of years Mandela fought for justice in South Africa.

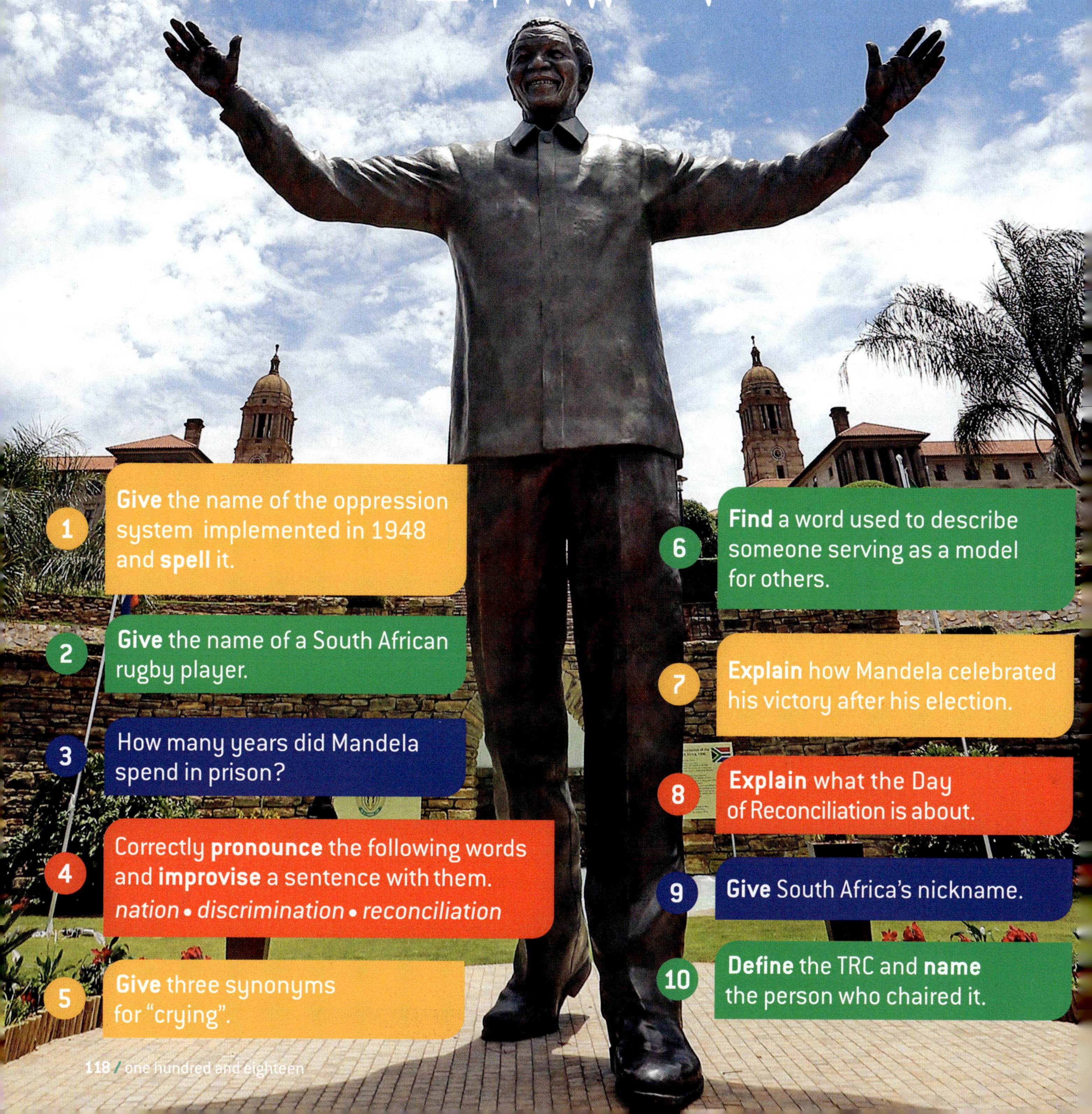

1. **Give** the name of the oppression system implemented in 1948 and **spell** it.
2. **Give** the name of a South African rugby player.
3. How many years did Mandela spend in prison?
4. Correctly **pronounce** the following words and **improvise** a sentence with them. *nation • discrimination • reconciliation*
5. **Give** three synonyms for "crying".
6. **Find** a word used to describe someone serving as a model for others.
7. **Explain** how Mandela celebrated his victory after his election.
8. **Explain** what the Day of Reconciliation is about.
9. **Give** South Africa's nickname.
10. **Define** the TRC and **name** the person who chaired it.

Build your English!

VOCABULARY

Les compléments numériques e-WB
lycee.nathan.fr/2sb118-119

EXERCISES → p. 230

MEMORISE your vocabulary

HEALING THE WOUNDS

Apartheid

- discrimination
- injustice
- oppression
- township = a segregated area
- racially-divided
- categorise
- mistreat = treat badly
- unfairly

Reconciliation

- perpetrator
- public hearing: *audition publique*
- the Rainbow Nation
- the Truth and Reconciliation Commission (T.R.C)
- forgiving
- truthful
- forgive
- testify
- undeniably : /ˌʌndɪˈnaɪəbli/

Remaining issues

- disparity
- shack: *cabane*
- polarised = divided
- unemployed
- face discrimination
- highly

Hopes for the future

- role model
- sense of community
- equal
- celebrate diversity
- embrace differences
- get closer to
- promote peace
- write a new page

Legacy

- equality ≠ inequality
- healing
- united
- bring together
- heal the wounds: *soigner les blessures*
- unite the nation
- annually

NOUN ADJECTIVE VERB ADVERB OR PREPOSITION

1 Match each definition with the corresponding word.

apartheid | the Rainbow Nation | testify | township

a. An expression used to promote South Africa's multiculturalism.

b. An area where black South Africans were sent to live outside cities.

c. A verb used to describe the fact of sharing your testimony.

d. A political system which targeted black citizens.

2 Find the antonym for each of the following words.

a. divided
b. equality
c. violence
d. hopeless

3 Choose the right noun in the following sentences.

a. *The Rainbow Nation* / *apartheid* lasted from 1948 to 1990.

b. With the Truth and Reconciliation Commission, Archbishop Desmond Tutu hoped to promote *inequality* / *forgiveness*.

c. Today, many South Africans live in *shacks* / *villas* in townships across the country.

d. Siya Kolisi hopes to serve as a *perpetrator* / *role model* to unite South Africa.

4 Write a post to react to the following event. You can use words from the wordmap.

Rugby team trophy tour, Durban, 2023.

+ EXERCISES → p. 236-237

A L'expression des regrets et des souhaits

GRAMMAR tuto

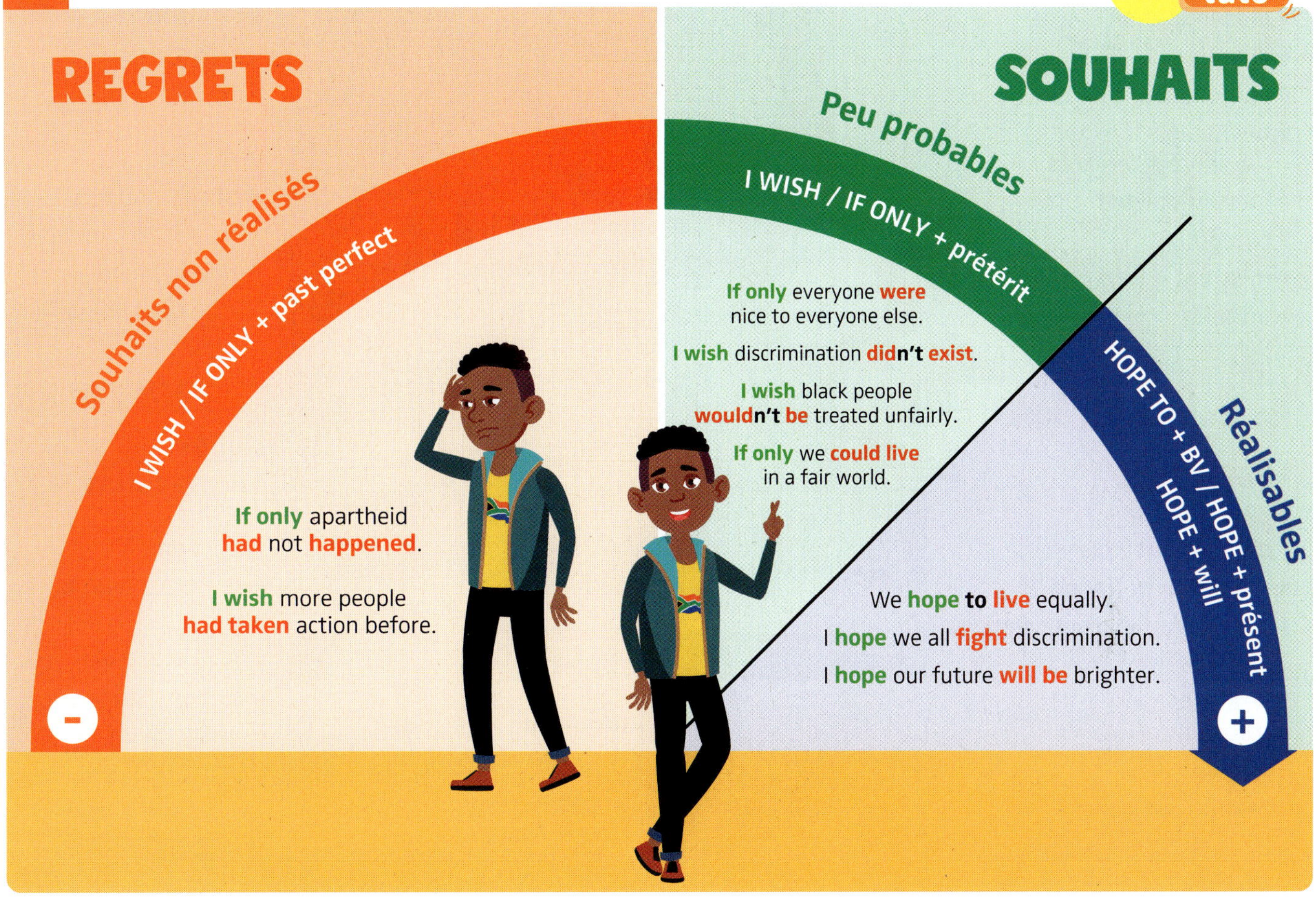

1 Indique pour chaque phrase si elle exprime le souhait ou le regret.

a. I wish I had met Mandela.

b. I wish we didn't have to fight for our rights.

c. If only South Africa hadn't been segregated.

d. He hopes to live in a peaceful country.

2 Conjugue le verbe entre parenthèses en fonction du sens de la phrase.

a. They wish more people (*fight*) apartheid. *regret*

b. If only people (*not live*) in townships. *souhait*

c. I wish black people (*have*) more freedom nowadays. *souhait*

d. If only people (*promote*) peace earlier. *regret*

3 Exprime des souhaits et des regrets à partir de ces réactions.

I wish… | *If only …* | *I hope …*

There are still differences between black and white people.

When I was a child, I couldn't have an education, I regret it.

My grandma suffered because of apartheid. I'm sorry for her!

Our nation? A role model? It's my dream!

4 Exprime les souhaits et les regrets de cette personne en utilisant les idées suggérées.

live in harmony

forgive but not forget

heal the wounds

people all over the world raise voices

countries help African people

not experience apartheid

Les compléments numériques
lycee.nathan.fr/2sb120-121

EXERCISES → p. 236-237

B Rapporter des paroles au discours direct ou indirect

GRAMMAR tuto

On peut rapporter des propos entendus tels quels **(discours direct)**, ou en les reformulant légèrement, pour plus de fluidité **(discours indirect)**. Dans les deux cas, on utilise un verbe introducteur :

say **tell** **explain** **answer** **ask** **wonder** **hear from**

DISCOURS DIRECT
Les propos entendus sont répétés **à l'identique** et **entre guillemets** par celui qui les rapporte.

DISCOURS INDIRECT
Les propos entendus sont **reformulés** par celui qui les rapporte, introduits avec un verbe **introducteur** mais **sans guillemets**.
⚠ Verbes, pronoms et adverbes sont modifiés.

PRÉSENT

Arthie **says**:
"I **see** our country is growing."
Les propos viennent d'être rapportés.

Arthie **says** (that)
he **sees** their country is growing.

PASSÉ

Madiba **explained**:
"I **want** sport to unite people."
Les propos ont été dits dans le passé.

On that day, Madiba **explained**
(that) he **wanted** sport to unite people.
Le jour où il parlait.

QUESTION

My friend **wondered**: "What is this flag?"
I **asked** him:
"Do you know South Africa?"
La forme reste interrogative.

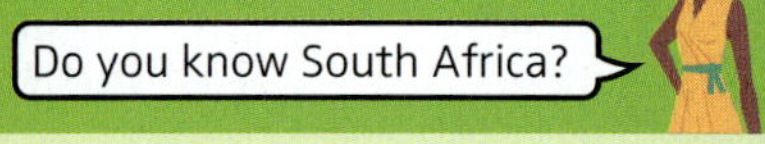

Last week, my friend **wondered** **what** that flag **was** so I **asked** him if he **knew** South Africa.

⚠ **L'impératif** se rapporte au **discours indirect** avec un verbe de **volonté** et une **proposition infinitive**.
"Take action!" → She **wanted** everyone **to** take action.

1 Indique pour chaque phrase si elle est au discours direct ou indirect. Attention à la ponctuation!

a. He asked, "Do you know South Africa?"
b. I told him not to worry about the future.
c. He said people hoped to promote equality and fairness.
d. "We hope that the future of South Africa will be a happy one for all," they said.

2 Rapporte les propos ci-dessous au style indirect. Utilise des verbes introducteurs au passé.

a. I want to stop discrimination. (Nelson Mandela)
b. We are a Rainbow Nation. (Desmond Tutu)
c. How long did Nelson Mandela fight apartheid? (my little brother)
d. Is discrimination over now? (student)

3 Réécris ces phrases au style direct.

a. She asked me when Reconciliation Day took place.
b. They asked me if I lived in a township.
c. Nelson Mandela said he wanted to promote peace.
d. My friend said he was proud to be part of the Rainbow Nation.

4 Rapporte ce dialogue entre deux amis au style indirect. Utilise des verbes introducteurs au passé.

"What is Mandela Day?"
"It is a day to celebrate Madiba, it is celebrated on July 18th."
"What do people do to celebrate?"
"Usually, people take action. For example, they volunteer to help their community."
"That's great! I want to take part. Volunteer with me!"

PHONOLOGY

Les compléments numériques
lycee.nathan.fr/2sb122

A L'accent de mots Audio

En anglais, chaque mot a un **accent principal**, dit **tonique**. L'accentuation varie d'un mot à l'autre. De plus, certains suffixes imposent des règles d'accentuation. Par exemple, dans les mots finissant en ***-ion***, ***-ity*** ou encore ***-ic***, l'accent tombe toujours sur la syllabe précédent le suffixe.

- *Nelson Mandela was a nati**o**nal p**u**blic figure. He promoted a more equal soci**e**ty and reconcili**a**tion for the Rainbow N**a**tion.*

1 Écoute les mots suivants, repère l'accent tonique et répète-les.

a. South Africa – nation – divided – equal – unity
b. segregation – annually – society –township

2 Lis ces mots. Quel est le point commun dans leur accentuation. Écoute et vérifie.

a. united – divided – included
b. oppression – commission – discrimination

B Les groupes de souffle Audio

- En anglais, on appelle **groupes de souffle** un ensemble de mots **énoncés à la suite**, avant une **pause**.
- La ponctuation peut parfois donner des indications sur ces pauses.
  - *In Johannesburg/ a South African group/ continues to spread Mandela's message/*
  - *Reconciliation and healing/ were the main goals of the TRC/*

1 Écoute les phrases suivantes et répète-les en prêtant attention aux groupes de souffle.

a. South Africa,/ which has 12 official languages,/ is a very diverse and multicultural country.
b. For many young South Africans,/ the dream of the Rainbow Nation/ hasn't been reached yet.

2 Lis ce post de la fondation *Nelson Mandela* en faisant attention aux groupes de souffle. Écoute et vérifie.

YOUR FINAL TASK

Record and publish a collection of testimonies on Day of Reconciliation.

With your team, get ready to celebrate Reconciliation Day with a series of testimonies you can post on an online platform.

1. **Get ready** and **gather** your ideas on:
   – the legacy of apartheid in South Africa today;
   – actions and events organised to celebrate the country's diversity;
   – South Africans' views on the Rainbow Nation and their relationship with their past.
2. In groups, **share** your work. **Prepare** and **record** audio testimonies, **write** a short post or **include** a poem or an illustration to prove your point.
3. **Use** an online platform to post your work.

AI Vous pouvez utiliser un outil d'IA pour **mettre en forme** votre projet (insertion de musique, transitions, etc.).

YES YOU CAN!

Record and/or write a series of testimonies

INTRODUCTION DU SUJET

Adresse-toi à tes lecteurs/auditeurs pour présenter ton projet de témoignages collectif.

Fitness and fun all in the name of Utata, a fitting way to lead into Mandela Day […] it's a fantastic opportunity for people to come and do something together and to bring the country together.

ILLUSTRATIONS ET EXEMPLES

Illustre des faits marquants et leur impact par des illustrations ou autres poèmes que tu pourras poster pour accompagner les témoignages. Tu peux reprendre des documents de l'unité ou intégrer des éléments de recherche personnelle.

"the Archbishop, chair of the commission,
laid down his head and wept.
That's how it began."

LES TÉMOIGNAGES

Enregistre des témoignages marquants. Utilise le discours direct si tu choisis de t'exprimer à la première personne ou le discours indirect si tu rapportes les paroles de quelqu'un.

"We're here just to share […], a little bit of Madiba magic that runs through our veins, here as a nation coming together saying this is what we can do together."

Organisers say sports was Madiba's favourite way to promote unity within a post-apartheid South Africa.

LE RÉCIT

Tu peux inclure des courts paragraphes rédigés pour mentionner l'impact des événements ou commenter les témoignages que tu as choisi d'inclure.

We wanted to encourage people […] to come and walk with us the same route that he used to and try and reflect about the state of our country…

CONCLUSION

Rédige ou enregistre un message positif pour conclure cette série de témoignages.

It was all left outside of the gates and everyone came here for a good time…

HOW TO SHINE IN WRITING/INTERACTING → p. 204/206

PRACTISE AND SHINE

Compréhension de l'oral

Nelson Mandela greets Francois Pienaar and his teammates during the Rugby World Cup, 1995.

Video
United in sports, *60 minutes*, 2022.

A1>A2 **Step 1** Before watching the video, **focus on** the title and the picture.

a. **Read** the video title and the picture caption. **Guess** the main topic of the video.

b. **Watch** the video without the sound and **make hypotheses** about it (type, speakers, topic).

TIPS
- **Récapitule** les connaissances culturelles de l'unité, et notamment le lien entre le sport et l'union de la nation. **Visionne la vidéo sans le son** et **appuie-toi** sur les images, légende et autres logos pour déduire la nature du document.

A2 **Step 2** **Watch** the video again with sound and **take notes** about:

a. the different speakers and their role;

b. the sports mentioned and the reasons for celebrating.

TIPS
- **Appuie-toi sur les différents interlocuteurs** pour en déduire leur rôle. Les différents **sons** ajoutés t'apportent également une indication sur le contexte de la vidéo et le ton.

A2>B1 **Step 3** **Watch** the video again and **pick out** details about:

a. the interviewees' feelings;

b. the role of sports;

c. the remaining issues.

TIPS
- **Identifie** les mots accentués importants, les répétitions et **prête attention** aux émotions des personnes interrogées qui te donneront une indication sur le message qu'ils souhaitent faire passer.

B1>B1+ **Step 4** **Recap.**

WAY 1. Gather your ideas and **recap.**

a. **Identify** the right elements to be used in your recap.

- The video is a **documentary** / **news report** / **talk show** from an **English** / **American** / **South-African** programme called '60 minutes'.
- It deals with the **rejection** / **positive role** of rugby in **England** / **South Africa** / **New Zealand**.

b. **Include** the following sentence in your recap: ***Siya Kolisi and Francois Pienaar both …***

c. **Mention** the role of sports and its impact on South Africans. You may use the following words:

enthusiastic | moving | equality | come together | unify

WAY 2. Rassemble tes idées et à l'aide des éléments de réponses, **récapitule** en français ou en anglais ce dont il s'agit.

B1+>B2 **Go further**

- **Explain** the goal of this document.

e-WB **Grille d'autoévaluation**

Compréhension de l'écrit

This weekend marks 30 years since Nelson Mandela was elected president of South Africa, officially ending the country's era of apartheid. NPR's Scott Detrow talks with journalist Redi Thlabi. […]

DETROW: You have kids, right–a 10 and a 7-year-old?

THLABI: Yes, 10 and 7...

DETROW: Can I...

THLABI: ...Both girls.

DETROW: ...Ask what you've told them–how you tell them the story of what happened in 1994 and what that moment felt like then?

THLABI: OK, so my children do appreciate the specialness, the uniqueness of coming from a country that produced Nelson Mandela. […]

My children have always gone to multiracial schools. And they talk about racism as something that shocks them, that I can't believe there was a time where this was not allowed. Why did it happen? Why did it happen? And I teach them that we shouldn't allow it to happen. I can't believe Nelson Mandela spent 27 years in jail. He wasn't the only one. We should never, ever build a world where people are sent to jail all because they want equality. So they understand that South Africa is a special place because of that. They understand that we chose reconciliation over war. […]

Nelson Mandela did not sell out[1]. He used the tools that he had–he and his peers[2]–to get us to a certain point. It is our responsibility then to build our country. He can't be blamed for the fact that we are not a caring society, we are not affording[3] socioeconomic rights to so many who are poor. So what I tell my daughters is that you are special because you come from South Africa, but you are not absolved[4] of your responsibility to build a just world.

Scott Detrow, *npr.org*, 2024

1. *trahir* 2. colleagues 3. give 4. freed

A1 › A2 **Step 1** Before reading the text **focus on** its source and **read** the introduction.

a. Think about all that you know about Nelson Mandela.

b. Observe the layout and **deduce** the nature of the text.

c. Guess what the text might deal with.

TIPS
- **Récapitule** les connaissances culturelles de l'unité, et notamment sur Nelson Mandela et la fin de l'apartheid.

A2 **Step 2** **Read** the text once and **take notes** about:

a. the occasion for the discussion; **b.** the journalist's questions;

c. Nelson Mandela.

TIPS
- **Repère** les mots-clés dans les questions pour identifier ensuite les éléments de réponse dans le texte.

B1 **Step 3** **Read** the text again and **pick out** elements on:

a. the children's reactions; **b.** the state of South Africa today;

c. the interviewee's hopes for the future.

TIPS
- **Repère** les différents pronoms personnels sujets et compléments pour **identifier** les éléments relatifs aux différentes personnes mentionnées dans le texte.

B1 › B1+ **Step 4** **Gather** your different ideas and **recap.**

a. Complete the introduction:
The text is an excerpt from … by an American … published to mark …

b. Explain the interviewee's main ideas using the following words and expressions:

reconciliation | remaining inequalities | condemn racism | younger generations | hopeful

B1+ › B2 **Go further**

- **Comment on** the last line "but you are not absolved of your responsibility to build a just world".

e-WB **Grille d'autoévaluation**

SHORTFILE 14

Walking in their tracks

▶ How is today's Australia shaped by ancestral cultures?

YOUR FINAL TASK

Write an article for the Darwin Aboriginal Art Fair (DAAF) website about the modernity of Aboriginal Art.

1. From generations to generations

1

▲ A First Nations warrior in front of Uluru.

Video

Living with the oldest culture on Earth, *Seek Discomfort*, 2023.

a. **Look at** the picture and **read** the title of the video. What issue do you think the video will deal with?

b. **Watch** the video and **pick out** the ancient civilisations and their time periods.

c. **Identify** what makes Indigenous Australian culture different from others.

d. **Explain** how Indigenous Australians preserve their history.

e. **Sum up** the challenge Indigenous culture faces in modern Australia.

VOCABULARY SPOT

- customs
- graphic novel
- landmark

- ancient /ˈeɪnʃənt/
- ancestral
- Indigenous = First Nations = Aboriginal

- inspirational
- intergenerational

- erase /ɪˈreɪz/
- pass on = pass down = transmit
- perpetuate traditions

MEMORISE your vocabulary

Les compléments numériques
lycee.nathan.fr/2sb126-127

2 e-WB Différenciation

Indigenous Alice Springs comic book artists Stick Mob put final touches on inspirational sequels

At a local arts centre in Alice Springs, a group of young Indigenous artists is preparing banners and merchandise ahead of launch day. The group, called Stick Mob[1], have been working diligently on the hotly anticipated second series of their comic books after breaking out into the niche industry in 2021. Born from the dreams of four high school students—and featuring mutants, cyborgs and phantasms—Stick Mob brings to life unique, central desert stories through their imaginative art.

Their inaugural releases—*Mixed Feelings*, *Exo Dimensions* and *Storm Warning*–took a deep dive into a range of topics, from climate change to intergenerational trauma and healing, set against the backdrop of life in Central Australia.

When their series launched in 2021, writer-illustrators Alyssa Mason, Seraphina Newberry and Lauren Boyle became the first female Aboriginal graphic novelists to be published in Australia. […]

Alyssa Mason, now in her early-20s, said the creations had filled the group with pride, and inspired them to keep making new work. […]

For Seraphina Newberry, the work is an opportunity to create a brighter future for her hometown of Alice Springs. She said many young Indigenous people, including herself, had faced adversity but that it does not need to define their lives.

"We're showing them that Alice Springs, or the youth, or whatever is happening in town, is not all bad," she said. "There's some really great stuff coming from this community, and the fact that we're all working together and we're actually thriving[2] and not, essentially, just being really closed off."

abc.net.au, 2024

1. Aboriginal term for a family or clan group 2. grow

▲ *The Rainbow Serpent by Alyssa Mason* from the Stick Mob collective.

a. **React** to the work of art.

b. **Read** the text and **find** information about Stick Mob.

c. GRAMMAR **Focus on** the expression "the group have been working diligently on ..." (l. 3). What does the *be* +V-*ing* form insist on?

d. **Explain** what their inspiration is and what their themes are.

e. **Comment on** the way Stick Mob's art reflects their culture and impacts young First Nations people.

YOUR TASK

DIFFÉRENCIATION

Interview a member of Stick Mob about cultural transmission.

WAY 1

Ask questions about the way she is transmitting her culture.

WAY 2

Ask questions about the way Aboriginal culture was transmitted and the way she is passing on her culture now.

Build your skills! Parler de l'importance de la transmission d'une culture

➔ Utilise la **forme en *be* + V-*ing*** pour parler d'une action en cours de déroulement :

- *A group of young Indigenous artists **is preparing** banners.*
- ***We're showing** them that Alice Springs is not all that bad.*

➔ Utilise des **marqueurs temporels** associés au prétérit :

- *The pyramids were built almost **5,000 years ago**.*
- *Their history was almost erased **over the course of 250 years**.*

Quiz TEST yourself

BUILD YOUR ENGLISH ➔ p. 132

2. The art of storytelling

1

Video

Emily Wurramara makes music with meaning, *NITV*, 2017.

▲ Emily Wurramara, the first Indigenous woman to win best adult contemporary album at the ARIA Awards, 2024.

a. **Watch** the video, **read** the subtitles at the beginning and **identify** who the singer is.

b. **Focus** on her song. **Say** what happened to her mother at boarding school and **explain** how it impacted her.

c. **Describe** how the singer uses her music to preserve her culture.

d. **Explain** the impact the singer hopes to have on other generations.

2

The grandfather of indigenous hip hop says he's inspired by the new wave of First Nations artists

Munkimuk AKA Mark Ross first got into rapping via breakdancing in the late 1980s and since then has been heavily involved as an artist, producer and mentor.

"The hip hop community just in general is populated by so many great First Nations artists that come from the mainland or Torres Strait Islands.

"If you go back to the 80s there weren't as many opportunities as there are now, so it's been a gradual thing and it's been an amazing journey to watch," he says.

Munkimuk feels there is a strong overlap[1] between his community, storytelling and hip-hop culture and this connection grew stronger in the 1980s.

"Our mob have been passing down stories for 100,000 years or so which is a reason why I think that First Nations people in this country gravitated towards hip hop in the '80s.

"You can go to any part of this country and you'll find people who were trailblazers[2] in their own communities that were doing hip hop or breaking.

"Our mob connects with hip hop so much because it's very similar in the way of stories being passed down. I think of graff and rock art, and dancing by ways of telling stories… I think that's the whole reason why First Nations mobs gravitate towards hip hop," he says.

Issy Phillips, *pedestrian.tv*, 2023

1. *chevauchement* 2. pioneers

◄ Baker Boy among finalists at National Indigenous Music Awards, 2022.

a. **Look at** the picture. **Describe** the rapper and the musical instrument.

b. **Read** the text and **identify** how Munkimuk first got into hip hop and his current roles in the industry.

c. **Describe** the similarities Munkimuk mentions between traditions and hip hop.

d. **Explain** how the hip hop scene for First Nations artists has changed over time.

CULTURE SPOT

The **Stolen Generations** were Indigenous Australian **children taken from their families** between the 1870s and the 1970s. Many were **sent to boarding schools** and **forced to forget their culture and language**. This caused deep suffering and still affects Aboriginal communities today.

3

communities at work

INDIGENOUS COMMUNITY STREET ART

▲ An Aboriginal mural at the Illoura Childcare Centre, Canberra, Australia, 2022.

▲ Steven Kennedy, local Aboriginal artist.

Video

Indigenous Community Street Art | Canberra, *Communities at Work*, 2022.

a. **Look at** the mural and **describe** it.

b. **Watch** the video and **identify** what the project at the Illoura Childcare Centre consists of.

c. **Describe** the symbols and elements in the artwork and what they represent.

d. PHONOLOGY **Focus on:** *Aboriginal* • *local* • *idea* • *awarded*. What is common about the pronunciation of <a>?

e. **Explain** how this artwork connects to the children and educators.

CULTURE SPOT

The Dreamtime is the period in which life was created according to Aboriginal culture.

The past of the **Spirit Ancestors** who live on in the legends are handed down through stories, art, ceremony and songs.

VOCABULARY SPOT

- dot
- elders
- generation
- handprint
- shape
- storytelling

- proud

- archive /ˈɑːrkaɪv/
- change
- evolve
- mean = signify
- preserve

MEMORISE your vocabulary

YOUR TASK

Write the script to a podcast about Indigenous art.

1. **Choose** one artist from this page and **recap** everything you know about his/her (origin, career, inspiration…).
2. **Write** the script and **highlight** his/her evolution as an artist.
3. **Record** your podcast.

Build your skills! **Raconter l'évolution d'un artiste**

Utilise le ***present perfect*** en ***be*** + V-***ing*** pour mettre l'accent sur la durée et le processus d'une action :

- *We **have been** passing down stories for 100,000 years.*
- *They **have been** working on the second series of their comic books.*

Quiz
TEST yourself

BUILD YOUR ENGLISH → p. 132

3. Preserving traditions

1

▲ Children from the Indigenous Literacy Foundation (ILF), 2021.

Video
First Languages Australia: The Importance of Language, *@DeptCommsAu*, 2019.

a. **Look at** the picture and **imagine** what the children are learning about.

b. **Watch** the video and **identify** the first languages spoken in Australia.

c. **Say** why Aboriginal culture is important for all Australians.

d. **Describe** the connection between language, identity, and culture.

VOCABULARY SPOT

- diversity
- heritage
- mother tongue
- root
- soul

- endangered = at risk
- important = crucial = essential

MEMORISE your vocabulary

CULTURE SPOT

There are **300 different languages** in Australia, including many Indigenous languages and dialects. These are vital for First Nations People, who represent 3% of the population, as they are part of their **cultural identity**. Today, many languages are at **risk of extinction** and communities are trying to preserve them and maintain **cultural diversity** in Australia.

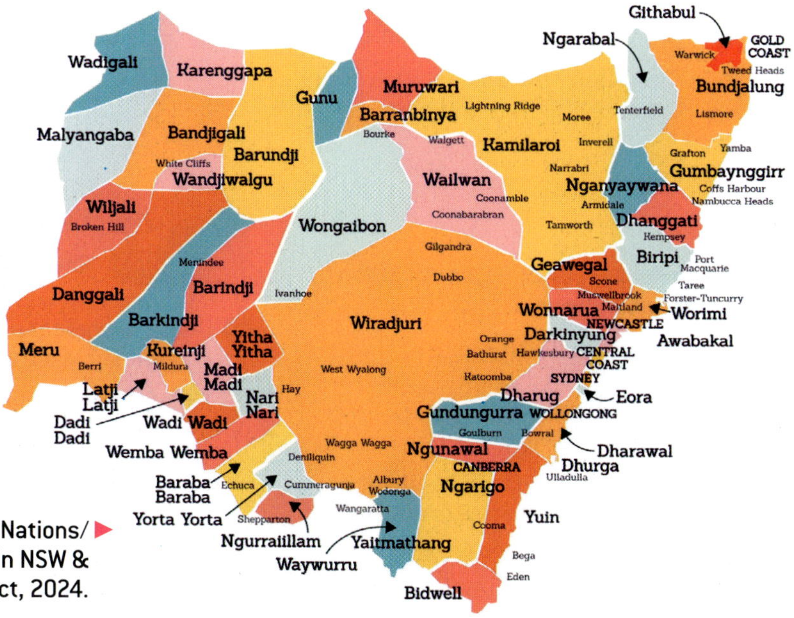

Aboriginal Nations/ Languages in NSW & Act, 2024.

2 e-WB Différenciation

Connecting with your Aboriginal culture through dance

Having grown up in a large family spread across different Australian states, I've always felt the need to maintain a strong connection to my culture and my loved ones. Despite the physical distances between us, I found a way to stay deeply rooted in my heritage through Aboriginal dance. It has become my lifeline, my source of joy and belonging. With every beat and movement, I feel an overwhelming sense of pride in my Aboriginal identity.

Dance has become my way of honouring my family, our traditions and the land that shapes us. It is a powerful tool for keeping the flame of our ancestry alive. Through my performances, I not only celebrate my cultural heritage but also hope to inspire others to embrace their own ancestral roots and find strength in that connection. Dance is the thread[1] that weaves[2] together my past, present and future, reminding me of who I am and where I come from.

When we learn our dances, we connect with our land and our culture, and we keep our culture alive and strong.

Dance has been an important part of Indigenous culture for thousands of years. It plays an important role in our ceremonies and celebrations and helps to maintain the culture of our people by passing down stories, songs and traditions from generation to generation. Dance has been used historically to communicate stories and messages about the land, animals and ancestral spirits. […]

It's an expression of our culture and reflects the diversity of all the different nations across Australia.

Samuel Wirrdapi Stubbs, *uwe.test.reachout.com*, 2023

1. *fil* 2. *tisser*

▲ Bangarra dancers in front of the Sydney Opera House, Australia, 2024.

a. **React** to the picture.

b. **Read** the text and **find** information about the narrator.

c. **Explain** what dance means to him.

d. **Explain** how dance helps pass down stories and traditions.

e. **Say** how it is related to the Dreamtime (p. 129).

YOUR FINAL TASK

Write an article for the Darwin Aboriginal Art Fair (DAAF) website about the modernity of Aboriginal Art.

1. **Define** what makes the essence and roots of Aboriginal art.
2. **Explain** how it has evolved through time.
3. **Focus on** some artists and **say** what they are doing to pass on traditions.

Build your skills! Décrire une démarche artistique

➔ Utilise ***by*** + V-*ing* et ***thanks to*** pour exprimer la manière :

- ***By*** *finding your mother tongue you will find yourself.*
- *Dance helps to maintain our culture* ***by*** *passing down stories.*
- ***Thanks to*** *hip-hop and rap, he became…*

➔ Utilise des expressions telles que ***to***, ***in order to***, ***so as to*** + BV, ***for*** + V-*ing* **pour exprimer le but** :

- *… it's a powerful tool* ***for keeping*** *the flame alive.*

Quiz TEST yourself

HOW TO SHINE IN GRAMMAR ➔ p. 218

Build your English!

GRAMMAR

Évoquer une action en cours ou faire un commentaire à l'aide de *be* + V-*ing*

Insister sur une action en cours de déroulement un processus (en train de...)	Exprimer un sentiment (admiration, agacement...)
TIP *Souvent associé à des expressions telles que : at the moment, listen, look...*	**TIP** *Souvent associé à un adverbe de fréquence : always, often...*

At the moment,
they **are meeting** a famous musician.
be au présent — *V-ing*

When he saw them,
they **were watching** an Aboriginal graffiti.
be au preterit — *V-ing*

We **have been studying** the Aboriginal culture **for 10 years**.
be au present perfect (have been) — *V-ing*

He**'s always creating** new graphic novels! Wow!
be au présent — *V-ing*

She **was often complaining** about her lack of inspiration.
be au preterit — *V-ing*

She **has been telling** the same story **over and over again**!
be au present perfect (have been) — *V-ing*

1 **Mets le verbe au temps qui convient en utilisant la forme *be* + V-*ing*.**

a. Aborigenes (pass down) stories for centuries.

b. These days, I (read) a lot of books about Australia.

c. Last night was fantastic: Aboriginal people (tell) stories and I (sing) with them.

d. I (travel) for a few years now.

2 **Pour chaque phrase, indique si la forme *be* + V-*ing* indique une action en cours ou un sentiment. Justifie ta réponse.**

a. This is how Aboriginal people are really keeping their traditions alive.

b. Today, I'm hiking to Uluru and we're meeting a tribe.

c. They've been living there for centuries.

d. You're always talking about the aboriginal culture, well, tell me more about it!

PHONOLOGY

La prononciation de la graphie <a>

La lettre <a> ne se prononce pas toujours de la même manière en anglais.

/æ/	/ə/	/eɪ/	/ɪ/	/ɑː/	/ɔː/	/ɒ/	/eə/
Aboriginal	*Aboriginal*	*erased*	*message*	*artist*	*called*	*what*	*share*

3 **Écoute et répète ces mots. Classe-les suivant la prononciation du <a>.**

family • image • traditions • wall • Australia • care • watch • large

/æ/	/ə/	/eɪ/	/ɪ/
/ɑː/	**/ɔː/**	**/ɒ/**	**/eə/**

4 **Lis ces phrases en te concentrant sur les sons de la lettre <a>. Vérifie ta prononciation en les écoutant, puis répète-les.**

Aboriginal artists all share a similar connection with nature and their ancestors. As First Nations people, they carry important messages about their language and their civilisation.

Les compléments numériques
lycee.nathan.fr/2sb132-133

VOCABULARY

EXERCISES → p. 230

MEMORISE your vocabulary

WALKING IN THEIR TRACKS

History and culture

- civilisation
- generation
- heritage
- ancient /'eɪnʃənt/
- era-defining
- archive /'ɑːrkaɪv/
- preserve ≠ erase

Community and identity

- diversity
- elders
- pride
- root
- sense of belonging
- soul
- proud
- belong to

Transmission

- mother tongue
- language
- spiritual
- storytelling
- Indigenous = First Nations = Aboriginal
- intergenerational
- pass down = transmit
- share

Art

- dot
- graffiti
- graphic novel
- mural
- painting
- shape
- committed to
- imaginative
- inspirational
- convey = express
- pay tribute to
- raise awareness

NOUN ADJECTIVE VERB ADVERB OR PREPOSITION

1 Complete these sentences with the right word.

graphic novel | pride | heritage | mother tongue

a. Aboriginal Australians are deeply connected to their ... .

b. She feels a strong sense of ... in her cultural roots.

c. At home, he speaks his ... with his family.

d. This ... combines text and illustrations to tell a story.

2 Match each verb with the correct ending.

pass down	a community
belong to	common values
pay tribute to	the ancestors
share	traditions

3 Put these word parts back together.

SERVE | BE | RATION | LONG | GENE | PRE | GENOUS | INDI

4 Write four sentences about this picture using words from above.

SNAPFILE 15 Royals 3.0

▶ **How has the representation of the royals evolved through time?**

YOUR FINAL TASK

You are a royal expert and **take part** in a special report on the Royal Family. **Explain** how the royals have adapted their communication over time.

FOLLOW THE STEPS

1

Video

Prince William and Taylor Swift don't shake it off, *Daily Mail Royals*, 2024.

▲ Taylor Swift with her boyfriend Travis Kelce and Prince William's family, Instagram, 2024.

▲ Coronation portrait of King Charles with heirs Prince William and Prince George, 2023.

a. **Observe** the pictures and **contrast** them (people, clothes, setting, framing…).
b. **Explain** their goals by showing what is similar to each other.
c. **Watch** the video and **pick out** details about the event.
d. **Explain** the organisation around the selfie.
e. **Comment on** the tools used by the Royal Family to promote their image.

PHONOLOGY SPOT

although • enough • through • daughter • thought • tough

En anglais, le **phonème <gh>** a **plusieurs prononciations** possibles.
Écoute et **entraîne-toi** à prononcer ces mots.

lycee.nathan.fr/2sb134-135

2 How Queen Elizabeth modernised the monarchy

The Queen's coronation was the first royal coronation to be televised.

Elizabeth II was crowned Queen on June 2, 1953, after the death of King George VI the year before. The ceremony had some traditional elements.

However, the Queen also modernised the coronation by allowing it to be televised for the first time in history, according to the royal website. An estimated 27 million people in the UK watched the ceremony, and for most people, it was the first time they had watched a live event on television, the website added.

Her Majesty invented the royal walkabout, forever changing the way the royals interact with the public.

The Royal Family often meet and shake hands with members of the public before official events, which has come to be known as a "royal walkabout." However, the practice of royals meeting the public didn't start until the Queen's tour of New Zealand and Australia in 1970.

The monarch also joined Instagram, writing her first post in 2019.

The Royal Family joined Instagram in 2013, but Her Majesty didn't write her first post until 2019.

On the official Royal Family account, she posted two photos of a letter written to Queen Victoria and Prince Albert from Charles Babbage, the world's first computer engineer, displayed[1] at London's Science Museum. She signed the post "Elizabeth R," her official signature as monarch.

Adapted from Mikhaila Friel, *businessinsider.com*, 2022

▲ Queen Elizabeth II greeting crowds during a walkabout, 2016.

1. *exposer*

VOCABULARY SPOT

- coronation
- event /ɪ'vɛnt/
- walkabout /'wɔːkəbaʊt/

- demure /dɪ'mjʊə/
  ≠ outrageous /aʊt'reɪdʒəs/

- attend an event
- greet

MEMORISE your vocabulary

a. Look at the picture and **guess** what the article is about.

b. Read the text and **account** for the actions taken by the Queen.

c. GRAMMAR **Pick out** the link word on l.6 and **explain** what it conveys about the Queen's goal.

d. Pick out the link words on l.15 and l.18 and **comment on** the Queen's attitude.

GRAMMAR SPOT

- *No William on stage,* ***although*** *we did see some great dad dancing*
- ***However****, the Queen also modernised the coronation …*

Quel mot de liaison exprime la **concession** ? L'**opposition** ?

STEP 1

Start your special report on the royal family. Prepare your first vocal memo on the modernisation of the Royal communication.

1 **Introduce** the topic with the way royal generations combine tradition and modernity in their communication.

2 **Explain** how Queen Elizabeth II transformed the monarchy for the modern era.

Build your skills! Témoigner d'un changement intentionnel

➔ Utilise des mots de liaison pour exprimer **opposition** et **concession** :
- *although, however, but …*

➔ Emploie ***by*** + **V-*ing*** pour donner les moyens utilisés :
- *… by allowing it to be televised for the first time in history …*

HOW TO SHINE IN GRAMMAR ➔ p. 218

3

A Cause That's Close to Her Heart

Princess Kate's newest initiative is supporting organisations that are making resources easily accessible to families across the United Kingdom.

This week, the Royal Foundation Centre for Early Childhood, a "hub" organisation Kate founded in 2021, announced the launch of the Baby Bank[1] Alliance, which will unite 300 baby banks in the U.K. and help them continue their work supporting children, parents, and caregivers.

The foundation shared the exciting news on Instagram, including photos of Kate's previous visits to various charities across the country. One snapshot shows Kate assembling gift bags with her daughter, Princess Charlotte, during a visit to a baby bank in Maidenhead, England, last December. (Kate's two other kids—Prince George and Prince Louis—also joined their mom in volunteering[2] at the bank.)

"Over the past few years, the Princess of Wales has visited several baby banks to highlight their crucial work in supporting families with babies and young children," the caption read. "Organisations like baby banks play a vital role in helping to give parents and carers[3] the capacity to provide the nurturing care which is so important to babies and young children." [...]

The alliance is the latest venture[4] for Kate in the realm of early childhood development, a cause she has long held close to her heart. For the past decade, much of her work as a member of the royal family has involved researching the connection between children's social and environmental experiences at a young age and their mental and physical development as adults.

Chelsey Sanchez, *harpersbazaar.com*, 2023.

1. a charity offering goods for babies and children. 2. *être bénévole*
3. *aidants* 4. project

▲ Kate Middleton at a baby bank, 2023.

a. **Observe** and **describe** the photograph.
Guess the Princess's activity.

b. **Read** the text and **identify** the cause supported by the Princess.

c. **Pick out** details about the charity's actions.

d. **Explain** how the Princess's initiative has been revealed.
Comment on the choice of the social media service she uses.

e. GRAMMAR **Spot** the verb form used on lines 13, 20, 22.
Explain what the journalist insists on with this tense.

f. **Imagine** why it is important for the Royal Family to do charity work.

CULTURE SPOT

Charity work and public engagement

Charities are very important in the UK. Since Princess Diana, **Royal members** have always got **involved in charity work** and up until today, use their **public engagement** to **promote important causes** such as homelessness, war victims or the environment.

VOCABULARY SPOT

- commitment: *engagement*
- public figure /'fɪgər/
- representative
- volunteer: *bénévole*

- dedicated /'dɛdɪkeɪtɪd/ to
- involved in

- promote a cause
- raise awareness
- use a royal platform to + *BV*

MEMORISE your vocabulary

Lycée Compagnon numérique

lycee.nathan.fr/2sb136-137

4

▲ King Charles (then Prince) speaks about the environment with schoolchildren in Clarence House gardens, his official residence, 2012.

Video

Charles III: the Climate King, *Pattrn*, 2023.

A LITTLE EXTRA

Video

Watch the video and **find out** more about Prince William's involvement at the Earthshot Prize.

a. **Look at** the video title and **identify** the King's nickname.

b. **Watch** the video. **Pick out** actions taken by him to justify this nickname.

c. PHONOLOGY **Focus on** the pronunciation of the three adverbs: *utterly – literally – urgently*. **Say** how they help the King express his message.

d. **Sum up** the speakers' views on the King.

e. **Explain** how promoting this cause has improved his image.

PHONOLOGY SPOT

- *We've got this **wonderful sustainable eco-friendly** king*
- *… for being **a climate champion, advocating for corporate action, working with animal and nature conservation groups, and even starting his own organic food company**.*

Dynamise ton reportage par une série d'exemples. **Prête attention à l'intonation** des listes d'exemples donnés.

STEP 2

Carry on with your special report. Record your second vocal memo on the Royals' involvement today.

1. **Mention** the different causes promoted by Royals.
2. **Explain** why their commitment plays an important role in the representation of the Royal Family.

→ **Your special report is now ready!**

Build your skills! **Décrire une évolution et énoncer des objectifs**

➜ Utilise le *present perfect* pour **dresser un bilan** :

- *Over the past few years, the Princess of Wales **has visited several** baby banks to highlight their crucial work …*
- *For decades, the staunch environmentalist **has used** his royal platform …*

➜ Pense aux infinitives pour **cibler des objectifs** :

- *… baby banks play a vital role in helping **to give** parents and carers the capacity **to provide** the nurturing care …*
- *We have **to reduce** the emissions urgently and take **action to tackle** the carbon already in the atmosphere …*

HOW TO SHINE IN GRAMMAR ➜ p. 214

Quiz
TEST yourself

FLASH FILE 16 Chicago skyline

▶ How does the architecture of Chicago reflect the evolution of the Windy City?

YOUR FINAL TASK — MÉDIATION

In teams, **watch** and **read** the documents. **Share** information about the architecture of Chicago. e-WB
Then **record** an audioguide for a guided tour of the city based on its architecture.

1

CHICAGO'S MUST-SEE BUILDINGS

Look at other US cities with skyscrapers, and you'll see that Chicago is home to some of the tallest buildings in the country, partly thanks to the famous fire that destroyed much of central Chicago and the near north side in 1871. Resources poured[1] into the city as it began to rebuild, creating a unique opportunity for building many iconic Chicago skyscrapers, and ushering[2] in the steel-frame[3] "skyscraper era."

Whether you're passing through on your way elsewhere, on a day trip, or visiting from far away — welcome to Chicago!

theskydeck.com

1. *affluer* 2. bringing 3. *charpente métallique*

1 THE MARINA CITY
(1964-68) – 588 feet[1]
KEY FACT: Often called the "corn cobs", it is considered to be a city within the city.

2 TRUMP TOWER
(2009) – 1,389 feet[1]
KEY FACT: This hotel designed to mirror the entire city is the second tallest building of the city after the Willis Tower.

3 JOHN HANCOCK CENTER
(1969) – 1,128 feet[1]
KEY FACT: Easily recognizable thanks to its black color, it reflects the industrial story of the city.

1. ft = 30,48 cm

2

Video
Architecture River Cruise in Chicago, *Viator*, 2020.

3

Video

Skydeck Chicago Admission at Willis Tower, Viator, 2013.

4

Video

Three Influential Architects All Worked on the Rookery Building, *WTT*, 2023.

A LITTLE EXTRA Video

Watch this video until 2'10 to discover how the Great Chicago Fire led to the city's architectural transformation.

VOCABULARY SPOT

- artistry = creativity
- landmark: *repère*
- masterpiece /ˈmɑːstəpiːs/: *chef d'œuvre*
- skyline
- skyscraper

- avant-garde = innovative
- breathtaking /ˈbreθˌteɪkɪŋ/
- futuristic /fjuːtʃəˈrɪstɪk/
- iconic /aɪˈkɒnɪk/
- sky-high

- blend
- marvel at
- reimagine
- reshape

MEMORISE your vocabulary

FILE 17 Still I rise

> *Today we are reminded of a delayed promise by this America—a promise that says independence, freedom, and justice for all. But are we all free?"*

Chelsea MILLER, Gen-Z activist and cofounder of Freedom March NYC, 4th of July 2020.

VOCABULARY SPOT

- demonstrator
- equality /ɪ'kwalɪti/
- legacy /'lɛgəsi/: *héritage*
- mob= a crowd of angry people

- enraged = angry
- inspiring /ɪnspaɪrɪŋ/

- galvanise= gather the nation
- honor /'ɑnɚ/
- pay tribute to /'trɪbjut/: *rendre hommage à*

MEMORISE your vocabulary

How are young generations walking in the footsteps of the leaders of the civil rights movement?

YOUR FINAL TASK

Record a podcast about the legacy of the civil rights and young people's actions today.

Video

Young marchers talk about Martin Luther King Day, *KCRA 3*, 2020.

A young boy walks past a painting depicting Dr. Martin Luther King Jr. (1929-1968), Los Angeles, 2020.

TEAM WORK

Team A
Look at the picture, **read** the caption and **react**.

Team B
Read the quote and **sum up** the Gen Z activist's idea.

Team C
Watch the video and **comment on** the legacy of MLK Jr.

- Now **share** your findings with the other teams and **explain** why MLK Jr.'s message is important for younger generations.

EXPLORE Key moments of the civil rights

Video
Former Little Rock 9 member shares her story, *WPLGLocal10*, 2023.

1

▲ In September 1957, nine black students volunteered to integrate an all-white high school in Little Rock, Arkansas.

1960 : Ruby Bridges was the first Afro-American child to attend formerly white-only School in New Orleans.

1955-1966 : Bus boycott launched following Rosa Parks's refusal to give up her seat and being arrested.

CULTURE SPOT

Free to go to school
In 1954, the US Supreme Court ruled that **segregation was unconstitutional**. From then on, it was illegal to separate black and white people at school.

TEAM WORK

Team A works on doc 1 and Team B on doc 2.

a. **Observe** the picture and **read** its caption. **Imagine** the situation on that day.

b. **Watch** the video and **pick out** information about the event.

c. **Describe** the atmosphere and people's actions.

d. GRAMMAR **Pick out** three verbs used to describe past events and **identify** the tense used.

e. **Share** your findings with the other team and **say** why both events were important in the civil rights movement.

A LITTLE EXTRA Video

Watch the famous *I Have a Dream* speech and **share** your impressions.

2

Video
Thousands rallied in Washington DC, *History Channel*, 2013.

▲ The March on Washington took place on 28 August 1963. On that day, Martin Luther King Jr. delivered his famous *I Have a Dream* speech.

Les compléments numériques
e-WB
lycee.nathan.fr/2sb142-143

CULTURE SPOT

Free to love each other

In 1967, the Supreme Court ruled in the ***Loving v. Virginia case*** that **interracial marriages were allowed by law**. Before that, mixed-race couples could be imprisoned for loving each other in many states including Virginia.

3

Audio version

Richard and Mildred Loving, husband and wife, lay in bed, sleeping, that warm, peaceful Virginia night in July 1958. Around 2:00 a.m., the stillness was shattered[1] when they were jolted[2] awake by the glare of three flashlights and rousted[3] out of bed by Sheriff Garnett Brooks and two deputies. [...] Standing beside the bed, Sheriff Brooks demanded to know what Richard was doing with the woman.

A quiet man, no doubt confused by the intrusion, Richard didn't immediately answer the sheriff's question. Mildred spoke up instead, saying, "I'm his wife."

Sheriff Brooks fired back: "Not here you're not." Richard pointed to the couple's marriage license that the newlyweds had hung on the bedroom wall, as if to prove Mildred's words were indeed fact, but the sheriff scoffed[4], saying, "That's not good here.'

Richard, a twenty-four-year-old bricklayer, and Mildred, a housewife just shy of her nineteenth birthday, had known each other most of their life. He was white. She was "colored" [...] Lifelong residents of Virginia, they lived in Central Point, a small rural area in Caroline County some fifty miles northeast of Richmond, the state capital.

Mixed marriages – those between a white person and a member of any other race – were against the custom in Virginia. They were also against the law.

Larry Dane BRIMNER, *Finding a Way Home: Mildred and Richard Loving and the Fight for Marriage Equality*, 2020.

1. interrupted. 2. shaken 3. *faire sortir* 4. laugh at him

a. Read the text and **pick out** information about the Lovings.

b. Sum up their reactions when the police walked in.

c. Explain the sheriff's reasons for coming to their house.

d. Read the last paragraph and **turn** to the Culture spot. **Say** what the Lovings did to change the situation.

A LITTLE EXTRA Video

Watch the trailer and **find out** more about the famous love story.

YOUR TASK

Write a short presentation for an upcoming exhibition on key moments in the civil rights movement.

1. **Describe** at least two key events (name, goal, and people involved).
2. **Talk** about the impact of those events in the fight for equality.

Build your skills! Décrire des faits passés importants

→ Utilise le prétérit et les marqueurs du temps pour situer les événements dans le passé :

- *The march **rallied** Americans to stand up against…*
- ***In May 1960**, she **graduated** from Central High School.*

BUILD YOUR ENGLISH → p. 150

Quiz

TEST yourself

EXPLORE

Passing on the torch

1

Audio version

Marching for freedom

Extract 1 [1963]. That morning in 1963, I woke up wanting to be free from all the inequities. I didn't want my aunt holding me down[1] anymore. I wanted the same good textbooks that my White counterparts had. Yes, I admit, I woke up that morning and my mind was on freedom! [...]

Extract 2 [nowadays]. [...] I talk about my decision to march, my arrest, and how my life changed from that point on.

Students always want to know if I got in trouble with my parents when I got out. They want to know if anyone failed to graduate because they marched. I've been asked why I decided to stay in Birmingham[2] after going through that. The educators want to talk more about what it was like going into that White school and the differences between what it was like in the all-Black school versus the all-White school. Sometimes I am asked how to inspire youth to be more concerned and more responsive to current affairs.

I have remained in Birmingham because I've always lived here and I didn't have a reason to leave. I saw some positive changes that took place after I participated in the Movement[3]. Some of the things I was protesting did indeed change for the better. I never wanted to leave because my family is here. Even after visiting other places, I saw some of the same kinds of situations that existed here. Moving probably would not have shielded[4] me from the race war.

I always tell young people who want to be involved to stand up for what they believe in. I tell them that they don't have to be leaders or in charge of a movement to make a difference. They can make a difference within their circle, and not just about race issues. They can include those who are physically challenged as a way to make a difference, or befriend the kid who is being bullied. I stress that they don't have to be a part of putting someone else down[5] because they're different.

Janice KELSEY, *I Woke Up with My Mind on Freedom*, 2017

1. *retenir* 2. a city in Alabama 3. the civil rights movement 4. protected 5. humiliating

▲ Book cover of a children book (2018).

a. **Observe** the title and the book cover. **Imagine** what the children were asking for.

b. **Read** the text and **find** information about the narrator.

c. **Explain** the reasons that led her to take action.

d. **Sum up** her actions when she was a child and their consequences.

e. GRAMMAR **Identify** the two verb forms in the sentence on lines 12-13 and **explain** why Janice Kelsey used those two tenses.

f. **Sum up** her message to the younger generations.

A LITTLE EXTRA Video

Watch the video and **take notes** on Janice Kelsey's and other marchers' memories of that day.

CULTURE SPOT

The Children's crusade

In May 1963, in Birmingham (Alabama), **children** left their schools to **march against segregation**. The **movement** led **President Kennedy to support the civil rights** movement.

Les compléments numériques
e-WB
lycee.nathan.fr/2sb144-145

2

e-WB **Différenciation**

Audio

Children's march 60 years later, *NPR*, 2023.

▲ Children's crusade reenactment, Birmingham (Alabama), May 2023.

a. **Listen** to the audio and **identify** the various speakers.

b. **Pick out** information about today's event.

c. **Explain** the past event which inspired it.

d. **Compare** and **contrast** the two events.

e. **Sum up** today's young people's new battles.

f. PHONOLOGY **Listen to** the words: ***h****istoric* • ***h****old* • ***h****ands* • ***h****onour*. Which <h> is not pronounced?

VOCABULARY SPOT

- jail /ˈdʒeɪl/ = prison
- placards /ˈplækɑːrd/ = *pancartes*

- determined
- involved in
- unexpected

- pass on a message
- march peacefully
- reenact = recreate
- set a good example = *montrer l'exemple*

MEMORISE your vocabulary

YOUR TASK

DIFFÉRENCIATION

For Black History Month, cover the Children's crusade anniversary.

WAY 1

Interview Janice Kelsey about her experience in the Children's crusade.

WAY 2

Interview a young demonstrator taking part in the Children's crusade reenactment.

Build your skills! Dresser le bilan d'une situation

➔ Pense au ***present perfect*** pour faire état d'une évolution présente par rapport au passé :

- *I* ***have remained*** *in Birmingham because…*
- *I* ***have been asked*** *why I remained in Birmingham…*
- *Millions of visitors* ***have learnt*** *about Carlotta's story in the museum…*

BUILD YOUR ENGLISH ➔ p. 150

Quiz

TEST yourself

EXPLORE Still fighting

1 e-WB Différenciation

▶ Video

Yolanda King evokes her grandfather's legacy, The Arena, NBA on TNT, 2022.

▲ Yolanda Renee King, 2024.

VOCABULARY SPOT

- activist
- discrimination
- inequality
- spokesperson /ˈspəʊkspɜːrsən/
- voting right
- committed to = *engagé*
- equal
- outraged = *révolté*

- launch a campaign
- raise awareness
- speak out

MEMORISE your vocabulary

CULTURE SPOT

Access to polls

Although the voting rights act was passed in 1965, **the access to voting places has been reduced in the 21st century**. Many polls have been closed in some states and voters had to cover long distances or face long queues to make their voices heard.

2 ▶ Video

Campaigning against voter suppression, Scripps News, 2020.

TEAM WORK

Team A works on doc 1 and Team B on doc 2.

a. **Watch** your video. **Identify** the type of document and the speakers.

b. **Explain** the problem(s) denounced by the activist.

c. **Sum up** what she/he wants for her/his country.

d. **Describe** the images used in the video and **say** how they help convey a message.

e. **Share** your findings and **comment on** the activists' common goal.

A LITTLE EXTRA ▶ Video

Watch the *More than a Vote* awareness campaign video online and be prepared to react.

Lebron James launched the *More than a Vote* campaign in 2020. ▶

Les compléments numériques

lycee.nathan.fr/2sb146-147

3

amandascgorman • Follow
Miami-Dade

I'm gutted[1]. Because of one parent's complaint, my inaugural poem, *The Hill We Climb*, has been banned from an elementary school in Miami-Dade County, Florida.
Books bans aren't new. But they have been on the rise–according to the ALA[2], 40% more books were challenged in 2022 compared to 2021. What's more, often all it takes to remove these works from our libraries and schools is a single objection. And let's be clear: most of the forbidden works are by authors who have struggled for generations to get on bookshelves. The majority of these censored works are by queer and non-white voices.

I wrote *The Hill We Climb* so that all young people could see themselves in a historical moment. Ever since, I've received countless letters and videos from children inspired by *The Hill We Climb* to write their own poems. Robbing children of the chance to find their voices in literature is a violation of their right to free thought and free speech.

What can we do? We must speak out and have our voices heard. That's why my publisher, Penguin Random House, joined PEN[3] America, authors, and community members in a lawsuit[4] in Florida's Escambia County to challenge book restrictions like these. To help, donate to and visit @PENAmerica and spread the word about these book bans.

Together, this is a hill we won't just climb, but a hill we will conquer.

-A

1. disgusted. 2. American Library Association
3. International author's free-speech organisation
4. *procès*

▲ Amanda Gorman, Instagram post, 23rd May 2023.

CULTURE SPOT

Book bans
In the past few years, several American states **removed books**, –especially books written by non-white writers, **from schools reading list and libraries**. Amanda Gorman's poem *The Hill We Climbed* was banned in Florida in May 2023.

a. **Read** the post and **describe** the problem faced by Amanda Gorman.

b. GRAMMAR **Focus on** "*my inaugural poem … has been banned*" (l.1-2). What effect does the use of the passive voice give?

c. **Explain** her feelings as a result.

d. VOCABULARY **Pick out** the linking words she uses and **say** how it helps her make her point.

e. **Sum up** the problem she is denouncing and the action she is taking to solve it.

f. **Comment on** her tone.

A LITTLE EXTRA

Video

Watch Amanda Gorman's reading of her famous poem and **pay attention** to her tone and message.

YOUR TASK

DIFFÉRENCIATION

Present an activist's cause.

WAY 1

You are Lebron James: **promote** your *More than a Vote* campaign.

1 **Present** your movement.

2 **Explain** your hopes and fears.

WAY 2

You are a journalist: **report** about Yolanda Renee King.

1 **Introduce** her role as an activist.

2 **Mention** her grandfather's legacy.

3 **Explain** her hopes and fears.

Build your skills! Faire campagne pour un message important

➔ Pense au ***present perfect*** pour poser un constat :
- *I **have** progressively **lost** voting rights.*
- *Authors who **have struggled** for generations*

➔ Utilise le **passif** pour parler des événements subis :
- *My inaugural poem […] **has been banned** from an elementary school.*
- *More books **were challenged** in 2022 than in 2021.*

BUILD YOUR ENGLISH ➔ p. 150-151

Quiz

TEST yourself

TEST YOUR CULTURE AND VOCABULARY

GEOCACHING IN DC

HOW TO PLAY

You are walking from the National Museum of African-American History and Culture and have to reach a secret destination.
Find the various geocaches on the way and **solve** the enigmas to reach your destination.

Name of Martin Luther King Jr.'s granddaughter?

Give three important battles for today's activists.

Explain the problem Amanda Gorman had to face with one of her books.

Word which describes a past event recreated not to forget it? Spell it.

Name the woman who refused to give up her seat in a bus.

Synonym for unconstitutional?
legal • illegal • allowed

Name of the Supreme court case which allowed mixed-race marriages?

Verb used to end segregation in schools? Spell it.

Name of Lebron James's campaign and its goal?

Give a quote from Martin Luther King Jr's famous "I have a dream" speech.

YOUR DESTINATION?

Build your English!

VOCABULARY

Les compléments numériques

e-WB

lycee.nathan.fr/2sb148-149

EXERCISES → p. 233

MEMORISE your vocabulary

STILL I RISE

The Civil rights

- the civil rights movement
- brave
- equal ≠ unequal
- unconstitutional=illegal
- denounce /dɪ'naʊns/
- march for freedom
- protest /prə'tɛst/
- raise awareness
- peacefully

Actions

- demonstrators
- demonstration
- strength /'strɛŋθ/
- determined
- change mentalities
- reenact /ˌriːɪn'ækt/
- take a stand

Segregation

- discrimination
- mob = crowd
- racism /'reɪsɪzəm/
- segregation≠desegregation /ˌdiːsɛgrɪ'geɪʃən/
- separate /'sɛpərət/
- desegregate /diː'sɛgrɪgeɪt/
- lynch
- not be allowed to + BV

Legacy

- heir
- legacy
- inspiring
- involved in
- follow one's footsteps
- inherit /ɪn'hɛrɪt/
- proudly

New fights

- activist
- book ban
- voting rights
- banned
- go to the polls = vote
- make a difference
- speak out

NOUN ADJECTIVE VERB ADVERB OR PREPOSITION

1 Choose the right verb in the following sentences.

a. The Little Rock Nine took part in a plan to (**legalise / desegregate**) school.

b. Lebron James wants to encourage American citizens to go to (**school / the polls**).

c. Yolanda King encourages youngsters to (**be quiet / speak out**).

2 Fill in the gaps with the correct adjective.

inspiring • banned • involved • voting

a. Yolanda Renee King fights for the protection of ... rights.

b. Janice Kelsey still speaks out to convince young people to get ....

c. Amanda Gorman denounces the current issue of ... books in the USA.

d. For many people, Martin Luther King Jr.'s *I Have a Dream* speech is still ... today.

3 Find the synonyms for the following words.

a. courageous b. angry crowd c. criticize d. quietly

4 Observe the picture and write the beginning of a speech to denounce book ban. Make sure you include words from the wordmap.

Build your English!

GRAMMAR

+ EXERCISES → p. 236-237

A Évoquer le passé avec le prétérit et lier passé et présent avec le *present perfect*

GRAMMAR tuto

On utilise le **prétérit** pour évoquer des actions ou des faits **passés, datés et achevés**.

On utilise le ***present perfect*** pour évoquer des actions ou des faits qui ont **commencé dans le passé** et **continuent dans le présent** **ou** pour évoquer les **conséquences d'une action passée sur le présent**.

Segregation **start**ed in the 1890s.
Black people **went** to segregated schools, they **did**n't **have** the same rights as white people.

Elizabeth Eckford bravely **walk**ed into a previously all-white school **years ago**.

Black people **have fought** for their rights **for years.**
(have : auxiliaire au présent ; fought : verbe au participe passé ; for : = durée)

Lebron James **has campaign**ed for equality **since 2020**
(since : = point de départ)

Segregation **has been** illegal **since 1954** but discrimination **has**n't **stopped**.

1 **Conjugue les verbes entre parenthèses au *present perfect* ou au prétérit selon la situation évoquée.**

a. Society (change) over the years but it (not / change) enough.

b. Segregation (end) in the mid-1950s in theory but black people (voice) their protest for decades.

c. The campaign (help) the cause since it was launched in 2020.

d. I (get) involved in the late 1990s, and since then, I (participate) in every march, I (not / miss) a meeting.

2 **Complète les phrases suivantes avec *for* ou *since*.**

a. Black people have fought for their rights ... the end of segregation, and they have voiced their protest ... decades.

b. Students have celebrated Martin Luther King Jr. every year ... the march on Washington.

c. Public figures have raised their voices ... years.

d. Black and white students have been to the same schools ... the early 1960s.

3 **Traduis les phrases suivantes en faisant attention au temps du verbe : prétérit ou *present perfect*.**

a. La ségrégation se termina officiellement dans les années 60.

b. En réalité, les discriminations n'ont pas cessé depuis la fin de la ségrégation.

c. C'est pourquoi les afro-américains continuent à se battre contre les inégalités depuis des décennies.

d. De nombreuses personnalités sensibilisent l'opinion publique depuis des années. Par exemple, Lebron James a lancé la campagne *More than a Vote* en 2020.

4 **Rédige des phrases au prétérit ou au *present perfect* pour rendre compte des évènements indiqués sur la frise.**

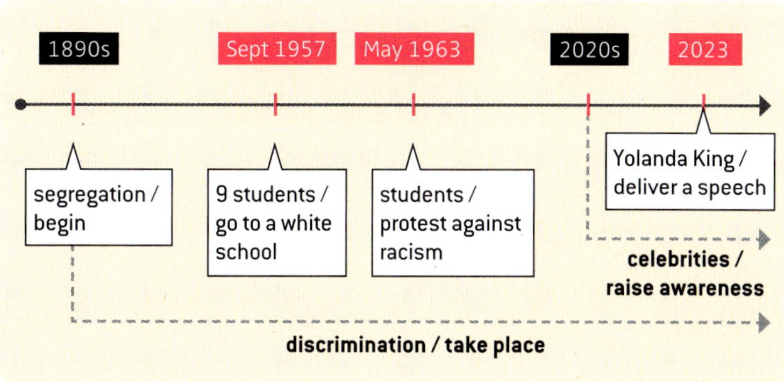

B Attirer l'attention sur le résultat d'une action avec la voix passive

GRAMMAR tuto

VOIX ACTIVE

Le sujet grammatical est responsable de l'action.

Sujet + **V conjugué** + **COD**

The crowd **insulted** the Little Rock Nine.

Many generations **have fought against** segregation.

Everybody **remembers** segregation as a dark period.

VOIX PASSIVE

Le sujet grammatical est l'objet de l'action, il la subit.

Sujet + ***be* conjugué (à tous les temps)** + **V au participe passé** + **complément d'agent**

The Little Rock Nine **were insulted** by the crowd.

Segregation **has been fought against** by many generations.

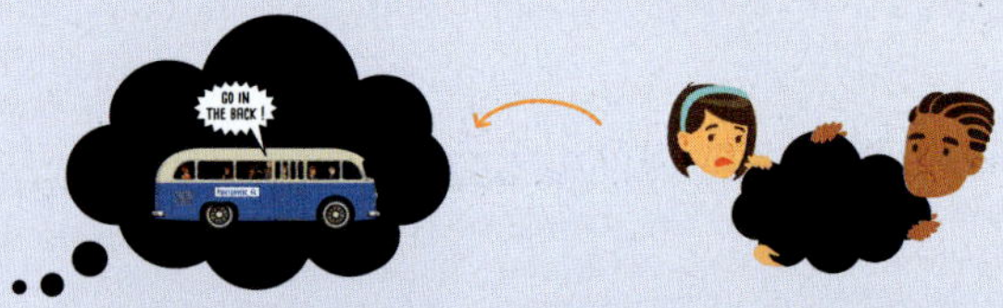

Segregation **is remembered** as a dark period.

→ *Agent non identifiable, général ou non essentiel à la compréhension = pas de complément d'agent à la fin de la phrase passive.*

1 Mets les phrases suivantes à la voix passive. Attention aux phrases avec deux compléments !

a. In the 1960s, they desegregated schools.

b. A white school accepted a few black students.

c. Virginia didn't recognise the Lovings' marriage license.

d. The government has denied Black people civil rights for decades.

2 Exprime ces faits passés à l'aide de la voix passive. Il faut parfois rajouter des articles, prépositions…

a. segregation • rule illegal • 1954

b. *More than a Vote* campaign • launch • Lebron James

c. MLK • honour • students

d. civil rights • not grant • to Black people in the 1960s

3 Mets les phrases actives suivantes à la voix passive et inversement.

a. MLK delivered the *I Have a Dream* speech in 1963.

b. Racial inequalities have been denounced for years.

c. Schools were segregated in the 1960s.

d. A poem was banned from an elementary school.

4 Pour chaque image, explique la situation en utilisant l'élément mis en évidence comme sujet. Utilise les verbes suggérés à la voix active ou passive selon le cas.

arrest • deliver • protest • sign • listen • hear

①

②

③

④

A La prononciation de la graphie <h> Audio

- En anglais, le <h> est **aspiré** dans la majorité des cas, c'est-à-dire qu'on le prononce en **expirant de l'air** : *high school* • *historic* • *huge* • *hundreds* ;
- Il est **muet** dans certains mots commençant par ***he-*** ou ***ho-*** : *heir* • *honor* • *hour*. Pour les noms, l'article indéfini à utiliser est alors *an* : *an heir*.

1 Écoute et répète ces mots, puis classe-les selon la prononciation du <h> (aspiré ou muet).

honest • honour • heir • high • historical • hold • hero

2 Écoute la liste de mots suivants

a. heir • highlight • honour • high school • honest • historical • hundreds • hour • huge

b. **En binôme, trouvez les mots dans lesquels le <h> est muet. Vérifiez à l'écoute.**

	A	B	C
1	*heir*	*highlight*	*honour*
2	*high school*	*honest*	*historical*
3	*hundreds*	*hour*	*huge*

B Les liaisons Audio

- Lorsque l'on parle, les mots s'enchainent de façon fluide. On appelle cela **des groupes de souffle**.
- Comme en français, on fait la liaison si un mot finissant par un son consonne est suivi d'un mot commençant par **un son voyelle**.
  - *It's an honour to be among other marchers today.*
  - *I had a friend whose mother was involved in the civil rights movement.*
- Si un mot commence par un <h> aspiré, on ne fait pas la liaison : *It was a great historical time.*

3 Écoute ces exemples et concentre-toi sur les liaisons indiquées, puis entraîne-toi à les répéter.

a. The Little Rock Nine were not afraid not to get into trouble to fight for our rights.

b. *More than a Vote* aims at encouraging people to get out and exercise their right to vote.

4 Lis les extraits du discours suivant et prononce-les en faisant attention aux liaisons. Écoute et vérifie.

Dr Martin Luther King Jr. was one of the greatest activists of all times.

I don't think I realised the significance of it all until I was 9 years old.

In my whole life I have always been around activism. I was lucky as I have always been hearing about these issues.

Martin Luther King Jr. Memorial, Washington, DC.

YOUR FINAL TASK

Record a podcast about the legacy of the civil rights and young people's actions today.

Present today's heirs of the civil rights movement in a podcast that will be posted on your school website.

1. **Get ready and gather your ideas on:**
   –historical milestones you want to mention and the issues addressed;
   –their legacy for today's generations;
   –today's new battles for young people.
2. **Record** your podcast and make sure to insist on the impact of the civil rights today.

YES YOU CAN!

Record a podcast

INTRODUCTION DU SUJET

Adresse-toi aux auditeurs pour attirer leur attention sur le sujet que tu vas traiter. Tu peux te présenter ou partir d'un fait précis pour ensuite décliner les informations.

On August 28, 1963, 250,000 people gathered in the nation's capital for the historic March on Washington for Jobs and Freedom.

FAITS ET EXEMPLES

Énonce des faits marquants, illustrés par des exemples. Explique leur impact.

The march took place at a critical moment in the civil rights movement. Tension and racial unrest had been building up throughout the years with anti-segregation demonstrators making headlines in Alabama and President John F. Kennedy announcing his intention to pass the civil rights legislation.

IMPACT ET HÉRITAGE

Mentionne l'impact de l'évènement et ce à quoi cela a mené.

Historians believe that the marches and King's speech were important catalysts in passing the Civil Rights Act of 1964 and the Voting Rights Act of 1965.

ATTITUDES, DEMANDES ET RÉACTIONS

Évoque les demandes des gens engagés, leurs attitudes et leurs réactions.

The time was right for a massive demonstration [...] But as it turned out, the marchers chose peace not violence that sunny Wednesday. The event featured speeches from prominent leaders and musical performances by Josephine Baker [...] and many others.

FLUIDITÉ

Adopte un ton posé et prête attention aux liaisons pour avoir un discours fluide.

The march is probably best remembered for Martin Luther King's Jr.'s acclaimed I Have a Dream *speech.*

HOW TO SHINE IN SPEAKING → p. 208

PRACTISE AND SHINE

Compréhension de l'oral

Video

60 years since *I Have a Dream* speech, *CBS News Miami*, 2023.

A1 › A2 **Step 1** Before watching the video, **focus on** the title and the picture.

a. **Browse** all that you know about *I Have a Dream* (speaker, date, place, topic, impact...).

b. **Name** all the elements you can see in the picture (name of the channel, people, pictures, title...).

c. **Make hypotheses** about the video (type, topic...).

A2 **Step 2** **Watch** the video once and **take notes** about:

a. the different speakers and their role.

b. the passages in black and white and the passages in colour.

A2 › B1 **Step 3** **Watch** the video again and **pick out** the key-words about:

a. the introduction by the journalists.

b. the women's statements.

B1 › B1+ **Step 4** **Recap.**

WAY 1. Link the ideas and **recap**.

a. **Choose** the correct answers:

- The video is a **documentary** / **news report** / **talk show** from an **English** / **American** / **South-African** channel called CBS News, Miami.
- It deals with the **commemoration** / **explanation** / **re-enactment** of the March on Washington that took place **40** / **50** / **60** years ago.

b. **Complete** the recap using the prompt: ***The March on Washington is ...***

c. **Add** the women's statements using some of the elements below:

enthusiastic | impressive | inspiring | galvanize | change

WAY 2. Mets en lien les informations recueillies et récapitule en français ou en anglais. Tu peux utiliser les aides contenues dans la *Way 1*.

Go further

- **Explain** the purpose of such a document.

TIPS

- **Récapitule** les connaissances culturelles de l'unité, et notamment la célèbre Marche sur Washington pour mieux comprendre le contenu de la vidéo.
- **Appuie-toi sur les différents interlocuteurs** pour en déduire leur rôle dans la vidéo. Un journaliste introduit un sujet et donne des informations, une personne interviewée délivre un témoignage.
- **Repère** les mots mis en relief par **l'accentuation et les pauses**, ce sont les mots les plus importants.

e-WB **Grille d'autoévaluation**

Compréhension de l'écrit

To the young peacemakers of America

Sixty years ago, in 1960, my life changed forever. [...]

I did not yet know I had stepped into the history books.

For my whole first-grade year I had to be escorted to and from school by four federal marshals, under the order of the president of the United States, because people were afraid for my safety. Going into and coming out of school every day, I walked through crowds of people yelling, screaming threats, throwing things at six-year-old me. They were against the integration of black and white children in the same school. I had been so excited to meet and make new friends at school and was met with something utterly different and terrifying.

[...] Some teachers even quit their jobs because they didn't want to teach black children.

My teacher, Barbara Henry, came all the way from Boston to teach me. For the entire year she sat alone with me in that classroom and taught me everything I needed to know. She really made school fun. We never missed a day that whole year. We knew we had to be at school for each other.

I felt safe and loved, and that was because of Mrs. Henry, who, by the way, looked exactly like the women in that screaming mob outside. But she wasn't like them. She showed me her heart, and even at six years old I knew she was different. Barbara Henry was white and I was black, and we mattered to each other. She became my best friend.

Ruby Bridges, *This is Your Time*, 2020.

A1 › A2 **Step 1** Before reading the text, **focus on** its source and the picture.

a. Remember all that you know about Ruby Bridges.

b. Deduce the nature of the text.

c. Make hypotheses about the content of the text.

> **TIPS**
> • **Récapitule** les connaissances culturelles de l'unité, et notamment la fin de la ségrégation scolaire.

A2 **Step 2** **Read** the text once and **take notes** about:

a. the narrator (I). **b.** the context (time, place, issue).

> • **Repère** les dates et les noms propres pour dégager le contexte.

B1 **Step 3** **Read** the text again and **find** the oppositions:

a. the girl's expectations *vs* the crowd's reaction;

b. the teachers' reaction *vs* Mrs Henry's;

c. the girl's different feelings.

> • Pour relever des contrastes, **appuie-toi** sur des **mots de liaison** tels que *although*, *but*, etc.

B1 › B1+ **Step 4** **Link** the ideas and **recap** in English.

a. Choose the correct answers:

• The text is an excerpt from **a(n) autobiography** / **novel**, written by Ruby Bridges, an American **activist** / **painter**. It deals with the **beginning** / **end** of school segregation in the USA.

b. Complete the recap using the prompt: ***Ruby was a ...***

c. Explain the different reactions using the elements below: go against the flow / refuse / reassure / be violently opposed to

B1+ › B2 **Go further**

• **Explain** the first line: "To the young peacemakers of America".

e-WB **Grille d'autoévaluation**

SHORTFILE 18 Take it S.L.O.W.

▶ How does the UK's youth embrace more sustainable ways of producing and consuming?

YOUR FINAL TASK

Take part in an interview about a "S.L.O.W. project" you would like to implement at school.

1. Produce better

1

Video

A realistic guide to sustainable fashion, *I-D*, 2018.

2

Knitting helps Tom Daley switch off

Olympian Tom Daley is the most decorated diver[1] in Britain's history. He is also an avid knitter. At the Paris 2024 Olympics Daley added a fifth medal to his collection–and caught the world's attention knitting[2] a bright blue "Paris 24" jumper while travelling to the games and in the stands. At the Tokyo Olympics, where Daley was first spotted knitting, he explained its positive impact on his mental health. "It just turned into my mindfulness[3], my meditation, my calm and my way to escape the stresses of everyday life and, in particular, going to an Olympics." [...]

Olympics-level sport relies on perfect scores and world records. When it comes to knitting, many of the mental health benefits are associated with the process, rather than the end result. Daley says knitting is the "one thing" that allows him to switch off completely, describing it as "my therapy". [...]

Knitting's been shown to have benefits relieving stress in high-pressure jobs beyond elite sport.

theconversation.com, 2024

1. *plongeur* 2. *tricoter* 3. *pleine conscience*

Tom Daley knitting as he watches a swimming event at the 2024 Paris Olympic Games. ▶

Doc 1

a. **Look at** the picture and **guess** what the video is about.

b. **Watch** the video and **find** information about fast fashion.

c. **Pick out** advice given by the speakers.

Doc 2

d. **Read** the text and **find** information about Tom Daley.

e. **Explain** the advantages of knitting.

Doc 1 and **Doc 2**

f. **Compare** the two approaches to fashion consumption and their advantages.

VOCABULARY SPOT

- overconsumption
- craft ≠ industry
- waste /weɪst/
- wellbeing
- handmade ≠ manufactured
- harmful to
- mindful of = aware of
- sustainable /sə'steɪnəbəl/: *durable*
- dispose of = throw away
- pollute /pə'luːt/

MEMORISE your vocabulary

Les compléments numériques

e-WB

lycee.nathan.fr/2sb156-157

3

CHIPPENDALE INTERNATIONAL SCHOOL of FURNITURE | Woodworking Courses | About Us | Exhibitions | News | Contact | APPLY

The Rise of Slow Furniture: Why Sustainable and Ethical Design is the Future

▲ A student at the Chippendale School of Furniture, Gifford (Scotland).

From food to fashion and even furniture, there has been a noticeable shift in consumer shopping habits in the past few years. A study found that shoppers are more socially conscious—reducing the number of new purchases and, when they do buy new, are now more inclined to choose brands based on their sustainability and ethical practices. […]

Keeping It Green

One of the primary benefits of buying 'slow' products is their minimal impact on the environment. Handcrafted[1] furniture is designed to last for generations, unlike mass-produced furniture which is not made with longevity in mind. Fast furniture often ends up in landfills[2], contributing to environmental degradation […].

Keeping It Local

Buying locally-made furniture is also better for the environment, eliminating pollution caused by transportation. Buying local has a more profound impact on the economy […]. Supporting local creates a ripple effect as fellow businesses in the area also benefit, from gift shops selling handcrafted items to timber merchants selling wood.

Moreover, by buying locally, you can be certain of the working conditions the furniture is produced in. You can be certain that the piece you have bought was created with care by a maker passionate about their craft–as opposed to made on a soulless (and potentially dangerous) factory line.

chippendaleschool.com, 2023

1. handmade 2. *décharges*

a. Look at the layout and **identify** the nature of the document.

b. Read the first paragraph and **identify** the conclusions of the study.

c. Read the subtitles and **find** the benefits of buying S.L.O.W. products.

d. VOCABULARY **Read** the article and **pay attention** to repeated verbs and **give** the detailed arguments in favour of S.L.O.W. furniture.

CULTURE SPOT

Originating from the Slow Food Movement in 1986, **the S.L.O.W. Movement** prioritises quality over quantity and mindful living.

S.L.O.W. also means **S**ustainable, **L**ocal, **O**rganic and **W**hole (not processed).

YOUR TASK

TEAMWORK **Enter a school contest for the most sustainable project!**

1. **Choose** a sustainable project from this page: fashion or making furniture.
2. **Imagine** a slogan and a short text and **say** why your project is the most ethical and sustainable.
3. **Create** a poster to promote it and **vote** for the best project.

Build your skills! **Mettre en place une action éthique et durable**

➜ Utilise le ***present perfect*** pour constater une situation :
- *There **has been** a noticeable shift in consumer shopping habits.*

➜ Emploie des **superlatifs** et des **comparatifs** :
- *Fashion is currently the second **biggest** polluter of the planet.*
- *Shoppers are **more** socially **conscious**.*

Quiz TEST yourself

HOW TO SHINE IN GRAMMAR ➜ p. 211, 215

EXPLORE 2. Consume better

1

No need for new toys, we have Team Repair

[...] We spoke to Anaïs Engelmann and Megan Hale from Team Repair. They run a 12-month fixing programme that could be a perfect gift for any young person in your life.

▲ Members of Team Repair, London, 2022.

Starting fixers young

The team of Team Repair is composed of five design-engineering graduates[1] who are linked by their passion for reducing e-waste[2]. Their company aims to introduce and teach children about repair and sustainability, each month sending them a new gadget to fix[3]. These gadgets include hand-held game consoles and remote-controlled cars—it's such a fresh and engaging approach to capturing children's minds.

Anaïs and Megan explain to us how they came to repair at different stages of their lives, proving that it is never the wrong time to learn these crucial skills. They believe that getting children interested in repair early is integral to inspiring our next generation of fixers and repair-friendly designers.

Another lovely aspect of the Team Repair model is encouraging generational skill sharing. Whether it is parents helping their children with the repair kits, or Team Repair themselves going into schools. At Restart, we recognise how important this skill sharing is in teaching younger people and also not letting this knowledge be lost to time.

Building in circularity

They tell us how a key feature of their project is building circularity into their work. It is not necessarily a popular approach with investors but Team Repair recognise the importance of this aspect of their work. In an effort to solve the issue of e-waste, it only makes sense to reuse the gadgets that they send out.

Their hope is that by educating children on repair and waste reduction, these skills will come in handy[4] when Right to Repair legislation also moves forwards in the coming years. It's a hope that we definitely share and are working towards making a reality all the time.

Team Repair's fixing programme is such a cool concept and we cannot wait to see how it develops and what other toys there are to fix!

therestartproject.org, 2022

1. *diplômés* 2. *déchets électroniques* 3. repair 4. *être utile*

VOCABULARY SPOT

- tool: *outil*

- cheap ≠ expensive
- secondhand ≠ (brand) new
- trendy ≠ old-fashioned

- engage in
- foster = encourage
- launch /lɔːntʃ/ = initiate
- prioritise /praɪˈɒrɪˌtaɪz/

MEMORISE your vocabulary

a. Look at the picture and the title and **guess** what Team Repair does.

b. Read the article and **pick out** information about Team Repair's activities.

c. Explain why Team Repair wants to work with schools.

d. GRAMMAR **Pay attention to** the determiner "each" (l.8) and **say** why it is used here.

e. Explain why Team Repair's programme is "such a cool concept" (l.30).

A LITTLE EXTRA Video

Watch the video and **explain** what the teenagers are doing.

Les compléments numériques
lycee.nathan.fr/2sb158-159

2

Video
Yard Sale, shewearsfashion, *Instagram*, 2024.

▲ Instagram post from Kavita (@shewearsfashion), 10 June 2024.

1. sign up = recruit 2. morally satisfying 3. stands

a. **Look at** the Instagram post, **read** the comments. **Say** what eco-friendly project is presented.
b. **Watch** the video and **list** all the items or activities available at this event.
c. **Explain** how it was organised.
d. PHONOLOGY **Focus on** the <u> in the words: *fun* • *cute* • *summer* • *jumper*. Which one is the intruder?
e. **Say** how the community and the participants are impacted.

YOUR TASK

Ask your school's headmaster/mistress to organise a yard sale!

1. **Gather** your notes about the benefits of a yard sale.
2. **Prepare** a speech for your school's headmaster/mistress to convince him/her to organise a yard sale.

Build your skills! Porter un projet

- Emploie des **quantifieurs** pour insister sur l'ampleur du projet :
  - ***lots of*** *kids* / ***lots of*** *cute clothes*
  - ***many*** *stalls*
- Utilise des **déterminants** ou **adverbes d'intensité** pour souligner son originalité :
  - *It's* ***such*** *a fresh and engaging approach.*
  - *This yard sale was* ***so*** *well planned.*

Quiz
TEST yourself

BUILD YOUR ENGLISH → p. 162
HOW TO SHINE IN GRAMMAR → p. 211

3. Live better

1

GEN ALPHA AND GEN Z WANT MORE GREEN SPACES...

and robots to pick up litter[1]

What is an obstacle to building greener cities?

Cost[2]: 46%

Lack[3] of knowledge: 17%

No opinion: 13%

What would you expect in a greener future?

More green spaces: 58%

Less plastic waste: 47%

Solar panels[4] on all buildings: 47%

Robots to pick up litter: 19%

What truly defines a 'green' future?

Cleaner air and less pollution: 58%

Electric public transport: 44%

Electric personal vehicles: 34%

1. *déchets laissés sur le sol*
2. *coût*
3. absence
4. *panneaux solaires*

Research carried out on behalf of *E.ON by 3Gem*, surveying 2,000 UK children aged 8 -16 years old, *express.co.uk*, 2024

a. Read the infographic and **say** what the questions are about and who they were asked to.

b. GRAMMAR **Observe** the questions and **say** how they are formed.

c. Say what Gen Alpha and Z want more in the future. Do you agree?

CULTURE SPOT

Gen Z refers to the generation of people born between 1999 and 2009, and **Gen Alpha** is those born from 2010 onwards.

VOCABULARY SPOT

- aim = goal
- cost
- litter = waste
- plastic tat = plastic junk

- involved in = committed to

- achieve /əˈtʃiːv/
- ban = forbid

MEMORISE your vocabulary

Les compléments numériques

lycee.nathan.fr/2sb160-161

2

e-WB Différenciation

Video
What is KAPTat, *Be Plastic Clever*, 2022.

▲ Skye Neville (left), with Amy and Ella, co-founders of KAP.

a. **Look at** the flyer. **Imagine** what KAP is and what the girls' role is in it.

b. **Watch** the video and **say** what KAP's action is about.

c. **List** the people the girls are asking help from and **say** who their target is.

d. **Describe** the potential impact of the KAPTat campaign on sustainability in the UK.

YOUR FINAL TASK

DIFFÉRENCIATION

Your British school has launched a "S.L.O.W. Innovation Challenge" to promote sustainable and mindful initiatives. Take part in an interview to present a S.L.O.W. project!

WAY 1

1 You're the interviewee. **Choose** a project from this file or **imagine** your own sustainable project.

2 **Take notes** about your project and **get ready** to be interviewed!

WAY 2

1 You're the interviewer. **Review** the documents to pick out questions you can ask on a sustainable project.

2 **Prepare** at least five questions.

Build your skills! **Discuter d'un projet**

- Utilise le **conditionnel** pour expliquer ce qui pourrait être fait :
  - *That **would be** awesome.*
  - *What **would** you **expect** in a greener future?*
- Utilise la **conjonction** *if* pour introduire une hypothèse :
  - ***If** we can get people involved, we **could make** it easier for you.*

HOW TO SHINE IN GRAMMAR ➜ p. 215, 218

Quiz
TEST yourself

Build your English!

GRAMMAR

Exprimer la quantité grâce aux quantifieurs

GRAMMAR tuto

INDÉNOMBRABLES
all
a lot of
much
a little
little
some
any
no

DÉNOMBRABLES
all
lots of
a lot of
many
several
a few
few
some
any
no

1 **Recopie ces phrases en choisissant le quantifieur qui convient.**

a. My brother doesn't repair *no* / *any* items: he throws away *all* / *many* of his broken objects!

b. We are facing *many* / *much* challenges at the moment and we hope *a lot of* / *little* people will set an example.

c. *Much* / *many* people over-consume and only *a little* / *a few* are aware of the issue.

d. We need *many* / *much* more time to make people change their habits.

2 **Recopie et complète les phrases suivantes avec le quantifieur qui convient.**

a few · many · few · a lot of · little · all · any

a. I don't have … clothes but I have … old dresses I want to sell next month.

b. This yard sale is quiet: there aren't … trendy items and there are … stalls.

c. Hurry up! We only have … time left before the yard sale tomorrow.

d. My cousin is very fashionable! She buys … clothes … the time!

PHONOLOGY

La prononciation de la graphie <u>

La graphie <u> peut se prononcer de différentes manières en anglais.

/ɜː/ nurse	/ʌ/ bus	/ə/ support	/uː/ blue	/juː/ computer

3 **Écoute et répète ces mots, puis classe-les en fonction de la prononciation de <u>.**

harmful • pollute • success • super • jumper • customer • purchase • reuse • overconsumption

/ʌ/	/ə/	/ɜː/	/uː/	/juː/

4 **Écoute et répète cette phrase en faisant bien attention à prononciation de la lettre <u>.**

Sustainability is the only way to pollute less. Manufacturers and consumers must find less harmful ways to produce and consume.

VOCABULARY

EXERCISES → p. 231

MEMORISE your vocabulary

TAKE IT S.L.O.W.

Buying and selling

- bargain: *bonne affaire*
- customer /ˈkʌstəmə/
- purchase
- stall /ˈstɔːl/
- cheap ≠ expensive
- new ≠ secondhand
- afford /əˈfɔːd/ = have enough money
- save: *économiser*

Sustainability

- environment /ɪnˈvaɪərənmənt/
- overconsumption
- waste /ˈweɪst/ = litter
- eco-friendly
- harmful = detrimental
- sustainable
- dispose of = throw away ≠ recycle
- engage in
- pollute
- reduce
- reuse

Production

- aim = goal
- factory
- handicraft: *travail d'artisanat*
- resource /rɪˈzɔːs/
- handmade ≠ manufactured
- involved
- local
- achieve /əˈtʃiːv/

Fashion

- fabric /ˈfæbrɪk/ = cloth = material /məˈtɪəriəl/
- fast fashion ≠ slow fashion
- casual: *décontracté*
- ethical
- old-fashioned ≠ trendy
- vintage /ˈvɪntɪdʒ/
- get dressed
- knit /nɪt/
- look good in
- responsibly

NOUN · ADJECTIVE · VERB · ADVERB OR PREPOSITION

1 Find the opposites.

old-fashioned · cheap · new · expensive · trendy · secondhand

2 Find the words corresponding to these definitions.

a. Get rid of something you no longer want: D SP S O

b. A table at a market where you can put things on sale: S A L

c. To make air, land or water dirty: P LL T

d. When people buy too many things or more than they need: O R SU ON

3 Write a short text about this image, using terms from the wordmap.

Designers wear their creations made exclusively from discarded rubbish to launch Junk Kouture, London, 2014.

4 VOCABULARY CHALLENGE!

a. In pairs, **choose** a slow project you have studied in the unit.

b. Take turns. You have 20 seconds to **make** a sentence about the project using words from the wordmap. A word can only be used once during the challenge.

The one who makes the most sentences in three minutes wins the challenge.

SNAPFILE 19

Building tomorrow's megacity

▶ How is Lagos dealing with the challenges of a rapidly growing population?

YOUR FINAL TASK

Write a report on the way Lagos deals with its urban issues.

FOLLOW THE STEPS

1

▲ Busy Lagos, Nigeria.

Video

Nigeria's Growth Is Unsustainable. Here's Why, *Faultline*, 2023.

NIGERIA FACTS

- 250 million inhabitants (most populous country in Africa, 6th in the world)
- Capital: Abuja
- 6th strongest African economy

LAGOS FACTS

- 15 million inhabitants
- 19th best city to visit in the world
- Most congested African city
- 4 main islands (Lagos, Iddo, Ikoyi, Victoria)
- Lagos territory **75%** land **25%** water

a. **Observe** the infographic and **give** the main facts about Lagos.
b. **Look at** the picture and **react** to the atmosphere it conveys.
c. **Watch** the video and **find** information about the population in Lagos.
d. **Take notes** on the problems mentioned.
e. **Recap** the situation.

VOCABULARY SPOT

- flooding /ˈflʌdɪŋ/: *inondation*
- informal (≠ proper) housing
- resilience: *résistance*
- sewage /ˈsuːɪdʒ/: *eaux usées*
- slum /slʌm/ = very poor quality housing

- traffic congestion
- transportation

- coastal = on the coast
- overcrowded /əʊvərˈkraʊdɪd/

- squalid
- tainted = polluted

- flood /flʌd/: *inonder*

MEMORISE your vocabulary

Les compléments numériques

lycee.nathan.fr/**2sb164-165**

2

e-WB **Différenciation**

Video

Life In a Floating Slum in Africa–Makoko, *The Journey*, 2024.

▲ People travel by boat in the Makoko area of Lagos, also known as the "Venice of Africa."

TEAM WORK

a. **Look at** the photograph and **say** why Lagos is called the 'Venice of Africa'.

b. **Imagine** these people's everyday life.

Team A

c. **Watch** the video and **find** the negative sides of Makoko.

d. **Explain** how boats help the community in their daily lives.

Team B

c. **Watch** the video and **find** the positive sides of Makoko.

d. **Describe** the way Makoko contributes to the life of other parts of the city.

e. Now **share** your findings and **explain** why Makoko is a 'contrasting community'.

PHONOLOGY SPOT

settlement • marketplace • complexity • transportation • craftsmanship • consequences

Écoute et **répète** ces mots.
Où la syllabe accentuée se situe-t-elle pour chacun d'entre eux ?

STEP 1

Report on the urban issues in Lagos.

1. **Create** an infographic displaying data on Lagos's issues.
2. **Write** a report commenting on them.

Build your skills! **Donner l'origine d'un problème**

Utilise des expressions exprimant la **cause** ou la **conséquence** :

- ***Due to*** *climate change, natural resources are impacted.*
- *The city is congested* ***because of*** *awful traffic jams.*
- *Lagos has a small land mass,* ***making*** *life difficult as the population is growing.*

HOW TO SHINE IN GRAMMAR → p. 218

3

Eko Atlantic: The Tale of Two Cities

On Victoria Island, which is next to Lagos, Nigeria, a brand-new coastal city called Eko Atlantic is being constructed. [...]

The modern city is expected to be the size of Manhattan's skyscraper district, standing on 10 million square meters of land that has been reclaimed from the ocean and shielded[1] by an 8.5-kilometer sea wall. It has cutting-edge[2] urban planning, its own power generation, clean water, cutting-edge telecommunications, open roadways, and tree-lined streets. It is self-sufficient and sustainable.

The location of Eko Atlantic City is situated on land reclaimed from erosion near the coast of Lagos. In order to protect the reclaimed land from flooding due to ocean surges, a coastal revetment known locally as the Great Wall of Lagos was constructed in 2009. [...]

Lagos' susceptibility to rising sea levels only seems to have drastic effects for poorer communities rather than wealthier parts. Just a few miles from the glitzy[3] Eko Atlantic construction are low-income communities like Magodo that are continually ravaged by the disastrous environmental effects of rising sea levels.

The stark contrast between Eko Atlantic and the reality of what many Nigerians face is very polarizing[4]. On the one hand, Eko Atlantic is seen to be this beacon[5] of economic prosperity to Lagos. The businesses and jobs the construction promises to provide will aid in boosting the overall economy of the state. However, the resources that are pumped daily to ensure the economic success of Lagos comes at a major disadvantage to their surrounding neighbors.

Obi NNADIKA, *hamiltoncs.org*, 2022

▲ An aerial view of the Eko Atlantic construction site, 2024.

1. protected 2. innovative 3. *clinquant* 4. *qui divise les gens* 5. *modèle*

GRAMMAR SPOT

- *The jobs **will aid** in boosting the economy of the state.*
- *It **will make** transportation more comfortable.*

Quel **temps** les actions en gras expriment-elles ?

a. **Look at** the picture of the construction site and **react**.

b. **Read** the text and **pick out** the characteristics of Eko Atlantic.

c. **Identify** the environmental issue mentioned.

d. VOCABULARY **Study** the formation of the following words and **use** the context to explain them: *tree-lined*, *self-sufficient*, *low-income*.

e. **Explain** the title : "*Eko Atlantic: the tale of two cities*".

VOCABULARY SPOT

- commuting
- inequalities
- relief: *soulagement*
- urban planning

- eco-friendly
- excessive = disproportionate
- wealthy /ˈwɛlθi/ = rich

- boost
- protect from

MEMORISE your vocabulary

4

Nigeria: Passengers celebrate as Lagos metro rail project begins operations

Nigeria's commercial capital Lagos on Monday began the first of commercial operations for its Blue Line Rail project.

Lagos State Governor, Babajide Sanwo-Olu, joined fellow Lagosians and state officials in celebrating the official launch of commercial operations for the Lagos Blue Line Rail.

The long-awaited commencement date, which had been postponed[1] multiple times, is expected to provide significant relief to the people of Lagos.

One passenger who had the opportunity to ride on the train exclaimed, "*It was a very smooth experience, everything was organised and there was, I like it, it was very organised actually.*"

An engineer, Joseph Akinpelu, said, "*It will allow people to be able to reach their destination faster and reduce the environmental pollution because it's run by electricity.*" Akinpelu added that, "*It will make transportation more seamless*[2]*, and more comfortable.*" [...]

With a population of over 20 million residents, the state has become synonymous with chaotic traffic situations.

The Blue Line Rail project was conceived as an innovative mode of intra-city commuting, with the specific aim of transitioning the state away from its heavy reliance[3] on a single transportation mode, for which it has been known. [...]

Upon full completion, the entire 27km Blue Line is expected to transport approximately 500,000 passengers daily, further alleviating the transportation challenges faced by Lagosians.

africanews.com, 2022

1. *reporté* 2. harmonious 3. dependence

a. **Look at** the picture and **brainstorm** on the advantages of this mode of transportation.

b. **Read** the text and **list** the advantages of the Blue Line.

c. **Explain** what problems Lagos residents hope the rail line will solve.

▲ The new train on Lagos's Blue Line metro rail, 2022.

A LITTLE EXTRA Video

Listen to users of the new Red Line (0'00 → 2'20) and **list** what they like about it.

Build your skills! **Donner des solutions à un problème existant**

→ Utilise le **passif** pour mettre l'accent sur les infrastructures réalisées :

- *A new coastal city **is being constructed**.*
- *The land **has been reclaimed** from the ocean.*
- *These challenges **are faced** by the Lagosians.*

→ Utilise des **adjectifs composés** pour apporter des précisions :

- *a **self-sufficient** city*
- ***tree-lined** streets*
- ***low-income** communities*

STEP 2

Report on the innovative projects in Lagos.

1. **Gather** all your notes about the innovative projects.
2. **Write** the second part of your report mentioning solutions and limits.

Quiz **TEST yourself**

HOW TO SHINE IN GRAMMAR → p. 211, 213

AXE 4. DÉFIS ET TRANSITIONS
→ Objet d'étude 2

FLASH FILE 20

Electric Route 66

▶ How can route 66 adapt to the electric revolution?

YOUR FINAL TASK

MÉDIATION

In teams, **watch** and **read** the documents. **Share** information about Route 66. Then **record** a vlog to promote EV road trips on route 66.

e-WB

1

Video

What is Route 66? A Very Brief History of "The Mother Road", *Travel Obscurer*, 2020.

VOCABULARY SPOT

- charging station
- electric vehicle /ˈviːɪkl/ = EV
- highway = main road
- rest area = rest stop

- iconic /aɪˈkɒnɪk/
- thrilling = exciting

- charge a car ≠ fill up a car with petrol /pəˈtrəʊl/
- drive across the country
- go on a trip
- lower running costs
- reduce carbon emissions

MEMORISE your vocabulary

2 A letter for change

October 18th, 2024

In their letter, the senators wrote: "The rich history and culture of Route 66 as a symbol of American freedom and adventure will draw millions of visitors to each of the eight states it runs through during the Centennial Anniversary of this iconic highway in 2026. In particular, we urge[1] the Federal Highway Administration and the Joint Office of Energy and Transportation to make significant investments in electric vehicle (EV) chargers along Route 66 through the second round of the Charging and Fueling Infrastructure (CFI) Discretionary Grant Program. We believe federal investment in EV charging will play a critical role in fostering[2] economic and infrastructure development in communities all along Route 66 during its Centennial Anniversary."

They continued: "More than 2 million people visit Route 66 every year, and our states are busy planning numerous events in 2026 to celebrate the anniversary and honor the Mother Road and its connection to American culture. Accessible charging infrastructure can help draw[3] visitors to historic sites and roadside attractions, as well as catalyze the revitalization of downtowns and main streets[4]."

▲ US Senator Martin Heinrich, Democrat, New Mexico, speaking at a Washington DC rally.

heinrich.senate.gov

1. encourage 2. encourage 3. attract 4. city centre

3 Electric Route 66

My name is Mike May, and I started Electric Route 66 in 2018 as a way to educate electric vehicle owners, small businesses, and travelers about using EVs to take classic American road trips, especially on the most classic road of all: Route 66.

I have only been an EV owner since late 2017, but I have been a road-tripper all my life. From childhood vacations with family, to solo trips starting at age 18 in the early 1990s, all the way to the present, I've always liked to visit interesting places and my preferred method of travel has always been by car.

My wife Jessica is my partner in road-tripping and all other ways, enthusiastic through our travels […]. We are a team, and I couldn't dream of adventuring without her.

Along with a new generation of electric vehicles, there comes a new set of challenges for travelers […], and a new set of opportunities for destinations to attract these drivers. As I learn how to integrate EV travel into my own life, I want to use Electric Route 66 to share my experiences and help others who are interested in the exciting new era of car travel that EVs represent.

electricroute66.com

▲ An electric car on an out-of-town excursion to the Fun Run in 2023.

FILE 21 Paths to freedom

"You know, when I was a girl, the idea that the British Empire could ever end was absolutely inconceivable. And it just disappeared, like all the other empires."

Doris LESSING, British writer (1919-2013), 2003.

Soldiers from the Coldstream Guards, Buckingham Palace, London, 2018.

Les compléments numériques
e-WB
lycee.nathan.fr/2sb170-171

How did British colonies gain their independence?

YOUR FINAL TASK

Create an illustrated panel on decolonisation for a school exhibition.

Video

Analysis: what is the Commonwealth?, *Euronews*, 2018.

VOCABULARY SPOT

- commitment
- decolonisation
- (a) flag-raising ceremony
- governance
- membership
- trade

- political

- celebrate
- collapse
- hold a flag
- set free from = emancipate from
- share values

MEMORISE your vocabulary

TEAM WORK

Team A
Describe the picture and **guess** why these soldiers are gathered.

Team B
Read the quote and **rephrase** the changes mentioned by the author.

Team C
Watch the video and **pick out** information about the Commonwealth.

- Now **share** what you have learnt to make the link between the British Empire and the Commonwealth.

EXPLORE A Crumbling Empire

1931 **Salt March** led by Mahatma Gandhi.

1947 Independence and Partition of **India.**

1952 The **Mau Mau Uprising** (Kenya).

1957 Independence of **Ghana.**

1963 Independence of **Kenya.**

1964 Independence of **Zambia**

20th century

1

Audio version

A British colonel attends a party hosted by an Indian family during the British Raj.

"Please, Colonel Sahib, please go into my house and the bearer will bring you a drink!"

Indrajit stepped in front of his son, his eyes lowered, and edged the colonel toward the interior of the bungalow. He had begun to sweat anxiously.

Alicia smiled at several of their acquaintances, nodding to the left and the right, and the colonel relaxed slightly.

"But what I do not understand is why so many of our countrymen do not question the supremacy of the British. Pah! It would seem to me that we are all too afraid of putting the situation right." Jagat Rai had his back to the rest of the party as he spoke to a small group of young men in the corner of his father's large open drawing room. "It would seem to me" he broke off as one of his friends jabbed[1] him in the ribs. The colonel was within earshot and had glanced several times in their direction: his ear was constantly tuned to any talk of unrest[2]. Jagat was undeterred[3]. "It would seem to me," he went on, but louder this time, his voice rising above the swell[4] of small talk, "that where the British are concerned, we are frightened of speaking our minds, it would seem to me"... Jagat received a sharp prod[5] with a bony elbow and turned toward his friend to protest. He saw then, quite clearly, that the colonel had stopped talking and was staring hard at him. The chatter around the room died away but he matched the colonel's stare.

Maria BARRETT, *Dishonored*, 1996

1. hit 2. agitation 3. not discouraged 4. *brouhaha* 5. *coup*

▲ Daily Life of the British in 19th century Colonial India.

CULTURE SPOT

The British Raj (1858-1947) was a period of British rule in India.

VOCABULARY SPOT

- contempt = disdain
- independence
- rule = control

- contemptuous = scornful defiant
- self-confident
- symbolic

- despise = look down on
- protest
- withdraw = leave

MEMORISE your vocabulary

a. **Observe** the picture and **comment on** the situation.

b. **Read** the text and **identify** the characters.

c. **Sum up** Jagat Rai's opinion about the British in India.

d. GRAMMAR **Observe** the sentence: "*Jagat Rai had his back [...] room.*" (l.12-14) **Explain** the link between the two propositions.

e. VOCABULARY **Read** the text and **pick out** the verbs of body movement. What do they show about the different characters?

f. **Comment on** the atmosphere of the scene.

Les compléments numériques
lycee.nathan.fr/2sb172-173

2

▲ Seamen's Hospital Booklet Cover: British Colonies' Crests, early 1900s

Video
The end of the British Empire, *Imperial War Museums*, 2020.

▲ Victorian lithograph of the personification of Great Britain and its Empire since Roman times.

a. Look at the two pictures and the motto at the top. What do they mean?

b. Watch the video and **pick out** elements about decolonisation (countries, dates).

c. PHONOLOGY **Focus on** <i> in these words: *pol**i**tical*, *decolon**i**sation*, *emp**i**re*. Which one is a vowel, a diphthong, a triphthong?

d. Give the reasons why British Empire collapsed.

A LITTLE EXTRA **Video**

Watch Trevor Noah performing a sketch about Britain's colonisation of India and **react**.

YOUR TASK

Write a post for the school website on Commonwealth Day.

1. **Present** the Commonwealth and the British Empire. **Use** the timeline to pick out dates.
2. **Explain** why British colonies wanted independence.
3. **Conclude** by evoking decolonisation.

Build your skills! **Présenter des faits historiques**

➔ Structurer son récit avec des **subordonnées et des marqueurs temporels** :
- *… took place more or less **around the middle decades of the twentieth century**.*
- *… **starting with** Ghana in 1957.*
- *… he broke off **as** one of his friends jabbed him…*

➔ Utilise la structure ***there*** + ***be*** pour mettre en valeur une nouvelle information :
- ***There was** more a sense that the national economy needed to be rebuilt.*

Quiz
TEST yourself

BUILD YOUR ENGLISH ➔ p. 180

The way to freedom

1

▲ *Lieutenant William Alexander Kerr during the Sepoy Revolt*, Engraving, 1857.

Challenging Imperialism: the Story of Protest in the British Empire

The history of the British Empire is a complex and multifaceted one, and the role of protest in its downfall is a crucial aspect to consider. Protests and uprisings within the empire played a significant role in challenging[1] the authority of the British and ultimately contributing to the empire's decline.

Throughout the centuries, ordinary people from all walks of life rose up against British rule, demanding their rights and freedoms. These protests took many forms, from peaceful demonstrations and strikes[2] to armed rebellions and revolutions. Each protest had its own unique set of circumstances and grievances[3], but they all shared a common goal–to challenge and dismantle the oppressive power of the British Empire.

betterprotest.org

1. question. 2. *grève* 3. complaint

a. **Look at** the title of the article and **guess** what it is about.

b. **Give** the different forms of protest.

c. GRAMMAR **Focus on** "*to challenge and dismantle*". What notion given l.13-14 does "to" express?

d. **Sum up** what the common goal of protests was.

e. **Look at** the painting and **say** what passage of the article it illustrates. **Comment on** the point of view given in the artwork.

CULTURE SPOT

The **Sepoy Revolt** (1857) was a rebellion in India against British rule. Indian soldiers (sepoys) and others fought due to unfair treatment and cultural clashes. It's seen by some as India's first independence war.

VOCABULARY SPOT

- attempt
- disobedience
- settler = colon
- uprising = rebellion

- colonial
- significant = important

- commit: *commettre*
- undermine = weaken
- urge = encourage

MEMORISE your vocabulary

2

Video

1930: Gandhi begins the Salt March, *HistoryPod*, 2022.

▲ Gandhi's Salt March, 1930.

3

Video

Mau Mau rebels, heroes of Kenya's independence, still seeking recognition, *France 24 English*, 2023.

▲ Kenyan President Jomo Kenyatta pardoning a Mau Mau leader, 1963.

a. Observe the pictures and **read** the captions (**docs 2** and **3**). **Deduce** the places and **make** hypotheses on the situations.

TEAM WORK

Team A works on doc 2 and Team B on doc 3.

b. Watch the video and **find** information about the protest campaign.

c. Explain its consequences.

d. Share your findings with the other team to compare the two countries' ways to independence.

A LITTLE EXTRA Video

Watch the video and **take** notes about the other independence movements in the British Empire.

YOUR TASK

Prepare sketchnotes about two independence movements.

1. **Gather** what you have learnt about the Salt March and the Mau Mau Rebellion.
2. **Complete** your sketchnotes.
3. **Compare** the two orally.

Build your skills! Synthétiser des relations

- Utilise *to* + BV pour exprimer le **but** :
  - *… which supported the idea of civil disobedience to achieve complete self-rule …*
  - *… a common goal–to challenge and dismantle the oppressive power of the British Empire …*
- Utilise le **passif** pour attirer l'attention sur les victimes plus que sur l'action :
  - *… 11,000 Mau Rebels were killed in the violence …*

BUILD YOUR ENGLISH → p. 181

Quiz
TEST yourself

EXPLORE New beginnings

1

e-WB Différenciation

Audio version

The birth of two nations

The narrator is a young girl who lives in Lahore (now Pakistan).

There is much disturbing talk. India is going to be broken. Can one break a country? And what happens if they break it where our house is? Or crack it further up on Warris Road? How will I ever get to Godmother's then?

I ask Cousin.

"Rubbish[1]," he says, "no one's going to break India. It's not made of glass!"

I ask Ayah.

"They'll dig[2] a canal...," she ventures. "This side for Hindustan and this side for Pakistan. If they want two countries, that's what they'll have to do—crack India with a long, long canal."

Gandhi, Jinnah, Nehru, Iqbal, Tara Singh, Mountbatten are names I hear.

And I become aware of religious differences.

It is sudden. One day everybody is themselves—and the next day they are Hindu, Muslim, Sikh, Christian. People shrink[3], dwindling into symbols.

Bapsi SIDHWA, *Cracking India*, 1988

1. nonsense 2. *creuser* 3. become smaller

2

▲ Shirin Shamsi, *The Moon from Dehradun: a Story of Partition*, 2022.

CULTURE SPOT

The **Independence of India** in 1947 created two separate nations, India and Pakistan, causing violence and displacement.

a. **Observe** the sources of the two documents and **find** information about the country and the context.

TEAM WORK

Team A works on doc 1 and Team B on doc 2.

b. **Sum up** the situation and its consequences.

c. **Explain** how the emotions are conveyed.

d. **Share** your findings with the other team. **Compare** and **contrast** the way a similar historic situation was tackled.

A LITTLE EXTRA Video

Watch the video on *what 'Commonwealth' and 'British Empire' mean to British people* and **react**.

Les compléments numériques

e-WB

lycee.nathan.fr/**2sb176-177**

3

▲ Jomo Kenyatta on *Newsweek* cover, 1963.

Video

Jamhuri Day Special: Jomo Kenyatta Speeches Highlights, *Citizen TV Kenya*, 2014.

a. **Study** the different elements of the cover and **explain** why Jomo Kenyatta made the cover of *Newsweek*.

b. **Watch** the video and **find** information about Kenyan independence.

c. **List** the positive elements mentioned in the document and **comment on** Jomo Kenyatta's goal.

d. **Explain** what future Jomo Kenyatta wanted for his country.

e. PHONOLOGY **Listen to** the following sentence focusing on pauses: "*At midnight on December the 12th 1963 at Uhuru Stadium, amid world leaders and multitudes of people, a new nation was born.*" **Repeat it**, making the proper pauses.

VOCABULARY SPOT

- displacement

- self-confident
- uncertain
- unknown (future)
- uprooted

- flee = escape
- look forward to the future
- look up
- move out

MEMORISE your vocabulary

YOUR TASK

For your school webradio, record a two-minute podcast to explain the post-independence period.

1. **Choose** either Kenya or India.
2. **Explain** what happened after the country was set free.
3. **Comment on** the impact on the population.

Tu peux utiliser un outil d'IA pour **mettre en forme** ton podcast (insertion de musique, transitions, etc.).

Build your skills! Exprimer un changement radical

Utilise des **parallélismes** :
- *this side for ... and this side for...*
- *one day... and the next day...*

Insère des **phrases courtes** et **percutantes** :
- *India is going to be broken.*
- *It is sudden.*

Quiz

TEST yourself

THE INDEPENDENCE CHALLENGE

HOW TO PLAY

Play in groups of six.

1. **Answer** quickly to reach Level 2!
2. **Time** yourself for each level.
3. **Compare** the results of all groups and **discover** who were the fastest!

Time Challenge!
The first to answer **wins 20' off** their total time!

ON YOUR MARKS, GET SET, GO!

LEVEL 1

1. How many countries are part of the Commonwealth?
2. What was the British Raj?
3. When did India gain Independence?
4. What was the Mau Mau Uprising?
5. What was the first African country to gain independence from British rule?
6. What role did protests play in the downfall of the British Empire?

LEVEL 2

7. What was the first South-Asian country to gain independence after World War II?
8. Name three countries in the Commonwealth.
9. Name one positive aspect of British rule in India.
10. Give two examples of the different forms protests took within the British Empire.
11. Name one reason why people protested against British rule.
12. Give the name of the Prime Minister of Kenya when it gained independence.

TIME CHALLENGE!

Name the two nations that were created after India gained independence.

Build your English!

VOCABULARY

Les compléments numériques
lycee.nathan.fr/2sb178-179

EXERCISES → p. 233

MEMORISE your vocabulary

PATHS TO FREEDOM

Unity in diversity

- commitment
- membership
- nation /ˈneɪʃn/
- trade
- fair
- shared (values)
- include

The post-independence period

- partition
- progress
- prosperity
- stability ≠ instability
- disturbing = troubling
- collapse

Leadership

- empire /ˈɛmpaɪə/
- governance
- settlers
- supremacy = domination
- imperial
- political
- govern
- rule = control

Protest

- civil disobedience
- march
- procession
- weaponry = weapons
- devastated
- jailed
- attack
- hit
- stare at sb: *fixer du regard qq*

Independence

- decolonisation
- emancipation
- freedom
- self-determination
- undoing
- achieve
- collapse
- promulgate = declare
- set free
- withdraw = leave

NOUN · ADJECTIVE · VERB · ADVERB OR PREPOSITION

1 Find the five hidden adjectives in the grid, then make a sentence with each of them.

F	J	S	Y	F	B	F	R	L	E
S	A	A	W	I	A	V	O	A	C
T	F	I	I	I	Z	J	X	C	U
G	E	Q	R	L	D	S	F	I	F
K	E	F	Y	E	E	W	P	T	O
X	G	T	R	N	P	D	O	I	A
Y	E	A	N	Y	B	M	E	L	S
T	H	F	S	E	H	J	I	O	P
S	W	T	K	N	M	T	K	P	L
D	I	S	T	U	R	B	I	N	G

2 Read the following sentences and find the missing words.

a. After many years of struggle, Kenya finally gained its ... in 1963.
b. Many people participated in the peaceful ... to demand their rights.
c. The British ... controlled vast areas of the world for centuries.
d. Mahatma Gandhi organised the famous Salt ... to challenge British authority.

3 Find the synonyms.

rule · troubling · supremacy · leave · domination · promulgate · disturbing · withdraw · control · declare

4 Find the verbs corresponding to these definitions.

a. Look at someone for a long time without moving your eyes.
b. Advancement toward a goal.
c. Successfully do something after putting in effort or working hard for it.
d. Make part of a whole.

Build your English!

GRAMMAR

EXERCISES → p. 237

A Situer les événements dans le temps

GRAMMAR tuto

Marqueurs de temps

Ils permettent de **situer des événements** dans le **temps** ou de les **dater**.

In + **année/mois/période** → Kenya gained independence **in 1963**.

On + **jour précis** → Kenya gained independence **on December 12th 1963**.

During + **période** → **During World War II**, the Commonwealth countries fought with GB.

By + **date butoir** → **By the end of the 1970s**, the British Empire no longer existed.

⚠ **Attention aux temps des verbes !**

Les subordonnées temporelles

Elles permettent de **relier** deux propositions et de les **situer** les unes par rapport aux autres sur l'**axe du temps**.

Indian people **obtained** independence
AFTER they **had organised** non-violent protest.

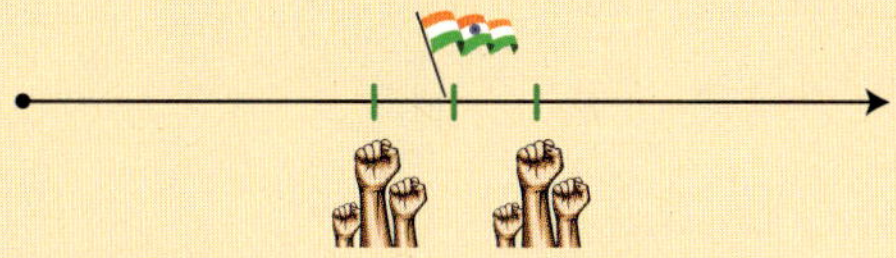

India **obtained** its independence **WHILE** other countries **were** also revolting against the British Empire.

India **broke apart**
WHEN it **got** its independence.

Indian people **celebrated** independence
AS SOON AS it **was proclaimed**.

1 **Choisis le marqueur de temps qui convient.**

a. Ghana has been an independent country *since*/*for* 1957.

b. *In*/*On* August 1947, India became independent.

c. Tensions rose *when*/*during* India and Pakistan were divided.

d. The British Empire controlled most of the world *in*/*by* the end of the 19th century.

2 **Recopie et complète ces phrases avec le marqueur de temps qui convient.**

a. The Commonwealth has existed ... 1931.

b. The British Empire declined ... many countries gained their independence.

c. Many people were displaced ... the partition of India and Pakistan.

d. Kenyan people celebrated ... they achieved independence.

3 **Recopie et complète ces phrases selon les marqueurs de temps proposés.**

a. Gandhi peacefully stood up **while ...**

b. Pakistan was created **as soon as ...**

c. Ghana fought for independence **after ...**

d. Kenya prospered **when ...**

4 **Prépare trois phrases pour accueillir des visiteurs au musée du Commonwealth. Utilise des subordonnées temporelles pour rendre compte de la chronologie des faits historiques.**

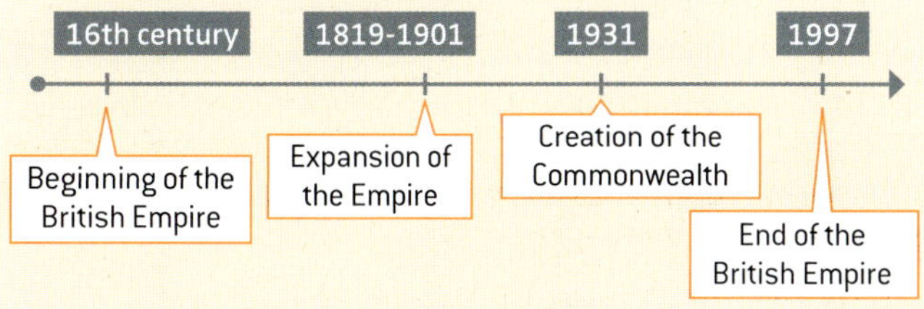

B Exprimer la cause, le but et la conséquence

GRAMMAR tuto

Pour exprimer la **cause**, le **but** ou la **conséquence**, on utilise des **connecteurs**.
La plupart sont des **conjonctions** qui introduisent une **subordonnée**, mais pas tous.

CAUSE

... **as**/**because**/**since** they felt oppressed. *(prop.)*

... **because of** the oppressive rules. *(GN)*

CONSÉQUENCE

... **as a consequence,** the Empire collapsed. *(prop.)*

... **so** they could have their own government. *(prop.)*

BUT

... **so as to**/**in order to** be free from the British rules. *(BV)*

... **for** their people **to** feel free. *(GN)*

1 Termine ces phrases de façon logique en t'aidant des amorces données.

a. Kenya asked for independence because of ...

b. Kenyatta successfully governed Kenya, as a consequence of ...

c. They organised a conference in London in order to ...

d. The Commonwealth was created because ...

2 Complète avec l'un des connecteurs ci-dessous. Attention au sens et à la construction !

in order to | as a consequence | because of | because

a. Tensions rose in many countries ... they asked for independence.

b. Gandhi fought peacefully ... get India's independence.

c. Many people died ... violent attacks.

d. They divided India into two countries ... India and Pakistan were created.

3 Relie les deux phrases par un connecteur exprimant la cause, la conséquence ou le but. Quelques changements peuvent être nécessaires !

a. Kenyans fought to get their independence. They had their own government a few years later.

b. The British Empire collapsed. Colonies could no longer put up with the British rules.

c. Gandhi organised a silent protest. The protest challenged the Empire.

d. Some countries joined the Commonwealth. They shared its values.

4 Tu travailles pour le site web du British Museum. Rédige un court paragraphe pour expliquer la cause, les conséquences et le but de la création du Commonwealth.

The British Museum | About | Projects | Discussions | SUPPORT OUR WORK

Dear visitors,
Do you know why the Commonwealth was created?
In fact, ...

Les compléments numériques

e-WB

lycee.nathan.fr/**2sb182**

A La prononciation des diphtongues et triphtongues (2)

En anglais, les **voyelles** peuvent former des **combinaisons** dans une même syllabe. Les sons formés par **deux sons voyelles** sont des **diphtongues** alors que les **triphtongues** sont composées de **trois sons voyelles**.

2 sons	3 sons
• join /ɔɪ/ • protest /əʊ/	• empire /aɪə/ • power /aʊə/

1 Écoute et répète ces mots, puis classe-les entre diphtongues et triphtongues.

hour • colonial • control • alliance • alliance • decolonisation • country • frightened

2 Entraîne-toi à prononcer ces phrases, puis écoute et répète-les.

a. Gandhi's nonviolent rebellion against the British viceroy played a crucial role in India's fight for freedom.

b. Jomo Kenyatta played a key role in Kenya's fight for independence and his leadership brought powerful changes to the nation's future.

B Les pauses

- Les **pauses en anglais** sont essentielles pour organiser le discours et améliorer la compréhension. Utilisées pour **séparer les idées** et **donner du rythme**, elles sont souvent placées après des éléments clés, comme les sujets ou les verbes importants, ainsi qu'entre les phrases.
- Les **pauses courtes** se placent généralement **après les virgules** pour séparer les éléments au sein d'une phrase, tandis que les **pauses longues** sont utilisées **après les points** pour marquer la fin d'une idée avant d'en introduire une nouvelle.

3 Écoute ces phrases en prêtant attention aux pauses, puis répète-les.

The end of the British Empire occurred gradually, throughout the 20th century, as former colonies gained independence. Starting with India, in 1947, this process marked a shift in global power dynamics, and the decline of British imperial influence.

4 Lis ce texte en marquant les pauses. Écoute et vérifie ton placement des pauses.

The Commonwealth was formed after the decline of the British Empire, as former colonies chose to remain connected. Today, it is a diverse association of nations, united by shared values, but with no political power over one another.

Painting of King George V (1865-1936), King of the United Kingdom and Emperor of India, hunting.

YOUR FINAL TASK

Create an illustrated panel on decolonisation for a school exhibition.

You school located in the UK organises an exhibition about the Commonwealth. You are in charge of the panel that deal with the key moments about independence from the British Empire.

1. **Present** the British Empire and its influence on the world.
2. **Explain** the reasons for decolonisation.
3. **Recap** the landmarks in Indian and Kenyan history.
4. **Finish** your panel with the post-independence period. You can add illustrations or original documents.

Tu peux utiliser un outil d'IA pour mettre en page ton panneau.

YES YOU CAN!

Prepare an illustrated panel

LES ILLUSTRATIONS

Choisis des photos emblématiques pour donner envie aux visiteurs de découvrir l'exposition.

L'OUVERTURE

Conclus ton exposition en faisant une ouverture sur l'évolution remarquée.

After their independence, the British colonies …

Nowadays, Kenya and India …

LE TITRE

Trouve un titre court et efficace qui présente le thème de l'exposition.

Paths to Freedom

Liberty and Independence

LA PRÉSENTATION

Développe le contenu de l'exposition et appuie-toi sur des repères temporels pour aborder des moments clés.

Organise tes informations pour un discours clair et structuré.

On 12 March 1930, Mohandas Gandhi began the 240-mile (390 km) Salt March to the coastal village of Dandi.

LES EXEMPLES

Utilise des exemples précis et concrets afin d'illustrer au mieux le contenu.

Gandhi chose to focus his protest on the 1882 Salt Act which placed a government monopoly on the collection and manufacture of salt.

Gandhi and 79 supporters departed his base on 12 March, and by the end of the twenty-four day march had built a procession that reportedly stretched for two miles.

HOW TO SHINE IN WRITING → p. 204

Compréhension de l'oral

◀ *A Friendly Power in Egypt*, by W.C. Horsley, 1900.

Audio

The British Empire: From Global Power to Decolonisation, *Another History*, 2024.

A1>A2 **Step 1** Before listening to the audio, **focus on** the title and the picture.

a. Gather the information you know about the British Empire (major dates, countries, events, consequences…).

b. Say what image of the British Empire the picture conveys and **link** it to the title of the video.

c. Make hypotheses about the video (type, topic…).

TIPS
- **Récapitule** les acquis culturels de l'unité afin de mieux appréhender les moments clés de la vidéo.

A2 **Step 2 Listen to** the audio once and **take notes** about:

a. the different countries and regions;

b. the dates and time periods and the events they refer to.

TIPS
- Grâce aux **dates** et aux **noms de pays** tu pourras mieux **comprendre** les **événements** dont on parle.

A2>B1 **Step 3 Watch** the video again and **make** the links between:

a. World War II and independence;

b. the Commonwealth of Nations and the legacy of the British Empire.

TIPS
- Mets les dates sur une **frise chronologique** pour comprendre l'**enchaînement des événements** et les **liens** entre eux.

B1>B1+ **Step 4 Recap.**

a. Identify the nature and the topic and **complete**:
- *The audio is a … and it deals with …*

b. Complete with three parts focusing on:

World War II | After World War II | The Commonwealth of Nations

c. Add elements about the legacy of the British Empire.

B1+>B2 **Go further**
- **Explain** why the British Empire's legacy is complex.

e-WB **Grille d'autoévaluation**

Compréhension de l'écrit

Empire stories are always mixed messages, with bad and good, fear and love, cruelty and beauty intertwined. This book is my personal mash-up, reader: memories of childhood overlaid with what I have learned as an adult, a coming to terms with some of the imperial ghosts that still haunt British psyches. […] And who am I, to tell these tales? A post-war baby-boomer, third son and middle child of five from an English mother and a Scottish father, born lower-upper-middle-class in northern England in 1950, the midpoint of the twentieth century. The place where I grew up from 1954 onwards, Kenya Colony and Protectorate, is another country–'So long, / So far away / Is Africa' as Langston Hughes wrote. But the place made me who I am and it is somewhere I feel compelled[1] to revisit in heart and mind and memory before I die.

For decades I put it all behind me. Like the UK itself, I turned my back on the British colonial past because it had become embarrassing. 'Colonialism is now a dirty word,' Elspeth Huxley wrote, 'arousing feelings of indignation in black breasts and guilt in white ones.'

Nicholas RANKIN, *Trapped in History: Kenya, Mau Mau and Me*, 2023.

1. forced

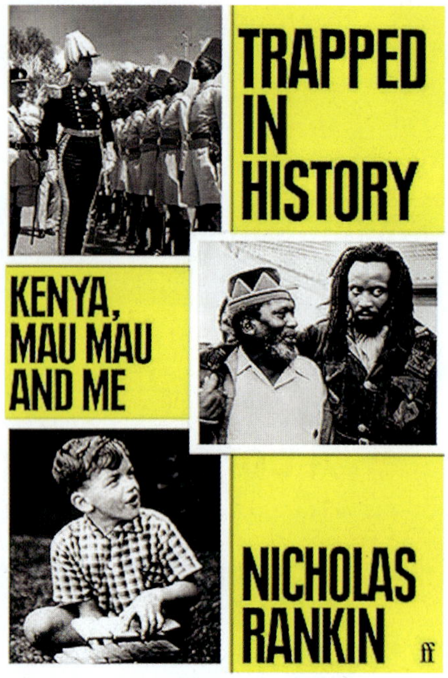

▲ Book cover, *Trapped in History: Kenya, Mau Mau and Me*, 2023.

A1 › A2 **Step 1** Before reading the text, **focus on** its source and the title.

a. **Remember** who the Mau Mau refer to.

b. **Look at** the personal pronoun used and **deduce** the nature of the text.

> **TIPS**
> • **Appuie-toi** sur la couverture pour comprendre qui parle et quelle est son histoire.

A2 **Step 2** **Read** the text once and **pick out** elements about:

a. the narrator;

b. the place where he grew up.

> **TIPS**
> • **Repère** les dates et les noms propres pour situer l'action et décrire le contexte.

B1 **Step 3** **Read** the text again and **explain**:

a. the British Empire's mixed messages;

b. what vision is given;

c. the reason why the author wrote the book.

> **TIPS**
> • Pour comprendre des situations, **appuie-toi** sur des champs lexicaux tels que la violence, les émotions, etc.

B1 › B1+ **Step 4** **Link** the ideas and **recap**.

a. **Choose** the correct answers:

• The text is an excerpt from a(n) **autobiography** / **article** / **novel** by an **American** / **British** / **Kenyan** writer. It deals with the colonial past in Kenya in the **19th century** / **in the 1930s** / **in the 1950s**.

b. **Complete** the recap using the prompt:

The author describes…

c. **Explain** the different ideas using the elements below:

identity | reasons for writing | mixed feelings | colonial past

B1+ › B2 **Go further**

• **Comment on** the title of the book.

e-WB **Grille d'autoévaluation**

SHORTFILE 22

Together in sport

▶ How does sport reflect the evolutions of the Commonwealth?

YOUR FINAL TASK

As a volunteer at the Commonwealth Games, **record** a video to express your opinion about the importance of this competition.

1. A common heritage

1

▲ Women's 200 metres final, Commonwealth Games, Gold Coast, Australia, 2018.

Video
The modern Commonwealth Games, *Commonwealth Sport*, 2018.

a. **Look at** the picture and **imagine** what the event may be about.

b. **Watch** the video. **Pick out** the positive elements of the event and **explain** why this is not just about sports.

c. PHONOLOGY **Listen** to these sentences: *It's more vital than ever before! / It's more important than ever before!* and **identify** the most stressed word. **Practise** repeating them.

d. **Look at** the source and **comment on** the goal of the video.

VOCABULARY SPOT

- athlete /'æθliːt/ = sportsperson
- event
- togetherness

- cross-cultural
- unifying /'juːnɪfaɪɪŋ/

- embody = represent
- strengthen /'strɛŋθn/

MEMORISE your vocabulary

Les compléments numériques

e-WB

lycee.nathan.fr/**2sb186-187**

2 Top 5 Facts About The Commonwealth!

The Commonwealth is an international organisation of 54 countries that work together to promote democracy, human rights and development. Here are 5 facts about the Commonwealth, from the organisation's rich history to its modern-day importance.

1. The Commonwealth originated from the British Empire.

Lots of countries were once ruled by Britain. It was called the British Empire.
When these countries started to become independent, they still had a link to the United Kingdom. Indeed, the Queen was the Head of the Commonwealth until her death in 2022. Now, Charles is King and he's not just the King of the UK… He is the King of some of the Commonwealth countries, including Australia and Canada.

2. The Commonwealth started in 1926.

This is when it changed from the British Empire to the Commonwealth.
It was agreed that certain countries would still have the Queen as their Head of State, however the United Kingdom would not rule over them any longer.

3. Around one third of the world is in the Commonwealth.

Around one third of the world is a part of it! There are around 2.5 billion people in Commonwealth countries.

4. There are 54 countries in the Commonwealth.

They are:
- In Africa: Ghana, Kenya, Nigeria, South Africa…
- In America: Jamaica, Canada…
- In Oceania: Australia, New Zealand…
- In Asia: India, Sri Lanka…

And of course the United Kingdom!

5. The Commonwealth Games is a sports event held every four years.

The Commonwealth Games is also known as the Friendly Games. It's a sports event where all of the countries in the Commonwealth compete against each other. It's held every four years.

Adapted from *funkidslive.com*

▲ Perry, the mascot for the Birmingham 2022 Commonwealth Games.

a. Read the text and **pick out** information about the construction of the Commonwealth and its characteristics today.

b. GRAMMAR **Observe** the first sentence. What does the pronoun *that* replace?

c. Explain how the Commonwealth Games contribute to strengthening the Commonwealth.

YOUR TASK

As an athlete who has just been chosen to be the flag-bearer for your country at the Commonwealth Games, write an Instagram post to say how meaningful this competition is for you.

1. **Decide** which sport you practise and which country you represent.
2. **Take notes** about this opportunity: the challenge, the symbol, the pride.
3. **Choose** a picture and **write** your message.

Build your skills! **Donner des précisions sur un événement**

Utilise des **subordonnées relatives** pour apporter des précisions.

- *It's a sports event **where all of the countries in the Commonwealth compete against each other**.*
- *The Commonwealth is an international organisation of 54 countries **that work together to promote democracy**.*

HOW TO SHINE IN GRAMMAR → p. 218

2. A unique sports tradition

1

e-WB **Différenciation**

Polo, often dubbed[1] as the "Sport of Kings," boasts a rich tapestry of history, extending back over 2,000 years. It's a game entwined[2] with nobility, strategic prowess[3], and most importantly, the enduring partnership between horse and rider. Let's journey back in time to explore the fascinating origins of this equestrian sport.

▲ Prince William, Jerudong Park trophy, 2017.

Around the 6th Century BC, in the expansive grasslands of Central Asia, the earliest forms of polo took root. Nomadic tribes, ancestors to the modern Mongols and Persians, played a rudimentary form of the game [...]. Fast-paced, physical, and requiring supreme equestrian skill, it was a means for warriors to hone[4] their cavalry skills, improve teamwork, and provide entertainment during times of peace.

But it was the British who globalized polo. British tea planters discovered the game in Manipur, India, in the 19th Century. Intrigued by this dynamic sport, they established the first polo club in Silchar in 1859. The sport, modified and codified, was transported back to England, where it took off among British aristocracy and military, becoming an emblem of the Empire's power and sophistication.

Today, polo is played in over 77 countries, and while it retains an air of exclusivity, the sport has become more accessible to a broader audience. It's more than a game; it's a cultural phenomenon that embodies skill, strategy, and an unspoken bond between horse and rider. Its rich history accentuates its appeal, rooting it in traditions that span[5] continents and millennia.

polovalley.com, 2023

1. call
2. combine
3. capacity
4. improve
5. *s'étendre sur*

a. **Read** the text and **identify** what the dates correspond to.

b. **Explain** in your own words how polo has evolved.

c. **Observe** the picture of Prince William. **Identify** which part of the text it illustrates.

d. GRAMMAR **Focus on** l.24. **Identify** the form that is repeated three times. **Explain** what it says about the place of polo today in the British world.

e. **Read** the *Culture Spot* and **comment** on the globalisation of the sport.

CULTURE SPOT

Polo around the world

Today, **polo** has been **exported** to all corners of the **world** and some of the most dynamic polo countries include New Zealand, Australia, Singapore, Argentina and the Caribbean.

VOCABULARY SPOT

- heritage
- legacy
- root

- cross-cultural
- former = previous

- long-lasting
- post-colonial

- have something in common

MEMORISE your vocabulary

Les compléments numériques
lycee.nathan.fr/2sb188-189

2

Video
How was cricket invented? *History of cricket*, 2024.

▲ A vintage illustration of cricket, London, 18th century.

▲ Harmanpreet Kaur, captain of the Indian women's national cricket team.

a. **Observe** the pictures. **Imagine** what the video is about.

b. **Watch** the introduction Video and **pick out** information about cricket (popularity, origin...).

TEAM WORK

Join your team and choose a video:

Video Australia Video India Video the Caribbean

c. **Choose** one part of the video. **Watch** it and **take notes** about the development of the sport and its specificities.

d. **Report** to your team to **identify** similarities and differences in the evolution of cricket.

A LITTLE EXTRA Video

Watch this video and **explain** how cricket both unites countries and highlights a major rivalry within the Commonwealth.

YOUR TASK

As a polo or cricket player, take part in a campaign to promote your sport all around the Commonwealth and record a short message.

1 **Choose** the country you come from and **take** a few notes: how your sport has spread, how it is part of your identity as a member of the Commonwealth.

2 **Record** your message in a dynamic way.

Build your skills! **Mettre en avant la portée d'un événement ou d'un sport**

➔ Fais des **comparaisons** :

- *The sport has become **more** accessible to a broader audience.*
- *It's **more than** a game.*
- ***As** the second most popular game in the world...*
- *Cricket spread **like** wildfire.*

BUILD YOUR ENGLISH ➔ p. 192

Quiz
TEST yourself

3. Commonwealth Games... but what for?

1

Is there a future for an event that some feel is a relic of Empire?

In April 2022, the Australian state of Victoria was awarded hosting rights for the 2026 edition, when over 70 nations were expected to participate. But just over a year later, it backed out. Organizers have not found it easy to find a replacement. Even if the next games go ahead, there are doubts as to whether it can survive into the second half of the century.

▲ Members of the British royal family attend the Commonwealth Games, 2022.

The Commonwealth Games, a quadrennial multi-sport event featuring nations that were formerly part of the British Empire, is in trouble. [...]

"One of the Commonwealth Games' biggest problems is identifying and emphasizing why it exists and what its role is," said Simon Chadwick, Professor of Sport and Geopolitical Economy. "In a post-colonial world, the event seems like an anachronism and out of kilter[1] with the strong sense of national self-identity and pride that many Commonwealth countries now have."

While many nations of the Commonwealth still have strong links with the United Kingdom, Chadwick sees a need for change. "It carries with it associations with colonialism, oppression, and enslavement," he said, adding that it needs rebranding and repackaging if there is to be any survival. [...]

Even that may not be enough. "I can't see a future," said Wong, former sports editor. "What are the Games but a celebration or reminder of a time of British colonialism? It's become a sporting relic and increasingly irrelevant competitively, and I won't be surprised if they cease to exist by 2040."

John Duerden, *dw.com*, 2024

1. *en décalage*

a. Look at the picture, the caption and the source of the text. **Identify** the nature of the document and the point of view.

b. Read the text and **identify** the problem that the organisers are facing with the 2026 Commonwealth Games.

c. Identify and **rephrase** the arguments questioning the relevance of the Games.

d. GRAMMAR **Observe** the sentence starting with *while* (l.18) and **explain** the ambiguity of the Commonwealth Games today.

VOCABULARY SPOT

- inclusive
- sportsmanlike
- tolerant

- achieve = accomplish
- embrace
- inspire
- reconcile /'rɛkənsaɪl/
- strive = try hard to
- turn a blind eye to: *fermer les yeux sur*

MEMORISE your vocabulary

Les compléments numériques

lycee.nathan.fr/2sb190-191

2

Video

Reconciliation Action Plan (RAP), *Gold Coast*, 2018.

a. **Look at** the pictures, **read** the culture spot, and **identify** the country that is being referred to.

b. **Watch** the video and **pick out** information about the unique project of the 2018 Commonwealth Games.

c. **Identify** concrete solutions to promote reconciliation.

d. **Imagine** how such an event may promote positive values both in Australia and around all the Commonwealth.

CULTURE SPOT

Reconciliation

Reconciliation is about strengthening **relationships** between **Aboriginal** and **Torres Strait Islander** peoples and non-Indigenous peoples, for the benefit of all Australians.

A LITTLE EXTRA Video

Watch this video from 0'47 min to pick out more arguments in favour of and against the Commonwealth Games.

YOUR FINAL TASK

As a volunteer at the Commonwealth Games, record a video to share your thoughts about the importance of this competition.

1. **Think** about what you did as a volunteer: mission, athletes you met…
2. **Take notes** about the international dimension of the event: atmosphere, sportsmanship, values expressed.
3. **Record** your message.

Build your skills! **Apporter de la nuance.**

Utilise des **tournures concessives** et des **formes d'opposition** :

- ***Even if*** *the next games go ahead, there are doubts.*
- ***While*** *many nations of the Commonwealth still have strong links with the United Kingdom, Chadwick sees a need for change.*
- *Things have happened* ***but*** *we are in control of ourselves right now.*

HOW TO SHINE IN GRAMMAR → p. 218

Quiz TEST yourself

Build your English!

GRAMMAR

Comparer des éléments et montrer des ressemblances

GRAMMAR tuto

Comparer des éléments

She is **more athletic than** her opponent and **bigger** too!
(athletic : *adjectif long* ; big : *adjectif court*)

Cricket is **as competitive as** polo.

This mascot is **less scary** than the other!

⚠ **aux modifications orthographiques au comparatif de supériorité !**
big → bigger • fit → fitter • friendly → friendlier

Montrer des ressemblances

William plays polo **like** John.
= *Tous deux jouent au polo.*

As in a typical polo match, the crowd was enthusiastic.
= *Ce match de polo est comme les autres.*

1 Mets les adjectifs entre parenthèses au comparatif suggéré : supériorité >, infériorité <, égalité =.

a. Some people think that the Commonweath Games are ... before. **(relevant <)**

b. Being part of the Games is ... being part of the Olympics. **(amazing =)**

c. The feeling of belonging is ... and ... ever before. **(deep >) (strong >)**

2 Choisis entre *as* et *like* et justifie ton choix.

a. *As* / *like* a professional Indian cricket player, Kiran has competed in the Commonwealth Games.

b. The Games are *like* / *as* a big family reunion for Commonwealth countries.

c. When the British settled in the colonies, they played cricket *as* / *like* in England.

d. Some people see the Games *as* / *like* a relic from the British Empire.

PHONOLOGY

L'intonation des phrases exclamatives

- À l'oral, pour **renforcer** l'expression d'émotions (surprise, enthousiasme, fierté...), on **accentue** plus fortement les mots sur lesquels on veut insister.
- L'intonation des phrases exclamatives est **montante** en début de phrase puis elle **descend** lentement.

  - *Around one third of the world is part of it!*

3 Écoute et répète ces phrases en veillant à bien respecter l'intonation.

a. It's such an honour to be the flag-bearer for my country.

b. I had always hoped to be part of it.

c. What an experience! Really incredible!

d. Let's go! Let's do this together and celebrate our diversity.

4 Lis ces phrases, associe-les aux émotions indiquées, puis entraîne-toi à les prononcer. Écoute pour vérifier.

admiration | surprise | déception | fierté | soulagement

a. What an incredible finish!

b. I wish I could have spent more time with the athletes!

c. I even got to hold the medals!

d. How exhausting! It was great but I'm glad it's over!

VOCABULARY

Les compléments numériques
e-WB
lycee.nathan.fr/2sb192-193

EXERCISES → p. 233

MEMORISE your vocabulary

A sports competition

- athlete /ˈæθliːt/
- opponent
- rivalry /ˈraɪvəlri/
- sportsman/sportswoman
- contest = compete in
- participate in
- strive /ˈstraɪv/ = try hard to
- achieve = accomplish

A unique atmosphere

- arena = stadium
- crowd /ˈkraʊd/
- pride /ˈpraɪd/
- team spirit
- gather
- hold one's breath
- outstanding
- sportsmanlike

A common heritage

- legacy
- cross-cultural
- former = previous
- independent from
- long-lasting = persistent
- post-colonial
- strengthen
- widely

Shared values

- sportsmanship = *fair-play*
- togetherness
- fair
- inclusive
- embody = represent
- empower = authorise
- inspire
- move forward

NOUN ADJECTIVE VERB
ADVERB OR PREPOSITION

1 Find the compound adjective behind each definition.

a. An influence that will last for a long time.
b. An experience shared by many nations.
c. Values that spread after colonialism.
d. A performance that really stands out.

2 How many words created from "sport" do you know? Use them all in a sentence.

3 Associate a word from each team to create common collocations.

ADJECTIVES	NOUN
former	values
shared	atmosphere
long-lasting	rivalry
vibrant	event
memorable	colonies
fierce	influence

4 a. Check the meaning of these idioms.

Rise to the challenge
The ball is in (your) court
Play by the rules
Play ball with somebody
Get the ball rolling

b. You are a sports coach. This is the last training session before the Games. Imagine your message to your team. How many idioms will you be able to include?

SNAPFILE 23

The Train from Rhodesia

▶ How does Nadine Gordimer's short story shed light on the consequences of colonialism in Africa?

YOUR FINAL TASK

Back in his village, the old man tells another vendor what happened at the station that day. Imagine his story.

FOLLOW THE STEPS

1

Video
"Zimbabwe Explained", *Opentiera*, 2024.

▲ Cecil John Rhodes (1853-1902).

a. Watch the video. **Pick out** dates and **create** Zimbabwe's historical timeline.

b. Say what Zimbabwe's former name was and **explain** why.

CULTURE SPOT

Cecil John Rhodes
English mining magnate and politician in southern Africa. He founded the southern African territory of Rhodesia (now Zimbabwe).

2

EXTRACT 1

Audio version

The train came out of the red horizon and bore down towards them over the single straight track[1]. The stationmaster came out of his little brick station with its pointed chalet roof. [...]. A stir of preparedness rippled through the squatting native vendors waiting in the dust; the face of a carved[2] wooden animal, eternally surprised, stuck out[3] of a sack. [...]

The train called out, along the sky; but there was no answer; and the cry hung on: I'm coming...I'm coming... [...]

Creaking, jerking, jostling, gasping, the train filled the station. Here, let me see that one—the young woman curved her body farther out of the corridor window. Missus? smiled the old man, looking at the creatures he held in his hand. From a piece of string on his grey finger hung a tiny woven basket; he lifted it, questioning. No, no, she urged, leaning down towards him, across the height of the train towards the man in the piece of old rug[4]; that one, that one, her hand commanded. It was a lion, carved out of soft, dry wood that looked like spongecake; heraldic, black and white, with impressionistic detail burnt in. The old man held it up to her still smiling, not from the heart, but at the customer. Between its Van Dyke teeth, in the mouth opened in an endless roar too terrible to be heard, it had a black tongue. Look, said the young husband, if you don't mind! And round the neck of the thing, a piece of fur[5] (rat? rabbit? meerkat?); a real mane[6], majestic, telling you somehow that the artist had delight in the lion.

Nadine GORDIMER, "The Train from Rhodesia", 1952

1. *voie* 2. sculpted 3. *dépasser* 4. *couverture* 5. *fourrure* 6. *crinière*

a. Focus on the title of the short story and **make** hypotheses about it.

b. Read the extract and **identify** basic information (place, characters, actions).

c. Pick out details about the lion. **Imagine** what it may represent to each character.

Les compléments numériques
e-WB
lycee.nathan.fr/2sb194-195

3 EXTRACT 2

Audio version

No, leave it, said the young woman, don't take it... Too expensive, too much, she shook her head and raised her voice to the old man, giving up[1] the lion. He held it high where she had handed it to him. No, she said, shaking her head. Three-and-six? insisted her husband, loudly. Yes baas! laughed the old man. Three-and-six?—the young man was incredulous. Oh leave it—she said. The young man stopped.

Don't you want it? He said, keeping his face closed to the old man. No, never mind, she said, leave it. The old native kept his head on one side, looking at them sideways[2], holding the lion. Three-and-six, he murmured, as old people repeat things to themselves.

The young woman drew her head in. She went into the coupe[3] and sat down. Out of the window, on the other side, there was nothing; sand and bush; and thorn tree.

Back through the open doorway, past the figure of her husband in the corridor, there was the station, the voices, wooden animals waving[4], running feet.

Nadine GORDIMER, "The Train from Rhodesia", 1952

1. abandon 2. *regarder de côté* 3. *compartiment* 4. *faire signe*

VOCABULARY SPOT

- dust: *poussière*
- passenger
- shape /ʃeɪp/

- desperate /'dɛspərɪt/
- dry ≠ humid
- filled with ≠ empty
- (newly) married /'mærid/

- beg: *mendier*
- grab: *attraper, saisir*
- starve = be deprived of food
- turn down = decline /dɪ'klaɪn/

MEMORISE your vocabulary

a. **Read** the extract and **describe** the scene.

b. GRAMMAR **Pay attention to** action verbs. What tense is mainly used and why?

c. **Pick out** verbs describing the old man's actions. **Explain** how his attitude reflects his social position.

d. **Comment on** the young woman's refusal to buy the lion.

GRAMMAR SPOT

- ***Creaking, jerking, jostling, gasping****, the train…*

Quelle forme verbale est utilisée pour la description ? **Commente** son effet stylistique.

STEP 1

Back in his village, the old man describes the scene to another vendor. Imagine his story.

1. **Describe** the atmosphere at the station and the arrival of the train.
2. **Tell** about negotiating with the couple:
   - the old man's hope when he saw potential customers;
   - his attempts to sell the lion;
   - the young couple's attitude.

Build your skills! Décrire une scène au passé

- Utilise le **prétérit simple** pour évoquer des actions brèves :
  - *… she **shook** her head and **raised** her voice …*
  - *… he **held** it high …*
- Ajoute des **adjectifs** pour enrichir tes descriptions :
  - *… **carved wooden** animals …*
  - *… **tiny woven** basket …*
- Emploie des **gérondifs** pour décrire une scène en cours de déroulement :
  - ***Creaking, jerking, jostling, gasping****, the train filled the station.*

HOW TO SHINE IN GRAMMAR → p. 211, 212, 214

4 EXTRACT 3

Audio version

The blind end of the train was being pulled helplessly out of the station. The young man swung in from the corridor, breathless. He was shaking his head with laughter and triumph. Here! he said. And waggled[1] the lion at her. One-and-six! What? she said. He laughed. I was arguing with him for fun, bargaining[2]—when the train had pulled out[3] already, he came tearing after...One-and-six Baas! So there's your lion. She was holding it a way from her, the head with the open jaws, the pointed teeth, the black tongue, the wonderful ruff of fur facing her. She was looking at it with an expression of not seeing, of seeing something different.

Her face was drawn up[4], wryly, like the face of a discomforted child. Her mouth lifted nervously at the corner. Very slowly, cautious, she lifted her finger and touched the mane, where it was joined to the wood. But how could you, she said. He was shocked by the dismay[5] of her face. Good Lord, he said, what's the matter? If you want the thing, she said, her voice rising and breaking with the shrill impotence of anger, why didn't you buy it in the first place? If you wanted it, why didn't you pay for it? Why didn't you take it decently, when he offered it? Why did you have to wait for him to run after the train with it, and give him one-and-six? One and six! She was pushing it at him, trying to force him to take the lion. He stood astonished, his hands hanging at his sides. But you wanted it! You liked it so much?—It's a beautiful piece of work, she said fiercely, as if to protect it from him.

Nadine GORDIMER, "The Train from Rhodesia", 1952

1. *remuer* 2. *marchander* 3. leave 4. *tendu*
5. disappointment and sadness

a. Read the text and **say** why the young man is happy at the beginning of the extract.

b. Pick out words and phrases describing the young woman's reactions. **Explain** how she feels towards the bargain.

c. Focus on the young woman's questions. What does she blame her husband for?

d. Pick out two adjectives describing the young man's feelings. **Compare** his reaction to the young woman's.

PHONOLOGY SPOT

know • would • whom • could • write

Écoute et **répète** ces mots. Que remarques-tu ?

VOCABULARY SPOT

- greed ≠ generosity
- trinket /'trɪŋkɪt/: *babiole*
- wealth ≠ poverty

- demeaning = degrading
- patronising ≠ respectful
- shameful = shameless

- blame sb for + V-ing = reproach sb for + V-ing
- be worth = have value
- swindle: *escroquer*

MEMORISE your vocabulary

Les compléments numériques

e-WB

lycee.nathan.fr/2sb196-197

5 EXTRACT 4

Audio version

She sat there, sick. A weariness[1], a tastelessness, the discovery of a void[2] made her hands slacken[3] their grip, atrophy emptily, as if the hour was not worth their grasp. She was feeling like this again. She had thought it was something to do with singleness, with being alone and belonging too much to oneself. She sat there not wanting to move or speak, or to look at anything even; so that the mood should be associated with nothing, no object, word, or sight that might recur and so recall the feeling again... Smuts[4] blew in grittily, settled on her hands. Her back remained at exactly the same angle, turned against the young man sitting with his hands drooping[5] between his sprawled legs, and the lion, fallen on its side in the corner. The train had cast[6] the station like a skin. It called out to the sky, I'm coming, I'm coming; and again, there was no answer.

Nadine GORDIMER, "The Train from Rhodesia",
The Soft Voice of the Serpent and Other Stories, 1952

1. *lassitude* 2. *vide* 3. become looser 4. *poussière de cendre*
5. *tombant* 6. *s'était dépouillé de*

Doc 5

a. Read the extract and **sum up** the end of the story.

b. Focus on the young woman's attitude and posture. **Describe** how she feels in this passage.

c. VOCABULARY **Explain** how the word "tastelessness" (l.2) reflects the young woman's emotional state.

d. Comment on the symbol of the train.

Doc 6

a. Listen to Nadine Gordimer's interview and **describe** the environment she grew up in.

b. Identify how apartheid impacted her relationships with others.

- **Read** the whole story again.

6

Video

Nadine Gordimer on racism, *Nobel Prize*, 2007.

▲ Nadine Gordimer.

CULTURE SPOT

Nadine Gordimer (1923-2014) was a South African novelist and short-story writer who was awarded the **Nobel Prize for Literature** in 1991. She opposed apartheid.

STEP 2

The old man discusses with another native vendor who points out that the bargain seems unfair. Write the dialogue.

1 **Imagine** what the Native vendor says to the old man.

2 **Describe** the old man's reaction.

Build your skills! **Écrire un dialogue au style direct**

➔ Utilise des **verbes introducteurs** au prétérit :
- *Three-and-six? **insisted** her husband, loudly.*
- *One-and-six! What? she **said**.*

➔ Ajoute des **adverbes** pour apporter des précisions :
- *It's a beautiful piece of work, she said **fiercely**...*
- *Why didn't you take it **decently**, when he offered it?*

HOW TO SHINE IN GRAMMAR ➔ p. 211, 213

Quiz

TEST yourself

FLASH FILE 24

From Westminster to Wellington

▶ How New Zealand and the UK have maintained political relationships since the creation of the Commonwealth?

YOUR FINAL TASK

MÉDIATION

In teams, **watch** and **read** the documents. **Share** information about the political relationships between New Zealand and the UK.

e-WB

Then, **write** a letter to apply for the position of New Zealand's representative at the upcoming Commonwealth Day celebrations in London.

1

Head of state : King Charles III
First Prime Minister: Henry Sewell (1856)
Government : modelled on the British Westminster system, adapted to meet New Zealand's circumstances.
Founding document : Treaty of Waitangi signed between the British Crown and Maori.

Member of the United Nations, the Commonwealth, and World Trade Organization.

- **1642** – Dutch explorer Abel Tasman sights the south island and charts[1] some of the country's west coast.
- **1840** – Treaty of Waitangi pledges[2] protection of Maori land and establishes British law in New Zealand.
- **1907** – New Zealand becomes dominion within British Empire.
- **1947** – New Zealand gains full independence from Britain.

British Rule | Dominion Status | Independence

1. *tracer* 2. formally promise

VOCABULARY SPOT

- ambassador
- application: *candidature*
- issue = problem
- current: *actuel*
- ongoing = continuing
- consider /kən'sɪdər/
- contribute to
- engage with
- look forward to V-ing: *attendre avec impatience*
- Dear Sir or Madam
- Yours faithfully, Sincerely yours

MEMORISE your vocabulary

A LITTLE EXTRA

Video

Watch the video and **learn** more about the role of High Commissioner.

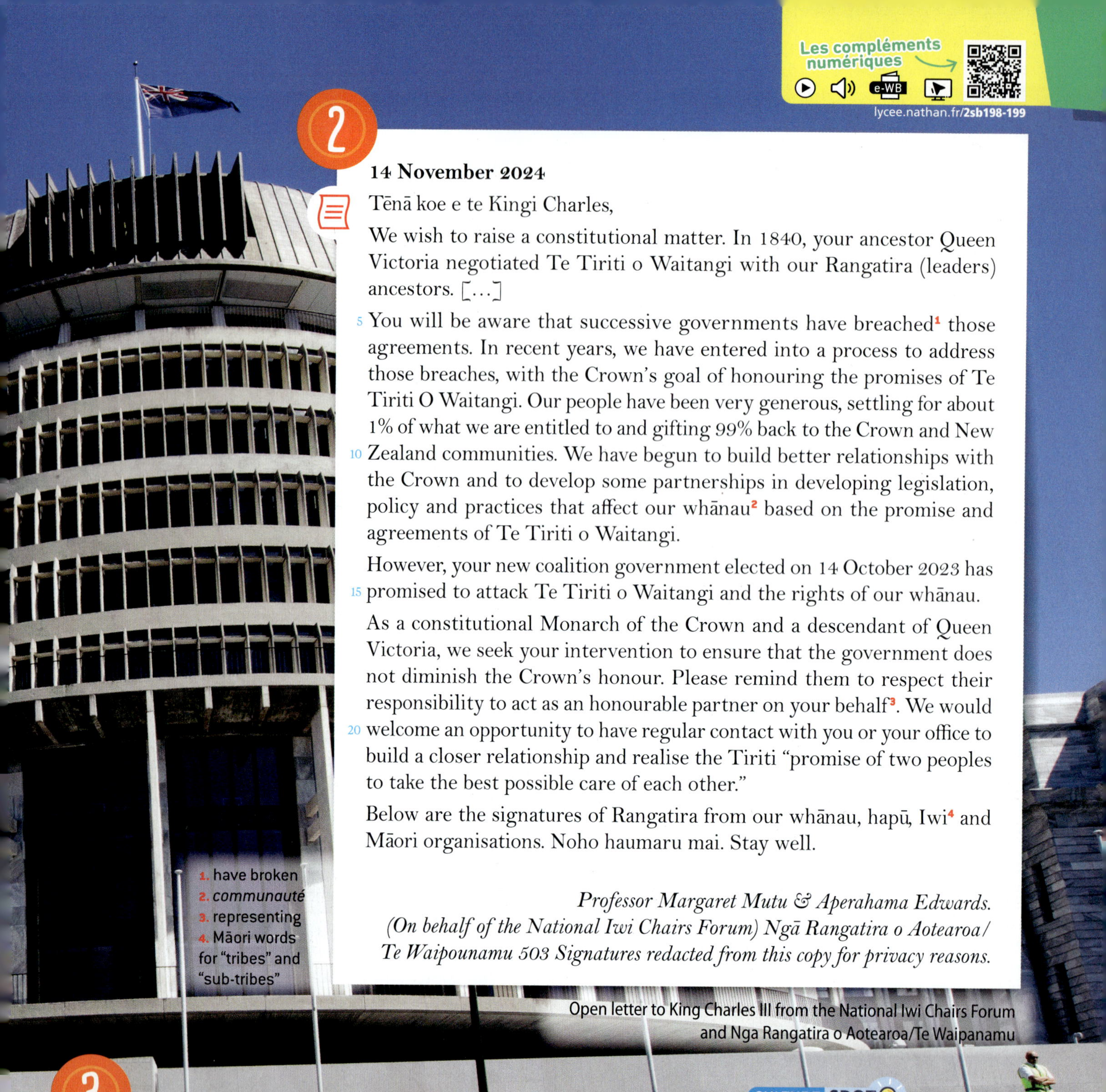

Les compléments numériques
e-WB
lycee.nathan.fr/2sb198-199

2

14 November 2024

Tēnā koe e te Kingi Charles,

We wish to raise a constitutional matter. In 1840, your ancestor Queen Victoria negotiated Te Tiriti o Waitangi with our Rangatira (leaders) ancestors. [...]

You will be aware that successive governments have breached[1] those agreements. In recent years, we have entered into a process to address those breaches, with the Crown's goal of honouring the promises of Te Tiriti O Waitangi. Our people have been very generous, settling for about 1% of what we are entitled to and gifting 99% back to the Crown and New Zealand communities. We have begun to build better relationships with the Crown and to develop some partnerships in developing legislation, policy and practices that affect our whānau[2] based on the promise and agreements of Te Tiriti o Waitangi.

However, your new coalition government elected on 14 October 2023 has promised to attack Te Tiriti o Waitangi and the rights of our whānau.

As a constitutional Monarch of the Crown and a descendant of Queen Victoria, we seek your intervention to ensure that the government does not diminish the Crown's honour. Please remind them to respect their responsibility to act as an honourable partner on your behalf[3]. We would welcome an opportunity to have regular contact with you or your office to build a closer relationship and realise the Tiriti "promise of two peoples to take the best possible care of each other."

Below are the signatures of Rangatira from our whānau, hapū, Iwi[4] and Māori organisations. Noho haumaru mai. Stay well.

Professor Margaret Mutu & Aperahama Edwards.
(On behalf of the National Iwi Chairs Forum) Ngā Rangatira o Aotearoa/ Te Waipounamu 503 Signatures redacted from this copy for privacy reasons.

1. have broken
2. *communauté*
3. representing
4. Māori words for "tribes" and "sub-tribes"

Open letter to King Charles III from the National Iwi Chairs Forum and Nga Rangatira o Aotearoa/Te Waipanamu

3

Video

Are you New Zealand's next representative to Commonwealth Day?, *NZ Parliament*, 2018.

CULTURE SPOT

The Treaty of Waitangi (Te Tiriti o Waitangi in Māori) established British sovereignty over New Zealand while aiming to protect Māori rights and possessions.

▲ New Zealand Parliament building : the Beehive, Wellington, New Zealand.

HOW to shine in… READING

Afin de t'aider à bien lire et comprendre différents types d'écrits, voici quelques conseils à suivre.

STEP 1
Anticiper le contenu

- Observer le **paratexte** (titre, auteur, date de publication, illustrations) pour **formuler des hypothèses** sur le contenu.
- **Observer** la mise en page pour identifier **la nature du document** (article, lettre, extrait de roman, etc.). S'agit-il d'un texte informatif, d'une fiction ou d'un récit ?
- **Lire les questions posées** sur le texte le cas échéant. Elles donnent de nombreux indices qui aident la compréhension.

STEP 2
Faire les premiers repérages

- Lire le texte une première fois pour en repérer la **structure globale** (y a-t-il des guillemets ? Indiquent-ils un dialogue ? des citations ? Combien y a-t-il de paragraphes ? sont-ils titrés ?)
- Repérer les majuscules indiquant des **noms propres** (identification des lieux, personnages, adjectifs de nationalité…), les **nombres** (identification de l'âge, des dates…) et les **mots transparents**.

A Cause That's Close to Her Heart

Princess Kate's newest initiative is supporting organisations that are making resources easily accessible to families across the United Kingdom.

This week, the Royal Foundation Centre for Early Childhood, a "hub" organisation Kate founded in 2021, announced the launch of the Baby Bank[1] Alliance, which will unite 300 baby banks in the U.K. and help them continue their work supporting children, parents, and caregivers.

The foundation shared the exciting news on Instagram, including photos of Kate's previous visits to various charities across the country. One snapshot shows Kate assembling gift bags with her daughter, Princess Charlotte, during a visit to a baby bank in Maidenhead, England, last December. (Kate's two other kids—Prince George and Prince Louis—also joined their mom in volunteering[2] at the bank.)

"Over the past few years, the Princess of Wales has visited several baby banks to highlight their crucial work in supporting families with babies and young children," the caption read. "Organisations like baby banks play a vital role in helping to give parents and carers[3] the capacity to provide the nurturing care which is so important to babies and young children."

Chelsey SANCHEZ, *harpersbazaar.com*, 2023

1. a charity offering goods for babies and children 2. *être bénévole* 3. *aidants*

▲ *Snapfile* 15, p. 136

▲ Kate Middleton at a baby bank, 2023.

STEP 3
Mettre en lien les informations

- Relire plus attentivement le texte et se demander qui parle, à qui et de quoi ?
- Identifier les pronoms et leurs antécédents pour suivre la logique du texte.
- Identifier les **connecteurs logiques** et les **marqueurs de temps** qui montrent la **progression** du texte et les relations entre les informations.

STEP 4
Aller plus loin

- Rechercher les **sous-entendus** et les **implicites culturels** en se basant sur le contexte historique, social, *etc.* du texte.
- Identifier les **figures de style** s'il y en a et analyser leur effet sur le texte.
- Repérer les **non-dits** et les **suggestions implicites** à travers le choix des mots et la structure du discours.
- Prendre en compte **les intentions de l'auteur**, l'effet qu'il cherche à produire sur le lecteur.

Your turn to shine!

READING

Sophie, Duchess of Edinburgh Strengthens Her Role in Royal Family with Latest Announcement

▲ The Duchess of Edinburgh meeting refugees in Chad, 13 October 2024.

The Duchess of Edinburgh will follow in her late father-in-law's footsteps by backing an organization that's at work in over 80 countries.

Sophie, the Duchess of Edinburgh is adding a role to her royal resume[1] to support a charity previously backed by her late father-in-law, Prince Philip.

On Nov. 25, Plan International UK announced Sophie, 59, as its new royal patron, taking over a post that the late Duke of Edinburgh held from 2015 until his death in 2018. The news was further circulated by King Charles and Queen Camilla's team on social media and the update came on the UN Day for the Elimination of Violence Against Women. […]

The announcement featured a photo of Sophie sitting with young women during her recent trip to Chad in October. The visit was significant as it marked the first time a member of the British royal family officially visited Chad. […]

The royal family's website describes Sophie as a "global champion" for the United Nations' Women, Peace and Security Agenda and a supporter of the United Kingdom's Preventing Sexual Violence in Conflict Initiative (PSVI). Raising awareness around the disproportionate impact of conflict on women and girls has become one of her close causes in recent years, and her new role with Plan UK will further this work.

Janine Henni, *People.com*, 2024

1. CV

STEP 1

- Observe le **paratexte** (photo, titre, etc.) : que peux-tu en anticiper sur le thème du texte ?
- Identifie la **source** : quelle est la nature de ce document ? Que peut-on en dire ?

STEP 2

- Lis le texte et fais tes **premiers repérages** : noms propres, pronoms personnels et à qui/quoi ils renvoient, nombres, mots transparents.
- Confirment-ils tes **hypothèses** ?
- Quelles **informations supplémentaires** t'apportent-ils sur le thème du document ?

STEP 3

- Lis le texte une deuxième fois et identifie **qui parle, à qui, de quoi** ?
- Repère les **champs lexicaux** utilisés, notamment les mots négatifs ou positifs.
- Repère les **structures grammaticales** (les temps, les formes…) et identifie ce qu'elles apportent au texte.
- Identifie les **connecteurs logiques** et en quoi ils matérialisent la progression du texte.

STEP 4

- Utilise tes **connaissances culturelles** pour mieux comprendre le texte.
- Relie la nature du document à l'intention de communication (une publicité → promouvoir ; un article → informer ; un édito → donner son opinion, etc.). Le texte est-il critique ? informatif ? élogieux ?
- Appuie-toi sur la photographie et le paratexte : en quoi confirment-ils tes réponses ?

Now recap!

What have you understood? Write a recap. Use the questions below to guide you if necessary.

1. **Be sure** to answer all the questions in: *who, what, where, when, how, why.*
2. **Concentrate on** the role the Royals choose to play.
3. **Explain** the link between that kind of media and the Royal Family.

HOW to shine in... WATCHING

Pour améliorer tes compétences en compréhension orale, il est essentiel de développer des stratégies efficaces qui te permettront de mieux appréhender et d'interpréter les vidéos que tu vas regarder. En voici quelques-unes !

STEP 1
Anticiper le contenu

Avant de regarder la vidéo ou d'écouter l'audio, s'appuyer sur le **titre du document** et/ou sur l'**image** s'il y en a une.

▲ A traditional Pookalam made to celebrate Onam.

▲ *File 5*, p. 57

- Appuie-toi sur la **source** pour déduire la nature de la vidéo : *a report? a documentary? an extract from a movie? a commercial?*
- Lis le **titre** du document : *immigrants from India or people of Indian descent? American = living in the USA? 2023 = nowadays? to keep tradition alive = which tradition?*
- N'oublie pas la **légende de l'image** s'il y en a une.

- Tu peux t'appuyer sur tes **connaissances personnelles** et dresser une **liste de mots que tu penses entendre** en lien avec le titre et/ou le visuel : *parents and children, Indian culture, meal, dishes, ingredients, rice, recipe, etc.*

STEP 2
Repérer le contexte et le sujet principal

- Regarder la vidéo une première fois **sans prendre de notes** et **vérifier ses hypothèses** concernant le contexte : quelle est la **nature** du document, **qui parle** et **qui sont les participants**, **où et quand** se déroule l'action ?
- **S'appuyer sur ce qui apparaît à l'écran pour obtenir des informations.** Par exemple, la bande de sous-titre indique que la vidéo est un reportage tandis que la présence du bus jaune au début de la vidéo montre que la scène se déroule aux États-Unis.

STEP 3
Identifier les informations essentielles

Regarder la vidéo une deuxième fois et **prendre des notes en même temps**.

- Relever **des informations sur les interlocuteurs** et/ou identifier leur rôle (journaliste ? spécialiste ? participant ? témoin ?).
- S'appuyer sur **les mots répétés** et **accentués** pour identifier les idées principales.
- Prêter également attention à la **musique**, aux **bruits de fond** ou à **l'intonation de la voix** pour dégager l'atmosphère du document (sérieuse ? tendue ? détendue ? inquiétante ?).

STEP 4
Relever les détails

Regarder la vidéo une troisième fois et **compléter ses notes.**

- Relever les **marqueurs de temps** ou les **dates** s'il y en a pour dégager la **chronologie des évènements**.
- Repérer les **connecteurs logiques** pour identifier **la manière dont les idées sont articulées** (liens de cause à effet, opposition, concession…).

- **Relis tes notes** entre chaque écoute et **organise-les** à l'aide de flèches ou d'annotations.

STEP 5
Rédiger un compte rendu

- Commencer par **présenter la vidéo** en indiquant sa nature, le sujet principal et le contexte (qui parle, de quoi, où et quand).
- **Résumer les points principaux** du document en respectant sa chronologie et/ou sa structure.
- Rapporter les **éventuels points de vue** et **identifier la fonction du document** (relater, informer, convaincre, critiquer, dénoncer, etc.)
- **Barrer** au fur et à mesure les notes sur le brouillon afin de s'assurer de ne rien oublier.

- Le but du compte rendu est de **montrer que tu as compris** le document. Tu n'as donc pas besoin de donner ton avis personnel sur le sujet.

Your turn to shine!

WATCHING

À toi de jouer ! Suis les différentes étapes indiquées pour écouter et comprendre le document suivant.

▲ Michelle Miller (on the left) and Indian Chef Surbhi Shani (on the right) in her restaurant Tagmo, New York city.

Video

Exploring Indian cuisine in the U.S, *CBS News Morning*, 2023.

STEP 1

▶ Regarde l'**image**, lis le **titre** et la **légende** et essaye de **trouver des indices** qui te permettront d'anticiper ce que tu as entendu :

- Quelle est la **nature** du document que tu vas entendre ?
- **Où** penses-tu que la scène va-t-elle se dérouler ? Dans quel pays anglophone ?
- **Qui** sont les personnes que tu vas entendre ?
- **De quoi** penses-tu qu'elles vont parler ?

▶ Liste les mots qui te viennent à l'esprit, puis prépare-toi à visionner la vidéo une première fois pour **vérifier tes hypothèses**.

STEP 2

▶ Regarde la vidéo et vérifie tes hypothèses : **lieu** ? **nombre de personnes** ? **de quoi** parlent-elles ? quel est le **ton**, l'**ambiance** ?

▶ Note ce que tu as compris tout en laissant de la place pour compléter.

STEP 3

▶ Regarde la vidéo une deuxième fois en prêtant attention aux **mots répétés** et aux **mots accentués**.

▶ Commence à **créer des liens entre les différentes informations** que tu as relevées et prépare-toi à l'écoute suivante afin de te focaliser sur les informations manquantes.

TIPS

- Ce n'est pas grave si tes hypothèses ne sont pas correctes. Le but est de te préparer à l'écoute et de noter en amont tout ce que tu n'auras pas à écrire plus tard.

STEP 4

Regarde la vidéo une dernière fois et complète tes notes avec :

▶ des **dates**, des **nombres** : à quoi correspondent-ils ?

▶ des **détails sur l'interlocutrice et sa famille** : pourquoi en parle-t-elle ?

Now recap!

Qu'as-tu compris ? Prépare-toi à rédiger un compte rendu de la vidéo en anglais ou en français. Utilise les questions ci-dessous pour te guider :

1. Quelle est la nature du document et quel est le sujet principal ?
2. Qu'apprends-tu sur l'interlocutrice principale ?
3. Quel est le lien entre sa vocation professionnelle et son histoire personnelle ?

HOW to shine in... WRITING

Pour briller en anglais à l'écrit, il est essentiel de développer des stratégies efficaces qui te permettront de communiquer tes idées avec confiance et style. Voici quelques conseils pour y arriver !

You are a journalist for "Teen Vogue magazine". Write an article to report on the evolution of beauty standards in the USA from the mid-20th century to today's beauty icons and trends.

▲ *File 9*, p. 93

You are an assistant screenwriter in Hollywod and you contribute to the writing of a movie's script. The movie aims at celebrating the 100 years of its creation. It will gather ten different short films each illustrating a theme linked to the film industry. Write the first page of your script.

▲ *File 1*, p. 33

STEP 1 Comprendre le sujet

S'assurer de bien **comprendre le sujet** en identifiant les éléments suivants :

- le **contexte** dans lequel tu vas écrire ;
- le **type de texte** que tu vas rédiger ;
- le **but** de ta production et le **destinataire**.

STEP 2 Trouver des idées

- **Partir du sujet** et noter toutes les idées qui te viennent à l'esprit.
- S'appuyer sur **les documents étudiés** en classe et les compléter avec des **recherches personnelles.**
- Organiser ses idées à l'aide **d'une carte mentale** ou dans **un tableau**.

TIPS

- Sur ton brouillon, mobilise le vocabulaire (noms, verbes, adjectifs, etc.).

STEP 3 Faire un plan au brouillon

Un plan est **indispensable** à la rédaction d'un texte car il permet de **structurer ses idées** et de **gagner en efficacité**. Le choix du plan dépendra du **type de texte** à écrire.

Écrit fictionnel → **Plan chronologique**
- Situation initiale
- Elément perturbateur → développement
- Situation finale

Écrit non-fictionnel

Plan thématique (explorer les différents aspects d'un sujet)
- Introduction
- Theme 1
- Theme 2
- Conclusion

Plan dialectique (discuter/débattre des différents aspects d'un sujet)
- Introduction
- Pour / avantages
- Contre / inconvénients
- Conclusion

- Tu peux préparer un plan de différentes manières : sous la forme d'un **tableau** en format paysage en deux ou trois parties, sous la forme d'une **liste de points** en format portrait, sous la forme d'un ***storyboard*** dans le cas des écrits fictionnels, etc.

STEP 4 Rédiger

- Penser à la **spécificité du texte** à rédiger et aux éléments qui caractérisent sa **mise en page**.
  – Article de presse : titre, sous-titre, date, illustration, paragraphes…
  – Script de film : indications scéniques, didascalies…
- **Développer ses idées** en utilisant des **propositions relatives** : *A decade ago in 2014 Aerie launched its first #AerieReal campaign featuring models* ***that*** *were not re-touched.*
- **Enrichir son propos** en s'appuyant sur **des adverbes** : *He leans back and chuckles* ***ruefully.***
- **Éviter les répétitions** en utilisant des **pronoms** ou des **synonymes** : *The afro is more than just a hairstyle,* ***it*** *was an incredibly powerful symbol of the Civil Rights movement.*
- **Structurer** son texte en utilisant des **connecteurs logiques et chronologiques** (however, moreover, consequently…) **ou des marqueurs de temps** (first, then, eventually…) : ***During and after the period of slavery in the United States,*** *…most Blacks styled in their hair in an attempt to mimic their oppressors.*

STEP 5 Relire sa production

Garder du temps pour la relecture en prêtant attention à :

- la **conjugaison** des verbes et aux **accords** (exemple : n'oublie pas le -s à la 3e personne du singulier au présent simple) ;
- l'**orthographe** (exemple : n'oublie pas la majuscule aux adjectifs de nationalité) ;
- la **ponctuation**.

Your turn to shine!

À toi de jouer ! Suis les étapes indiquées pour rédiger le texte correspondant à l'un de ces deux sujets.

You are a member of the team organising a "World Fashion history" exhibition in your school. Write a thematic panel about the evolution of beauty standards in the USA from the mid-20th century to today.

Aerie's #AerieReal campaign, spring 2019.

You are a young writer and you take part in a short story competition. The theme is: "The Hollywood industry". Write the beginning of your story.

Universal Studios' entrance, Hollywood.

STEP 1

Lis bien le sujet et demande-toi :

- Quel **type d'écrit** est attendu ici ?
- Quel est le **thème** et l'**objectif** du sujet ?
- Quel est ton **rôle** ? Et **à qui** s'adresse ton texte ? Dans quel **contexte** ?

STEP 2

- **Pars du sujet** et **réponds aux questions** : *Who? Where? When? What? Why? What for?*
- **Reprends chaque document** que tu as étudié en classe et **dresse une liste** des aspects du sujet qui y sont abordés.
- Complète cette liste avec des **connaissances** ou des **recherches personnelles** si besoin.
- Surligne d'une même couleur les **idées similaires** pour commencer à élaborer ton plan.

STEP 3

- **Choisis le plan approprié** :
  Ton écrit est-il **fictionnel** ?

Oui	Non
↓	↓
Plan **chronologique**	Plan **logique**

STEP 4

- Demande-toi quel est le **temps** et la **forme** des verbes que tu vas le plus utiliser : présent, passé ou futur ?
- Si tu n'es pas sûr(e) de toi, commence par **rédiger des phrases simples** (sujet + verbe + complément) : *Mia entered the elevator. There were two women. She did not look at them.*
- Puis, enrichis ta production avec des **relatives**, des **adjectifs** ou des **adverbes**: *Mia **quickly** entered the elevator **where** there were two **thin** women, but she didn't look at them.*
- Pense à utiliser des **connecteurs logiques ou chronologiques** pour relier tes idées : ***Then**, she rushed to the director's office and knocked at the door.*
- Dans un écrit non fictionnel, n'hésite pas à partager ton opinion et à illustrer tes arguments avec des exemples : *I'm **convinced** that … • I firmly **believe** that … • **For example**/ for **instance** …*
- Enfin, pense à la **mise en forme** de ton texte : y a-t-il besoin d'un titre ? Ta production est-elle structurée en paragraphes ?

STEP 5

Relis ton texte et **vérifie les points suivants** :

- As-tu utilisé les bons **temps** ?
- As-tu vérifié toutes les **bulles d'accord** (accords sujet-verbe ; noms au pluriel) ?
- As-tu utilisé les bons signes de **ponctuation**, notamment dans les dialogues ou le discours direct rapporté ?

HOW to shine in… SPEAKING

Prendre la parole en anglais sur un sujet, même familier, peut être intimidant mais avec les bonnes stratégies et de l'entraînement tu peux gagner en confiance et en fluidité. Qu'attends-tu pour libérer ta parole en anglais ?

Record a 2-minute video on the evolution of the American family in TV shows. You are a Youtuber and a fan of American family sitcoms. Study the documents and gather information about the representation of the American family over time.

▲ *Snapfile* 7, p. 74

STEP 1 Comprendre le sujet

Lire attentivement la consigne et identifier :

- la **nature de la tâche** ;
- le **sujet de ta présentation** ;
- le **contexte** dans lequel se déroule l'intervention et **à qui elle s'adresse** ;
- la **durée** de l'intervention.

STEP 2 Rassembler ses connaissances et ses outils

Comme pour réaliser une bonne recette, il y a des « ingrédients » indispensables pour bien se préparer :

- Des **connaissances culturelles** et des **exemples concrets** que tu pourras rassembler sur le sujet en parcourant les documents que tu as étudiés en classe et en effectuant des recherches complémentaires sur d'autres séries que tu connais.
- **Des structures grammaticales et du lexique** pour communiquer tes idées comme :
  - le prétérit simple (pour décrire des faits passés) ou le *present perfect* (pour faire un bilan présent) ;
  - le génitif pour décrire les liens entre les différents personnages ;
  - le lexique de la famille et des séries télévisées.

STEP 3 Organiser sa prise de notes

- Organiser ses idées **sous forme de notes** dans **un plan simple et clair**.
- Le **plan** du développement variera selon le sujet :
  - **Thématique** : développer les différents aspects d'un sujet ;
  - **Chronologique** : montrer l'évolution d'un sujet au fil du temps ;
  - **Logique** : exposer les causes et conséquences ou avantages et inconvénients.

1. Introduction	2. Développement	3. Conclusion
= expliquer brièvement ce dont on va parler • Expliquer brièvement que la représentation de la famille américaine a évolué au cours des dernières décennies. • Noter l'intérêt du sujet en soulignant pourquoi il est intéressant d'explorer cette évolution.	= exposer les idées sous forme **chronologique** • Tu peux réaliser **une frise chronologique** pour t'aider : **1950s-1970s** → The traditional family → "I Love Lucy" "All in the Family" "Father Knows Best" **1980s-2000s** → Breaking traditions → "Who's the Boss" "The Cosby Show" **2000s-Today** → Modern Families → "Modern Family" "This is Us"	= résumer brièvement ce qui a été dit et remercier l'auditoire • Souligner le parallèle entre l'évolution des modèles familiaux et leur représentation dans les séries télévisées. • Ouvrir (si possible) sur une question telle que : à quoi ressembleront les familles américaines dans les séries de demain ?

STEP 4 S'entraîner

- **Accueillir l'auditoire** et **le remercier** à la fin de son intervention : *Good morning/afternoon everyone! • Welcome to my channel. • Today we're going to … • Thank you for listening.*
- Prévoir des **synonymes** pour éviter les répétitions : *represent = portray = depict • sitcoms = TV shows = series*
- Utiliser des **connecteurs** pour passer d'une idée à l'autre sans transition : *In the 1970s, … • Then, in modern TV shows… • Last but not least/Finally, …*
- S'entraîner à **prononcer** les **mots clés**.

TIPS

• Tu peux utiliser un outil d'IA pour répéter des mots et soigner ta **prononciation** : *show • 2020 • modern • nuclear • father • popular.*

STEP 5 Captiver son auditoire

- Poser ses notes pour avoir les mains libres et **parler de façon naturelle** avec son auditoire.
- Garder un **contact visuel** avec son auditoire (ou la caméra).
- Parler suffisamment fort et articuler pour que la présentation soit **audible**.
- Adapter le **débit** de parole : ni trop lent, ni trop rapide.
- Utiliser des **supports visuels** (des images ou des extraits vidéos) pour illustrer les exemples choisis.

Your turn to shine!

À toi de jouer ! Suis les étapes indiquées pour prendre la parole en continu sur le sujet ci-dessous.

As a specialist of TV shows, make a 2-minute speech at a Comic Con about the representation of the American family in recent TV shows.

STEP 1

Lis le sujet et identifie les **informations clés** de la consigne :

- Quel **rôle** incarnes-tu ? Dans quel contexte ?
- **À qui** vas-tu t'adresser et **pourquoi** ?
- Sous quel **format** vas-tu t'exprimer et **pendant combien de temps** ?
- Quel est **l'objectif** (informer, convaincre, etc.) de ton intervention ?

STEP 2

- **Rassemble des informations** sur la famille américaine d'aujourd'hui et sur la manière dont elle est représentée dans les séries télévisées depuis les années 2000. Tu peux classer ces séries en fonction des thèmes qu'elles abordent : la famille traditionnelle ? la famille monoparentale ? la diversité culturelle ? la famille moderne et inclusive ?
- **Dresse une liste des structures grammaticales et du lexique** dont tu auras besoin pour rendre compte de cette représentation dans les séries récentes.

Representation of the American family

- **TV shows**: accurately • depict=represent • biased • incredible • celebrate
- **Family**: nuclear • traditional • idealised • diverse • dysfunctional
- **Audience**: shape • expectations • challenge • stereotypes
- **Compare and contrast**: On the one hand,... On the other hand,... • Similarly = Likewise,...

STEP 3

Fais un **plan rapide** avant de prendre la parole.

1. Présente le sujet et son intérêt

- Quelle représentation de la famille américaine ces séries TV nous donnent-elles à voir ?
- Ces représentations reflètent-elles les valeurs et les normes sociales de notre époque ?

2. Explique comment la famille américaine est représentée dans les séries actuelles

- La famille nucléaire et traditionnelle comme modèle persistant.
- La famille moderne et inclusive plus représentative de la diversité culturelle et sociale moderne.

3. Clôture ton discours

- Résume brièvement ce que tu viens de dire.
- Suggère une piste de réflexion si nécessaire.

STEP 4

Pendant la présentation :

- **salue** ton auditoire, **présente-toi** et **introduis le sujet** : *Thank you for being here today at Comic Con... My name is... and together we're going to explore the fascinating topic of how the American family has been represented in recent TV shows ;*
- utilise des **connecteurs** pour **articuler tes idées** : *In **today's** TV landscape,... **Then**, there are also dramas like... **Finally**, recent TV shows **such as**...*
- utilise **uniquement des notes** pour parler de façon naturelle et dynamique ;
- **conclus** et **remercie** ton auditoire : *So, we can say that these varied portrayals enrich our understanding of what it means to be an American family in today's world... Thank you for your attention.*

HOW to shine in... INTERACTING

La capacité à interagir avec les autres est essentielle dans l'apprentissage d'une langue. Voici quelques techniques que tu peux adopter pour développer cette compétence à l'oral et à l'écrit.

Take part in an interview to present a S.L.O.W. project.

Partner A Get ready to be the interviewer or the interviewee. Imagine what questions could be asked.

Partner B Get into a conversation and react about the S.L.O.W. project.

Shortfile 18, p. 161

STEP 1 Comprendre le sujet

Lire attentivement le sujet et repérer :

- le **contexte** et la **nature** : dans quel cadre cet échange a-t-il lieu ? Est-ce une discussion entre amis de longue date ? Entre professionnels ? Y a-t-il un public ?
- l'**objectif de cette interaction** : obtenir des informations ? convaincre son auditoire ? proposer des idées ? débattre ?
- les **participant(e)s** : comment les interlocuteurs échangent-ils, quel registre de langue devra-t-il être utilisé ?

STEP 2 Préparer ses idées

En fonction du rôle tenu dans cette interaction, noter au brouillon les **idées et informations utiles** pour que l'échange soit riche et réponde ainsi à la consigne. Il est aussi utile de **prévoir les réactions de l'interlocuteur(rice)** et de prendre des notes supplémentaires pour s'y préparer.

⚠ Ne pas rédiger des phrases complètes au brouillon, mais simplement des mots et expressions.

The interviewer	The interviewee
– Nature / Name of the project? – Origin / inspiration / objectives? – What is easy/difficult? – Partners / funding / help? – Progress?	– a public bookcase at school, in the hall – sharing books / used books / discovering new stories and authors – finding an old bookcase / rejuvenating it / repainting it – help from other students / the school librarian – should be finished this month

STEP 3 Interagir

Rendre l'interaction vivante en fonction de son rôle.

- **Pour l'élève qui interviewe** :
  – accueillir et remercier la personne qui participe à l'interview ;
  – présenter le sujet de l'échange, donner un point de vue ;
  – poser des questions précises ;
  – relancer la discussion en élargissant le sujet…
- **Pour l'élève interviewé(e)** :
  – présenter précisément son projet ;
  – répondre aux questions de manière concise sans transformer l'échange en monologue ;
  – donner un point de vue…

Écouter attentivement l'autre pour que l'échange reste spontané :
– montrer de l'intérêt aux questions (ou réponses) ;
– réagir aux propos tenus : curiosité, surprise, désaccord, etc. ;
– reformuler sans couper la parole…

Avoir une attitude et une posture adaptée :
– bien articuler ;
– prendre soin de son intonation ;
– regarder les interlocuteurs dans les yeux ;
– ne pas utiliser de français mais plutôt des *gap fillers* ou faire des pauses.

TIPS

Et à l'écrit ?

- **Respecter le format du support et le registre de langue** : par exemple, sur un forum, utiliser des paragraphes pour plus de clarté ; sur un SMS ou un chat, être plus concis et utiliser des emojis : *Hey! What's up?*
- **Être clair et concis** : éviter les longues phrases et aller droit au but. Un long paragraphe risque d'être lu en diagonale et mal compris ! Se relire avant d'envoyer le message.
- **Utiliser des marqueurs d'interaction et rendre l'échange vivant** : poser des questions, réagir, mentionner quelqu'un, *etc.* *Good point, @Emily! • I totally agree! What do you guys think?*
- **Faire attention au ton et à la ponctuation**, éviter les malentendus en utilisant des emojis ou en précisant son intention (humour, ironie) : *OK, cool!* vs. *OK, cool.* et des abréviations : *lol • fyi*… Ne pas abuser des majuscules, qui donnent l'impression QUE L'ON CRIE.

Your turn to shine!

À toi de jouer ! Suis les étapes indiquées pour prendre part à cette conversation.

As a defender of local sustainability, you want to get your friends involved in a S.L.O.W. project. Take part in a conversation to convince them to participate in a community yard sale.

STEP 1

Lis le sujet et repère les éléments suivants :

- Quel est le **contexte** ?
- Quel est l'**objectif** de cette interaction ?
- Quels sont les différents **rôles** à tenir dans cette interaction ?

TIPS

- **Donner des précisions, expliquer** : *S.L.O.W. movement is about… • It helps… • It's in reaction against… • It's generally in the street…*
- **Convaincre, encourager :** *This will help many people. • You should do it! Come on, let's do this!*
- **Demander des précisions :** *What do you want us to do? • What kind of objects would you like to buy/sell? • What are the benefits for the community?*
- **Exprimer clairement ton point de vue** : *I think/believe that it's a great idea • I don't want to sell my things! • I don't share your opinion about…*

→ Pour d'autres expressions utiles dans l'interaction, consulte le rabat à la fin de ton manuel !

STEP 2

Choisis ton rôle dans la conversation et prépare tes interventions.

Tu proposes ce vide-greniers à tes ami(e)s.

- Rassemble des **notes** sur les bienfaits d'une action liée au mouvement *S.L.O.W.*
- Entraîne-toi à **expliquer** en quoi consiste un vide-greniers et comment il est organisé.
- Trouve des **points de vue** ou des **exemples** pour **convaincre** tes amis de participer.

Ton ami(e) te propose cette idée.

- Rassemble des **idées** et des **opinions** sur le mouvement *S.L.O.W.* et/ou les vide-greniers.
- Imagine des **questions** à poser à ton ami(e) pour en apprendre davantage sur l'organisation de ce vide-greniers.
- Prépare-toi à **réagir** à ce que ton ami(e) va te dire et à **expliquer** pourquoi tu acceptes ou refuses de participer.

STEP 3

Tu proposes ce vide-greniers à tes ami(e)s. | **Ton ami(e) te propose cette idée.**

Début de conversation

Tu proposes ce vide-greniers à tes ami(e)s.

- **Salue** tes ami(e)s et annonce-leur que tu veux leur **présenter un projet**.
- **Présente** rapidement ce que tu veux faire.

Ton ami(e) te propose cette idée.

- **Écoute** ton ami(e) et **demande-lui des précisions** au fur et à mesure de sa présentation.

Explications et discussion

Tu proposes ce vide-greniers à tes ami(e)s.

- **Donne des précisions** sur ce projet et sur le mouvement *S.L.O.W.* en général.
- **Persuade tes amis** de participer.
- Sois **convaincant(e)** et **relance** régulièrement sur l'intérêt du projet.

Ton ami(e) te propose cette idée.

- **Demande davantage d'informations** sur le projet.
- Explique **pourquoi tu acceptes/refuses** de participer.

Attitude et posture pendant la conversation

- **Regarde ton/tes interlocuteurs(trices)** et parle clairement.
- **Écoute attentivement** les autres s'exprimer et ne transforme pas la conversation en monologue en t'accaparant la parole tout le temps. **Ne coupe pas la parole.**
- Aide tes camarades en **relançant une question** s'ils semblent hésiter.
- Évite de répondre uniquement par *yes* ou *no* pour **garder l'échange vivant**.

Le bon déroulement de la conversation dépend de tou(te)s !

HOW to shine in... GRAMMAR

Le groupe nominal

Pour construire une phrase, tu as besoin de noms. Tu peux ajouter des éléments pour donner des indications ou des précisions.

Le nom

→ Il peut être **dénombrable** ou **indénombrable**.
a child *sugar*

→ S'il est **dénombrable**, il peut être au **singulier** ou au **pluriel**.
a brother *brothers*

Pour former un **pluriel**, on ajoute un ***-s*** à la fin du mot, sauf pour les exceptions : *bus**es**, match**es**, part**ies**, wol**ves**, fish, m**e**n, wom**e**n, child**ren**, f**ee**t, t**ee**th*...

→ Il peut être **simple** ou **composé**.
a home *a girlfriend*

My family is so cool!

Les articles et les démonstratifs

Ils **précèdent** le nom pour apporter une information supplémentaire.

→ On emploie **l'article indéfini *a*** (ou ***an*** devant un son voyelle) pour désigner **un élément isolé**.
- ***a** story / **an** event*

→ On n'utilise **pas d'article *(Ø)*** pour désigner **plusieurs éléments indéfinis**.
- *They watch **Ø** Bollywood movies together.*

→ On emploie ***the*** pour parler d'un élément ou de plusieurs éléments dont on a déjà parlé.
- ***The** film we watched together was great!*

→ Pour désigner une **généralité**, on n'utilise **pas d'article** (**Ø**).
- *He likes **Ø** dancing and **Ø** cooking!*

→ Lorsque tu veux être très **précis** pour désigner quelque chose, tu peux utiliser un **démonstratif**.
- ***this** woman → **these** women* (proximité)
- ***this** time → **those** times* (éloignement)

La possession

Pour exprimer une **relation** entre deux éléments, on utilise :

→ Des **déterminants possessifs** devant un nom :
my, your, his/her/its, our, your, their
ou des **pronoms possessifs** :
mine, yours, his, hers, its, ours, yours, theirs.

→ Le **génitif** : *Kunal**'s** family*
possesseur ┘ └ ce qui est possédé
- *the neighbour**'s** car* (la voiture du voisin = singulier)
- *the neighbours**'** car* (la voiture des voisins = pluriel)

GRAMMAR

Les adjectifs

- Ils donnent une **indication sur le nom**.
- Ils sont **invariables**.
- Ils peuvent être **simples** ou **composés**.
  united *close-knit*
- Lorsqu'ils sont associés à un nom, ils se placent toujours **devant le nom** selon la règle **TAFCOM** : **T**aille – **Â**ge – **F**orme – **C**ouleur – **O**rigine – **M**atière.
- Ils sont utilisés dans le **comparatif** et le **superlatif** :

Comparatif	Superlatif
less nice than… (moins sympa que…) *as nice as…* (aussi sympa que…) *nicer than…* (plus sympa que…) *more complicated than…* (plus compliqué que…)	*the least difficult situation* (la situation la moins difficile) *the nicest family* (la famille la plus gentille) *the most complicated story* (l'histoire la plus compliquée)

adjectif court · adjectif long (comparatif)
adjectif court · adjectif long (superlatif)

Les degrés

Pour exprimer le **degré**, on utilise :

- des **adverbes** qui servent à nuancer les adjectifs (***very** joyful*, ***so** fabulous*) et les noms (***such** a big family*) ;

⚠ Enough est placé après l'adjectif mais avant le nom.
• *They are good **enough**!*
*They have **enough** guests.*

- des **quantifieurs** avec des noms :

	Noms indénombrables	Noms dénombrables
Quantité nulle	*no money*	*no trains*
Petite quantité	*little milk* (peu) *a little milk* (un peu)	*few eggs* (peu) *a few eggs* (quelques)
Quantité incertaine	*some work* *any work*	*some/several days* *any day*
Grande quantité	*much water* *a lot of water*	*many biscuits* *a lot of biscuits*

Train and memorise!

Ma fabrique de noms

Crée des groupes nominaux pour décrire cette situation en utilisant des articles, des démonstratifs, des quantifieurs, des adjectifs, des noms…

▲ Indian family birthday party.

Je m'entraîne :
SNAPFILE 3 p. 45 • **FILE 5** p. 61 • **SNAPFILE 7** p. 77 • **SHORTFILE 10** p. 102 • **SNAPFILE 11** p. 106 • **SHORTFILE 18** p. 162 • **SHORTFILE 22** p. 192

Le groupe verbal

Pour construire une phrase, tu as besoin de verbes que tu vas modifier pour rendre compte des actions.

La base verbale, l'infinitif et le gérondif

→ La **base verbale** est la forme la plus simple du verbe.
- *watch* • *read* • *sing*

Elle s'utilise après les **modaux, et les verbes *help*, *let* ou *make***.
- *You can **watch** the movie!*
- *She helped her **learn** her lines.*

→ **L'infinitif** est la base verbale précédée de ***to***.
Elle s'utilise après **les verbes de volonté** : ***expect***, ***want***, ***would like***, ***ask***…
- *She expects him **to book** the tickets.*

→ Le **gérondif** est la base verbale suivie de ***-ing***.
Il s'utilise après les expressions ***prefer, like, hate, don't mind, look forward to…***
- *I prefer **reading** the novel!*
- *I am looking forward to **watching** Wicked with you!*

"Have you ever seen *Wicked*?"
"Yes, I have. What an incredible musical!
I've never seen such a good performance!"

Les énoncés affirmatifs

→ Ils suivent l'ordre : Sujet Verbe Complément
- *She bought the tickets.*

→ On peut utiliser l'auxiliaire ***do*** (***did*** au prétérit) pour donner du poids à ce que l'on dit.
- *I **do** like Wicked!*

Les énoncés exclamatifs

Ils se forment :

→ avec ***what*** + groupe nominal (introduit par ***a/an*** au singulier).
- ***What a** wonderful play!*
- ***What** brilliant actresses!*

→ avec ***how*** + adjectif.
- ***How** beautiful this show is!*

La négation

→ Les énoncés négatifs se forment grâce à un **auxiliaire**. C'est sur cet auxiliaire que porte la négation le plus souvent exprimée par ***not***.
- *I **don't** want to go to the theatre.*
- *She **will not** come with us.*
- *I **am not** leaving now!*

→ Je peux utiliser des mots comme ***no***, ***nobody***, ***nothing*** ou ***never***. Le verbe est à la forme affirmative.
- *I play **no** instrument.*
- *I **never** bought it.*
- *She met **no one** there.*

→ Je peux garder la négation avec ***any*** et ses composés.
- *I **do not** play **any** instrument.*
- *I **didn't** meet **anyone**.*

Les questions

Il y a plusieurs types de questions :

→ Les questions **fermées** ou ***yes-no questions*** : elles appellent une réponse commençant par oui ou non. Elles se construisent selon le schéma : **Auxiliaire Sujet Verbe Complément**
• *Do you know this story?*

→ Les questions **ouvertes** ou ***wh- questions*** : elles demandent une information et sont introduites par un **pronom interrogatif**.
What = nature d'un objet : ***What** do you like?* • ***What instrument** do you play?*
Which = quel(le) ? ***Which musical** is your favourite?*

Who = identité d'une personne : ***Who** is this actress?*
Whose = identité du possesseur : ***Whose book** is it?*
Where = lieu : ***Where** is this theatre?*
When = date, heure : ***When** do you want to go there?*
Why = cause : ***Why** have you chosen this play?*
How = manière : ***How** did you find it?*
ou associé à un adjectif pour une demande de renseignement :
***How much** is it?* (prix)
***How popular** is it?* (notoriété)
***How long** have you been staying here?* (durée)
***How often** do you go to the theatre?* (fréquence)

Les adverbes

→ Pour qualifier, intensifier ou nuancer une action, on peut utiliser des **adverbes**.

Adverbes	Exemples
Lieu : *here, there…*	*The theatre is **far away**.*
Temps : *yesterday, now, today, soon…*	*They will watch it **tomorrow**.*
Fréquence : *never, sometimes, often, always…*	*I **rarely** watch musicals.*
Manière : *quickly, slowly, well…*	*She left **immediately**.*

La voix passive

→ Pour attirer l'attention sur **l'objet** ou **la victime** de l'action, on peut utiliser la voix passive.

→ La voix passive se forme grâce à l'auxiliaire ***be*** (conjugué au temps voulu) et au **verbe au participe passé**. Lorsque l'agent (l'auteur de l'action) est mentionné, il est introduit par la préposition ***by***.

Voix active	Voix passive
*Her teacher **writes** musicals.*	*Musicals **are written by** her teacher.*
*Her teacher **is writing** a new musical.*	*A new musical **is being written by** her teacher.*
*Her teacher **adapted** the novel.*	*The novel **was adapted by** her teacher.*
*She **has prepared** this musical for three years.*	*This musical **has been prepared** for three years.*
*She **will publish** her new novel soon.*	*Her new novel **will be published** soon.*

Train and memorise!

Ma fabrique de phrases

Fabrique le plus de phrases possible pour décrire cette situation.

◄ Street signs and advertisements at Times Square, New York City, 2011.

Je m'entraîne :
FILE 1 p. 31 • **FILE 17** p.151

Les temps

Pour construire une phrase ou un paragraphe, tu as besoin de décrire des actions au moyen de verbes. Tu conjugueras les verbes au temps qui convient.

Le présent simple

→ Il se forme avec la **base verbale** à laquelle on ajoute un ***-s*** à la 3e personne du singulier.
- *I **enjoy** Australian dot art.*
- *He **enjoys** Australian dot art.*

→ Pour former une **question** ou un énoncé **négatif**, on utilise l'auxiliaire ***do***, ou l'auxiliaire ***does*** à la 3e personne du singulier.
- *What **do** you **study**?*
- *What **does** she **play**?*
- *I **don't play** the didgeridoo.*
- *He **does not play** an instrument.*

→ Il est employé pour **caractériser** quelqu'un ou quelque chose ou évoquer une **habitude**.
- *They **live** in Australia.*
- *She **loves** singing.*
- *She **takes** singing lessons every week.*

Le *present perfect*

→ Il se forme avec l'auxiliaire ***have* au présent** et le **participe passé** du verbe.
- *I **have lived** in Australia for two years.*
- *He **has lived** in Australia since 2023.*

→ Pour former une **question**, ***have*** conjugué au **présent** est placé avant le sujet.
- *What **have** you **studied**?*

→ Pour former un énoncé **négatif**, on ajoute ***not*** à l'auxiliaire.
- *They **have not seen** her concert yet.*

→ Il fait le **bilan** d'une situation **passée** ou présente les **résultats présents** d'une action **passée**.
- *Their situation **has changed** over the years.*

L'impératif

→ Aux **2e personnes** du **singulier** et du **pluriel**, il se forme avec la **base verbale**.
- ***Look**! He's an artist!* • ***Listen** carefully!*

→ À la forme **négative**, on ajoute ***don't*** devant le verbe.
- ***Don't be** afraid!*

→ À la **1re personne** du **pluriel**, le verbe est précédé de ***Let's***.
- ***Let's listen** to the story!*

→ À la forme **négative**, on ajoute ***not*** à ***let's***.
- ***Let's not forget** what happened!*

→ On utilise l'impératif pour donner un **ordre** ou une **consigne**.

Le présent en *be* + V-*ing* et le prétérit en *be* + V-*ing*

→ On utilise l'auxiliaire ***be* au présent** ou au **prétérit + V-*ing***.
- *She **is visiting** the Australian Museum.* (présent)
- *She **was visiting** the Australian Museum.* (passé)

→ Pour former une **question**, on place ***be***, conjugué au présent ou au prétérit, avant le sujet.
- *What **is** she **doing**?* (présent)
- *What **was** she **doing**?* (passé)

→ Pour former un énoncé **négatif**, on ajoute ***not*** à l'auxiliaire ***be*** conjugué au **présent** ou au **prétérit**.
- *She **is not complaining** about the situation!* (présent)
- *She **was not complaining** about the situation!* (passé)

→ Il est utilisé pour insister sur le fait que l'action est ou était **en cours de déroulement**.
- *Right now she **is visiting the Australian Museum.*** (présent)
- *She **was visiting** the museum when he called her.* (passé)

Le prétérit simple

- Il se forme en ajoutant **-*ed*** à la base verbale. Les **verbes irréguliers** ont des formes particulières qu'il faut connaître par cœur (→ p. 234-235).
  - *She **started** to sing when she **was** a child.*
- Pour former une **question** ou un énoncé **négatif**, on utilise l'auxiliaire ***did***.
  - *What **did** you **study**?*
  - *He **didn't know** them very well.*
- Il est employé pour exprimer un **fait passé et terminé**. Il peut être associé à des repères temporels passés.
  - *In 2020, she **released** her first single.*

Munkimuk AKA Mark Ross first got into rapping via breakdancing in the late 1980s and since then has been heavily involved as an artist, producer and mentor.

"The hip hop community just in general is populated by so many great First Nations artists that come from the mainland or Torres Strait Islands."

Le *past perfect* (ou *pluperfect*)

- Il se forme avec l'auxiliaire ***have*** au **prétérit** et le **participe passé** du verbe.
  - *She **had lived** in Australia before moving to London.*
- Pour former une **question**, ***have*** conjugué au **prétérit** est placé avant le sujet.
  - *What **had** she **done** before becoming a singer?*
- Pour former un énoncé **négatif**, on ajoute ***not*** à l'auxiliaire.
  - *When they went to her concert, they **had not heard** her songs.*
- Il marque **l'antériorité** d'un fait par rapport à d'autres faits **passés**.
  - *He **had not heard** her songs before he went to her concert.*

L'expression du futur ou du conditionnel

En anglais le futur n'est **pas un temps**.
Il peut être exprimé :

- Avec le modal ***will*** pour prédire l'avenir grâce à une **certitude personnelle**.
  - *He **will** become a storyteller to pass on traditions.*
- Avec ***be going to*** + BV pour prédire l'avenir grâce à des **critères objectifs**.
  - *Look at her! She's **going to** sing!*
- Avec ***be about to*** + BV pour dire ce qui est **sur le point de se réaliser**.
  - *Hurry up! The concert **is about to** start!*
- Le conditionnel, ou **futur dans le passé** est exprimé grâce à ***would***.
  - *She said she **would** become a storyteller.*

Train and memorise!

Ma fabrique de phrases

Utilise ce *cartoon* pour faire des phrases à différents temps.

◀ Mark Lynch, *Boomerang*, 2019.

Je m'entraîne :
FILE 1 p. 30 • **SHORTFILE 2** p. 42 • **FILE 5** p. 60 • **FILE 17** p. 150 • **SNAPFILE 19** p. 167

HOW to shine in… GRAMMAR

Les modaux ou équivalents

Les verbes de ta phrase peuvent être modifiés en utilisant des modaux qui expriment des notions comme la capacité, l'obligation, la probabilité, etc.

La capacité

→ On utilise ***can*** + **BV** pour exprimer la **capacité** physique, intellectuelle, ou autre, **au présent**.
• *They have enough money. They **can** rent a flat in London.*

→ On emploie ***could*** + **BV** pour exprimer la **capacité** physique, intellectuelle, ou autre, **au passé**.
• *He **could** buy a flat in London but he preferred to keep his money.*

→ **L'incapacité** est exprimée par ***cannot*** (***can't***) au présent et ***could not*** (***couldn't***) + **BV** au passé.
• *He **cannot afford** it.*
• *He **could not afford** it.*

→ On utilise aussi l'expression ***be able to*** + **BV**, notamment pour exprimer la **capacité future**.
• *He **is able to live** in a skip.*
• *He **was not able to live** in a skip, so he sold it.*
• *He **will not be able to live** in a skip. It's too small.*

L'obligation, l'interdiction

→ On utilise ***must*** + **BV** pour exprimer **l'obligation**.
• *She **must find** a place to live.*

→ On emploie ***mustn't*** + **BV** pour exprimer **l'interdiction**.
• *You **mustn't sublet**!*

→ **L'obligation** peut également être exprimée par **un équivalent *have to* + BV**, notamment **au futur**.
• *She **will have to share** her flat.*

→ Lorsque **l'obligation** est liée à une nécessité, on peut utiliser ***need to*** + **BV**.
• *She **needs to find** a room for her sister.*

They must find a place to live in London, but they cannot afford it. They may opt for flatsharing.

Le conseil

→ On utilise le modal ***should*** + **BV** pour **conseiller** quelqu'un.
• *You **should buy** a home with your friend.*

→ On emploie l'équivalent ***ought to*** + **BV** pour exprimer un **devoir moral**.
• *Her parents **ought to help** her.*

→ On utilise aussi l'expression ***If I were you, I would*** + **BV**.
• ***If I were you, I would** commute.*

La permission et la suggestion

→ On utilise ***may*** + **BV** pour demander la **permission**.
• ***May** I **come** with you?*

→ On peut utiliser ***might*** + **BV** pour **suggérer**.
• *You **might want** to ask the owner first.*

La probabilité

→ Les modaux de probabilité indiquent les **chances de réalisation** d'un fait.

Certitude →	**must:** *She **must be reading** the small ads.*
Possibilité logique →	**can:** *She **can find** a solution with her parents.*
Possibilité moindre →	**could:** *They **could find** a solution if they kept on seeking.*
Possibilité moindre →	**may:** *The roommates **may become** friends.*
Probabilité restreinte →	**might:** *The roommates **might buy** a house together.*

Les adverbes de probabilité

→ La probabilité peut également s'exprimer grâce à des **adverbes** : *certainly, surely, probably, maybe…*
- ***Maybe** it will rain today.*

Certitude →	*They have **certainly/surely** found an expensive flat.*
Possibilité logique →	*It will **possibly** happen today!*
Possibilité moindre →	*She will **probably** share a house with her best friend.*
Probabilité restreinte →	***Maybe/Perhaps** he wants to buy a skip!*

La probabilité au passé

→ Pour exprimer une probabilité d'un fait passé, on peut utiliser un **modal de probabilité + *have* V-EN**.
- *He **may have found** a flat in Redbridge.*
*= **Perhaps** he found a flat in Redbridge…*

Train and memorise!

Ma fabrique de phrases

Exprime des hypothèses pour décrire cette scène de recherche de logement à Londres.

Je m'entraîne : **SHORTFILE 2** p. 72

HOW to shine in... GRAMMAR

La phrase complexe

Pour construire un paragraphe, tu as besoin de lier des idées entre elles. Pour cela, tu peux utiliser des phrases complexes.

Les propositions relatives

→ Elles sont introduites par un **pronom relatif** qui a pour antécédent un **groupe nominal** ou une **proposition**. Elles permettent d'éviter une répétition.

Groupe nominal :

- Fashion designers create clothes. / The clothes should be for everybody.
- Fashion designers create ***clothes***, **which** should be for everybody.
- The USA is a country. / In the USA, celebrities promote body positivity.
- The USA is a ***country*** **where** celebrities promote body positivity.

Proposition :

- ***He wants to keep his locks***, ***which*** *is impossible.*

→ Les **pronoms relatifs** :

Fonction du pronom relatif	Antécédent humain	Antécédent non-humain	Antécédent exprimant le lieu, le temps, la cause
Sujet	***who*** • *The model* ***who*** *promoted self-acceptance is Ashley Graham.*	***which*** • *The suit* ***which*** *was gender-neutral was popular.*	
Complément	***Ø, that*** • *Ashley Graham is the model* ***that*** *she prefers.*	***Ø, which, that*** • *The material* ***that*** *she chose for this dress is organic cotton.*	***where, when, why*** • *The country* ***where***... • *The time* ***when***... • *The reason* ***why***...

Les mots de liaison

→ Ils permettent de **relier deux éléments**.

- *He went to the school with his locks,* ***and / that's why / so*** *he was not accepted in class.*

→ Les mots de liaison expriment différents sens :

Le temps : *then, afterwards...*
L'opposition : *but*
La concession : *however, yet...*
L'addition : *and, moreover, also...*
La précision : *indeed, in fact...*
La conséquence : *so, that's why...*
La cause : *for...*

She said, "I have called the school several times and they have told me that if my son did not cut his locks then he would be suspended."

Les propositions subordonnées

→ La **proposition principale** et la **proposition subordonnée** sont reliées entre elles par une **conjonction de subordination**.
Le sens dépend de la conjonction :

La condition : *if* (si), *whether*
- ***If*** *they decide to promote self-acceptance, they will launch a new campaign.*

Le temps : *when* (quand), *while* (pendant que), *as soon as* (dès que), *until* (jusqu'à)
- ***When*** *she is older, she will become a fashion designer.*

La cause : *because*
- *He likes this jacket* ***because*** *it is organic.*

Le but : *in order to, to, so as to*
- *They used this material* ***to*** *create a new dress.*

L'opposition : *while, whereas* (alors que)
- *He likes second-hand clothes* ***while*** *his sister prefers brand new items.*

La concession : *although, even if* (bien que)
- ***Although*** *they know social media filters, they never use them.*

Les discours direct et indirect

LE DISCOURS DIRECT

→ Une personne rapporte directement la parole de quelqu'un en utilisant des **guillemets**.
- ***Billie Eilish says**, "I never wore pants or shorts."*

LE DISCOURS INDIRECT

→ Une personne rapporte les paroles de quelqu'un en **faisant des modifications.**
- ***She said that** she had never worn pants or shorts.*

→ Quand le verbe introducteur est **au présent**, les changements affectent seulement la **ponctuation** (disparition des guillemets, du point d'interrogation), les **pronoms**, les **possessifs**, **l'ordre des mots** et parfois l'ajout de ***that*** (affirmation) ou de ***if*** (question fermée).
- *She says, "I got obsessed with this brand."*
→ *She says (**that**) **she** got obsessed with this brand.*
- *The journalist asks her, "Do you like it?"*
→ *The journalist asks her **if she** likes it.*

→ Quand le verbe introducteur est **au prétérit**, les changements affectent aussi les **temps**, les **démonstratifs** et les **repères de temps ou de lieu.**
- *She said, "I became obsessed with this brand."*
→ *She said that **she had** become **obsessed** with **that** brand.*

Changements :

Discours direct	Discours indirect passé
présent simple / en *be + ing*	prétérit simple / en *be + ing*
prétérit simple / en *be + ing*	*past perfect* / en *be + ing*
present perfect	*pluperfect*
will	*would*
can	*could*
here	*there*
yesterday / tomorrow	*the day before / the day after*

Verbes introducteurs :
say to somebody, tell somebody, ask somebody, answer, reply, retort…

Train and memorise!

Ma fabrique de phrases

Fabrique le plus de phrases complexes possible pour décrire cette situation.

Je m'entraîne :
FILE 9 p. 90-91 • **FILE 13** p. 120 • **SNAPFILE15** p. 137 • **FILE 21** p. 180-181

HOW to shine in... VOCABULARY

Comprendre le sens des mots (1)

Lorsque tu découvres un document (à l'oral ou à l'écrit), il est normal de ne pas connaitre tous les mots. Le contexte peut t'aider à comprendre ce mot ou à avoir une compréhension globale.

1 S'appuyer sur le contexte

▶ Si tu rencontres un mot inconnu dans le titre d'un document, tu peux souvent l'élucider avant même de commencer à lire ou écouter. Pour cela, prends en compte toutes les informations du **paratexte** : une illustration, un auteur, une légende, etc. peuvent t'aider à comprendre le sens.

EXEMPLE

Living months in the bush with Indigenous Australians...

Im drawn to the unknown, I thing we all are. Most of us here in Australia are living in a country with little to no understanding of its...

YouTube • Wild Reaches • Jul 23, 2023

La miniature de la vidéo, l'hébergeur et la courte description du document peuvent te permettre de comprendre le sens de *bush* dans le titre de ce document.

▶ Au cours de ta lecture ou de ton écoute, garde en tête le **thème** du document. Repère le **sujet principal** dès le début du document en t'appuyant sur les différents **mots clés.**

EXEMPLE

Écoute l'audio. Les mots *sneakers*, *collection*, *several pairs* doivent te permettent de comprendre le thème global de la phrase. Tu peux déduire le sens de *closet*, en te demandant où ranger toutes les paires de cette collection.

▶ Dans certains cas, la difficulté peut se trouver en début de phrase. Il faut continuer à **lire ou à écouter jusqu'au bout** pour repérer des **indices** qui vont t'aider à construire le sens.

EXEMPLE

• *The scars of apartheid run deep, leaving a legacy of segregation, discrimination and inequality.*

L'énumération en fin de phrase (*legacy of segregation, discrimination, inequality*), indique des conséquences négatives. L'expression *run deep* doit t'indiquer que le bilan est lourd et profond afin de comprendre la métaphore.

2 Comprendre les idées générales

▶ Dès que tu abordes un sujet complexe, tu peux rencontrer des termes précis, parfois un peu techniques, que **tu n'as pas besoin de comprendre parfaitement pour saisir l'idée générale**. Tu peux accepter de remplacer dans ton esprit le mot précis par la catégorie générale.

EXEMPLE

My mother, she worked long hours, and like many working parents, she leaned on a trusted circle to help raise us. None of them family by blood, and all of them family by love. Family who taught us how to make gumbo, how to play chess and sometimes even let us win.

Kamala Harris talking about her childhood.

Tu n'as pas besoin de savoir exactement ce dont il s'agit pour comprendre qu'on parle d'un plat typique et d'un jeu. Essaie de remplacer les mots inconnus par d'autres mots que tu connais (*Family who taught us how to cook, how to play games*). C'est suffisant pour comprendre le lien qui unit Kamala Harris aux personnes qui l'ont entourée étant enfant.

Les compléments numériques

lycee.nathan.fr/2sb220-221

Your turn to shine!

À TOI DE JOUER ! Relève ces challenges pour vérifier que tu as bien compris !

CHALLENGE 1

- **Quote 1:** "I am stuck here. I have nowhere else to go."
- **Quote 2:** "In 2014, a film called *Kingsman: The Secret Service* was released, [...] Now, two years later, comes *The Golden Circle*, which takes place directly after the events of the original. This follow up seemed to be everything that made the first one so fun, just turned up to eleven."

Jarrod Flaherty, *The Hudsonian Student Newspaper*, 2017.

- **Quote 3:** "Stingy people have often been forced to give when they were very, very young, when they weren't ready. And generous people have often been really appreciated when they were very young." Fred Rogers (American television host)

a. Lis la citation 1 et appuie-toi sur la seconde phrase pour déduire le sens du mot souligné.

b. Lis la citation 2. Repère la **paraphrase** qui te permet de déduire le sens du mot souligné.

c. Lis la citation 3. Repère l'**antonyme** qui te permet de déduire le sens du mot souligné.

d. Vérifie tes hypothèses dans le dictionnaire.

CHALLENGE 2

a. Fais une première lecture en te concentrant sur le sens global. De quoi parle ce texte ?

- Appuie-toi sur le titre et la source pour guider ta première lecture et te demandant ce qui fait de Chicago une ville moderne. Repère les champs lexicaux utilisés.

b. Relis le texte et interroge-toi :
- Quelle est la nature des mots surlignés ?
- Certains d'entre eux ont-ils une racine que tu connais ?
- Appuie-toi sur les mots qui précèdent ou suivent les mots inconnus.

c. Relis le texte en essayant de déduire le sens de tous les mots. Tu peux comparer avec ton/ta camarade pour voir si vous parvenez à émettre les mêmes hypothèses.

Chicago Architecture : Skyscrapers and the Birth of the Modern City

The City of Chicago has significantly impacted the history of architecture, often referred to as the "birthplace of the skyscraper." Its pivotal role in shaping the modern skyline began with the development of the Chicago and Galena Railroad in 1848, positioning the city as a major transportation hub, followed by its recovery after the Great Fire in 1871. The Great Chicago Fire of 1871 destroyed much of Chicago's central district, leaving a blank slate for innovation and a necessity to rebuild quickly.

Juanita HALIM, *parametric-architecture.com*, 16 October 2024

CHALLENGE 3

Video

A superfan on David Bowie's legacy, *TVO Today*, 2016.

a. Regarde la vidéo afin d'appréhender le message dans sa globalité. Tu dois repérer qui est cette fan et à quelle occasion elle a rencontré David Bowie.

b. Regarde de nouveau la vidéo en cherchant à comprendre plus précisément **comment elle a pu créer une complicité avec David Bowie** lors de leur rencontre.

- Appuie toi sur le rythme pour repérer les groupes de sens et comprendre qu'on change d'idée.
- Essaye de visualiser la scène décrite afin de comprendre comment elle a pu s'approcher de lui en repérant les différentes étapes : *wait in line, parking lot, stage.*

HOW to shine in… VOCABULARY

Comprendre le sens des mots (2)

La construction d'un mot ou d'une expression peut aussi t'aider à en déduire le sens.

1 S'appuyer sur les préfixes et les suffixes

Lorsque tu rencontres un mot inconnu, tu peux souvent en déduire le sens en t'appuyant sur sa construction.

- Repère le **radical** et les **préfixes**.

TIPS

- Tu peux télécharger la liste suivante avec les principaux préfixes et leur sens. e-WB Fiche

EXEMPLE

- *Some TV shows are perpetuating **un**realistic beauty standards.*

- Prends le temps de **bien lire**, car dans les mots qui commencent par *dis-* ou *un-* par exemple, ce ne sont pas forcément des **préfixes privatifs.**

EXEMPLE

- *Modern cowboys **dis**regard traditional methods of farming, opting instead for more efficient, technology-driven approaches that distinguish them from their ancestors.*

Ici, on a un vrai préfixe privatif dans le premier cas, Mais attention, il n'y en a pas dans le verbe *distinguish*.

- Repère le **radical** et les **suffixes**.

TIPS

Pense à faire la différence entre :

- les **suffixes qui changent le sens du mot** (*-ation, -ise, -y, -ness, etc.*) et aussi souvent sa catégorie grammaticale ;
- les **suffixes grammaticaux** qui ne modifient pas le sens du mot mais apportent des précisions sur le temps (*-ed, -ing*), le degré (*-er, -est*), etc.

EXEMPLE

- *Kate has made count**less** appearances wearing her favourite trainers.*
- *Sport is not just a form of entertainment or competition but a power**ful** tool for social cohesion and economic development.*

Tu connais les mots *count* et *power*. Les suffixes *-less* et *-ful* te permettent de comprendre un **sens négatif ou positif.**

2 S'appuyer sur la formation des mots composés

- On trouve en anglais de nombreux mots composés : ceux-ci sont constitués de deux éléments, qui, ensemble, créent **une nouvelle unité de sens.**

TIPS

- Lorsque tu vois deux mots associés, sans savoir s'ils forment une unité de sens, tu peux **vérifier dans le dictionnaire**. Tu trouveras surement le mot composé à la lettre du premier des deux mots, ainsi qu'un renvoi dans l'article du deuxième mot.

MOTS COMPOSÉS

Le sens

Quelle que soit la graphie, le premier mot **modifie** ou **précise** le sens du second :

- *A screenwriter is a writer who writes for the screen.*
- *An award-winning performance is one that can make you win awards.*

L'écriture

La graphie des mots composés peut varier. Pour parler du cinéma, on peut par exemple trouver :

- en **un seul mot** : *screenwriter, blockbuster*
- avec un **tiret** : *box-office, award-winning*
- en **deux mots séparés** : *movie star, red carpet*

La construction

On peut associer des mots de **nature** différente pour composer des mots composés de plusieurs **catégories grammaticales**. Par exemple, pour parler des standards de beauté, on trouvera :

- des **noms** : *bodyshape* (nom + nom), *make-up* (verbe + préposition) ;
- des **adjectifs**: *photo-ready* (nom + adjectif), *flawless-looking* (adjectif + verbe) ;
- des **verbes**: *body-shame* (nom + verbe), *whitewash* (adjectif + verbe).

Your turn to shine!

À TOI DE JOUER ! **Lis le texte ci-dessous et suis les conseils pour déduire le sens des mots surlignés.**

On August 15, 2024, the Indian diaspora across the globe celebrated India's 78th Independence Day with unmatched zeal and fervor. Indian-origin communities worldwide came together, showcasing their love for their homeland.

Across different corners of the world, Indian ambassadors orchestrated similar events, highlighting unity within the diaspora. From ceremonial flag-hoisting to cultural performances, these gatherings acted as home away from home for many. While exchanging stories and songs, members of the diaspora cherished their cultural heritage, reflecting on their decades-long narratives of migration and integration.

This momentous occasion underlines how far Indians have made strides beyond their motherland through cultural and communal unity. With every note of the anthem sung and every flag raised, the sentiment of pride and nostalgia connects each individual to India's limitless pursuit of freedom.

Thus, as every celebration unfolded, it became clearer: Independence Day is not just marked on calendars; it's felt deeply by Indians everywhere.

Source *indiandiaspora.org*, 2024

▲ Members of the Indian diaspora, streets of New York City.

STEP 1

Lis le texte et focalise-toi sur les **mots dérivés**.

▶ Identifie les **radicaux** et leur **sens** : ***orchestra**ted* ➜ *orchestre*.

▶ Retrouve les **suffixes** et les **préfixes** et demande-toi **comment ils influencent le sens** du mot et sa catégorie grammaticale : *limit**less*** ➜ *less* + adjectif = marque la privation.

▶ Déduis le sens de chaque mot, puis vérifie dans un **dictionnaire**.

STEP 2

Porte maintenant ton attention sur les **mots composés**.

▶ **Décompose** les mots composés en t'interrogeant sur **le sens de chaque élément**.

▶ Déduis le sens de chaque mot composé, puis vérifie dans un **dictionnaire**.

- Si tu connais le sens de chacun des éléments, interroge-toi sur **la façon dont l'un détermine l'autre** et **les précisions que cela apporte**.
- Si tu ne connais le sens que d'un des deux éléments, trouve **la nature du mot que tu ne connais pas** et replace le mot dans son contexte pour donner du sens de façon plus globale et vérifier que ton hypothèse de compréhension est pertinente.

Exemple : *decades-long narrative* ➜ assure-toi que le sens que tu identifies pour *decades-long* est pertinent par rapport à *narrative*.

HOW *to shine in...* VOCABULARY

Mémoriser le lexique

Apprendre ton vocabulaire, oui mais comment ? Il y a des techniques à utiliser !

1 Crée-toi des outils de révision

▶ Choisis la méthode qui te correspond le mieux :

- une ***mindmap*** comme dans le manuel. Pour chaque catégorie, ajoute une phrase de synthèse en essayant de regrouper tous tes mots : il est toujours plus facile d'apprendre un mot dans un contexte !
- des **cartes de vocabulaire** personnalisées comme par exemple :

1. Écris le mot en mettant en exergue la syllabe accentuée (couleur, soulignement)

2. Écris une phrase avec ce mot et identifie sa nature par 1 couleur
   - nom
   - adjectif
   - verbe
   - adverbe

household	
My household is composed by my parents and me.	family house live together

3. Tu peux associer 1 image ou 1 symbole au mot.

4. Tu peux également associer des mots clés.

TIPS
- Tu peux écrire un synonyme, un antonyme, un mode de la même famille, une expression.

TIPS
- Tu peux aussi utiliser un outil d'IA pour créer des flashcards de révision. Tuto video

▶ Au fur et à mesure de l'étude du chapitre, note les **mots clés** à retenir et classe-les par **champs lexicaux** (4 ou 5 par chapitre).

▶ Quand tu as fini de créer tes outils, pense à bien **vérifier l'orthographe** pour ne pas apprendre des mots mal orthographiés !

TIPS
- Tu peux t'inspirer de la *mindmap* du chapitre pour créer tes catégories.
- Pour chaque champ lexical, efforce-toi de trouver au moins un nom, un verbe et un adjectif.

2 Apprends, mais comment ?

▶ **Apprends des phrases** plutôt que des mots isolés : un nouveau mot hors contexte est très difficile à mémoriser. Mais si tu l'associes à une phrase, ce sera plus facile pour toi de le mémoriser. De même, quand tu dois apprendre une liste de mots, il sera plus efficace de les placer dans une phrase que de les apprendre isolément.

EXEMPLE

Traditions
- customs = habits
- heritage = legacy
- roots
- long-standing = ancient /ˈeɪnʃənt/
- nostalgic
- celebrate = commemorate
- honour /ˈɒnə/
- live on: *perdurer*
- stick to = preserve

*Traditions are **long-standing customs** and **heritage**, our **roots** in the past, which evoke a **nostalgic** feeling when we **celebrate** and **honour** them, so that they may **live on** as we **stick to** them.*

- Mémorise l'orthographe correcte des mots : pense à **épeler les mots** quand tu révises.
- Apprends les mots avec leur **prononciation**.
- **Espace tes révisions** : tu n'apprendras pas tout en une seule fois ! Par exemple, apprends une catégorie de ta *mindmap* par jour jusqu'à ta tâche finale. Chaque jour, pense à réviser les mots travaillés la veille.

TIPS

- Attention aux mots qui s'écrivent **toujours avec des majuscules** (*African-American*), aux variations entre **l'anglais britannique et l'anglais américain** (*honour v. honor*), aux **lettres muettes** (*island, subtle*), aux **doubles consonnes** (*necessary, committed*) et aux **pluriels irréguliers** (*life → lives*).
- Tu peux réécouter les mots de la *mindmap* et des encadrés *Vocabulary Spot* grâce à 🔊. Réécoute les documents audio et vidéo du chapitre pour **mémoriser la prononciation en contexte**.

Your turn to shine!

À TOI DE JOUER ! À deux, relevez ces challenges pour vérifier vos connaissances.

1 DEFINE IT!

- Chacun(e) d'entre vous choisit **5 mots du chapitre**. À tour de rôle, vous énoncez le mot et l'autre doit le définir en anglais **le plus rapidement possible**.

EXEMPLE *household → A **household** is a house and its occupants.*

2 GUESS IT!

- Chacun d'entre vous prépare **5 définitions d'un mot du chapitre**. À tour de rôle, vous proposer une définition à l'oral et l'autre doit deviner le mot **en moins de 30 secondes**.

EXEMPLE *It's a **verb** we use to say that traditions continue → live on*

- Indique à ton/ta camarade la catégorie grammaticale du mot à trouver.

3 SPELL IT!

- Chacun d'entre vous choisit **10 mots du chapitre**. À tour de rôle, vous proposer le mot et l'autre doit **l'épeler ou l'écrire** correctement.

4 LINK IT

- Chacun d'entre vous choisit **10 mots du chapitre** et les écrit sur des cartes. À tour de rôle, vous **tirez une carte** et **faites une phrase** pour expliquer le lien du mot avec le thème de l'unité.

EXEMPLE *Diaspora, because there is an important Indian diaspora.*

5 MAKE IT SOUND

- Choisissez un son et trouvez à tour de rôle un mot qui le contient. Celui qui trouve le plus de mots a gagné.

EXEMPLE [ai] *diaspora • migrate • pride • childhood • ...*

- N'oublie pas que tu as aussi de nombreux outils numériques dans ton manuel pour réviser le vocabulaire via les activités. MEMORISE your vocabulary

HOW to shine in... VOCABULARY

Utiliser le lexique : du vocabulaire pour quoi faire ?

1 Pour exprimer un point de vue

▶ Certains mots permettent de **décrire une situation** de façon plutôt neutre ou au contraire **d'exprimer un point de vue**. A toi d'analyser la situation pour savoir quel type de lexique utiliser.

TIPS

- En situation de compréhension (écrite ou oral), être attentif(ve) à ce lexique te permettra d'accéder à **des éléments de sens implicites** et de **repérer le point de vue** exprimé.
- Tu peux utiliser des **adverbes** pour **atténuer** ou **renforcer** le point de vue exprimé : *obviously, undeniably, somewhat, seemingly, etc.*

EXEMPLE

Avec des verbes de parole et d'opinion :

- Verbes neutres : *say, believe, think...*
- Verbes de paroles et d'opinion exprimant une opinion ou une conviction personnelle : *reckon, assume, claim...*

EXEMPLE

Avec des adjectifs :

- *A **long** film ➜ An **endless** film.*
- *The water is **polluted** ➜ It is **disgusting**.*

plus neutre ⟷ plus subjectif

2 Pour exprimer des nuances de sens

▶ Plus ton vocabulaire sera précis, plus tu pourras t'exprimer clairement et ainsi faire ressortir tes connaissances et **le lien entre langue et culture**.

▶ Un vocabulaire précis va aussi te permettre **d'exprimer tes idées avec plus ou moins d'intensité**.

EXEMPLE

A building?

- *If we are in Chicago ➜ a skyscraper*
- *If we are in the UK countryside ➜ a cottage*
- *If we are by a Canadian lake ➜ a cabin*
- *If we are in London ➜ a Victorian House*

EXEMPLE

- *David Bowie's influence on the music scene was **important** < **significant** < **profound** < **ground-breaking**.*

3 Pour s'adapter à la situation d'énonciation

▶ Ton vocabulaire va te permettre de **t'adapter à la situation de communication** en faisant varier les **registres de langue.**

EXEMPLE

- *As an athlete writing a message on social media: "I'm so proud to be part of the Olympics! It's a dream come true, and I can't wait to represent my country. Let's do this!! »*
- *As a country official delivering a speech: "It is with immense pride that I welcome you to the Commonwealth Games. This prestigious event is not only a celebration of sport, but also the embodiment of the spirit of unity and collaboration that transcends borders".*

4 Pour développer ton propos

▶ Un vocabulaire précis va permettre d'**enrichir tes productions** en exprimant des **détails**.

▶ Développer ta connaissance du lexique va aussi te permettre **d'éviter les répétitions** et ainsi de **donner du rythme** à ton propos.

EXEMPLE

- Level 1: *I grew up in India with all my **family**.*
- Level 2: *I grew up in India in a **joint family** with all my **relatives**.*

EXEMPLE

- *When you speak about electric cars along Road 66: cars or EVs or Vehicles.*
- *When you speak about the heirs of the Civil Rights: They keep fighting for the society to be fairer or more inclusive or more egalitarian.*

Your turn to shine!

À TOI DE JOUER ! **Lis le texte ci-dessous et suis les conseils pour déduire le sens des mots surlignés.**

1 SAY IT CLEARLY

Hollywood is a big industry that makes a lot of money by producing films. The studios invest a lot of money in movies that they think will be popular and make them a profit. They choose actors, directors, and stories that will attract a large audience. Hollywood films are shown all over the world, and they influence what people like to watch.

a. Lis ce texte afin d'identifier le **propos**.

b. Reformule-le en exprimant **ton point de vue**.

- Si tu veux exprimer un point de vue **positif**, pense à utiliser ces expressions : *high-quality • wisely • It helps bring… • it offers… etc.*
- Si tu veux **critiquer ce système**, appuie-toi sur ces expressions : *It mainly focuses on… • again and again • It prioritises … over … • There is little room for…*

2 ENRICH IT!

a. Réécris cette phrase en ajoutant une information.

GenZ people are concerned with climate issues.

b. Donne ta nouvelle proposition à ton/ta camarade. À lui/elle d'ajouter un nouvel élément à la phrase, et ainsi de suite. **Jusqu'où pourrez-vous l'enrichir ?**

- Utilise des adverbes pour insister ou nuancer : *significantly • most of the time • deeply*
- Donne des informations supplémentaires grâce à des subordonnées : *GenZ are people born after 2000. • Nowadays people know that natural resources are limited.*
- Utilise des adjectifs pour **décrire la situation :** *urgent • climate-conscious.*
- Fais des comparaisons pour mettre en évidence des évolutions : *more and more • more … than …*

3 THE FORBIDDEN WORD

a. Révise ton chapitre en choisissant des mots mystères. Pour chaque mot mystère, impose-toi 3 ou 4 mots interdits.

b. Élabore une **définition** afin de faire deviner le mot mystère à tes camarades, **sans avoir recours aux mots interdits**. Cela va te forcer à trouver des synonymes et à exprimer des nuances.

- Fais des **comparaisons** pour contourner les mots interdits et exprimer des nuances : *It's almost like … except that …• It's more recent than …*
- Pose des questions à ton/ta camarade pour l'amener à utiliser à son tour un maximum de mots de vocabulaire : *Do you know the …? • Do you remember the video …?*

4 THE FINAL CHALLENGE

a. Choisis une unité, relis la problématique de l'unité et garde ta *mindmap* sous les yeux.

b. Demande à un camarade de faire l'arbitre et de lancer le chronomètre. Tu as **deux minutes pour répondre à la problématique** en essayant d'utiliser **le plus de mots possible**. Ton/Ta camarade pourra les compter. Ensuite, échangez les rôles.

c. Envie d'un challenge supplémentaire ? Demande à ton/ta camarade de faire l'arbitre. Si tu répètes un mot de la *mindmap* plus de deux fois, tu as perdu. À toi de trouver la solution pour éviter les répétitions.

Build your English!

Exercise bank

AXE 1 REPRÉSENTATION DE SOI ET RAPPORT À AUTRUI

1 Assemble chaque mot avec son contraire.

challenge · friendly · open-minded · shy · narrow- minded · embrace · support · hostile · outgoing · conform · reject · criticise

2 Remets les lettres dans l'ordre pour obtenir des mots en lien avec l'admiration.

a. IOFASHN = trend (noun)
b. DREAMI = look up to (verb)
c. TTRSU = believe in (verb)
d. CESSUCORS = heir (noun)

3 Ajoute les lettres manquantes pour former des mots sur les apparences.

a. AP_E_ _A_C_	E	P	A	N	R
b. _I_ER_I_	Y	D	T	V	S
c. I_ _L_E_ _E	F	N	N	U	C
d. I_C_U_I_IT_	Y	N	S	V	L
e. C_R_ _CE_U_	S	U	V	A	O

4 Forme des mots en associant chaque radical à un préfixe et/ou un suffixe.

UN- · DIS-

REAL · TREND · ICON · RESPECT · TRUST · FRIEND

-SHIP · -FUL · -LESS · -ISTIC · -Y · -IC · -WORTHY · -ING

5 Remplace les mots soulignés par des synonymes.

a. James often <u>mimics</u> his friends.
b. David Bowie was an amazing <u>innovator</u>. He started so many trends.
c. I know I can tell her my secrets, she's <u>reliable</u>.
d. People's relationships have <u>changed</u> over the past years.

6 Associe les mots à leur définition.

trustworthy · relate to someone · sympathetic · identify with · self-esteem

a. Feel that you can share the feelings of someone else.
b. Be able to have a friendly relationship with someone.
c. Feeling concern about someone.
d. Someone who can be trusted and believed.
e. Favourable impression of oneself.

7 Cette jeune bloggeuse veut écrire un *post* sur l'acceptation de soi sur ses réseaux sociaux. Aide-la à rédiger un paragraphe de six lignes. Cherche la signification de ces expressions, puis utilise-les dans ton *post*.

Get along with someone
Open up to someone
Speak one's mind
Be on the same wavelength
Take someone for granted

8 Avec un(e) ami(e) anglophone, discute des caractéristiques d'un(e) vrai(e) ami(e) : *What makes a true friend?* Choisis deux mots dans chaque exercice ci-dessus pour t'aider à exprimer tes pensées.

AXE 2 VIVRE ENTRE GÉNÉRATIONS

9 Retrouve les neuf mots cachés dans la grille. Choisis-en trois et écris trois phrases sur l'axe 2.

G	O	T	R	E	S	P	E	C	T	A
P	E	Y	H	S	U	X	T	B	F	O
O	J	N	K	N	W	C	R	I	K	A
L	I	U	E	E	M	I	A	E	T	D
F	Z	R	L	R	G	O	D	B	I	V
Y	C	S	D	U	A	N	I	N	A	I
O	L	D	E	L	P	T	T	C	Y	S
J	O	E	R	M	A	L	I	L	O	E
U	N	I	O	C	D	I	O	O	U	C
P	A	R	E	N	T	S	N	E	N	V
M	O	D	E	R	N	N	O	I	G	D

10 Associe les mots par paires contraires.

modern – remember – conservative – young – progressive – different – traditional – similar – old – forget

11 Dans chaque liste, trouve l'intrus. Explique pourquoi.

a. siblings – grandparents – children – difference
b. inclusion – gap – values – respect
c. misunderstand – support – rely on – trust
d. change – progress – evolution – conflict

12 Ajoute les lettres manquantes pour retrouver les mots.

a. E_ _ER_ _NC_ — E E P X I
b. R_ _PE_ _F_L — S T C E U
c. W_ _ _ _ _ — O M S I D
d. C_N_L_ _TIN_ — C F I G O
e. RE_ _T_ _ _S — A L E I V

13 Associe les expressions suivantes à leur signification.

Look for compromise.
Bridge the generation gap.
Live in harmony.
Make the most of differences.
See things from a different perspective.

a. Reunite two generations.
b. Look at things with a different vision.
c. Find a way to satisfy everyone.
d. Live peacefully.
e. Use differences as an advantage.

14 Pour chaque mot, propose au moins un synonyme (mot ou expression) et un antonyme.

open-minded = ... ≠ ...
change = ... ≠ ...
modern = ... ≠ ...
look after = ... ≠ ...

15 Complète chaque ligne avec l'élément manquant. Aide-toi de l'exemple.

nom	adjectif	verbe
change	changing	change
communication		
		support
	dependent	
		respect

16 En tant que journaliste, rédige un court article sur : *What are the advantages and disadvantages of living in multi-generational households?* Utilise deux expressions de l'exercice 13 et un mot de chaque exercice.

Exercise bank

AXE 3 LE PASSÉ DANS LE PRÉSENT

17 Remets les lettres dans l'ordre pour trouver les mots correspondant aux définitions.

a. What you get from the past. YAGECL

b. Something that is too old and is no longer adapted. OUDATTDE

c. A movement towards the future. WORFADR

d. An important moment in history. MISTLEONE

18 Associe les étiquettes pour former des mots en lien avec la mémoire.

COMME · RE · NOR · MORATE · RE · HO · VIVE · LIVE · PRE · TIME · LESS · SERVE

19 Ces mots ont été mélangés dans le tableau. Range-les par champ lexical, puis trouve les titres.

...	...	...
history change modernisation revolution	uprising progress evolution discovery	heritage past innovation tradition

20 a. Recherche la définition de ces expressions.

social change
developing countries
technological advancement
step forward
cultural exchange

b. Interview un personnage historique de ton choix. Imagine son message pour notre époque. Combien d'expressions réussiras-tu à utiliser ?

21 Forme des mots en associant deux ou trois types d'étiquettes, en modifiant l'orthographe si nécessaire. Puis construis des phrases.

RE- · DIS- · MODERN · CULTURE · CONNECT · HISTORY · TRADITION · SOCIAL · -AL · -ICAL · -ATION · -ISE · -ION

22 Remplace les mots soulignés par des synonymes.

a. We must <u>preserve</u> Aboriginal culture.

b. The commissions often left opinions <u>polarised</u>.

c. Some people <u>reshape</u> history.

d. Stories <u>convey</u> First Nations wisdom.

23 a. Battle ! En une minute, note tous les mots qui te viennent à l'esprit en lien avec l'axe. Puis compare-les à ceux d'un(e) camarade et créez une carte mentale.

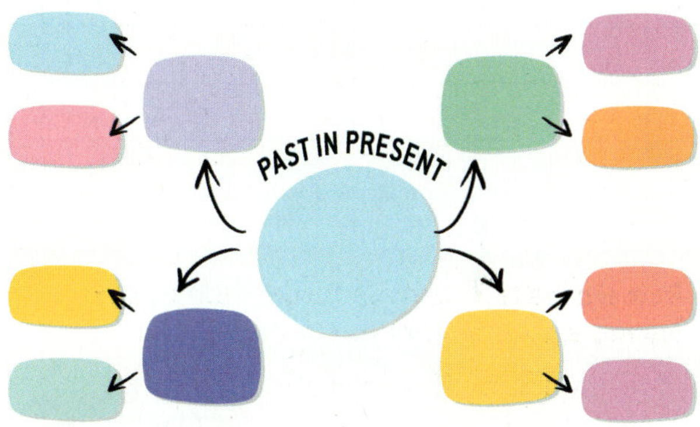

b. À l'aide de cette carte mentale, décris ce photo-montage réalisé par un photographe sud-africain, et réagis.

▲ Photomontage, Howard Klaaste, *Non-white man sits on a bench*, South Africa, 2024.

24 **Retrouve les dix mots cachés dans la grille. Choisis-en trois et écris trois phrases sur l'axe 4.**

C	H	A	L	L	E	N	G	E	T
E	T	H	I	C	S	O	S	R	R
I	Y	F	U	T	U	R	E	F	A
G	H	K	T	E	O	L	N	A	N
I	M	P	A	C	T	D	I	I	S
M	A	U	J	S	Q	E	A	R	I
A	C	T	I	O	N	E	T	C	T
A	D	V	E	R	S	I	T	Y	I
T	R	I	G	H	T	S	C	I	O
F	O	S	O	L	U	T	I	O	N

25 **Remets les lettres dans l'ordre pour trouver les mots correspondant aux définitions.**

a. Get the better of in a struggle. = VOECEROM (v)

b. Adjust yourself to situation. = TDAAP (v)

c. Capable of recovering from illness, misfortune. = RTNEIESIL (adj.)

d. Attempt to get free. = SGGURLTE (n)

26 **Trouve les lettres manquantes dans chaque mot. Aide-toi des indications données.**

a. E_ _O_ ER = give power

b. P _ O _ _ ESS_VE = having modern ideas

c. E_ _L V_ = synonym for change

d. H_ R _ S _ _ P = synonym for difficulty

27 **Retrouve l'intrus dans chaque liste. Justifie ton choix.**

a. adversity – difficulty – success – hardship

b. adapt – evolve – transform – struggle

c. challenge – progress – evolution – transformation

d. inequality – difference – disparity – inclusion

28 **À partir du mot donné trouve d'autres mots par dérivation et/ou composition.**

Dérivation	Composition
happy → unhappy	camp + site → campsite

a. sustain → ...

b. transform → ...

c. reduce → ...

d. protect → ...

e. power → ...

f. improve → ...

29 **Trouve le ou les synonymes de chaque mot ou expression.**

overcome a problem – improve – combat – address an issue – struggle – make better – transform – turn into – tackle a problem – fight – change – deal with an issue

30 **Recopie et complète ces phrases à l'aide des mots ci-dessous.**

ENVIRONMENT TECHNOLOGIES SUSTAINABLE GLOBAL WARMING URBANISATION

a. This company grows ... crops.

b. ... threatens coastal cities.

c. Uncontrolled ... destroys natural habitats.

d. Bad ... hurt the ... .

31 **Écris quatre phrases pour décrire cette image. Utilise le vocabulaire de cet axe.**

Exercise bank

AXE 5 CRÉER ET RECRÉER

32 Ajoute les lettres manquantes pour retrouver les mots.

a. _R_A_I_ _ — T C N E O
b. IN_ _IR_TI_NA_ — P A O S L
c. _E_TS_L_I_G — L N B E S
d. A_KN_ _LE_ _E — W O C D G

33 Retrouve l'intrus dans chaque liste de mots. Justifie ton choix.

a. creative – common – innovative – experimental
b. invent – recycle – create – design
c. painting – sculpture – photograph – canvas
d. prototype – creation – experiment – modify

34 Associe les mots ayant le même sens.

homage – change – alteration – model
tribute – form – pattern – shape

35 Complète les phrases avec les mots correspondant aux définitions données.

a. State of being widely known. F... (n)
b. Very popular film. B... (n)
c. Triumph. S... (n)
d. Art of writing scripts. S... (n)

36 Range les mots par champ lexical puis donne un titre à chaque groupe.

...	...	...
drama	villain	Stetson
denim	comedy	fantasy
symbol	spurs	horror
lasso	myth	hero

37 Associe les syllabes afin de reconstituer des mots sur le cinéma.

TYPE – PLAY – ADAP – SIDER – OUT
SCREEN – DOM – ARCHE – TATION – STAR

38 Associe chaque expression anglaise à son équivalent français. Aide-toi du vocabulaire que tu connais déjà.

think outside the box – avoir une idée
être un facteur de changement radical
be a game-changer
brainstorm ideas – concrétiser une idée
bring an idea to life – penser différemment
come up with an idea
réfléchir intensément à de nouvelles idées

39 Retrouve les lettres qui ont été effacées sur ce *flyer*.

In the 1900s, a group of filmm_____ began to ___ate a new kind of a__. They used the latest ______logy to tell stories. They were pion____, and they helped to create the __th of Hollywood. They also created a new kind of cele_____, the __vie star.

AXE 6 LES PAYS DU COMMONWEALTH

40 **Retrouve les dix mots cachés dans la grille.**

E	A	D	O	M	I	N	I	O	N	A
M	T	I	I	O	L	M	H	T	E	O
P	I	V	S	T	A	T	E	L	C	A
I	E	E	C	Q	U	A	X	L	U	D
R	S	R	G	E	R	S	I	E	L	V
E	E	S	A	T	W	P	S	G	T	I
R	H	I	S	T	O	R	Y	A	U	S
N	E	T	W	O	R	K	G	C	R	E
I	T	Y	F	L	V	B	E	Y	E	C
C	O	L	O	N	I	E	S	I	O	V

41 **Complète le texte suivant au sujet du Commonwealth à l'aide des mots donnés ci-dessous. Attention il y a des intrus !**

independence • cooperation • association • colonies • empire • continents • democracy • political • Commonwealth

The Commonwealth is an ... of 56 countries, most of which were once part of the British ... . It was formed to promote peace, ..., and development around the world. The idea began in the 19th century, but the modern ... took shape after World War II, when many former ... gained ... .

42 **Associe les mots deux par deux et retrouve des expressions en lien avec les pays du Commonwealth.**

shared — common — post — multi — Commonwealth

culturalism — Games — values — colonialism — history

43 **Ajoute les lettres manquantes pour retrouver les mots.**

a. _E_ _T_ _E — G H I A R

b. A_ _AN_E_ _NT — M V D C E

c. _D_ _T_ _Y — T N I I E

d. M_G_ _T_O_ — R I N A I

44 **Remets les lettres dans l'ordre pour trouver les mots correspondant aux définitions.**

a. NODCTAOSENOLII = restoration of a country's autonomy (n)

b. CENDPNIDEDNEE = self-reliance (n)

c. TAOCORENIPO = working with (n)

d. MEFROED = lack of restriction (n)

45 **Associe par deux (ou trois) les mots ayant le même sens. Puis invente trois phrases sur le Commonwealth.**

bonds — ties — cohesion — conflicts — borders — legacy — struggle — tensions — limits — fight — unity — strive — boundaries — heritage

46 **Poste l'explication de cette photo sur la page Instagram de l'agence de presse pour laquelle tu travailles.**

▲ Queen Camilla during a visit at the Commonwealth War Graves, Kenya, 2023.

Build your English!

Les verbes irréguliers

	Base verbale	Prétérit	Participe passé	Traduction
	Trois formes identiques			
C	cut /ʌ/	cut /ʌ/	cut /ʌ/	*couper*
H	hurt /ɜː/	hurt /ɜː/	hurt /ɜː/	*blesser*
L	let /e/	let /e/	let /e/	*permettre, louer*
P	put /ʊ/	put /ʊ/	put /ʊ/	*mettre, poser*
R	read /iː/	read /e/ (Orthographe inchangée mais prononciation différente)	read /e/	*lire*
S	set /e/	set /e/	set /e/	*fixer*
	shut /ʌ/	shut /ʌ/	shut /ʌ/	*fermer*
	Prétérit et participe passé identiques			
B	bend /e/	bent /e/	bent /e/	*(se) courber*
	bring /ɪ/	brought /ɔː/	brought /ɔː/	*apporter*
	build /ɪ/	built /ɪ/	built /ɪ/	*construire*
	burn /ɜː/	burnt /ɜː/	burnt /ɜː/	*brûler*
	buy /aɪ/	bought /ɔː/ (Ne pas confondre avec *boat*)	bought /ɔː/	*acheter*
C	catch /æ/	caught /ɔː/	caught /ɔː/	*attraper*
D	dream /iː/	dreamt /e/	dreamt /e/	*rêver*
F	feel /iː/	felt /e/	felt /e/	*(se) sentir, éprouver*
	fight /aɪ/	fought /ɔː/	fought /ɔː/	*se battre, combattre*
	find /aɪ/	found /aʊ/	found /aʊ/	*trouver*
G	get /e/	got /ɒ/	got /ɒ/	*obtenir*
H	have /æ/	had /æ/	had /æ/	*avoir*
	hear /ɪə/	heard /ɜː/	heard /ɜː/	*entendre*
	hold /əʊ/	held /e/	held /e/	*tenir*
K	keep /iː/	kept /e/	kept /e/	*garder*
L	lead /iː/	led /e/	led /e/	*mener, guider*
	learn /ɜː/	learnt /ɜː/	learnt /ɜː/	*apprendre*
	leave /iː/	left /e/	left /e/	*laisser, quitter*
	lend /e/	lent /e/	lent /e/	*prêter*
	light /aɪ/	lit /ɪ/	lit /ɪ/	*allumer*
	lose /uː/	lost /ɒ/	lost /ɒ/	*perdre*
M	make /eɪ/	made /eɪ/	made /eɪ/	*faire, fabriquer*
	mean /iː/	meant /e/	meant /e/	*signifier, vouloir dire*
	meet /iː/	met /e/	met /e/	*(se) rencontrer*
P	pay /eɪ/	paid /eɪ/	paid /eɪ/	*payer*
S	say /eɪ/	said /e/	said /e/	*dire*
	sell /e/	sold /əʊ/	sold /əʊ/	*vendre*
	send /e/	sent /e/	sent /e/	*envoyer*
	shoot /uː/	shot /ɒ/	shot /ɒ/	*tirer*
	sit /ɪ/	sat /æ/	sat /æ/	*être assis*
	sleep /iː/	slept /e/	slept /e/	*dormir*
	smell /e/	smelt /e/	smelt /e/	*sentir (odorat)*
	spend /e/	spent /e/	spent /e/	*dépenser, passer (le temps)*
	stand /æ/	stood /ʊ/	stood /ʊ/	*être debout*
	stick /ɪ/	stuck /ʌ/	stuck /ʌ/	*coller*
	strike /aɪ/	struck /ʌ/	struck /ʌ/	*frapper*
T	teach /iː/	taught /ɔː/	taught /ɔː/	*enseigner*
	tell /e/	told /əʊ/	told /əʊ/	*dire, raconter*
	think /ɪ/	thought /ɔː/	thought /ɔː/	*penser*
U	understand /ʌ/ə/æ/	understood /ʌ/ə/ʊ/	understood /ʌ/ə/ʊ/	*comprendre*
W	win /ɪ/	won /ʌ/	won /ʌ/	*gagner*

	Base verbale	Prétérit	Participe passé	Traduction
	Deux formes identiques			
B	beat /iː/	beat /iː/	beaten /iː/ə/	*battre*
	become /ɪ/ʌ/	became /ɪ/eɪ/	become /ɪ/ʌ/	*devenir*
C	come /ʌ/	came /eɪ/	come /ʌ/	*venir*
R	run /ʌ/	ran /æ/	run /ʌ/	*courir*
	Trois formes différentes			
B	be /iː/	was /ɒ/ / were /ɜː/	been /iː/	*être*
	bear /ɛə/	bore /ɔː/	borne /ɔː/	*supporter*
	begin /ɪ/ɪ/	began /ɪ/æ/	begun /ɪ/ʌ/	*commencer*
	bite /aɪ/	bit /ɪ/	bitten /ɪ/ə/	*mordre*
	blow /əʊ/	blew /uː/	blown /əʊ/	*souffler*
	break /eɪ/	broke /əʊ/	broken /əʊ/ə/	*casser*
C	choose /uː/	chose /əʊ/	chosen /əʊ/ə/	*choisir*
D	do /uː/	did /ɪ/	done /ʌ/	*faire*
	draw /ɔː/	drew /uː/	drawn /ɔː/	*dessiner*
	drink /ɪ/	drank /æ/	drunk /ʌ/	*boire*
	drive /aɪ/	drove /əʊ/	driven /ɪ/ə/	*conduire*
E	eat /iː/	ate /e/	eaten /iː/ə/	*manger*
F	fall /ɔː/	fell /e/	fallen /ɔː/ə/	*tomber*
	fly /aɪ/	flew /uː/	flown /əʊ/	*voler*
	forbid /ə/ɪ/	forbade /ə/eɪ/	forbidden /ə/ɪ/ə/	*interdire*
	foresee /ɔː/iː/	foresaw /ɔː/ɔː/	foreseen /ɔː/iː/	*prévoir*
	forget /ə/e/	forgot /ə/ɒ/	forgotten /ə/ɒ/ə/	*oublier*
	forgive /ə/ɪ/	forgave /ə/eɪ/	forgiven /ə/ɪ/ə/	*pardonner*
	freeze /iː/	froze /əʊ/	frozen /əʊ/ə/	*geler*
G	give /ɪ/	gave /eɪ/	given /ɪ/ə/	*donner*
	go /əʊ/	went /e/	gone /ɒ/	*aller*
	grow /əʊ/	grew /uː/	grown /əʊ/	*grandir, faire pousser*
H	hide /aɪ/	hid /ɪ/	hidden /ɪ/ə/	*(se) cacher*
K	know /nəʊ/	knew /njuː/	known /nəʊn/	*savoir, connaître*
L	lie /aɪ/	lay /eɪ/	lain /eɪ/	*être étendu*
R	ride /aɪ/	rode /əʊ/	ridden /ɪ/ə/	*aller (à cheval / vélo)*
	ring /ɪ/	rang /æ/	rung /ʌ/	*sonner*
	rise /aɪ/	rose /əʊ/	risen /ɪ/ə/	*s'élever, se lever*
S	see /iː/	saw /ɔː/	seen /iː/	*voir*
	shake /eɪ/	shook /ʊ/	shaken /eɪ/ə/	*secouer*
	show /əʊ/	showed /əʊ/	shown /əʊ/	*montrer*
	sing /ɪ/	sang /æ/	sung /ʌ/	*chanter*
	speak /iː/	spoke /əʊ/	spoken /əʊ/ə/	*parler*
	steal /iː/	stole /əʊ/	stolen /əʊ/ə/	*voler, dérober*
	swear /ɛə/	swore /ɔː/	sworn /ɔː/	*jurer*
	swim /ɪ/	swam /æ/	swum /ʌ/	*nager*
T	take /eɪ/	took /ʊ/	taken /eɪ/ə/	*prendre*
	tear /ɛə/ (ne pas confondre avec **tear** /ɪə/)	tore /ɔː/	torn /ɔː/	*déchirer*
	throw /əʊ/	threw /uː/	thrown /əʊ/	*jeter, lancer*
U	undergo /ʌ/ə/əʊ/	underwent /ʌ/ə/e/	undergone /ʌ/ə/ɒ/	*subir*
W	wake (up) /eɪ/ʌ/	woke (up) /əʊ/ʌ/	woken (up) /əʊ/ə/ʌ/	*(se) réveiller*
	wear /ɛə/	wore /ɔː/	worn /ɔː/	*porter (des vêtements)*
	write /aɪ/	wrote /əʊ/	written /ɪ/ə/	*écrire*

Build your English!

Exercise bank

1 Transforme ces phrases actives en phrases passives.

a. My Indian family bought this house in the 1990s.

b. Yesterday, they found the new model for their next campaign.

c. They build a lot of skyscrapers in Lagos.

d. They sell tickets for *Wicked, the Musical* in this shop.

2 Mets ces phrases passives à la voix active.

a. She has been made famous thanks to the «Love your body» campaign.

b. This medal was won by the British team.

c. These sneakers will be worn by the greatest stars!

d. This song was sung by Bowie's fans during the concert.

3 Recopie ces phrases en conjuguant les verbes entre parenthèses au *present perfect* ou au prétérit selon le sens et les indications de temps.

a. Cowboys (make) people dream for decades.

b. I (leave) India and (go) to the USA to study in 2013; now, I (come) back to India.

c. Many colonies (fight) for independence after WWII, they then (get) their independence.

d. My family (keep) our traditions alive since the early 1890s!

4 Identifie les formes au prétérit ou les participes passés dans ce serpent de mots. Recopie-les et indique s'il s'agit du prétérit ou du participe passé et donne la base verbale.

sentshotstrucklenthadgotburntbroughtsetcut
wonmeanteatenflewspokentakenthrew

5 Utilise cette frise pour rendre compte des événements en utilisant le prétérit, le *past perfect* et le *present perfect*.

TIPS

• Souviens-toi : le *past perfect* permet de montrer l'antériorité d'un événement par rapport à un autre au passé.

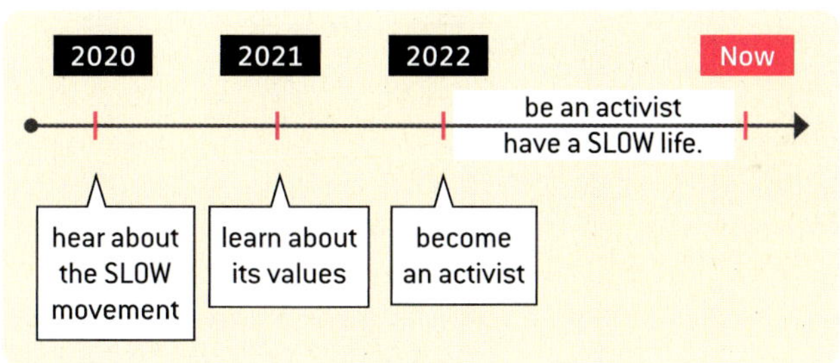

6 Recopie ce texte en conjuguant les verbes au temps qui convient : prétérit, *present perfect* ou *past perfect*.

I remember when I (be) a child, I (dream) of becoming an actor! I (spend) hours watching films.

When I finally (become) one a few years later, I (think) of all the times my mom (take) me to Hollywood to see the filming. Once, I (see) a film crew in the street and I (meet) my favourite actor! At that moment, I (feel) so excited: I (freeze) and I (stand) still, watching him. Then, he (shake) my hand and we (speak) for a few minutes.

I'm sure he (forget) me, but I (forget / not) that moment.

7 Remets les lettres dans l'ordre pour retrouver les participes passés irréguliers. Indique ensuite pour chacun sa base verbale et sa forme au prétérit.

a. VONFRIGE
b. LEPST
c. KNASHE
d. GNUR
e. GATHTU
f. TOLS
g. NIRVED
h. GUATCH
i. WNLOB

8 Utilise chaque verbe de l'exercice précédent dans une phrase, à sa forme prétérit ou participe passé (voix passive, *present* ou *past perfect*).

9 Retrouve 6 formes de participes passés et 10 formes de prétérit. Pour chaque verbe trouvé, indique de quelle forme il s'agit et donne sa base verbale et sa traduction.

R	T	H	R	O	W	N	K	R
I	F	E	L	L	B	A	N	O
S	O	P	W	R	O	T	E	D
E	R	A	H	B	L	E	W	E
N	G	I	V	E	N	P	B	T
H	A	W	O	K	E	N	E	O
I	V	A	C	H	O	S	E	R
D	E	U	F	L	O	W	N	E

10 Assemble les étiquettes afin de retrouver pour chaque verbe la base verbale, la forme prétérit et le participe passé. Quel est l'intrus ?

SANG — LEND — FALL — FORGOT — SEEN
SUNG — LENT — FALLEN — FEEL — LEFT
SING — FORGET — FELL — SEE — LENT
SAW — FORGOTTEN — FELT — FELT

11 **Recopie et complète les verbes au prétérit avec les lettres manquantes. Aide-toi des bases verbales entre parenthèses si besoin.**

a. They st...d up against oppression. (stand)

b. I h...r... that the housing prices in London r...e last year. (hear / rise)

c. My father t...l... me he m... Aborigines whenever he went to Australia. (tell / meet)

d. Apartheid t...u...t us all a lesson about discrimination. (teach)

12 ***Battle!* Tu as 30 secondes pour réaliser chacun des défis suivants. Compare ensuite avec ton voisin : celui qui trouve le plus de mots a gagné.**

a. Trouve le maximum de participes passés finissant par en *-en*.

b. Trouve un maximum de verbes irréguliers dont les 3 formes sont identiques.

c. Trouve un maximum de verbes irréguliers dont le *d* final devient *t*.

13 **Rends compte de la vie de ce cowboy en te servant des éléments suggérés.**

teach him to ride a horse (father)
grow up in the West • first ride at 3 years old
buy ranch at 20 years old • catch a thief at 22

His father taught him to ride a horse, and he first...

14 **Rapporte les propos suivants en utilisant un verbe introducteur au passé. Utilise un verbe différent à chaque fois.**

a. I give you my word, I swear to fight for equality! (Madiba)

b. These days, I see sneakerheads everywhere in the street, they wear expensive sneakers. (a journalist)

c. I dream of winning a medal. (an athlete at the Commonwealth games)

d. Did David Bowie sing this song? Did he write it? (a fan)

15 **Remets ces paroles au discours direct.**

a. Sara said she had a flat in London but the rent rose every month.

b. Jack told me he fought every day to reduce his waste and that he regularly bought second-hand clothes and sold his on the internet.

c. My great grandma told me she had met Gandhi.

d. John said he had won the medal because he had swum faster than the other competitors.

16 **La snowboardeuse Brenna Huckaby a participé à la campagne #AerieReal célébrant la *body positivity*. Utilise les verbes irréguliers ci-dessous conjugués aux temps appropriés pour rédiger un *post Instagram* sur son expérience lors de cette campagne.**

learn a lot • teach kindness • feel confident and proud • write about the experience • sell plus-size clothes

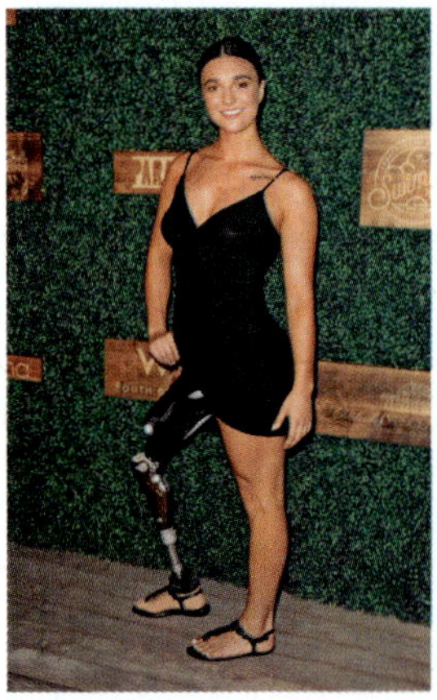

◄ Brenna Huckaby walks the red carpet at the 2018 Sports Illustrated Swimsuit show, Florida, July 15, 2018.

17 **Tu écris une biographie de Ghandi. Aide-toi de cette image et des verbes suggérés pour en rédiger un passage.**

fight for independence • teach peace • bring pride and hope • lead the Indians • swear to help

▲ Statues depicting Gandhi at the head of the Salt March, Delhi (India).

Les sons

Voici les symboles phonétiques de l'anglais.

Il existe des sons longs et des sons courts en anglais. Les sons longs sont signalés par les deux points **:** Prononce bien les voyelles courtes et les voyelles longues, autrement le sens du mot n'est pas le même !

VOYELLES

/æ/	hat	/hæt/
/ɑː/	car	/kɑː/
/ə/	ago	/əˈɡəʊ/
/e/	bed	/bed/
/iː/	sea	/siː/
/ɪ/	fill	/fɪl/
/ɒ/	not	/nɒt/
/ɔː/	door	/dɔː/
/ʊ/	put	/pʊt/
/uː/	moon	/muːn/
/ʌ/	sun	/sʌn/
/ɜː/	burn	/bɜːn/

= 2 sons voyelles à la suite !

DIPHTONGUES

/eɪ/	page	/peɪdʒ/
/aɪ/	five	/faɪv/
/ɔɪ/	boy	/bɔɪ/
/əʊ/	no	/nəʊ/
/aʊ/	now	/naʊ/
/ɪə/	hear	/hɪə/
/eə/	hair	/heə/
/ʊə/	sure	/ʃʊə/

= 3 sons voyelles à la suite !

TRIPHTONGUES

/aɪə/	fire	/faɪə/
/eɪə/	player	/ˈpleɪə/
/ɔɪə/	royal	/ˈrɔɪəl/
/aʊə/	flower	/ˈflaʊə/
/əʊə/	lower	/ˈləʊə/

Elles sont plus « explosives » qu'en français. Mais certaines peuvent être muettes : *climb, doubt, subtle, muscle, handkerchief, Wednesday…*

CONSONNES

/p/	peace	/piːs/
/b/	bug	/bʌɡ/
/t/	tea	/tiː/
/d/	doll	/dɒl/
/k/	colour	/ˈkʌlə/
/ɡ/	great	/ɡreɪt//
/m/	machine	/məˈʃiːn/
/n/	new	/njuː/
/ŋ/	song	/sɒŋ/
/f/	fool	/fuːl/
/v/	village	/ˈvɪlɪdʒ/
/θ/	thin	/θɪn/
/ð/	there	/ðeə/
/s/	son	/sʌn/
/z/	zero	/ˈzɪərəʊ/
/ʃ/	shop	/ʃɒp/
/tʃ/	change	/tʃeɪndʒ/
/ʒ/	leisure	/ˈleʒə/
/dʒ/	journalist	/ˈdʒɜːnəlɪst/
/r/	root	/ruːt/
/h/	hello	/heˈləʊ/
/w/	well	/wel/
/j/	yellow	/ˈjeləʊ/
/l/	lie	/laɪ/

Consonnes sonores : /b/ /d/ /ɡ/ /v/ /ð/ /z/ /ʒ/ /dʒ/ /w/ /m/ /n/ /ŋ/ /r/ /j/ /l/

Consonnes sourdes : /p/ /t/ /k/ /f/ /θ/ /s/ /ʃ/ /tʃ/ /h/

Évite le piège du **<th>** : jamais /s/ ni /z/, mais toujours la langue contre les dents… Avec un peu d'entraînement, c'est facile !

Prononce le **<h>** au début des mots sauf dans *honour, hour, honest, heir*.

ACCENT DE MOT

Accent principal : /ˈ/ → /ɪkˈstrɔːdɪnri/ extraordinary

Accent secondaire : /ˌ/ → /ˌɪntəˈfɪə/ interfere

Your turn to shine!

Tu penses que tu ne sais pas prononcer correctement ? Suis ces conseils pour t'entraîner et tu verras, ce n'est pas si difficile !

STEP 1

Pour bien prononcer l'anglais, il est utile d'apprendre les **symboles phonétiques**. Observe-les p. 156 et entraîne-toi à les **répéter** en écoutant les audios.

STEP 2

Anticipe la prononciation des mots que tu rencontres ! Il y a quelques règles pour deviner la prononciation des sons voyelles notamment.

- Par exemple, le **<i>** dans *write* se prononce /ai/ alors que dans *written* il se prononce /ɪ/. Pourquoi ? Car dans *written*, le **<i>** est suivi de deux consonnes, ce qui l'empêche de diphtonguer !
En revanche, dans *write*, **<i>** est suivi d'une consonne et du **<e>** final.
- La lettre **<a>** se prononce /ɑː/ lorsqu'elle est suivie d'un **<r>** sans lettre après elle comme dans *car*, *bar*, *far*… Lorsqu'elle est suivie d'un **<e>** comme dans *care*, *bare*, *fare*, elle diphtongue.
- Tu peux repérer les combinaisons de lettres qui reviennent souvent, comme les lettres **<ower>** qui se prononcent presque toujours /aʊə/ comme dans *flower*, *power*, *tower*… (mais pas dans *lower* /'ləʊə/ dont le radical est *low* !).

STEP 3

N'aie pas peur de te lancer ! **Entraîne-toi devant un miroir** à prononcer des mots et regarde les **mouvements** que font ta bouche et tes lèvres. Exagère ces mouvements et garde-les en mémoire lorsque tu t'exprimes en anglais.

Train and memorise!

1 Anticipe la prononciation des lettres en rouge, puis écoute et classe les mots en fonction de leur prononciation.

/ɪ/	/ɪə/	/iː/	/aɪ/

screen • ride • dream • script • movie • musical • society • time • green • ecological • divide • sneakers • empire • exhibition • here • rise • healing • year

2 a. Recopie ces mots et entoure d'une même couleur ceux dont les lettres en rouge ont la même prononciation. Un mot n'a pas de son commun avec les autres, lequel ?

cast • farm • American • evolution • culture • Australia • sustainable • revolution • shape • family • ecological • fame • cars

b. Écoute et vérifie.

3 Lis les mots suivants en anticipant leur prononciation.

a. Écoute, répète, puis entraine-toi à prononcer ces mots.

fiction • evolution • nature • culture • ecology • figure • biodiversity • question • beauty • representation • generation • consume • sport • relation

b. Que remarques-tu pour :
- les mots finissant en *-tion* ?
- les mots finissant en *-ture* ?

Attention, ces mots s'écrivent (presque) comme en français mais ne se prononcent pas pareil !

Crédits photographiques

Couverture : Sergii Figurnyi /AdobeStock (New York) ; StockImageFactory.com/shutterstock (famille indienne) ; Bd IR Stone/Shutterstock

Intérieur :15 b © The Open University ; 16 h g Photo12/Alamy/Witold Skrypczak ; 16 h d Photo12/Alamy/D. Hurst ; 16 b g Photo12/Alamy/darekm101, RooM the Agency ; 16 b d Lubomir/AdobeStock ; 17 h Benny Dayal/Shefali Alvares/DR ; 17 b Collection Christophel / Kanchana 3, 2019. Réal.Lawrence Raghavendra © Raghavendra Productions / Sun Pictures ; 18 g Phumelele Tshabalala ; 18 h d Sokari Douglas Camp / Photo © Jonathan Greet ; 18 b d Brian Otieno ; 19 © Haka Tours ; 20-21 COLLECTION CHRISTOPHEL / ONCE UPON A TIME IN HOLLYWOOD, Quentin Tarantino, 2019 © Sony Pictures Entertainment - Heyday Films - Visiona Romantica ; 21 d © Tidbits of History / DR ; 22 h Sean Pavone / Alamy /Photo12 ; 22 b Eric Charbonneau/Getty Images for Warner Bros ; 23 Collection Christophel / La la land 2017 Réal. Damien Chazelle. © Black Label Media / Gilbert films / Impostor Pictures / Marc Platt Productions / Summit Entertainment ; 26 h From The Queen of Sugar Hill. Copyright © 2024 by William Morrow Paperbacks. DR ; 26 b Aliah Anderson/ Getty Images AFP ; 27 COLLECTION CHRISTOPHEL / THE BRUTALIST 2024 de Brady Corbet, avec Adrien Brody, Guy Pearce, Joe Alwyn, Felicity Jone,s Raffey Cassidy, Alessandro Nivola. © Universal - Brookstreet Pictures - Kaplan Morrison - Intake Films - Andrew Lauren Productions - Lip Sync - Richmond Pictures - Meyohas Studio - Carte Blanche - Pierce Capital Entertainment ; 28 Eloi_Omella/iStockphoto ; 28 (Oscar) Cedric Gibbons / DR ; 28 (Walk of Fame) Periera and Luckman / DR ; 29 h COLLECTION CHRISTOPHEL / BABYLON 2022 de Damien Chazelle P.J. Byrne, Olivia Hamilton. © Scott Garfield - Paramount Pictures - C2 Motion Picture Group - Marc Platt Productions - Material Pictures - Organism Pictures - Wild Chickens Productions 1920's / DR ; 29 bas COLLECTION CHRISTOPHEL / ONCE UPON A TIME IN HOLLYWOOD 2019 de Quentin Tarantino Brad Pitt, Leonardo DiCaprio, Al Pacino. © Andrew Cooper - Sony Pictures Entertainment - Heyday Films - Visiona Romantica ; 30 COLLECTION CHRISTOPHEL / ONCE UPON A TIME IN HOLLYWOOD 2019 de Quentin Tarantino. Margot Robbie, Robert Richardson (directeur photo, à la caméra) sur le tournage /© Andrew Cooper - Sony Pictures Entertainment - Heyday Films - Visiona Romantica ; 31 John Shearer/WireImage/ Getty ; 32 Kevin Winter/Getty Images/AFP ; 33 fabioderby/iStockphoto ; 34 Photo12/Alamy/ AFF ; 35 From Warner Bros.: Hollywood's Ultimate Backlot. Copyright © 2014 by Taylor Trade Publishing/DR ; 37 From The Sixth Gun Volume 2: Crossroads. Copyright © 2011 by Oni Press/DR ; 38 © American Experience | PBS/DR ; 39 © Samuel Goldwyn Films / Tara Cowell-Plain / 2024/DR ; 41 Kevin Mazur/Getty Images ; 43 OwenPrice/IStock ; 44, 46 b COLLECTION CHRISTOPHEL / WICKED 2024 de Jon M. Chu Cynthia Erivo. D'après le roman de Gregory Maguire, d'après les personnages créés par L. Frank Baum © Universal Pictures - Marc Platt Productions ; 45 Collection Christophel / Le Magicien d'Oz (The wizard of Oz), 1939 réal. Victor Fleming. Judy Garland © Action Gitanes ; 46 h © Headline / 2024/DR ; 47 © WICKED The Musical/DR ; 48-49 Everett Collection / Aurimages/ West Side Story - Dir : Jerome Robbins, Robert Wise (1961) Natalie Wood, Richard Beymer, 1961 / DR ; 48 bas From Shakespeare's Romeo and Juliet: A Graphic Novel. Copyright © 2024 by Franklin Watts/ DR ; 50-51 Visuals Stock / Alamy / Photo 12 ; 50 b © MEA / 2021/DR ; 51 © Let's Go/DR ; 52 h Dimple Bhati/ iStockphoto ; 52 b Ghajendrra Bhati/ AdobeStock ; 53 COLLECTION CHRISTOPHEL / The Namesake, 2007 Réalisatrice Mira Nair / © Fox Searchlight Pictures / Cine Mosaic ; 54 h © The Oxford Union ; 54 b COLLECTION CHRISTOPHEL © CBS - Warner Bros. Television - Chuck Lorre Productions THE BIG BANG THEORY série TV créée par Chuck Lorre et Bill Prady 2007- USA affiche américaine de la saison 2 ; 55 Idrees MOHAMMED / AFP ; 56 Photo12/Alamy/Dinodia Photos RM, Dinodia Photos ; 57 Santosh Varky / Alamy / Photo12 ; 58 stockpexel/Shutterstock ; 59 Ira Berger/Alamy/Photo12 ; 61 Imageplotter/ Alamy Live News/Photo12 ; 63 © NewsHour Productions LLC ; 64 © harshibar / DR ; 65 Photo12/Alamy/Dinodia Photos RM, Dinodia Photos ; 66 Photo12/Alamy/Vuk Valcic ; 67 valdisskudre/iStockphoto ; 68 h © IWC Media / DR ; 68 b krblokhin/iStockphoto ; 69 h Standard by Ruth Bloomfield ; 69 bas © Politics JOE ; 70 From Number 11*. Copyright © 2016 by PENGUIN / DR ; 71 The Flatshare © 2019 by Flatiron Books ; 73 h Delpixart/ iStockphoto ; 73 b Photo12/Alamy/Vuk Valcic ; 74 © Houston National Insurance ; 75 I LOVE LUCY © Desilu Studios/DR ; 76 h Father Knows Best ; 76 b Embassy Television / Columbia Pic (c) CHRISTOPHEL ; 77 Kathy Hutchins/Shutterstock ; s_buckley/Shutterstock ; DFree/ Shutterstock ; 78-79 Nathan Denette/CP/ABACAPRESS.COM ; 78 m © Elisplace ; 80-81 © Good American/DR ; 81 Lustre Art Group /AdobeStock ; 82 hg COLLECTION CHRISTOPHEL / My week with Marilyn 2012, Réal. Simon Curtis. Michelle Williams. © Lipsync Productions / Trademark Films ; 82 hd © 5 Points Records/DR ; 82 m © RuPaul's Drag Race 2015/DR ; 83 h Alberto Rodriguez/GA/The Hollywood Reporter via Getty Images ; 83 bas Vittorio Zunino Celotto / GETTY IMAGES EUROPE / Getty Images via AFP ; 84 h © The Take/DR ; 84 bas Photo12/Alamy/Doug Peters ; 85 Aeria/DR ; 86 Hulton Archive/Getty ; 87 h © Scripp News / DR ; 87 b © Channel 4 News / 2013 / DR ; 88 Photo12/Alamy/AlessandroBiascioli ; 89 PeopleImages.com - Yuri A/Shutterstock ; 92 h Photo12/Alamy ; 92 mg Jim Spellman/ WireImage/Getty ; 92 md et bas Dfree/Shutterstock ; 93 © Teen Vogue / DR ; 94 © CVS Health ; 95 FabrikaSimf/Shutterstock ; 96 The Origins of Sneakers by PBS Voices ; 96 g © Matthew Laurence Knott/DR ; 96 d © Mimi Yoon / DR ; 97 Photo12/Alamy/Landmark Media ; 98 h Frank Micelotta Archive /Hulton Archive/Getty ; 98 b JEFF HAYNES / AFP ; 99 Michael Ochs Archives/Getty Images ; 100 © Puma / Fenty / 2024/DR ; 101 © furyblades.com/ Image générée par un outil d'IA ; 103 © Run DMC / DR ; 104 g DR ; 104 d Photo12/Alamy/ adrian lourie ; 105 © Vitoria Bas/DR ; 106 g © The Advocate / 2020 / DR ; 106 d Simone Joyner/Getty Images ; 107 g Kevin Winter/Getty Images for The Recording Academy ; 107 d Lynn Goldsmith/Corbis/VCG via Getty Images ; 108-109 Peter Nahum at The Leicester Galleries, London / Bridgeman Images ; 108 Photo12/Alamy/ICP, incamerastock ; 109 h National Trust/John Pittwood / Bridgeman Images ; 109 b Photo12/Heritage Images/Fine Art Images ; 110-111 Per-Anders Pettersson/Getty Images ; 111 © NewsHour Productions LLC ; 112 Keystone-France/Gamma-Keystone via Getty Images) ; 113 From Nelson Mandela: The Authorized Comic Book. Copyright © 2009 by W. W. Norton & Company. DR ; 114 DR ; 115 Kwazulu-NataMuseum Instagram/DR ; 116 © Rise/DR ; 117 h © AFP News Agency/ DR ; 117 m © eNCA ; 118 J. Countess/Getty Images ; 119 h Susan Winters Cook/Getty Images ; 119 b Gallo Images / GETTY IMAGES EUROPE / Getty Images via AFP ; 122 Arun P V/Alamy ; 123 © eNCA ; 124 © 60 Minutes / CBS / DR ; 125 Scott Detrow / NPR ; 126 Grant Faint/Getty ; 127 Alyssa Mason/DR ; 128 h Emily Wurramara / NITV/DR ; 128 b Wendell Teodoro /Getty/AFP ; 129 © Communities at Work/DR ; 130 h © Indigenous Literacy Foundation/DR ; 130 b © Aboriginal Nations/Languages in NSW/DR ; 131 Don Arnold/Getty ; 133 h Dylan Burns / AFL Photos / GETTY IMAGES ASIAPAC / Getty Images via AFP ; 133 b chameleonseye/iStockphoto ; 134 g Taylor Swift on Instagram ; 134 d George Rogers/SIPA ; 135 Max Mumby/Indigo/Getty Images ; 136 Photo by Jeremy Selwyn - WPA Pool/Getty Images ; 137 Photo by Rota/ Anwar Hussein/Getty Images ; 138-139 f11photo/AdobeStock ; 138 de haut en bas Photo12/Alamy/Gina Rodgers/ Bertrand Goldberg / DR ; 4kclips/ AdobeStock / Adrian Smith / DR ; SOMATUSCANI/AdobeStock/ Fazlur Khan, Bruce Graham / DR ; 139 ht Photo12/Alamy/Richard Ellis/ Fazlur Khan, Bruce Graham/DR ; 139 b © WTTW/ DR ; 140-141 Jae C. Hong/AP/ SIPA Press ; 141 © CBS 8 San Diego/DR 141 © CBS 8 San Diego/DR ; 142 h Bettmann/Getty ; 142 m Tanarch/Shutterstock ; 142 b Granger Coll NY ; 143 Loving 2016 Real Jeff Nichols. Collection Christophel © Raindog films / Big beach films ; 144 Let the children march / Monica Clark-Robinson / Frank Morrison/DR ; 145 Zuma Press/Maxppp ; 146 h EPA/MAXppp ; 146 b Harry How/Getty Images North America/AFP ; 147 Image Press Agency/SIPA USA/SIPA ; 149 Andrew Harnik,/AP ; 152 Andrew Harnik,/AP ; 154 © CBS News Miami/DR ; 155 UN Photo/Eskinder Debebe/DR ;156 © i-D/DR ; 157 © Chippendale School of Furniture/DR ; 158 © TeamRepair/DR ; 159 © shewearsfashion / DR ; 160 © Express UK / 2024/DR ; 161 © Kids Against Plastic ; 163 h Renata Angerami/ iStock ; 163 b © Junk Kouture/Getty ; 164 Juno/Stocksy/AdobeStock ; 165 Photo12/Alamy/ ZUMA Press, ZUMA Press, Inc. ; 166 Kehinde Temitope Odutayo /iStockphoto ; 167 DR ; 168-169 Photo12/Alamy/Martina Birnbaum ; 168 drmakkoy/Getty ; 169 electricroute66. com ; 170-171 Christopher Furlong / GETTY IMAGES EUROPE / Getty Images via AFP ; 171 © Euronews ; 172 DR ; 173 b Photo12/Alamy/Lordprice Collection ; 174 PVDE / Bridgeman Images ; 175 h Sharif Shaik/DR ; 175 m Pictorial Press Ltd/Alamy ; 177 © Newsweek/DR ; 179 Photo12/Alamy/Imageplotter Travel ; 182 Photo12/Ann Ronan Picture Library ; 183 DR ; 184 Photo12/Alamy/Classic Image ; 186 MICHAEL STEELE / GETTY IMAGES ASIAPAC / Getty Images via AFP ; 187 hairul_nizam/Shutterstock ; 188 Photo12/Alamy/WENN, WENN Rights Ltd ; 189 m Mark Nolan/Getty Images/ AFP ; 190 Chris Jackson/Getty Images ; 191 © Commonwealth Sport ; 193 Michael Dodge / Intermittent/Getty via AFP ; 194 g Photo12/ Alamy/Peter Horree ; 194 d © Opentiera/DR ; 197 Leonardo Cendamo/Getty Images ; 198-199 ChameleonsEye/Shutterstock ; 199 © NZ Parliament/DR ; 200 Reprise p. 136 ; 201 Stefan Rousseau/PA Images ; 202 Santosh Varky / Alamy /Photo12 ; 203 © CBS Mornings / DR ; 204 Reprise p. 57 ; 205 Reprise p.85 ; 207 NBCUniversal/DR ; 210 triloks/iStick ; 211 Visuals Stock/Alamy ; 212 Donald Cooper/Alamy ; 213 Allen.G/Shutterstock ; 215 © CartoonStock ; 221 © TVO Today/DR ; 223 ANI/DR ; 224 sa-photo/Image générée à l'aide de l'IA ; 227 eamesBot/Shutterstock ; 229 SHUTTERSTOCK/KPDMedia ; 230 © Howard Klaaste (Photomontage) ; 233 Pool/Getti Images ; 237 d Antonov Maxim/Shutterstock ; 237 gh Photo12/Alamy/Media Punch, MediaPunch Inc ; 237 gb Arthur Simoes/Shutterstock. + Freepik ; 29, 43, 58, 59, 60, 62, 89, 90, 91, 102m, 102b, 103h, 120, 121, 132, 160, 178, 228, 229, 231, 233, 217, 219, 220, 239

Crédits des textes

23 Collection Christophel / La la land 2017 Réal. Damien Chazelle. © Black Label Media / Gilbert films / Impostor Pictures / Marc Platt Productions / Summit Entertainment ; 24 h © iNews ; 24 m © Complex ; 24 b © Tampabay ; 25 © 20th Century Fox / Ethan Coen / 1991 / DR ; 26 From The Queen of Sugar Hill. Copyright © 2024 by William Morrow Paperbacks. DR ; 27 Kelsey Weekman, 2024 ; 35 From Warner Bros.: Hollywood's Ultimate Backlot. Copyright © 2014 by Taylor Trade Publishing/DR ; 39 © The Atlantic ; 40 From No Excuses: A Steamy Older Heroine Grumpy Vs Sunshine Small Town Romance (Willow Creek: A Small Town Romance Series). Copyright © 2024 by Andrea Jenelle. DR ; 41 Max Berlinger / GQ ; 45 From The Wonderful Wizard of Oz by L. Franck Baum / DR ; 46 ht From Wicked. Copyright © 1995 Gregory Maguire. DR ; 46 b © WICKED The Musical / DR ; 49 From These Violent Delights. Copyright © 2020 by Margaret K. McElderry Books. DR ; 53 The Namesake by Jhumpa Lahiri. Copyright Houghton Mifflin Harcourt. ; 55 Sanya Jain / The Hindustan Times ; 56 h © HuffPost by Gaura S. Majmudar ; 56 b From Dancing in the Family: An Unconventional Memoir of Three Women © 2005 by Houghton Mifflin Harcourt ; 65 © Today / DR ; 67 Elsie McDowell / The Guardian Foundation ; 68 © GFY / DR ; 69 Standard by Ruth Bloomfield ; 70 From Number 11*. Copyright © 2016 by PENGUIN. DR ; 71 The Flatshare © 2019 by Flatiron Books ; 75 © Peabody Awards / DR ; 76 Melissa Camacho. Common Sense Media ; 78 The Guardian ; 82 Copyright The Fashion Guide of Marian ; 84 © Independent ; 85 Indigo 9 digital by Tricia McKinnon / 2024 ; 86 © Essence / DR ; 95 Racquel Coral / Chicago Defender / DR ; 97 From Cottonable ; 98 Copyright High Snobiety ; 101 Ankitamishra in Fury Blades. 2024 ; 105 © meer / DR ; 107 From CWA ; 109 Amina Khan in Artic, 2023 ; 114 Terrestrial things / Kwela / Snailpress / 2002 / DR ; 116 © Rise / DR ; 125 Scott Detrow / NPR ; 127 © ABC Australia / DR ; 128 Copyright Pedestrian TV, 2023 ; 131 Samuel Wirrdapi Stubbs ; 135 Business Insider ; 136 © Harpers Bazaar / DR ; 143 From Finding a Way Home: Mildred and Richard Loving and the Fight for Marriage Equality by Larry Dane Brimner, 2020 ; 144 I Woke Up with My Mind on Freedom by Janice Kelsey ; 147 Amanda Garman on Instagram ; 155 © Ruby Bridges, This is Your Time / 2020 / DR ; 156 © The Conversation / DR ; 156 The Chippendale School ; 157 From therestartproject.org ; 166 Obi Ndadika in Hamilton CS, 2022 ; 167 © Africa News / DR ; 169 h © Heinrich.senate.gov / DR ; 169 b © electricroute66.com ; 172 From Dishonored. Copyright © 1998 by Grand Central Publishing/DR ; 174 © Better Protest / DR ; 176 From Cracking India by Bapsi Sidhwa / 1998/DR ; 185 Trapped in History: Kenya, Mau Mau and Me ; 187 Adapted from the Fun Kids Live website ; 188 © Polo Valley / DR ; 190 John Duerden / dw.com ; 194, 195, 196, 197 The Train from Rhodesia by Nadine Gordimer / 1952 ; 199 Professor Margaret Mutu & Aperahama Edwards/DR

Direction éditoriale : Marie Lucas
Édition : Christelle Pelletier, assistée par Gaspard Jolly et Louise Noury
Édition numérique : Pauline Boyeau
Relecture : Seonaid Cruickshank
Iconographie : Candice Renault
Conception de la maquette : Élise Launay
Conception de la couverture : Clémentine Largant
Mise en pages : Laure Gros, Patrick Droit, Charline Husson
Illustrations : Coline Girard, Gonzalo Izquierdo
Infographies : Marie Van Der Marlière, Johanna Crainmark, Charline Husson

N° de Projet : 10302098 - Dépot Légal : Mai 2025 - Achevé d'imprimer en Mars 2025 par Rotolito S.p.A. Italy

Les programmes de la classe de 2de

Les programmes de 2de en anglais sont organisés autour de 6 axes culturels, déclinés chacun en 4 objets d'étude qui te permettront de progresser en anglais tout en découvrant la diversité culturelle des pays anglophones !

En anglais LVA, le niveau du CECRL visé en fin de 2de est B1+. En LVB, le niveau visé est A2+.

	Compréhension de l'oral et de l'écrit	Expression orale et écrite	Interaction orale et écrite,médiation
A2+	• Je peux repérer et comprendre les informations principales relevant de situations prévisibles ou de sujets familiers, exprimées dans un vocabulaire fréquent dans une gamme variée de textes, ainsi que dans des conversations ou émissions, à condition, en compréhension de l'oral, que le propos soit clair et lent.	• Je peux présenter ou décrire des aspects de mon environnement quotidien, tels que les gens, les lieux, des projets, des habitudes et occupations journalières, des activités passées et des expériences personnelles. • Je peux donner des explications pour justifier pourquoi une chose me plaît ou me déplaît, et indiquer mes préférences en faisant des comparaisons de façon simple et directe.	• Je peux interagir avec une aisance raisonnable dans des situations bien structurées ou prévisibles. • Je peux faire face à des échanges courants ou sur des thématiques connues sans effort excessif. • Je peux poser des questions, répondre à des questions et échanger des idées et des renseignements sur des sujets familiers dans des situations familières et prévisibles. • Je peux transmettre des informations pertinentes présentes dans des textes informatifs bien structurés, assez courts et simples, à condition qu'elles portent sur des sujets familiers et prévisibles.
B1+	• S'agissant de sujets familiers, je peux suivre une présentation et y distinguer les idées principales des détails qui s'y rapportent ainsi que comprendre l'information contenue dans la plupart des documents enregistrés ou radiodiffusés d'intérêt courant, à condition que la langue soit standard et clairement structurée. • Je peux comprendre des textes factuels ou courts sur des sujets familiers ou d'intérêt courant dans lesquels les gens donnent leur point de vue, lire dans des journaux et des magazines des comptes rendus de films, de livres, etc., qui ont été écrits pour un large public et en comprendre les points principaux. • Je peux identifier le schéma argumentatif suivi sans en comprendre nécessairement le détail.	• Je peux développer une histoire, décrire assez précisément un événement, exprimer clairement mes sentiments par rapport à quelque chose que j'ai vécu et expliquer pourquoi je ressens ces sentiments. • Je peux développer une argumentation suffisamment bien pour être comprise sans difficulté la plupart du temps en donnant des raisons simples pour justifier un point de vue sur un sujet familier. • Je peux rédiger une critique ou un compte rendu structuré sur un film, un livre ou un programme télévisé, en utilisant une large gamme de structures adaptées et un vocabulaire assez étendu.	• Je peux démarrer une conversation sur des sujets familiers et aider à la poursuivre en posant des questions assez spontanées sur une expérience ou un événement particulier, et exprimer mes réactions et mon opinion. • Je peux soutenir des conversations relativement longues sur des sujets d'intérêt général, à condition que l'interlocuteur fasse un effort pour faciliter la compréhension. • Je peux résumer (en langue Y), l'information et les arguments contenus dans des textes (en langue X), sur des sujets d'ordre général ou personnel. • Je peux résumer (en langue Y) un court récit ou un article, un discours, une discussion, un entretien ou un reportage (en langue X) et répondre à des questions portant sur des détails. • Je peux expliquer les différents rôles des participants lors d'un travail collectif, donner des consignes claires pour un travail en groupe. • Je peux demander à mon interlocuteur(rice) de préciser son propos. • Je peux demander aux parties en désaccord d'expliquer leur point de vue et peut répondre brièvement à ces explications, à condition que le sujet me soit familier et que les interlocuteurs(rices) parlent clairement.

92 avenue de France, 75702 Paris cedex 13 - contact@nathan.fr - ISBN 978-2-09-5042813 - code éditeur: 264265

Nouveau programme 2025

W0370884

Shine Brighter

A2+ > B1+

2de

Sous la direction de **Corinne Escales**

Corinne Escales
IA – IPR
Académie de Versailles

Élodie Deglos
IA - IPR
Académie de Versailles

Sabrina Benkhaled
Professeure certifiée
Lycée polyvalent Romain Rolland, Goussainville (95)
Formatrice, Académie de Versailles

Cindy Ferrere
Professeure agrégée
ND Les Oiseaux, Verneuil sur Seine (78)
Académie de Versailles

Ève Grandin
Professeure agrégée
Lycée Bellevue, Le Mans (72)
Académie de Nantes

Lynda Itouchène
Professeure agrégée
Lycée Jean-Jacques Rousseau, Sarcelles (95)
Formatrice, Académie de Versailles

Hadrien Morand
Professeur agrégé
Collège de Sèvres (92)
Formateur, Académie de Versailles

Sophie Robin-Boudjenane
Professeure agrégée
Lycée Louis Bascan, Rambouillet (78)
Formatrice, Académie de Versailles

Odette Toneatti
Professeure agrégée
Collège-lycée Le Caousou, Toulouse (31)
Académie de Toulouse

Les auteurs remercient chaleureusement Patrick Marques, enseignant d'Histoire-Géographie au lycée Anita-Conti de Bruz (35), et formateur dans l'Académie de Rennes, pour la rédaction de la double page « L'IA, un allié pour apprendre »

SPEAKEASY NEWS

Nathan